About

Cara Colter shares ten ac... ... ...with her real-life hero Rob, ten ho... dog, and a cat. She has three grown children and a grandson. Cara is a recipient of the Career Achievement Award in the Love and Laughter category from *RT Book Reviews*. Cara invites you to visit her on Facebook!

Rosanna Battigelli loved reading Mills & Boon novels as a teenager and dreamed of writing them one day. Rosanna is the author of: a Gold IPPY Award winning historical novel, *La Brigantessa*; a fiction collection, *Pigeon Soup & Other Stories* (a 2021 Finalist, American BookFest Best Book Awards); and two children's books. Rosanna is thrilled that her early dream has come true, with five Mills & Boon novels published so far.

Award-winning author **Jennifer Hayward** emerged on the publishing scene as the winner of the So You Think You Can Write global writing competition and recipient of a *Romantic Times* Reviewer's Choice Award. Jennifer's careers in journalism and PR, including years of working alongside powerful, charismatic CEOs and travelling the world, have provided perfect fodder for the fast-paced, sexy stories she likes to write.

Tempted by the Tycoon

Tempted by the Tycoon

A Surprising Encounter

CARA COLTER

ROSANNA BATTIGELLI

JENNIFER HAYWARD

MILLS & BOON

First Published in Great Britain 2023
by Mills & Boon, an imprint of HarperCollins*Publishers* Ltd,
1 London Bridge Street, London, SE1 9GF

www.harpercollins.co.uk

HarperCollins*Publishers*
Macken House, 39/40 Mayor Street Upper,
Dublin 1, D01 C9W8, Ireland

ISBN: 978-0-263-31909-5

MIX
Paper | Supporting
responsible forestry
FSC™ C007454

This book is produced from independently certified FSC™ paper
to ensure responsible forest management.

For more information visit: www.harpercollins.co.uk/green

Printed and Bound in the UK using 100% Renewable Electricity
at CPI Group (UK) Ltd, Croydon, CR0 4YY

SWEPT INTO THE TYCOON'S WORLD

CARA COLTER

To Kymber, the man my daughter has
given her heart to.

CHAPTER ONE

"WHO IS THAT?" Chelsea's whisper was breathless.

Bree Evans shot her young assistant an exasperated look. "You've got to stop it. We were asked at the briefing not to gawk at the celebrities. It's part of our agreement to provide sample products and a display for this event. To be strictly professional. No staring. No autographs. No—"

Chelsea, unaware, or uncaring, that she was jeopardizing Bree's big break, was not paying the least bit of attention to her boss. Instead she was standing completely frozen, a neatly gift-wrapped box of Kookies for All Occasions' Love Bites in her hand. Bree followed her gaze, looking toward the outside door that led into the foyer area of the concert hall, where they were setting up.

Oh, no.

"Who *is* that?" Chelsea whispered again.

Oh, no. Had she said it out loud?

He was everything Bree remembered, only more. She had not seen him, in person, anyway, for six years. Though it hardly seemed possible, in that time his *presence* had multiplied. He had lost any hint of boyish slenderness, and the gorgeous lines of his face had settled into maturity. His dark brown hair, which she remembered as untamed, touching his collar and sweeping across his forehead, was now cut short and neatly groomed, as befit his position.

"It's Brand Wallace," Bree said carefully. She positioned herself with her back to the doorway he was coming through. Her heart was beating way too fast. Good grief. Her palms were sweating.

"Like in *Braveheart*?" Chelsea gasped.

"That was Mel Gibson," Bree explained with what was left of her patience. "Gibson *played* the part of William Wallace—he *wasn't* William Wallace."

Still, even though she didn't want to, Bree understood why Brand would make her young assistant think of brave hearts. There was something about him, and always had been—a way of moving with supreme grace and confidence that suggested a warrior, a man who was certain in his own strength and courage and capabilities.

Chelsea was still totally distracted. "I have never seen a more stunning example of the male of the species. Never."

Despite ordering herself not to, Bree slid another careful look at the doorway. She had to give Chelsea that. Brand Wallace was a stunning example of the male species!

He'd stopped just inside the double glass doors, his head tilted toward Shelley Grove, organizer of the Stars Come Out at Night, a charity gala to help fund the construction of a new wing for Children's Hospital.

Shelley had her hand cozily on his arm and was beaming up at him. He was steel, and women were magnets drawn to him.

Though the room was beginning to fill with well-known celebrities, many of whom were in Vancouver—"Hollywood North," as it was sometimes called—filming television series and movies, he stood out from all of them.

Even surrounded by some of the world's most dazzling people, there was something about him that was electric. It sizzled in the air around him, sensual and compelling.

He was in a sports jacket that, by the cut, hang and fit, was obviously designer. It showed the breadth of his shoulders, the power in him. White shirt—no doubt silk—and no tie. The shirt was tucked into dark jeans that clung to the hard lines of his thighs.

He was as fit and muscular, as outdoorsy-looking, as he had been when he'd worked as a summer student for her dad's landscaping company.

Brand made the extremely famous actor, who was standing a short distance away from him, look small and very, very ordinary.

"I'm sure I know who he is," Chelsea said, her tone mulling. "I've seen him in something. *Warriors of the New Age?* No, I know all of them. Maybe that new series. You know the one? Where the lady time-travels and the gorgeous guy—"

"He's not an actor," Bree said. "Chelsea, please put the cookies out. We only have twenty minutes until the official start time and I—"

She had to what? Leave, obviously. Before he saw her.

"But I know who he is," Chelsea said. "I'm sure of it." She unwillingly turned back to emptying the cookie-filled boxes, her body angled sideways so she could keep casting glances his way.

"You probably saw him on the cover of *City* magazine," Bree said. "That's why you feel as if you know who he is. Could you put a row of Devilishly Decadent at the end of the display?"

"Brand Wallace," Chelsea announced, way too loudly. "The billionaire! You're right! *City* had him on the cover. I couldn't turn around without seeing that glorious face on every newsstand! I don't usually buy it, but I did. He founded an internet start-up company that went insane with success—"

Bree shot a look to the doorway. Apparently he had heard Chelsea yelling his name like a teenager who had spotted her rock-star idol. He was casting a curious look in their direction.

Bree did not want him to see her. She particularly did not want him to see her in her Kookies outfit. She and Chelsea were both wearing the uniforms she had designed, and Chelsea had sewn. Until precisely three minutes ago, she had been proud of how she had branded her company.

Kookies sold deliciously old-fashioned cookies with a twist: unexpected flavors inside them, and each different type claimed to hold its own spells.

And so the outfits she and Chelsea wore were part sexy witch, part trustworthy grandmother. They both had on granny glasses, berets shaped like giant cookies, and their aprons—over short black skirts and plain white blouses—had photos of her cookies printed on them, quilted to make them look three-dimensional. It was all so darn *cute*.

Somehow she did not want the man her father had convinced to escort her to her senior prom to see her as cute. Or kooky. She certainly did not want him to see her with a giant cookie on her head!

In fact, she did not want Brand Wallace to see her at all. He belonged to another time and another place. A time when she had still believed in magic. A place that had felt as if her world would always be safe.

She shot another glance at the doorway. He was still looking in their direction—she could see he was trying to extricate himself from the conversation with Shelley.

"He's coming this way," Chelsea sighed. "How's my hair?"

Out of the corner of her eye, Bree saw Chelsea flicking her hair. She also saw there was an emergency exit just a little behind and to the left of their table. For some reason, it felt imperative to get out of there. And out of the apron. And the beret. Especially the beret.

It was trying to remove both at once that proved dangerous. She was twisting the apron over her head and taking off the beret with it, when, too late, she saw the corner of a box of Little Surprise cookies that was jutting out from under her display table. At the last second she tried to get her foot over it and failed.

The toe of her shoe caught on the box, and it caught the leg of the table, which folded. Apron and beret twisted around her neck, she had to make a split-second decision whether to save the cookies or herself. The cookies, which represented so much hard work, and her future—being invited to participate in this event was a huge coup for her company—won.

She dove under a cascade of Spells Gone Wrong boxes, which fell on her, one by one, until she was very nearly buried in them.

Really, it was a slow-motion and silent disaster, except for the fact she had managed to break the fall of the delicate cookies.

The incident probably would have gone completely unnoticed if Chelsea had not started shrieking dramatically.

And then he was there, moving the avalanche of boxes gently out of the way to reveal Bree underneath them. He held out a hand to her.

"Miss, are you—"

He stopped. He stared at her.

She blinked where she was lying on the floor, covered in boxes, and remembered. She remembered his eyes, the glorious deep brown of them, warm as dark-roasted coffee. She remembered that very same tilt of his mouth, something faintly sardonic and unconsciously sexy in it.

She remembered the *feeling* of his gaze on her, and a forbidden warmth unfolded in her that made her feel boneless.

"Bree?" he said, astounded.

She heard Chelsea's cluck of astonishment.

"Breanna Evans," he said slowly, softly, his voice a growl of pure sensuality that scraped the nape of her neck. And then his hand, strong and heated, closed around hers and he pulled her to her feet, the cookie boxes, which she had sacrificed her escape to save, scattering. His grasp was unintentionally powerful, and it carried her right into the hard length of him. She had been right. The shirt was silk. For a stunned moment she rested there, feeling his heat and the pure heady male energy of him heating the silk to a warm, liquid glow. Feeling what she had felt all those years ago.

As if the world was full of magical possibilities.

She put both hands on the broadness of his chest, and shoved away from him before he could feel her heart, beating against him, too quickly, like a fallen sparrow held in a hand.

"Brand," she said, she hoped pleasantly. "How are you?"

He studied her without answering.

She straightened the twisted apron. Where was the beret? It was kind of stuck in the neckline of the apron and she yanked it out, and then shoved it in the oversize front pocket, where it created an unattractive bulge.

"You're all grown up," he said, in a way that made her blush crimson.

"Yes," she said, stiffly, "People do tend to do that. Grow up."

She ordered herself not to look at his lips. She looked. They were a line of pure sexy. The night of her prom she had hoped for a good-night kiss.

But he hadn't thought she was grown up then.

Did it mean anything that he saw her as grown up now?

Of course it did not! Chances of her tasting those lips were just as remote now as they had been then. He was a billionaire, looking supersuave and sophisticated, and she was a cookie vendor in a bulging apron. She nearly snorted at the absurdity of it.

And the absurdity that she would still even *think* of what those lips would taste like.

But she excused her momentary lapse in discipline. There wasn't a woman in the entire room who wasn't thinking of that! Chelsea's interest, from the first moment she had laid eyes on him, had made it clear Brand Wallace's sex appeal was as potent as ever.

"You know each other?" Chelsea asked, her voice a miffed squeak, as if Bree had kept state secrets from her.

"I was Bree's first date," he said softly.

Oh! He could have said anything. He could have said he was a summer student who had worked for her father. But oh, no, he had to bring *that* up.

"I don't recall you being my *first* date," she said. "I'd had others before you." Freddy Michelson had bought her a box lunch at a fifth-grade auction. That counted. Why did he think he'd been her first date?

No doubt her well-meaning father had told Brand that his bookish, introverted daughter had not been asked to her senior prom. Or anywhere else for that matter.

She could have felt annoyed at her father spilling her secrets, but no, she felt, as she always did, that stab of loss and longing for the father who had always acted as if she was his princess, and had always tried to order a world for her befitting of that sentiment.

"Your first date?" Chelsea squealed, as if Bree had not just denied that claim.

Bree shot Brand a look. He grinned at her, unrepentant, the university student who had worked for her father during school breaks. The young man on whom she had developed such a bad crush.

She turned quickly to the fallen table, and tried to snap the fallen leg back up. It was obstinate in its refusal to click into place.

"Let me," Brand said.

"Must I?"

"You must," Chelsea said, but Bree struggled with the table leg a bit longer, just long enough to pinch her hand in the hinge mechanism. She was careful not to wince, shoving her hand quickly in her apron pocket.

"Here," he said, an order this time, not an offer. Bree gave in, and stepped back to watch him snap the leg into place with aggravating ease.

"Thanks," Bree said, hoping her voice was not laced with a bit of resentment. Of course, everything he touched just fell into place. Everything she touched? Not so much.

"Is your hand okay?"

Did he have to notice every little thing?

"Fine."

"Can I look?"

"No," Bree said.

"Yes," Chelsea breathed.

Bree gave Chelsea her very best if-looks-could-kill glare, but Chelsea remained too enamored with this unexpected turn of events to heed Bree's warning.

"Show him your hand," she insisted in an undertone.

To refuse now would just prolong the discomfort of the incident, so Bree held out her hand. "See? It's nothing."

He took it carefully, and she felt the jolt of his touch for the second time in as many minutes. He examined the pinch mark between her thumb and pointer, and for a stunning moment it felt as if he might lift her tiny wound to his lips.

She held her breath. Somewhere in the back of her mind she heard Chelsea's sigh of pure delight.

Of course, one of the most powerful men in Vancouver did not lift her hand to his lips. He let it go.

"Quite a welt," he said. "But I think you're going to live."

Feeling a sense of abject emptiness after he'd with-drawn his hand, Bree turned her attention to the boxes of cookies scattered all over the floor, and began to pick them up. He crouched beside her, picking them up, too.

"Please don't," she said.

"Thank you for your help," Chelsea said firmly, clearly coaching her boss how to behave around an ex-traordinary man.

"I can get them," Bree said.

But Brand stayed on the floor beside her, reading the labels out loud with deep amusement. His shoulder was nearly brushing hers. An intoxicating scent, like the forest after rain, tingled her nostrils.

"'Little Surprises,'" he said, reading the boxes. "'Love Bites. Devilishly Decadent. Spells Gone Wrong.' These are priceless," he said.

His appreciation seemed genuine, but she now felt the same about her cookie names as she had just felt about the apron and the beret. She felt *cute* rather than *clever*. She wished she had come up with an organic makeup line, like the woman at the booth set up across the foyer from her.

"Bree, are these your creations?"

"Yes, Kookies is my company."

"I like it all. The packaging. The names. I'm glad you ended up doing something unusual. I always won-dered if it would come true."

The fact that he had wondered about her, at all, knocked down her defenses a bit.

She stared at him. "If what would come true?"

"That night, at your prom. Don't you remember?"

She remembered all kinds of things about that night. She remembered how his hand felt on her elbow, and how his same forest-fresh scent had enveloped her, and how every time he threw back his head and laughed her heart skipped a beat. She remembered dancing a slow dance with him. And she remembered that she, school bookworm and official geek, had been the envy of every other girl in the room. She remembered, when the evening had ended, leaning toward him, her lips puckered, her eyes closed, and him putting her away.

"Do I remember what?" she asked, her voice far more choked than she would have liked it to be!

"They gave out all those titles in a little mock ceremony partway through the dance. Most likely to succeed. Mostly likely to become prime minister. You don't remember that?"

"No."

"Most likely to become a rodeo clown, most likely to win the Golden Armpit for bad acting."

"Those weren't categories!"

"Just checking to make sure you were paying attention."

As if anyone would *not* pay attention to him. His grin widened, making him seem less *billionaire* and more *charming boy from her past*.

She remembered this about him, too—an ability to put people at ease. That night of the prom, gauche and starstruck, she had wondered if it was possible to die from pure nerves. He had teased her lightly, engaged her, made himself an easy person to be with.

Which was probably why she had screwed up the nerve to humiliate herself by offering him her lips at the end of the evening.

"Now that I've jarred your memory, do you remember what your title was?"

"I hardly remember anything about that night." This was not a lie. She remembered everything about *him*, but the other details of the night? Her dress and the snacks and the band and anyone else she had danced with had never really registered.

"Most likely to live happily ever after. That was the title they bestowed on you."

The worst possible thing happened. Not only was she here on the floor, picking up her mess with the most devastatingly attractive man she had ever met, in a silly apron, with her hair scraped back in a dumb bun and granny glasses perched on her nose, but now she was also going to disgrace herself by bursting into tears.

CHAPTER TWO

No!

Bree Evans was not going to cry in front of Brand Wallace. She had a broken dream or two, but so what? Who didn't?

She bit the inside of her cheek, hard. She made herself smile.

"Of course they did," she said. "Happily-Ever-After. Look. Here's the proof." She bought a moment away from the intense gaze of his eyes on her face. She picked through the boxes of cookies.

There they were, the favorite kooky cookie for when she supplied weddings. She opened a box and pulled a cookie from its wrapping.

Shortbread infused with strawberries and champagne.

She passed it to him, and he took a quizzical bite.

"There you go," Bree said, and hoped he could not hear the tight, close-to-tears note in her voice. "Happily-Ever-After."

She watched as his eyes closed with pleasure. He was distracted, as she had hoped.

When he opened his eyes again, he smiled at her.

"That is one of the oddest—and tastiest—combinations of flavors I've ever experienced. Ambrosia."

"Thank you. I'll tuck that away for a new cookie name."

But then she saw she might not have distracted him quite as completely as she hoped, because he was watching her way too closely. She felt as if his eyes locked on the faint quiver of her lip.

"My company has an event coming up, a charity ball in support of this same goal, to raise funds for the new wing of Children's. Do you think I could get you to supply some of these?"

Bree's mouth fell open.

"Of course," Chelsea said smoothly.

"I'm sure they will be planning some kind of mid-night snack or party favor," Brand said. "Have you a card? I'll give it to my event planner, and she'll be in touch."

Being around him was a roller-coaster ride, Bree thought, as she turned, flustered, to get him her business card. For a stunning moment she had thought he was showing interest in her. He'd quickly doused that by saying his event planner would be in touch.

This kind of opportunity was exactly why she was at this event, Bree reminded herself firmly, turning with a bright, hopefully professional, smile to give him the card.

He slipped the card into his inside jacket pocket, and popped the rest of the cookie into his mouth. It drew her attention, unfortunately, to the rather sensuous curve of his lips as he chewed.

"Do you want to go for a quick coffee?" he asked her.

A roller-coaster ride!

The invitation seemed to take him by surprise as much as it did her.

"R-right now?" she stammered. "Things are just about to begin. See? People are going through to the auditorium. The program said Crystal Silvers is going to sing first."

"I don't care about that."

One of the most sought-after performers in the Western world, and he didn't care about that? He cared more about having coffee with her?

This was dangerous territory indeed.

Bree gestured helplessly at her display. "Oh, I couldn't possibly—"

"You're going for coffee," insisted Chelsea, who had never had a stubborn moment in her life—she was certainly changing things up tonight. Her tone was firm, brooking no argument.

"No." Bree aimed her best who-is-the-boss-here? look at her assistant.

Chelsea ignored it. "Go, I can handle this."

"No, I—"

"Go!" Chelsea said, and then, under her breath, she added, "Live dangerously, for Pete's sake."

"Unless your husband would object," Brand said smoothly.

Chelsea snorted in a most unflattering way.

Brand's gaze slid to Bree's ring finger. She wanted to hide it behind her back as if its nakedness heralded some kind of failure.

"Boyfriend, then."

Chelsea rolled her eyes. "She doesn't have a boyfriend."

She was as oblivious to the daggered look Bree gave her as she had been to the who-is-the-boss-here? look.

"The last guy she met on e-Us was a loser."

Since Chelsea was so adept at ignoring Bree's looks, dancing happily with insubordination, Bree managed to step hard on her foot before she could elaborate on the e-Us thing. Chelsea gave her a sulky look, but clamped her mouth shut.

Even so, damage had been done. Bree could see him registering what e-Us was.

One thing that was obvious about someone like Brand Wallace? He'd never been on a site like e-Us in his life.

"We'll just go around the corner," he said persuasively. "Two old friends catching up."

"Old friends," Chelsea breathed. "Do *you* have, uh, a significant other, Mr. Wallace?"

"Does my dog count?"

Chelsea gave Bree a not-so-subtle nudge on her shoulder.

"I don't think—" Bree began.

"I'm interested in your business. You'll be back in half an hour," he assured Bree. "The first set will have hardly started. These things never go off quite on time."

Meaning he was very familiar with *these things*. Big surprise.

"I'll have you back before intermission."

"I bet he won't stick you with the bill, either," Chelsea said helpfully, sidling out of the way before Bree could get her foot again.

The firm line of his mouth registered disapproval as he registered that morsel of information about the sad state of Bree's dating life.

"Your young assistant looks more than capable of finishing the setup here." His voice was suave.

Chelsea preened. "More than capable," she said, and flipped her hair.

It would seem churlish to refuse. It would seem like she was *afraid* of him, and life and surprises and the very thing she tried to bake into all her cookies.

Magic.

It was that magical thinking that always got her in trouble, Bree reminded herself. He had mentioned business. She was not in a position to turn down this kind of connection to the business world.

"All right," she said, resigned. "A quick coffee."

Bree came face-to-face with her truth. She was terrified of believing in good things.

And terrified especially to believe in the happily-ever-after that men like him had made women like her yearn for since the beginning of time.

"For goodness sake," Chelsea said in an undertone, "lose the apron. And do something with your hair."

She ran a hand through it, and followed Brand, tilting her chin at him when he held the door open for her.

It was a beautiful spring evening in Vancouver, and Bree was aware her senses felt oddly heightened. The air smelled good from a recent rain, and plump crystal droplets fell from the blossom-laden branches of the ornamental cherry trees that lined the sidewalk.

There were two coffee places around the corner from the concert hall, and Bree liked it that Brand chose the independent shop, Perks, rather than the one that was part of a big chain.

It was cozy inside, with mismatched sofas and scarred old tables with brightly painted chairs clustered around them. It smelled heavenly, of coffee and exotic spices.

"Have you been here before?" he asked her.

"Just to introduce them to Kookies. They passed."

"Fools."

Brand said it with such genuine indignation. It was going to be hard to keep her defenses about her. But she had known that when she was trying to refuse his invitation.

"Thank you for saying so. But it wasn't personal. They already had a contract with someone."

"Humph."

She had managed to get rid of her apron, but remembered Chelsea's instruction to do something with her hair. "If you'll excuse me for just a sec, I'll go freshen up."

"What can I get you?"

She was going to say hot chocolate; coffee was out at this time of evening. But in the spirit of living dangerously and allowing life to astonish her, she didn't. "Surprise me," she said.

"Oh. That sounds fun."

Somehow, she was not at all sure he was talking about beverage selection! She excused herself hastily before he could see the blush moving up her neck.

She found the washroom, slipped inside and looked at herself in the mirror. What she saw was so ordinary as to be discouraging. Her light brown hair, average at the best of times, was pulled into a tight bun—even worse. She had gone very light on the makeup, so faint freckles stood out on her nose. She had on no lipstick, and she had worn glasses tonight instead of her contacts. A wholesome, old-fashioned look was exactly what she wanted when she was behind the table giving out cookie samples.

To have coffee with an old crush—who could coax a blush out of her with a turn of phrase—not so much!

She pulled her hair out of the bun. It fell, stick-straight, to her shoulders. She rummaged in her purse for a brush and added a touch of lip gloss.

It was an improvement, but she was aware she still felt very ordinary, the kind of workaday girl who was virtually invisible.

"Not in his league," she told herself. But then she saw the plus side of that: she could just relax. It was just old friends catching up, after all. Nothing would ever come of it, except maybe a beneficial business connection.

She went back out into the main room. He had chosen two love seats facing each other with a round coffee table in between. She walked over and sat opposite him.

"You've let your hair down," Brand said.

Physically, not figuratively, despite her intention to relax. She hoped he didn't think she had done it to impress him.

"More comfortable," she said.

"I always liked the color of your hair. It reminds me of sand on a sun-warmed beach."

He had remembered the color of her hair? She gawked at him. *Sand on a sun-warmed beach?*

Do not gawk at the celebrities, she ordered herself. *And do not take it personally*, she also ordered herself. It was obvious he knew his way around women. He had found her one redeeming feature and flattered her about it. And it had worked some terrible magic on her. She could feel her nerves humming so hard it felt as though her skin was vibrating.

"I always considered it mousy brown," she said.

"That is ridiculous."

If she wasn't careful, she was going to gawk again. Probably with her mouth hanging open.

Thankfully, the beverages were delivered. Two steaming cups were set in front of them. She took hers, blew on it gently so as not to blow a blob of foam right onto his forehead and took a sip.

"What is this?" she asked, delighted.

"So I did manage to surprise! You've never had it before?"

"No."

"It's a chai latte. Spiced sweet tea with steamed milk. You like?"

"Wonderful. I can taste the tea, which is so ordinary, but then the spices and the mound of sugar-crusted foam raise it to a new level."

Suddenly she wondered why he had picked it for her. And she found herself looking at *ordinary* in a different light.

"And what are you having?" she asked him.

"Coffee, black."

"Given the variety on the menu, that seems unadventurous."

"I save my adventuring for other arenas."

She was going to blush again! No, she was not. She would not give him the satisfaction.

"You have had some great adventures in business," she said, pleased that she did not miss a beat. "I've been reading about you, Brand," she said. "You've done so well."

"Ah, the *City* article. I had no idea that magazine was so widely read."

Bree doubted it had been before they featured him on the cover!

"I must say I didn't treasure anonymity nearly enough when I had it. Everyone suddenly knows who I am. It's a little disconcerting. But thank you. The success part seems to be luck and timing. I jumped on an opportunity."

"My dad loved the quote—'opportunity meets preparation.' He always thought very highly of you. He admired your work ethic. He was fond of saying, 'That young man is going places.'"

"He used to say the same thing to me. When not another person in the world was. I feel as if he was the first person who truly believed in me. That goes a long way in a young man's life, especially one with no father figure. I don't think I ever had a chance to tell him that. What his faith in me meant. I regret it, but I'm glad I've been given this opportunity to tell you."

It became evident to her this was why he'd invited her for coffee. It was an opportunity to tell her what her father had meant to him.

It was lovely.

So, why did she feel faintly resentful—as if she was a chai latte that had just been demoted to a very ordinary cup of Earl Gray?

He watched her now over the rim of his coffee cup. "I called several times after your dad died. I spoke to your mother. Did she tell you?"

"Yes, she said you had called and asked after me."

"One day I called and the number was out of service. I dropped by the house and it was empty. For sale, if I recall."

Bree took a sip of her drink, and let the spicy aroma

fill her nostrils and warm the back of her throat before she replied. "I left for college. My mother felt lonely in the house, so she sold it quite quickly. Then she remarried and moved to San Francisco."

"Is she happy?"

"Yes, very." She did not say it seemed her mother had moved on to happiness with unseemly swiftness. Bree had felt so abandoned. Of course, there was nothing like feeling abandoned to leave a young woman looking for love in all the wrong places.

"What did you take? In college?"

Heartbreak 101.

"I took a culinary program. I'm afraid I didn't finish."

He cocked his head at her. "That doesn't seem like you, somehow."

She cocked her head back at him. "Doesn't it?" she asked, deliberately unforthcoming, and letting him know that really, he knew very little about her, past or present.

"In some ways, you are very changed," he told her.

For a moment, she felt panicked, as if the sad ending of the pregnancy that had forced her to leave school was written all over her. She hoped her face was schooled into calmness, and she made herself release her stranglehold on her mug.

He *still* made her nervous.

"Your confidence in high heels for one thing."

Relief swept through her at his amused reference to her clumsiness on the night of the prom.

"Oh, geez, you must have had bruises on your arm the next day. I should have practiced. I clung onto you most of the night."

"And I thought you were just trying to feel my manly biceps."

Despite herself, she giggled.

"It was a really nice thing for you to do," she said. "To take the boss' dateless daughter to her senior prom. I don't think I thanked you. Of course, it didn't occur to me until later that it probably wasn't your idea."

"It wasn't," he confessed. "I didn't date girls like you."

"Girls like me?"

"Smart," he said. "Sweet."

Not quite as smart as anyone had thought.

"I bet you still don't," she said wryly.

"I'm more the superficial type."

He made her laugh. It was as simple as that.

"So," he said, leaning forward and looking at her intently, "tell me how you have passed the last years. For some reason, I would have pictured you the type who would be happily married by now. Two children. A golden-retriever puppy and an apple tree in the front yard."

Happily-ever-after.

She could feel that same emotion claw at her throat. It was exactly the life she had wanted, the dream that had made her so vulnerable.

He had her pegged. Well, you didn't rise as fast in the business world as he did without an ability to read people with some accuracy.

There was no sense denying it even if it was not in vogue.

"That is my type. Exactly," she said. She heard the catch in her voice, the pure wistfulness of it.

"It's what you come from, too. I can see that you would gravitate back to that. Your family was so…"

He hesitated, lost for words.

"Perfect," she said, finishing his thought.

"That's certainly how it seemed to me. Coming from one that was less than perfect, I looked at the decency of your dad and the way he treated you and your mom, and it did seem like an ideal world."

One she had tried to replicate way too soon after the passing of her father, with a kind of desperation to be loved like that again, to create that family unit.

It was only now, years after her miscarriage, that she was beginning to tiptoe back into the world of dating, looking again to the dream of happily-ever-after. So far, it had been a disaster.

"Are you, Bree? Happy?"

She hesitated a moment too long, and his brow furrowed at her.

"Tell me," he commanded.

Ridiculous that she would tell him about her happiness, or lack there of. He had worked for her father a long time ago, and somehow been persuaded to take the hopeless daughter to her prom. They were hardly friends. Barely acquaintances.

"Deliriously," she lied brightly. "My little company builds a bit each day. It's fun and it's rewarding."

"Hmmm," he said, a trifle skeptically. "Tell me, Bree, what do you do for fun?"

The question caught her off guard. She could feel herself fumbling for an answer. What could she say? Especially to someone like him, who moved in the sophisticated circles of wealth and power?

She couldn't very well say that she had all the Harry

Potter books and reread them regularly, with her ancient cat, Oliver, leaving drool pools on her lap. That after Chelsea, seamstress extraordinaire, had showed her how, she had individually quilted each of the cookies on her aprons. That she was addicted to home-renovation shows, especially ones hosted by couples, who had everything, it seemed, that she had ever dreamed of. That she trolled Pinterest features about homes: welcome signs, and window boxes, and baby rooms.

It would sound pathetic.

Was it pathetic?

"My business takes an inordinate amount of time," she said when her silence had become way too long.

"So you don't have fun?"

"Maybe I consider developing new cookie recipes fun!"

"Look, my business takes a lot of time, too. But I still make time for fun things."

Just then a man came over and squatted on the floor beside her. He stuck out his hand. "Miss Evans? I'm the manager here. Mr. Wallace leads me to understand you have a line of cookies. We'd love to try them. Have you got a minute?"

She looked over the manager's shoulder at Brand. He was smiling. He nodded encouragingly at her.

"Yes, I have a minute," she said. The manager got up and sat beside her. She started to tell him about Kookies.

When she looked over at Brand, he was gone. The love seat across from her was empty.

No goodbye.

But at least he hadn't stuck her with the bill.

Fifteen minutes later, she left Perks. They were going to give Kookies a trial term of six months.

She walked back to the concert hall. Outside the door, before going in, Bree debated only for a full five seconds before she pulled out Brand's business card with his phone number and called him.

"Hello?"

She had been expecting it to go to voice mail, since she thought he was probably now in the front row for the Crystal Silvers performance. But there was no background noise.

"I was expecting to leave a message," she said.

"Bree. What an unexpected pleasure."

"I was rehearsing my message!"

"Okay, just pretend this is my voice mail."

"All right. Hello, Brand. Thank you for a pleasant evening and for buying me coffee. I wanted you to know Perks is going to try my cookies for a trial period."

"Excellent!"

"Voice mail does not respond," she reminded him primly.

"Oh, yeah. Forgive me. Continue."

She took a deep breath. "Thank you, but you didn't have to use your influence for me."

"Of course I didn't *have* to. But what exactly would be the point of having influence if you didn't use it to help others?"

And then he was gone, no goodbye again. She contemplated the kind of man that would make a statement like that.

This was what her father had always seen: the decency of Brand Wallace, a guy who could be trusted to do the right thing, even with a starry-eyed eighteen-year-old girl, desperate to be kissed.

His innate decency made her feel shivery with

longing. He appeared to be the polar opposite of Paul Weston, the college professor who had taken what was left of her heart after the death of her father and run it through the meat grinder.

But it would be a form of pure craziness to think that a woman like her could ever have a man like Brand Wallace.

On the other hand, who had ever looked at her hair before and seen sun-kissed sand?

She went in the doors, and could hear the music blasting out of the auditorium. Chelsea, looking a little worse for wear, was behind a completely rummaged-over sample table, dancing enthusiastically by herself to the loud music spilling out into the foyer. She danced salsa competitively and managed to look ultrasexy even in the cookie apron and beret.

She stopped when she saw Bree coming toward her. Sadly, it did not appear her sudden cessation of movement was because it had occurred to her it might be inappropriate that the table in front of her was badly in need of straightening.

"Did you have wine?" Chelsea demanded.

"No, I had a chai latte." Bree decided, then and there, she probably would never have one again. Those smoky, spicy exotic flavors would remind her of a surprisingly pleasant evening—and forbidden longings—for as long as she lived.

"Oh, you're all glowy."

Bree was pretty sure *glowy* was not a word, not that she wanted to argue the point.

"What has happened to the table?" Bree asked, not wanting to encourage an interrogation from Chelsea. "It's a mess."

"Oh! About ten minutes before Crystal Silvers started to sing, the people just started to pour through the front door. They were on me like the barbarian hordes. Just grabbing things, ripping open boxes, uninvited. I have tidied, you know. There were wrappers all over the place. Anyway, somehow samples made it back to the lady herself. She sent out an assistant to tell me she loved our cookies, to expect a big order for her birthday blowout."

It was more than Bree had hoped for! So why did she feel curiously flat about it?

If that came through, along with the extra business from Perks, there would be no time for thinking about happily-ever-after, or lack thereof, as the case might be.

Thank goodness.

"Oh, there goes the glowy look," Chelsea said. "The frown line is back. Miss Worry rides again."

Bree deliberately relaxed her forehead. She hadn't even realized until tonight she was endangering her chances of aging gracefully because of her perpetual frown. Despite the fact she knew better than to encourage Chelsea, she could not stop herself from asking.

"What color would you say my hair was?"

Chelsea regarded Bree's hair, flummoxed, clearly thinking this was a trick question that she was not going to answer correctly.

"Brown?" she finally ventured.

Bree nodded sadly. "Just as I thought."

CHAPTER THREE

YOU DIDN'T HAVE to use your influence for me.

After Brand had disconnected the phone and put it back in his pocket, he made his way through the rain-glittered streets. He had decided to walk home. Going back to the gala after being with Bree Evans would have felt like getting dumped onto an eight-lane freeway after being on a quiet path through the country.

Despite her new proficiency with high heels, and the way she filled out her trim white blouse, she was still sweet and smart. Definitely adorable. Totally earnest.

And completely refreshing.

Those words—*you didn't have to use your influence for me*—just reinforced all those impressions of her.

Everybody wanted him to use his influence for them. Even the manager at Perks had approached him, not the other way around. He'd recognized him from that blasted *City* article.

Brand came to his house, and stood back for a second, gazing at it through the walkway opening in the neatly trimmed hedge. His architect had called it colonial, a saltbox, and, thankfully, it was less ostentatious than most of the mansions on his street.

Inside, Beau, who seemed to be largely telepathic,

had figured out he was home, and gave a deep woof of welcome.

When people asked why he'd gone with a single-family house instead of a superglamorous condo, he said he'd purchased the Shaughnessy heritage home because it was close to his office tower in downtown Vancouver, his golf course and the VanDusen Botanical Garden.

That seemed much easier than admitting he had purchased the house because he thought his dog would prefer having a tree-shaded backyard to a condo balcony.

He opened the front door he never locked. Anyone with the nerve to try and get by his one-hundred-and-thirty-pound bullmastiff deserved a chance to grab what they could before dying.

The dog nearly knocked him over with his enthusiastic greeting, and Brand went down on his knees and put his arms around him. They wrestled playfully for a few minutes, until Brand pushed away Beau, stood up and brushed off his clothes.

"You stink."

The dog sighed with pleasure.

"I met a woman tonight, Beau," he told the dog. "More terrifying than you."

Beau cocked his head at him, interested.

"And that was before she laughed."

Since the events of this evening were about the furthest thing from what he had expected when he'd headed out the door, it occurred to him that life was indeed full of little surprises. He had the renegade—and entirely uncomfortable—thought that maybe her cookies held predictions in them after all.

And he had eaten that one.

Happily-Ever-After.

But one lesson he had carried from his hardscrabble childhood, left far behind, was an important one.

Fairy tales belonged to other people. People like her.

Except, from the stricken look on her face when he'd asked her about her happily-ever-after, somehow her great ending had evaded her. Or she thought it had. She was way too young to have given up on a dream.

And it was none of his business why it had, or why she had given up hope on it, but he felt curiously invested— as if that night he had taken her to the prom, he had made a promise to her father, a man who had been so good to him, that he would look out for her.

Brand also felt, irrationally perhaps, that he had given Bree a dream he couldn't have and she had let him down.

She was, in many ways other than just the high heels, very different. All grown up, as he had noted earlier. Her hair had been very long, but now, once she had let it down, he'd noticed it was shoulder-length and very stylishly cut. She used makeup well, and it made her cheekbones stand out, high and fine. She hadn't had on lipstick when he'd first seen her, but when she had sat down across from him at the coffee shop, her lips had the faintest pink-tinged gloss on them, shining just enough to make a man's eyes linger there for a moment.

And yet her eyes, huge and brown with no makeup at all, were almost exactly, hauntingly, as he remembered them—owlish and earnest, behind spectacles.

Almost, because now there was a new layer there. Sorrow. For her father, of course, but maybe something deeper, too.

She had pegged it. He'd never dated a girl like her before her prom, and to be honest, never had again.

"And I'm not about to start now," he told the dog. He took off his jacket and threw it in a heap on the floor, then undid his shirt and took off his shoes and socks. He padded barefoot through his house.

The architect had kept the outer footprint of the house, as the historical society demanded, but the inside had been stripped to the bones and rebuilt in a way that honored the home's roots, yet still had a clean, modern aesthetic.

The kitchen was no exception. Except for the Elvis cookie jar in the center of a huge granite island, his kitchen was a modern mecca of stainless steel and white cabinets, photo-shoot ready.

The designer had convinced him to go with a commercial kitchen, both for resale value and for ease of catering large events at his home. So far, there had been no large events at his home. As good as it sounded on paper, he didn't like the idea of boisterous gatherings in *his* space. Home, for him, was a landing strip between business trips, one that was intensely private. It was what it had never been when he was growing up—a place of quiet and predictability.

The cookie jar was stuffed with Girl Guide cookies. Brand shared a fondness for them with his dog, but he wondered if his enjoyment was now compromised for all time after sampling Bree's wares. Not feeling ready to admit to that, Brand passed on the cookies, grabbed a beer from a fridge that could have stocked a cruise ship for a month and went to the media room.

The media room was bachelor heaven: deep reclining leather seats, set up theater style, and a wall-to-wall television set with surround sound. There were Elvis posters on every wall. He flopped into one of the chairs, while Beau took up guard in his dog bed at his feet. He turned on the TV set, and let the comforting rumble of sound fill the room. He flipped through to the hockey game that had been recorded in his absence.

"This is the life," he told Beau, a little too forcefully.

Beau moaned, and he was aware of an echo, as if this room, filled with everything any man could ever want, was empty.

Bree had done that, made him aware of emptiness, in one single encounter.

If there was one thing Brand was really good at, in the business world and wherever else it mattered, it was heeding the subtle first tingles of a warning.

She was the kind of woman that would require more of a man.

No doubt most men would find her quite terrifying. That included him.

So, he knew what he had to do. Nothing. Absolutely nothing. Disengage. He'd already done way too much. In a moment of madness he'd actually given her his phone number. She had already shown she wasn't afraid to use it.

Or maybe she had been afraid, and used it anyway, which was much, much worse.

See? That's the kind of woman she was. Simple things could become complicated way too fast.

He thought of the new layer of sadness in her eyes. Was that from the death of her dad, or had something else happened to her? He thought of her trying to get that business off the ground by herself. He thought of her not having an answer about having fun. He thought of her assistant letting it slip that Bree was on a dating site, and was meeting losers who stiffed her with the bill. He thought about how good her father had been to him.

He took her business card out of his pocket. It was a well-done card. Glossy. Colorful. Professional. Memorable. Kookies for all occasions. Her number was already in his phone, because she had called him.

He took a deep breath, scrolled through to her information and added it to his contact information. He hesitated and pressed the green phone symbol.

She wouldn't answer. She was in the middle of—

"Hello?" Her voice was breathless.

He had the renegade thought he would like to make her breathless in quite a different way. It nearly made him end the call, because what the hell did a thought like that have to do with honoring her father by helping her out a bit? But there was no placing an anonymous call these days, so he sucked it up.

"Can't get the taste of your cookies out of my head," he said.

Funny that thinking about taste made a vision of her lips pop into his mind.

"I try to warn people," she said. "Spells and enchantment."

He thought of her lips again! That must be it. He was spellbound. Now would be a great time to tell her he had pocket-dialed.

"Aside from my charity function, I thought we should talk about the possibility of you supplying my office staff room. And meetings."

She was silent.

"Bree?"

"It's very kind, but—"

There was suddenly a great deal of noise.

"I'm sorry," she said, "it's intermission. I'm going to have to—"

"Meet with me next week."

"Um—"

Geez! He was offering her a huge opportunity here. What was the problem? While the rest of the world was yapping at his heels wanting things from him, she was resistant—the lone exception.

"I'll be in the office all day Wednesday," he said smoothly, "if you want to drop by and we'll figure out the details."

Again there was hesitation, and then she asked, "Around ten a.m.?"

"Perfect. My office is—"

"I know. It's in the article."

"The *damn* article," he said.

She rewarded him with that laugh, soft, like a brook gurgling over rocks. "Okay. Wednesday at ten. Dear Lord."

"What?"

"Crystal Silvers is walking toward me. Good grief. She hardly has any clothes on."

And then she was gone. Brand stared at his phone. "Beau?"

The dog lifted his head and gave him a watery-eyed look.

"You're an expert on all things stinky. I stink at relationships, right?"

The dog laid his head back down with a groan as if there was no point in having bothered him with such a self-evident question.

"That's what I thought. I'm putting on my big-brother shirt."

He remembered the refreshing innocence about her. Crystal Silvers had been walking toward her, the chance of a lifetime, possibly, and she focused on the no-clothes-on part.

Innocent in a world that was fast. Old-fashioned in a world that could be slick. Real in a world that distracted with shock.

So, she needed a bit of coaching. His offer to get her under contract to supply his office was perfect. Of course, he could have left the details up to his office manager, but this way he would be able to check up on her a little bit, and make sure some great business opportunities came her way. And maybe, subtly, move her in the direction of happiness, which she so richly deserved.

"Not that I'm any expert on happily-ever-after," he muttered.

The dog wagged his stump of a tail in approval. One thing that both Brand and Beau knew was that Brand was not cut out for relationships. Brand's father had abandoned him and his mother. At six he had become the man of the family. He'd been there for his mom, and he still was, but he was pretty damn sure that his father's genetics ran strong through his blood.

"Ask Wendy," he said out loud.

The dog's tail stopped thumping, no doubt a coincidence, but still Beau and Wendy had never seen eye-to-eye. It had been okay when Brand was just seeing her, as he had been exclusively for two years.

But then, she'd moved in. You thought you knew a person until they took down your Elvis posters and replaced them with original works of abstract art. He'd had to rescue the cookie jar from the garbage. People as svelte as Wendy did not let cookies touch their lips.

Within twenty-four hours, she was planning a Christmas extravaganza. Here. In their home. In their private space. She thought they could easily host two hundred people!

Thankfully, in short order, Beau had chewed through the sofa she had brought with her, a ridiculous antique thing that wasn't even comfortable. Next on the menu had been three pairs of her shoes, imported from Italy. For dessert, Beau had eaten her Gucci wallet, with her credit cards in it. All that had been left was three gooey strands of leather and one slimy half of her Gold card.

She had said, "It's the dog or me."

He'd paid for the wallet and shoes and sofa, and chosen the dog. But in his heart he knew it wasn't really about the dog. It was about being unsuitable for the kind of cozy domestic future she was envisioning. It had all been great when he could pick her up at her house, and take her out to dinner or a function, without her cosmetics and hair products all over his bathroom counter.

Something in him had already been itching to move on, three days after she'd moved in. He was pretty sure he would have got out of it, one way or another, way before the Christmas extravaganza, just as his father had done.

After Wendy's departure from his home and his life, Brand put the Elvis posters back up. The Elvis memorabilia had been his mother's pride and joy. Her suite in the seniors home had not been able to accommodate even a fraction of her collection. Always emotionally fragile, she'd gone into hysterics trying to decide what she could keep and what she could part with.

Another reason for a rather large house in Shaughnessy.

Okay, it wasn't the most pragmatic reason to buy a house. But when he picked up his mother on Sunday afternoons and brought her to his home, she was so happy to see it. Somehow, having them around him, reminded him of exactly what he came from. And that might be the most important lesson not to forget.

As if on cue, his phone went off—it was the quacking ringtone he reserved for his mom, a private joke between them. He glanced at the clock. Late. He could feel himself tensing ever so slightly.

"Hi, Mom."

"There was a movie tonight," she told him. "*Abracadabra.* Have you seen it?"

"No, I heard it was good, though. Tell me about it." The tension left him as her happy voice described the movie.

It was, Bree told herself firmly as she glanced at her wavering image in the polished steel elevator cage that was whisking her up to the forty-third floor, a second chance to make a first impression. Technically, her third chance, if she counted the prom.

Even though she was going to pitch a cookie contract to Brand's office, there was no cookie beret today and no quilted apron.

Something in his voice when he had called her offering her the contract had given her pause. It was why she had hesitated. Did he consider her a charity that would benefit from his generosity? It was as if he had relegated her to a perpetual little-sister position in his life. No doubt he had done the same the night of the prom! No wonder he had refused her lips that night. Not that she was offering her lips today. Or even letting her mind wander in that direction.

No, today, Breanna Evans was erasing *cute* from his impression of her, erasing a cookie beret and a quilted apron. Today, she was going to be one-hundred-percent professional. Polished. Pure business.

And grown up!

Even the night of the gala, when he had pronounced her all grown up, it seemed to her now, in retrospect, it was something said to a thirteen-year-old that you had last seen when she was ten.

Toward this goal, Bree had dug deep into her resources and purchased a stunning deep red, bordering on burgundy, Chloë Angus hooded cloak to wear over her one and only business suit, a nondescript pantsuit in a color that might be best described as oatmeal. The cloak made her hair, piled up on top of her head in an ultrasophisticated look, seem like sun-kissed sand.

Then, to compound the insanity, she had bought a matching pair of heels. The shoes made her look quite a bit taller than she really was, and hopefully, more powerful, somehow, like a busy CEO. She wasn't quite as graceful in them as she wanted to be, but she wasn't planning on running a marathon wearing them, either—she just wanted to make a crucial impression.

The one to erase all other impressions.

"CEO," she muttered to herself in the elevator, and then more firmly said, "Chief executive officer. Who got a contract to provide Crystal Silvers with five thousand cookies for her birthday blow-out? You! That's who!"

She hoped the elevator didn't have security cameras that recorded sound. A security guard somewhere would be having a good laugh at her expense.

She was carrying two large, rectangular white bakery boxes of cookie samples, which she always took, as a gift, when she was pitching an office contract. Unfortunately, the samples would not fit into a briefcase. Or maybe that was fortunate: who knows what kind of money she would have spent on that power item?

The elevator stopped. Despite her pep talk to herself, her heart fell to the pointy toes of her new red shoes. She considered just riding back down. She felt overcome by nerves, despite all the money she had spent trying to shore up her confidence with the beautiful, subtle raven-imprinted cloak.

But when the doors whispered open on the penthouse floor of one of Vancouver's most exclusive downtown office towers, Bree took a deep breath and forced herself to be brave. The world did not reward cowardice after all!

She stepped out into a gorgeous foyer, and her feet sank into a deep carpet. Hard surfaces would have been so much better for the heels! The lighting was low, and she noted two white leather sofas facing each other. Beyond them was a receptionist desk, currently empty of a receptionist, in some kind of exotic wood. On the far wall, to the right of the elevator, a stone wall had water trickling down its face, and was embossed with shining, wet gold letters that announced she was at the right place, BSW Solutions.

It looked like a solid wall behind the receptionist's desk, but then a sliver of light appeared in it, and Bree realized there was a door hidden in the wall. It pushed open a little more, swinging out into the room.

And then it was flung back with such force that the door hit the wall. Bree took a startled step back just as a monster shot out the door and galloped toward her! Her surprised mind grappled with the fact it was a dog. Not just any dog, but the largest one she had ever seen. He was brindle-colored with a head the size of a pumpkin. He was dragging a leash, and slobber was flying from his mouth as he covered the distance between them in three gigantic bounds.

Was he going to jump on her? Her own safety was not as paramount in her mind as the new cloak and her cookies.

She let out a little shriek and took a step back. Her heel caught in the extravagant pile of the carpet, and she lost her footing and dropped the cookies. She wind-milled her arms, trying to stay upright, but to no avail.

She fell on the floor and closed her eyes tightly, re-signed to being killed by a beast in the luxurious foyer of Brand Wallace's business. Why did nothing ever go quite as she planned it?

After a full second of anticipating her imminent death, nothing happened.

She opened an eye and sat up. The beast had skid-ded to a stop, and as she watched he nudged open the lid of a box and began to gobble up three dozen or so Spells Gone Wrong cookies.

"Beau!" The tone commanded the dog's complete respect. He sat immediately at attention, eyes on his master, his cookie-encrusted muzzle the only evidence he had done anything untoward.

"Bree. Oh, my God, I'm so sorry."

Brand was standing over her, his forehead puckered with concern, his eyes on her face. He reached down to her and his hand, strong and warm, closed around hers. He pulled her up and then he just stared at her, as if he'd never seen her before. Somehow, he forgot to let go of her hand.

He was dressed casually, far more so than he had been the night of the gala. He was wearing a jacket over a T-shirt, faded jeans and a nice pair of leather loafers with tassels on them.

The stunned look on his face made the Chloë Angus cloak and the shoes worth every penny of the investment.

"Are you okay?" he growled.

"Yes, I think so. Just in a bit of shock. You don't expect, er, *that* in an office like this."

"No, I know. I apologize. It's unforgivable, really."

"Brand," she said firmly, "I could tell you a thing or two about unforgivable, and believe me—" she looked at the dog, comic in his contriteness "—he doesn't even register."

She was shocked she had said that, as if she was ready to share confidences from her sordid past with him, which she most certainly was not. His hand was still holding hers. That was the problem. She had just been attacked by a monster beast, but her hand in his made her feel safe and protected.

And about as far from a CEO as you could get!

"Are you sure you're all right?"

"Positive, though I do think we have to stop meeting like this."

He realized he was still holding her hand. He looked down at their joined hands with surprise, and then let go abruptly. He looked at his hand. He looked at her hair, and lifted his hand as if he was going to touch the scattered tendrils of what was left of her lovely up-sweep. Then he looked at her cloak. It seemed as if he was debating whether or not he should be brushing her off, and then thought better of it. He jammed his hands in his pockets. Bree actually found herself smiling, and then chortling.

She could tell it took a lot to rattle Mr. Brand Wallace, but he was rattled now.

"This is not a laughing matter," he told her sternly, and then looked to the dog. "Bad dog."

The dog flinched at the reprimand, but then turned a repentant gaze to Bree. His stub of a tail thumped hopefully.

"It's okay," she told the dog. He came out of his seated position. His whole monstrous back end wiggled.

"It's not!" Brand said. The dog sat back down.

Just then a breathless girl came out the door that both the dog and Brand had come through.

"Mr. Wallace, I'm so sorry. He's never done that before! I was just bringing him in off the terrace, when he bolted. I just wasn't expecting it. One minute I had the leash, and the next I didn't."

Brand looked really annoyed, despite the explanation. "Jennifer, he knocked over our guest."

"No—no, he didn't," Bree said quickly. "He startled me and I took a step backward. I fell over all on my own."

The girl was close to tears. It was obvious she had a bad case of hero worship for her boss and felt far more terrible that she had let him down than that their guest had taken a spill in the main foyer.

"I'm so sorry," Jennifer said tremulously.

"I take the blame," Bree said, still smiling. She picked up the open, and now empty, box of cookies and held it up. Spells Gone Wrong was clearly written across the lid. "Things always go off the rails whenever I make them. When it's combined with Little Surprises, watch out!"

"Oh," Jennifer said knowingly. "Cookies."

"That dog could not have possibly smelled cookies through that door," Brand said. "It's impossible."

He looked hard at his young employee, and seemed to realize she needed forgiveness. Nothing could be changed now. Unfortunately, Bree's sense of him being somehow safe in a stormy world intensified when his tone softened as he addressed the girl.

"Cookies are his weakness. I'm afraid I give him the odd one. Keep a firmer hold on him next time, Jenn."

Jenn heard the *next time* and beamed. "He likes the vanilla Girl Guide cookies," she told Bree. "Mr. Wallace has a closet full of them for the days he brings Beau to work with him."

The girl's attitude reminded Bree so much of Chelsea being altogether too revealing about Bree's personal life that she laughed out loud. Brand—one of the most successful men in Vancouver's business community—owned the world's ugliest dog. And brought him to work with him. And fed him Girl Guide cookies.

"He probably won't eat Girl Guide cookies ever again now," Brand said woefully, looking at the empty box and the dog's cookie-encrusted muzzle.

"I'll take him, Mr. Wallace."

"No, it's okay, I've got him now. If you could look after this mess I'd appreciate it." He stooped and picked up the leash, though it was probably entirely unnecessary. The dog was stuck to him like glue, as he leaned into his leg.

The dog made a moaning noise, as the mashed cookies were packed up, and Bree looked at him. He gave her a woebegone look that she could not resist. She got down on one knee in front of him.

"Don't touch him," Brand warned, too late. "He stinks."

But she already had the dog's big, wrinkly face between her hands. "Did you call him Beau?"

"He mostly answers to 'bad dog,'" Brand offered, "but sometimes I call him Beau."

"Beau," she said softly. "You are not a bad dog. You have one of the most beautiful souls I've ever seen."

The dog regarded her thoughtfully, and then his big, ugly chops spread into an unmistakable grin. His big tongue whipped out and removed most of her makeup before she could move her face away. She laughed, and stood back up, while wiping at her face with a corner of her brand-new cloak.

She stopped, aware Brand was staring at her.

"What?" she said.

He was looking at her with the oddest look.

As if he had found a treasure he had waited his whole life to find. A woman lived for a look like that.

CHAPTER FOUR

BUT THEN HE spoiled it all when he said, "You look just like Little Red Riding Hood."

Just the look she was going for! Should she tell him he looked just like the Big Bad Wolf? Before she could, he spoke again.

"I've provided the wolf, I'm afraid. Beau usually doesn't like people."

Hmmm, he thought the dog was the wolf.

"Not that he's nasty or anything," Brand continued, "just colossally indifferent."

That look she thought she had seen was gone from his face and, in fact, Bree wondered if it wasn't her ever fertile imagination going into overdrive. She'd thought she had made a breakthrough in being perceived as an adult woman, but he was seeing a character out of a fairy tale!

"Let me show you around," Brand said, then led her to the door and held it open for her. Beau sat as she passed.

"Look at him," Brand said, "anxious to prove he's the perfect gentleman, and *not* the Big Bad Wolf."

As she went by him, Bree had the impression that Brand was uncomfortable, as if he knew, in that split second, he had revealed something he didn't want to reveal, and was now covering his tracks as quickly as possible.

If his intention was to distract, the room she found herself in certainly did that!

It was like nothing she had ever seen before.

It was a huge open space, scattered with deep fabric chairs that could have been mistaken for boulders, if people were not sunk so deeply into them. A cat was curled up in one young lady's lap.

Bree shot Beau a look, but he was looking off into the distance, regally indifferent to the cat.

"The cat and him sorted things out a long time ago," Brand said. "He's terrified."

"People bring their pets to work?" she asked, astounded. It was one thing for the boss to bring his dog on occasion, but it was startling to see the cat.

Brand nodded. She noticed a colorful hammock was suspended by ropes from the arched wooden beams of the ceiling, and a bearded fellow swung gently, as he tossed a beanbag in the air above his head and caught it. At the far end of the room the whole wall was covered in the colorful footholds and handholds of a climbing wall. There was a ball pit, of all things, filled to overflowing with bright yellow and red and blue balls. Music, a flute she thought, flooded the area.

A guy walked by them in bare feet. "Hiya, boss. Beau."

The dog, as Brand had predicted, was indifferent to the greeting. Brand took her elbow and guided her through the rock chairs and past the hammock bed hanging in the middle of the room.

He ushered her into his office and dropped Beau's

leash. The dog padded across the floor to a large doggie bed.

The office was beautiful and expansive. Floor-to-ceiling windows looked out over the cityscape, and beyond that she could see the ocean and mountains, still white-capped at this time of year. A gorgeous desk, possibly rosewood, with deep chairs in front of it, anchored the room, but off to one side two love seats faced each other over a glass-and-steel coffee table.

"This seems like the only conventional space on the whole floor," she said. "Except, of course, for Beau, who is, um, hardly conventional."

The dog did several circles on the bed, then with a happy sigh, laid down.

"What on earth is his breeding?" she asked. "I think the floor shook when he settled!"

"He's part bullmastiff. And part rhinoceros. I've held off on letting the world know there was a successful interspecies breeding. He's introverted. I don't think he could handle the attention."

"I can clearly see he's introverted," she laughed.

"I suspect you smell overwhelmingly of cookies. He really is introverted, as I said, largely indifferent to people, with the exception of me. Have a seat." He gestured to the love seats, rather than the seats in front of his desk. "Can I get you something?"

"No, thanks." She sank into the masculine, distressed leather, and Brand took a seat on the identical one across from her. "Is that a Lalique?" she said of the vase on the coffee table between them.

"A leak?" he said, and looked around puzzled.

"The vase."

Then she saw he was teasing her. His eyes sparkled with devilment.

"Yeah, their Midnight Blue collection. According to my designer, an investment." He rolled his eyes.

She knew she should be entirely professional, and just get down to business, but as always, he had a gift for putting her at ease. Curiosity overwhelmed her. "Tell me about that space out there. I have never seen anything like it."

"The thing about a business like mine is you can't just go with one idea. You have to be looking for the next one, and the next one after that. You have to be continually evolving and you have to be light-years ahead of the competition and the copycats.

"I'm good at business," Brand said, "and maybe even great at it. But I'm not strong in creativity, and I don't have top-of-the-line tech skills. And so I want to attract the best and brightest computer and creative working minds in the business. And I want to keep them. I've researched what makes a happy and productive workplace, and it's evolving it. That guy in the hammock, tossing the beanbag? His name's Kevin. He had an idea that made the company ten million dollars last year. He is one guy I make sure to talk to every single day."

"That's a lot of cookies," she said with a gulp. "The article—correction, the damn article—never said how it all began."

She still felt nervous, and a little off balance. But, of course, here she sat, Little Red Riding Hood, hair in shambles, her makeup licked off and her cloak askew. It would be good if she could get him talking until her wits came back!

"I had an idea a few years back—kind of Uber meets

Facebook, only in real time. I was traveling overseas for the company I worked for at the time. I was in Copenhagen and had a couple of hours on my hands. I thought, I wonder if I could find a pick-up game of hockey anywhere?"

She couldn't help herself. She laughed.

"What's so funny?"

"It's just so Canadian. And so *guy* somehow."

He smiled. That smile! So charming. So sexy! He leaned forward. His gift, or one of his gifts, was that he could make anyone feel as if they were the only person in the world that mattered to him.

"I know. A more sophisticated guy probably would have been checking out the museums and art galleries and restaurants. But I'd been on airplanes and in meetings for three days and I just wanted to blow off some steam and get very physical."

She felt her admiration for him grow even more. Because, really? If a guy like him wanted to get physical… She had to wrestle the blush that was threatening back down her throat.

Instead, her tone completely professional, she said, "It seems ironic that this hugely successful company came out of a desire to play hockey."

"I know, there is a bit of a bizarre element to it. Even more so because I was in no way unhappy with what I was doing. Loved my company. Loved the job. But this idea wouldn't let me go."

She actually had a general idea, from the magazine article, exactly where his thought of playing hockey in Denmark had taken him, but she was enjoying hearing about the birth of his company from him, directly and in detail.

"Intents was born. I liked how the name said one thing, but if you said it out loud it sounded like another—intense.

"The premise is you find yourself in a strange city, or country, but you like playing hockey or you like rock climbing or you like going to the opera or you like playing chess. An app shows you where to find those activities, and also people nearby who might be available to do them with you. You've been security-checked, they've been security-checked. It's all totally free. The pop-up ads on the website and app pay for it."

"It's quite brilliant," she said.

"Thanks, I'm proud of it. One of the things that surprised me, but is very satisfying, is how deep, lasting friendships come out of these connections sometimes. It's simply a great way to meet people who like the same things as you. We've had several weddings as a result."

"That isn't a dig at me meeting a guy on e-Us is it?"

"Who stiffed you with the bill," he reminded her.

"Thank you, Chelsea," she said. They both laughed, but when the laughter died, he was looking at her intently.

"What did you mean when you said you could tell me a thing or two about unforgivable?" he asked softly.

"Wh-what?" she stammered.

"When I said the dog knocking you over was unforgivable, you said—"

"I know what I said. A slip." She was *not* telling him. She clamped her mouth firmly shut and folded her arms over her chest. "Let's talk about cookies," she said brightly.

"I don't think you should be meeting people on e-Us," he said.

"Really?" she said. He did not appear to hear the coolness in her tone. "That's the accepted way of meeting people in this day and age."

"Well, it sucks."

She thought back over the majority of her experiences on e-Us. He had her there. "How would you suggest meeting people?"

"You like books? Go to a bookstore and tap some guy on the shoulder. Ask him what he's reading."

"That seems very forward. And maybe even dangerous."

"Unless he's in the memoirs-of-serial-killers section, you're probably okay," he said drily. "Geez, meeting a complete stranger, whose profile you've seen on the internet, is better somehow?"

"It's always in a public place. For a cup of coffee. Not very different than what we did the other night."

"I am not a complete stranger! I'm sure you knew, from our former acquaintance, I wasn't going to wait outside in the parking lot and club you over the head. Or follow you home. And I'm sure you knew I wasn't going to stiff you with the bill."

"Thank you, again, Chelsea."

"Not that I've been on one of them—"

She'd guessed right on that account!

"But it seems to me the problem with dating sites would be you can't get a read for people, the way you do when you meet them in person. The site is filtering all the facts. Even the picture can be a lie, can't it?"

She would certainly not admit that her last date had looked at least ten years older than he had in his profile picture.

"Plus there's the problem of sitting across from

someone you barely know in a coffee shop. How does that not end up feeling awkward? Like an interview?"

She hated it that he, who had never been on a dating site, was picking up the weaknesses of the system.

Why was it that this meeting, which was supposed to be an interview of sorts, did not feel like one at all?

"If you'd seen that guy in the bookstore, your little hinky sense would have told you—jerk. Something about the way he was standing, or the hole in his jeans, or the kind of book he was reading."

"Especially if he was in the serial-killer section!"

"More subtle. *How to Get Your Internet for Free, Collecting Coupons for Dummies.*"

She had the awful thought this was why she was really here. Despite her every effort to be the consummate professional, to correct those first impressions, here they were again.

With him feeling some kind of obligation to take care of her!

She had to get this back on track. The encounter with the dog had literally knocked down her defenses!

"All right," she said brightly. "I'll get the Intents app on my phone. Next time I'm in Denmark, I'll meet some fellow Harry Potter fans. I'll probably end up marrying one."

Harry Potter? Had she really said Harry Potter? She, who wanted to appear so grown up?

"Is that guy on the hammock out there single?" she said in a rush to correct impressions. "Maybe, on my way out, I'll just stop and ask him what he's throwing around. Is he single?"

"He is," Brand said drily, "but you have to speak Klingon to interest him."

"Klingon," she repeated, playing along. "I could learn. How often would I have to watch *Star Wars* to pick it up?"

"*Star Trek*. A mistake I'm okay with. Kevin? Not so much."

He was smiling. As if he found her intensely amusing! And here she was playing along with him. Well, enough was enough!

"Is that why I'm really here? Not to sell you cookies, but so that you can give me unsolicited advice about my personal life?"

CHAPTER FIVE

BREE KNEW SHE should stop right there, but she didn't.

"Despite playing the role at my senior prom, you are not my big brother!"

"You're right," Brand said. "I'm sorry. I've overstepped. I was acting like your protector, and—"

So, she *had* guessed right. She was here out of some form of sympathy. Support for the old boss' daughter. Okay, just the tiniest bit of weakness unfolded in her when he said *protector* like that. Oh! To have a protector such as him! She felt as if she had been on her own, with no one to lean on, for so long.

But, no! She was not giving in to that weakness. She was here to correct that very impression. That somehow she needed something that only he could give her.

She knew she was never going to be able to dislodge that first impression, not even if she went out and bought four hundred Chloë Angus capes. It was set in his mind. He was always going to see her as a hopelessly naive young girl. Nothing she had done today, from tripping over carpets to kissing dogs, had corrected that impression. Even the fact that she was sophisticated enough to recognize a Lalique had gone completely over his head!

Brand Wallace was buying her cookies, entering a business arrangement with her, out of pity! Out of some misguided desire to help her.

Suddenly she knew one way to correct his impression of her. To make him realize he didn't know her at all. The boldness it required stole her breath. It made her realize maybe her impressions of *herself* also needed a bit of tweaking.

She got up. She felt like a soldier going into battle. Her heart was beating so hard that surely he could see it hammering, right beneath the cloak. Some sort of momentum carried her across to his sofa. A granite determination overtook her as she sank into the seat beside him.

She could hear the frantic roar of her own heart in her ears.

She leaned closer to him, put both hands on either side of his face and drew him to her. Her heart went still. A great and surprising calm overtook her.

His cheeks, beneath her fingertips, were ever so slightly whisker-roughened, as if she was touching sandpaper. His scent was pine and rain and man. His eyes were the deepest brown she had ever seen, and the devilment in them had been replaced by surprise. And understandable wariness.

He was a man not accustomed to being caught off balance, and she had put him off balance. He was a man accustomed to calling the shots, and right now, in this surprising instant, she was calling the shots.

If she dared.

She saw it in his eyes that he knew what was coming, but was not sure she had the nerve.

She hesitated for one moment at the edge of the cliff,

terrified of the dizzying height she stood at. And then she jumped.

And felt the exquisite and glorious freedom of free-fall. She kissed him. She kissed him hard, and she kissed him passionately. She kissed him until neither of them could breathe. She kissed him until any resistance from him melted and his hands were tangled in her hair and he was kissing her back, his delicious lips nuzzling her own, exploring her own, claiming her as his own.

She lost the point of the exercise. Somewhere, she lost herself. Her world became so small, only this: his lips, the taste of them and the texture of them and the suppleness of them and the force of them. Her world became so large, only this: the stars in the sky, and the birds in the trees and the rivers flowing endlessly to the sea. All the mysteries were in this one small thing.

It seemed it might go on forever. There was that word, *forever*, that beautiful, enticing, enigmatic word from fairy tales.

But then the whole love seat seemed to groan, and his lips left hers.

"Beau!"

The dog had hefted himself up on the couch, and inserted his bulk gingerly between them. His huge tongue was flattened across the whole of Brand's cheek, slurping upward in slow motion.

With an impatient shove, he put the dog off the couch and wiped at his soggy cheek with the sleeve of his jacket.

Before she could lean back in and offer her lips again, Brand leaped off the love seat. He stared down at her. He ran a hand through his hair. He paced away from her.

"Harry Potter fans of the world, beware," he muttered. "What the hell was that about?"

Bree made herself sit up straight. She took a deep breath. She adjusted her cloak. She touched her hair. Her upsweep was now totally unswept.

Still, she made her voice firm. "I am not some cute child who has showed up at your office selling cookies, like a Girl Guide going door-to-door," she said.

"Okay, I think you've made that point."

"And I am not the gauche girl who was so innocent you could not risk a kiss good-night after her senior prom."

He swore under his breath. He was looking at her way too closely. "Have you been nursing that little grievance all these years?"

"No!"

"I think you're lying," he said softly.

"Well, you don't know anything about me."

He touched his lips. "That's true," he conceded.

Suddenly, she was mortified. She had just kissed Brand Wallace! What would he think she *was* selling? She thought of apologizing, and then she thought better of it.

Okay, it might not have been the most professional thing she had ever done, but really? From the look on his face, he was never going to think of her as a child again!

And really? She felt alive, and powerful. She felt she was practically sizzling with energy and life and passion.

"Now," she said, "are we ready to talk business?"

Under his breath, he said something that sounded

like a word a sailor might say. He looked downright wary. That was better!

"I'm not sure we're done discussing *that*."

"We are," she said firmly.

"If you didn't think of it for six years, where did that come from?"

"It's Spells Gone Wrong," she said, lifting a shoulder. "Again. Deadly, in combination with Little Surprises."

"You must have brought some Devilishly Decadent, too," Brand said drily.

He remembered the names of her cookies! *Stay on track*, Bree ordered herself.

"You're right, I must swear off delivering that particular combination of cookies. And speaking of cookies, how many people are in your office? I usually recommend starting with two cookies per person per day. Initially, I'll send quite a variety, but I'll give you a voting sheet to put on the coffee table. Then I'll start sending what people like best. If I was going to guess for this office? Earth Muffin. Vegan cookies..."

Brand watched Bree. She seemed composed enough after what happened, but if he was going to guess? She probably didn't usually talk this much.

Still, as she detailed her ordering and billing procedures, he noticed that, despite the rather shocking interchange that had just occurred between them, she had a really good business head on her shoulders. Nothing *kooky* about that part of her.

This whole fiasco was his own fault.

He'd been rattled since the first moment when he'd found her on the floor. His sense of not being in control had deepened when he had seen how she had reacted to the dog licking off her makeup.

No shrieking. No hysterics.

And she hadn't been putting it on to impress him, either. She genuinely loved animals.

But nobody loved Beau!

Except him.

This suddenly felt like one of the scariest moments of his life: she looked like Little Red Riding Hood, and kissed like a house on fire. She wove spells into her cookies. And she could see the souls of dogs.

He had known she was going to kiss him. He'd known it as soon as she sank down on the couch beside him.

He'd known and yet, he had not moved. He'd been caught in some spell of curiosity and enchantment.

He had to get her out of here, and out of his life. She was right. Absolutely right. She was totally grown up. One-hundred-percent pure woman. She'd proven that beyond a shadow of a doubt. There was nothing brotherly about the way he was feeling about her.

"Okay," he said abruptly. "Where do I sign?"

"I'll email you a contract with the terms we've just discussed."

City magazine would love to see him now. The man they'd declared to be the businessman of the decade was going to be emailed a contract and he had not the slightest idea what was in it, or what they had just discussed.

He forced himself to focus on her. A mistake. Her hair was scattered around her face. She was glowing. Her lips looked faintly bruised. She looked more like a woman who had just had some loving laid on her than one who had just made a great sale.

"Cookie delivery will start on Monday," Bree said, a complete professional *now*. "The cookies have a shelf life, not refrigerated, of six days. I like to leave them only for a maximum of three. My delivery guy will change out any older cookies when he comes midweek. We donate them to a kitchen that feeds the homeless. Is that okay with you?"

"Fine," he said.

She stood up. "Thank you for your business, Brand." For a moment, her in-charge businesswoman persona faded. She took her hand out of her cloak, looked at it and looked at him as if she was considering offering it.

He could feel himself holding his breath. He really did not want to risk the temptation touching her again would no doubt create!

Thankfully, she saw his hesitation, tucked her hand back under her cloak and went out the door. He was aware, as it whispered shut behind her, that he was exceedingly tense.

He deliberately rolled back his shoulders, shrugged them up to his ears, then let them slide back down. He shot his dog a dirty look.

"Traitor."

Beau opened one eye and thumped his tail a few times. If he could talk Brand was pretty sure he'd say, "Look, buddy, we both kissed her. How is it I'm the traitor?"

"What did I just order, anyway?"

Bree rode the elevator down. "CEO of the century!" she told her reflection. Despite things going slightly off the rails—well, a lot off the rails if it came to that—it was a great contract.

She was not going to think about that kiss! Or the taste of him. Or the way he had looked after she had kissed him. Baffled and off-kilter and aware of her in a whole new way!

She was not going to think about what strange madness had overtaken her. She suspected he was right.

It was comeuppance for his rejection of her lips all those years ago. She probably had thought of it way more than she should have. Well, now she knew. She knew what he tasted like. She knew she could make him see her as a woman, not a child. She knew and she could put that all behind her.

She was not thinking of that anymore. He could be the worst possible kind of distraction. She was going to keep him at arm's length. She didn't have to see him again, and she was not going to indulge the little swoop of loss she felt right in her tummy at the thought of not seeing him again.

She was thinking of her business. How could she be in close proximity to those lips and still think about her business? So, proximity was out.

Between this, the new Perks contract and her special order for Crystal Silvers, Kookies for All Occasions was in the best shape it had been in since she had started the company.

Her phone vibrated in her pocket just as she exited the office building.

It was Chelsea, and she was talking loudly and rapidly, on the verge of hysteria. Bree had to hold her phone away from her ear.

"Chelsea, slow down. What happened?"

The story came out, bit by disjointed bit. When Bree understood completely, she froze in shock. But this is what she should have remembered about life: for her, good things were followed by disaster.

Since her father had died, it seemed that lesson got hammered home again and again. She had fallen in love with Paul, head-over-heels in love, shamelessly blinded by what she had felt for him. It had been, she thought, the best thing that ever happened to her.

The pregnancy had shown her his true colors. She had been shocked by how, underneath all that charm, he was self-centered and mean-spirited. He had accused her of doing it on purpose! Paul had seemed like the most romantic of men, but it had really been nothing more than manipulation of a vulnerable, very young and hopelessly naive woman. His abandonment had been complete and immediate.

That's what she knew about unforgivable!

Still, there had been the pregnancy, acting as a beautiful buffer to complete heartbreak. Of course she had been afraid. Of course her life had been disrupted. But underneath all that had been a little hum of joy that walked with her, a constant, through her days.

A baby. Her baby, growing beneath her heart. She sang it lullabies of pure love. She talked to it of hopes and fears.

But her joy stopped abruptly with the miscarriage, and never, if she thought about it, ever really came back. Not completely.

"I am not thinking about that right now!" she said fiercely, out loud, not caring who sent wary glances her way.

No, she was not going to pathetically catalog her heartbreaks and disappointments because of the blow Chelsea had just delivered.

She was harnessing the energy of her visit with
Brand. The aliveness of it. The powerful surging energy, a sense of not being able to do anything wrong.

"I am the CEO of the century," Bree reminded herself. "I've been given a problem. A big one, but there
is no point in crying over spilt milk. I need to find a
solution, not fold up my tent and creep into the night!"

But forty-eight hours later, exhausted and broken, she
admitted defeat.

With what was left of her strength she called his
number. For some reason, it felt as if it was going to be
her hardest call and so she made it first.

"Bree! I've been waiting for that contract."

She had steeled herself to sound only businesslike.
Did he have to sound so happy to hear from her?

"I'm sorry."

"Bree?"

"There isn't going to be a contract."

"Are you crying?"

"No."

"Not because of what happened here, I hope."

"I am not crying." But she was. Still, he couldn't see
her, red-faced and snotty-nosed, the antithesis of the
woman she had been two days ago.

So, he was still thinking of that kiss. Well, so was
she. The taste of his lips—and the surprising boldness
that she was capable of—was one of the few things
that had sustained her through forty-eight hours of hell.

"*If* I was crying it would have nothing to do with
what happened there."

"What's wrong?"

She found herself unable to speak.

"You *are* crying, aren't you? Where are you?" he asked.

"I'm at my apartment."

"I'm coming over."

"No, I—"

"Give me the address."

Oh, the temptation. There it was again, that foolish weakness, not wanting to be so alone with it all. To just lean on someone else, even for a little while.

"There's been a…situation, and I need to shut the company down temporarily." She had planned to tell him she hoped perhaps she would be up and running again in a few months, but she knew she could not keep control, so she quickly ended the call. "Goodbye, Brand. It was nice connecting with you again. Thank you for the opportunity."

"Bree—"

She disconnected.

She looked at herself. Of course he couldn't come over. Her whole apartment was smaller than his office. It was three o'clock in the afternoon and she was still in her pajamas. Her hair was tied up on top of her head with a neon orange shoelace. Her eyes were puffy. She wandered into the kitchen and opened the fridge. There was nothing in it. Well, a bottle of unopened wine, left over from a girls' night several weeks ago.

She could not have a drink. That was no way to deal with sorrow. It would be the beginning of the end.

Defiant of the bleak future the wine promised, she took the bottle out of the fridge. It wasn't even good wine. An Australian screw-top. If she ordered a pizza, it would be okay to have a glass. Lots of people—grown-ups—had a glass of wine with their pizza.

It might be a good idea to eat something, come to

think of it. Chocolate ice cream and the broken cookies she'd brought home could not sustain her forever. Plus, she was out of the ice-cream part of the equation. She called for a pizza, and took the wine into her tiny living room. Her cat, Oliver, was in her favorite chair, so she took the less comfortable couch.

She poured a glass of wine and eyed it. Red. She didn't even like red wine. It generally gave her a headache. She closed her eyes without sampling the wine.

The doorbell rang. Had she fallen asleep? She glanced at the clock. Only a few minutes had passed.

The pizza place was just down the street, but that was fast, even for them. She looked at her disheveled state: Oliver-approved pajamas with cats on them, furry slippers that looked like monster feet, her hair uncombed, her face unwashed.

She didn't owe an explanation to the pizza-delivery boy! He probably saw it all. Wasn't there even a commercial about that? Where a guy goes to the door in his underwear to get his pizza? Still, she found herself formulating a story about the flu as she opened the door.

The shock was so great, she tried to close it again.

CHAPTER SIX

"GET YOUR FOOT out of my door," Bree said. She shoved hard on the door. She felt like a mouse trying to move a mule.

"No."

"What are you doing here? I never gave you my address." Having failed to shut the door, she tucked herself behind it and peeked out at him. This was worse than being seen in her Kookies apron and beret. She was an absolute mess.

He, of course, was not. A mess. Or anything close to it. He was supremely put together in a light blue button-down shirt, dark chinos, boots, a black leather jacket and a scarf. She thought one man in a thousand could wear a scarf well. Naturally, he would be that one.

"I work with the world's best computer geeks," Brand said smoothly. "Your address, to them? Child's play. A great big yawn. Not even a challenge. Had it in my hand forty seconds after I asked for it."

"I'm not sure if that is completely ethical," she said crisply, from her station behind the door.

He cocked his head at her. "I'm not sure it is, either," he said thoughtfully. "But you should think of how easy it was next time you are arranging to meet a stranger on e-Us."

"How did you get in the front door of the building?"

He blinked at her twice, slowly, demonstrating his hypnotic charm. "This is a face that inspires trust, particularly in a little old lady trying to manage an unruly beagle and a bag of groceries at the same time."

"Mrs. Murphy," she said, annoyed. "Why are you here, Brand?"

And why did he have to look so good? Strong, and put-together, and sure of himself, the kind of guy a woman in a weakened state might want to throw herself at.

"I wanted to make sure you were okay."

"Well," she said, "you can clearly see I'm okay."

"You're hiding behind a door. How do I know if you're okay? Maybe one of your computer dates hit you over the head with a club."

She stepped out from behind the door. "See?"

He looked her up and down. He looked insultingly unconvinced about her okayness. He stared at her feet for a long time before he looked up again.

"You look as if you've been crying," he said softly.

"I have the flu, sick to my stomach, cold symptoms, runny nose, puffy eyes. You know," she said, relieved she had prepared an excuse for the pizza-delivery boy.

Who chose that minute to get off the elevator, in his distinctive red ball cap and shirt, and come to her apartment door.

"Your front-door security clearly sucks," Brand noted in an undertone.

"Medium, everything on it, double anchovies?" the delivery boy asked cheerfully.

Brand raised an eyebrow at her. "Flu food?"

She glared at him and turned to get her wallet out of her pint-size kitchen. When she returned the pizza boy was gone, and Brand was inside, holding the box, her door shut firmly behind him.

"Really? Double anchovy?" he asked.

"My weakness."

"Mine, too."

She searched his face for the lie and found none.

"Can we share it?" he asked. He was grinning that boyish grin, the same one that had, no doubt, sucked Mrs. Murphy into letting him into the building. Bree found herself as helpless as Mrs. Murphy. Who on earth could resist this overpowering charm?

"Since you paid for it, would it seem churlish to refuse?"

"Yes."

"You didn't have to come."

"No, I didn't. What can I say? I find a damsel in distress irresistible."

Somehow, with Brand, there was no point telling him he did not have to do the decent thing.

"I seriously doubt there is one thing about me that is irresistible at the moment," she said as she led him through to the tiny living room. Oliver gave him a disdainful look and curled into a tighter ball, which left them the option of sharing a too-small couch. Brand sat down on it.

"I should go get dressed. I'm at my worst."

"Well, I've already seen it, so I wouldn't get too twisted. It's not as if I can unsee it."

She flopped down on the couch beside him. "The

old 'no point shutting the barn door after the horse is out,' eh? That bad?"

He slid her a look. "Kind of adorable."

"Adorable," she said glumly. He was ready for his *GQ* cover and she was adorable. "Like a Pomeranian puppy?"

"More like a Yorkie. It's the furry-feet slippers. And the bow in your hair. You know how Yorkies wear those little bows on their heads?"

She reached up and yanked the shoelace out of her hair.

He sighed. "The adorable factor just went down, oh, maybe five points."

Don't indulge him, she ordered herself. "On what scale?"

"Out of a hundred. Being a perfect hundred before and now minus the five points."

"If I take off the pajamas?"

He went very still.

"I didn't mean it like that." She gave him a good hard punch in the arm.

He held his arm and made a face of exaggerated pain. "Oh. Okay. I just couldn't be sure. Because of that kiss—"

She punched him again. "Don't ever mention that to me again!"

"Bossy. Another five points off. And ten for each time you hit me in the arm."

"I should be a rottweiler pretty soon then. I can only hope. People respect rottweilers," she muttered, though inwardly she was greatly enjoying his banter. Only because it was proving a distraction from the last few days, which had been so without lightness of any kind.

"You have the feet for a rottweiler," he suggested.

She kicked off the slippers.

"Minus two for losing the slippers. Cute feet, though. Are your toenails lime-green? Plus twenty."

"With flowers." She held one up for him to inspect.

"Impressive. Plus twenty-five."

"It's not really my style, but Chelsea wants to work in a spa someday, once she gives up salsa dancing. Her toes are always showing for competitions, so she's very good at nail polishes. Still, she likes to practice on other people, namely me. I don't let her touch my fingernails, though, just the parts of me that usually don't show!"

He eyed the glass of wine, the bottle beside it. "For someone a little inhibited it seems like it might be a bit early for that," he said.

"Too early for anchovies?" She grabbed her wineglass. She took a defiant sip. Inhibited? Who had kissed whom?

"You better tell me what's going on." His shoulder was touching hers. Warmth radiated through his jacket. The leather was soft and supple, and if expense had a smell, the scent coming off the jacket would be it. Brand put the pizza box on the hassock and opened it.

She set down her wine and took the piece of pizza he offered. There was no way to eat an everything-on-it with any kind of decorum, but it was too late to make a good impression now, anyway. She was suddenly starving.

Come to think of it, she was all done making impressions. She took a huge bite of the pizza and chewing it gave her a few moments to put her thoughts together.

"You can see from the size of this place, I wasn't making cookies here." She kept her voice firm. "I rented space in a commercial kitchen. It burned to the ground two days ago, just as I was leaving your office, actually. Chelsea was there. I don't want to say Chelsea burned it to the ground, but she does get distracted practicing her routines while the cookies bake. There's some talk of a lawsuit. The building owner advised me to retain a lawyer."

"Ouch."

"Do you know what that costs?"

"Unfortunately."

"If that wasn't bad enough, I lost all my stock and some of my equipment and inventory. Insurance will cover some of the stock and inventory—unless Chelsea is found liable. Then I would have to sue her personally, which I don't think I could do, under any circumstances, even if she was practicing salsa dancing and got distracted and caught the kitchen on fire. She's so upset already."

"Do you have another wineglass?"

"Kitchen cupboard beside the range."

He got up and she watched him go. His shoulders practically touched either side of the galley-kitchen door frame. Her place was small, and now it seemed smaller, as if he was filling it—not just the floor space, but the air. He would leave, but still be here. She would breathe him in forever. She might have to move. On top of everything else.

She sighed heavily. Brand came back with a coffee mug instead of a wineglass. He poured himself some wine. He sampled it cautiously. "Not as bad as I thought it would be."

"My story?"

"No, that's worse than I thought it would be. The

wine's pretty good, though I'm just drinking this to keep you from downing the whole bottle yourself. Not that you don't have reason, but I don't want to see you get drunk. Lose your inhibitions—"

She cocked her fist at him.

"I wasn't going to mention the thing that must not be mentioned." His eyes went to her lips, and stayed there for a heated second until he looked away.

Had he deliberately paraphrased a very famous line from a series of books she had admitted, in an unguarded moment, to liking? Did that mean he had read them?

Possibly just seen the movies, which was way more resistible.

"A gentleman until the end," she said wryly.

"I try," he said.

"This is one of those surreal moments," she decided. "Here I am in my hobbit-sized apartment with a view of the side of the building next door, serving cheap wine in a coffee mug to the man being lauded by *City* magazine as the billionaire businessman of the decade."

"Don't forget the furry-feet slippers and the shoelace," he said, beautifully unimpressed with himself.

"This could only happen to me."

"You're probably right. Cheers."

"Cheers," she said. They rapped their glasses together.

"I like your hobbit-sized place," he said. "It's homey."

"Humble."

"Don't worry about it, Bree. I'm not really a gentleman."

"What? Of course you are!"

He wagged his eyebrows fiendishly at her, but there

was something in his voice when he spoke again. "I'm just a pretender at the genteel life. What I come from makes this place look like a palace."

"Really?" But then she remembered something he had said the night of the gala. He had said her family looked perfect, particularly to someone who came from one that was not. He had mentioned he had no father figure.

He nodded.

Suddenly, she *needed* to know. She needed to know something deeper about him, needed to know he could be vulnerable, too.

"Tell me about that," she insisted softly.

He hesitated. She thought he might distract with charm. But he didn't. After a long moment, he spoke.

"My dad left my mom and I when I was six." His voice had a roughness around the edge of it that it did not normally have. "My mom was ill. We lived in places smaller than shoeboxes. On one memorable occasion, we lived in a car for three days. Sometimes we went to McDonald's and stole creamers because she didn't have money for milk. She would have considered this wine champagne."

Somehow his revealing this part of himself was the most extraordinary of gifts. This was authentic, the edge of raw pain in his voice was real. That he had found her worthy of entrusting with this secret part of himself felt like the best thing that had happened to her in a long time.

Maybe even better than that kiss. Well, maybe not.

The moment of feeling he trusted her was extraordinarily brief. "I don't know why I said that," he said with a regretful shake of his head.

"You can trust me with it," she said softly.

"Thanks," he replied, but his tone was clipped.

She had questions, but assumed from the growl in his voice and his use of the past tense when talking about the champagne, that his mother was dead, and that it still caused him pain to think about it.

"Did my dad know how things were for you?" she asked.

He looked like he was very annoyed by the fact she was continuing the conversation, but after a moment he answered.

"Not all the details, but he knew I was shouldering a lot of responsibility. He helped me apply for scholarships at college. He wrote me letters of endorsement. I think he paid me more than I was worth when I worked for him. Your dad was one decent guy, Bree."

"So are you."

He lifted a shoulder.

"I think that's why you're such a decent guy," she said softly. "You know firsthand what it's like to have it tough."

Maybe it was the wrong thing to say, because a veil went down completely in his eyes, as if he regretted sharing the confidence as much as she welcomed it.

"We'll save my tales of woe for a different day," he said smoothly. "Right now I want to hear the rest of yours."

She would have liked to talk about him some more, but she could clearly see he had said all he was going to say for one day. She appreciated his confidence and did not want to appear to pry. So, she took a fortifying gulp of her wine before launching into the rest of the story.

"I thought I could rent another kitchen, but I've been

unable to find a suitable space in my price range. I'm behind on orders. You can see I can't work out of here. I'm going to have to cancel the Crystal Silvers contract. And Perks. I'm going to have to let Chelsea go, and she's already a mess, poor kid. I know I will eventually get back on my feet, but for now—" Despite that fortifying gulp of wine her voice cracked.

"For now, I'm done," she choked out. She finished her wine in one long pull. When she went to refill, he took the bottle and put it out of her reach, beside him on the floor.

"Bree, I might be able to help you out."

So, here they were again. He was going to help her out. He still felt as if he owed her dad a debt of gratitude.

But she didn't want to fight it anymore. She was so tired. She just wanted to sink into his strength. To let him take care of her. To let him rescue her from her life. There were worse things than letting a super successful man—who had a good heart and was decent to boot— look after you, take your troubles away.

Okay, so she had taken ten giant steps back from the woman in the beautiful cloak and high heels that she had been just two short days ago. She might never see that woman again, she realized sadly. The cloak was probably going to have to go to a consignment store. She couldn't in good conscience take it back. The dog had slobbered on it.

"You probably have a team of lawyers," she said. "Thank you."

"Wasn't even thinking of the legal aspects of your dilemma, but yes, I'll run your liability issues by my legal eagles."

"What were you thinking about?"

"A place for you to work."

"I appreciate you wanting to help, but believe me," she said, "I've already tried everything. I even hoped maybe I could rent a restaurant kitchen, after hours, work all night if I had to, but I just couldn't turn anything up. Again, it's the budget. And I don't want you to offer to rent me a kitchen over my budget, because the cookie business can't sustain that. It's still a business, not a charity, and if I can't run it in the black—"

"Bree, be quiet."

She sighed. Was he hearing her?

"I have a kitchen," he said softly. "In your price range. I have a commercial kitchen. That's completely empty. And available. That no one ever uses."

"Yeah, as if that would be in my price range."

"It's in your price range."

"You don't even know what my price range is. It's laughably small."

"The kitchen is free."

"Are you kidding me?" She could not keep the skepticism out of her voice. "I would have to hate you forever if you rented a kitchen for me, and then told me it was free out of some kind of misguided—"

"I would never lie to you like that. Never. And I would never risk having you hate me forever."

She could feel herself falling toward the most frightening thing of all: hope. She searched his face. She could see the innate trustworthiness of him. She felt that hope flutter to reluctant life in her chest.

"If you're kidding me, I'll have to kill you. You know that, don't you?"

"I understand completely. I mean, it's just theoretical, because I have a kitchen, but how would you go about killing me?"

"I'd have to think about it," she said regally.

"Because I'm quite big, and you're quite small. It's not like I would just stand there, with my arms open, saying, 'okay, kill me now.' And to be honest, you don't seem very threatening. I think it may be the slippers you took off a while ago that ruin your killer image."

"Maybe those slippers shoot…things. Like in a James Bond movie."

"You'd have to be more specific to convince me. Bullets? Darts? Cookies?"

She loved this bantering back and forth, but she had to know.

"Brand, please do not keep me in suspense another moment! We can discuss your potential demise another time. Tell me about the kitchen! No one *has* a kitchen, just sitting around, at their disposal."

"Well, I do."

Don't get your hopes up, she told herself. She was crying. She couldn't help it. "Where is it? Brand, I need to start right away. I'm so far behind. If I work night and day I might be able to get the Crystal Silvers birthday cookies done. Maybe."

"You'll get them done," he said, with such absolute confidence in her that she cried harder.

"How can I thank you? Where is it?"

"It's at my house."

Her heart dropped, and the tears of relief stopped. She tried not to replace them with the despairing, hopeless kind.

She took a deep breath, and did her best not to sound

too skeptical. But she'd already resigned herself to it. It was too good to be true.

"You have a commercial kitchen in your house? No one has a commercial kitchen in their house. Why would a bachelor have a commercial kitchen in his house?"

"When I bought the house, I renovated it, top to bottom. The designer told me a commercial kitchen was an investment. She said the kind of house I have is where large functions are catered."

Of course he'd have that kind of house. Brand was a billionaire. Still, Bree was a little awestruck all the same.

"I gave my poor designer a pretty hard time about that kitchen. She just kept insisting that someday I'd be really glad I had it. And you know what?"

"What?" Bree breathed.

"She was absolutely right."

His voice was soft and strong at the same time, the voice of a man who could make someone believe, all over again, even when they knew better, that magic was part of the fabric of life, that miracles happened all the time.

That when you had totally given up, when you had no hope left, life could surprise you all over again with how good it could be.

CHAPTER SEVEN

BREE EVANS WAS in his house.

Brand recognized, on the danger scale, the needle was edging toward the top of the red zone.

Because she was so very complex. Adorable. But smart. An astute businesswoman. The daughter of a man who had helped him. A woman whose kiss he could not get out of his head.

He'd confided in her that he'd once lived in a car. No one but his mother knew that about his life. What kind of moment of ridiculous weakness had that been?

Brand watched her race around his kitchen, nearly beside herself with excitement, and it felt as if every ounce of that danger he had invited into his life was worthwhile.

She stopped at the Elvis cookie jar. She took out a cookie and examined it as if she had found a bug.

"Beau's?" she said.

"He does have a weakness. Despite what Jenn said, I restrict him to one or two a week. He mostly gets dog biscuits, which he only tolerates."

"When I get caught up, I'll try making something for him that's healthier and that he'll love." She put the cookie back in the jar, and examined the jar itself. "Somehow I didn't figure you for an Elvis kind of guy."

The less she figured out about him, the better. Especially now that he had given her hints. Especially now that she was under his roof. Making herself at home.

No, that wasn't quite right. She wasn't making herself at home, she was making it feel like home.

Without even trying. She was making it feel like home even *before* she tried baking cookies for his dog.

"What exactly would you consider an Elvis kind of guy?" he asked, intrigued despite himself.

"Sleazily oversexed?"

"Elvis?" he said, with pretended hurt. "That's slanderous. You have enough legal problems without slandering the King."

"I think e-Us matched me with him once. Complete with the sweaty scarf." She shuddered delicately.

"Okay, here's the deal. I said the kitchen was free, but it's not."

"Don't do this to me," she moaned.

"No more e-Us. That's the price."

"Deal," she said, way too fast.

He eyed her suspiciously.

"I've got my sights set on Kevin."

"I hope you don't."

"I do," she said and whipped her phone out of her back pocket. "Look. There's an app that teaches you to speak Klingon."

He saw she was teasing him. Or he was pretty sure she was teasing him. But she did know about the app.

"I'm going to be way too busy to have a social life," she declared happily.

Why was he happy, too? What did he care about her social life or lack thereof?

She was dashing around the kitchen again, opening drawers, looking in cupboards. She ran reverent hands over one of the ovens. "A steam oven. I could not have dreamed."

She opened it up. "You've never used this," she said with faint accusation.

"How do you know?"

"The racks have cardboard on the corners."

"Oh."

"Three ovens," she whispered, looking around. "Have you used any of them? Oh!" she squealed, before he had a chance to answer. "Look at this!"

He came over to see what was causing such excitement. She had changed out of her pajamas, and put her hair up with a band. He liked the shoestring better, not that he wanted her to know he'd noticed. She was wearing snug jeans and a white top.

She was bent over a lower cabinet looking inside it. He could look at that particular sight for a long time, but it made him feel like an oversexed Elvis so he made himself focus on what she was looking at. Something huge and ugly and red was in his cupboard.

"What is that?" he asked, astounded.

"It's in your kitchen. You don't know?" She tossed an amused look over her shoulder.

"See that thing over there?" he said, and pointed. "It's called a microwave. I know that. And the fridge. I've used the coffeemaker a couple of times."

"That explains why it's so clean in here."

Actually, a cleaning staff kept it clean in here, but it seemed so pretentious to say it, that he didn't.

"Well, this—" she tugged, and the whole shelf slid out and began to rise "—is a stand mixer. Sometimes called a batch mixer."

He was so startled at it moving by itself that he took a step back. He actually took her shoulders and moved her back, too.

The monstrous apparatus rose silently and then stopped at counter level.

"If it moves toward you, run," he whispered.

He loved her giggle. She sounded like Goldie Hawn.

"It's not dangerous," she assured him. She reached out as if she was going to pet it.

He grabbed her hand. "Don't touch. I think it may be HAL."

"HAL?"

She had to ask. He wouldn't break it to her just yet that she didn't have a hope with Kevin. He didn't care about her and Kevin. Shoot. He cared about her and Kevin. And her and some guy who had stiffed her for coffee. And her and the sleazy oversexed guy with the scarf. He was still holding her hand. He dropped it like it was hot.

"2001: A Space Odyssey."

She was all over that ugly red space alien piece of machinery. "I'm not familiar with it."

Kiss Kevin goodbye.

"It's a movie. Old. Sci-fi."

"Hmmm, you don't look like a sci-fi kind of guy."

Or an Elvis kind of guy. He was going to ask her how she knew a sci-fi guy from one who wasn't, but she'd probably dated one.

Instead he said, "I'm not really a sci-fi guy, but when you work with the geek squad, you pick up on what they consider to be the essentials of life. Consider it like being immersed in a continuous episode of *The Big Bang Theory*."

She was very focused on the apparatus in front of her but laughed at his joke. She was obviously very familiar with the ugly red space alien. Was she caressing the damn thing?

Don't ask. "What kind of guy would you say I am?" he asked.

"The best kind," she said with a smile. "The kind with a commercial kitchen *and* a stand mixer."

"I have other sterling qualities."

"Where's your bedroom?"

His jaw dropped. He, who considered himself virtually unshakable, felt like he was turning the same color as the darned mixer.

"That's not what I meant," he said. His voice sounded like a squeak.

She actually turned her attention away from the attractions of the mixer and stared at him. And then her eyes widened. And then she giggled, that funny little Goldie Hawn giggle. And then the giggle deepened into something even better. She laughed. She laughed until she doubled over from it. She laughed until the tears were squirting out her eyes.

"Oh, my God, Brand."

"What's so damn funny?"

"I wasn't suggesting you had sterling qualities in the bedroom. Not that you don't. I mean maybe you do."

Her laughter dried up, just like that. Now they were both standing there with faces as red as the mixer.

"I'm going to be trying to catch up on my orders." She was speaking very fast, her words tumbling over one another. "I need to call Chelsea. We'll probably work all night. I wanted to know where your bedroom was so we wouldn't disturb you. So I know how quiet I need to be. We usually work with music. And equipment like this—" she patted that mixer with disturbing affection again "—is quite loud."

"Oh." He said. "That's a relief." Well, kind of a disappointment, but mostly a relief.

She actually looked faintly hurt. "Yes, isn't it?"

"My bedroom's a long way away. Play anything you want. As loud as you want."

"Do you have a favorite Elvis song?"

The soundtrack of his childhood. He could tell from which one was playing when he walked through the door after school how his Mom was going to be that evening. Or maybe more accurately, who she was going to be.

He could have never told Wendy about that. Had never wanted to.

And yet, at this precise moment, there was an ache to tell Bree. It felt as if he would die of loneliness if he didn't tell her.

But he didn't.

Instead, he forced his tone to be smooth and light, and answered, "Must I pick only one? Impossible. Yours?"

She didn't hesitate. "'I Can't Help—'"

She stopped. She stared at him. She stammered, "Uh, I can't think of one. 'Jailhouse Rock' maybe."

He should tell her never to take up poker. She was a terrible liar.

They were definitely in the danger zone right now, right this instant. He could feel the chemistry between them. The needle was edging up into red. He'd made a mistake inviting her into his space. He could clearly see that.

"Don't worry about disturbing me at all," he said. "I was just going to pack a bag, anyway."

"You were?"

"Yes, I have a business trip. We're opening a new physical location. Bali." He hadn't been planning on going to the opening until thirty seconds ago. Suddenly it felt imperative to put a world of oceans between them.

"Bali," she said.

He thought of her in Bali. Carefree. He wondered if she'd ever snorkeled. Or surfed. That was where he had learned to do both. He felt an unfortunate curiosity about what she would look like in a bikini.

"Okay," he said, hastily "if you've got everything you need, I'll go pack."

"Yes," she said formally. "I've taken enough of your time."

He moved away from her, edging toward the door. Edging back toward the world where he controlled everything. Where there were surprises, of course there were, but in a way, even though they were surprises, they were predictable kind of surprises. Like deciding to go to Bali on a moment's notice.

Nothing that made his heart do what it was doing right now.

Thank goodness!

"Yes, you do that," she said, as insultingly eager to get rid of him as he was to go. "Go to pack. Do I need a key? To get in and out? I'll need to go for supplies."

He started to say he didn't lock it. But suddenly he didn't want his house unlocked with him away and her coming in and out. What if she was coming in with her arms full of groceries and there was an intruder, already inside? Or what if she was inside making a bunch of noise, so much noise she might not hear an intruder? Beau would be left at the office while he was away. Should he leave him here with her instead? To protect her?

No. The dog would probably compromise the health standards of the kitchen. There was a keypad on the front door that Brand had never used. He was going to have to figure it out. He'd call one of his technical geniuses.

It occurred to him he'd never thought he had anything of value in here. It was valuable stuff, but he recognized, right this minute, he had no attachment to any of it.

It felt as if Bree Evans was the only valuable thing in his world.

Her and Beau.

Beau could look after himself.

"I have to get going," he said again. He could hear the desperation in his own voice. He was pretty sure there was a line of sweat breaking out over his top lip.

She waltzed over to him. She looked as if she was going to kiss him again. He backed away from her rapidly.

"Make yourself at home while I'm away," Brand said. "If you need a break there's a media room through that door. The freezer has microwavable stuff in it, if you get sick of eating cookies. There are guest bedrooms upstairs if you need a snooze. There's four, no, five powder rooms, so take your pick."

There was that look again, as if she might kiss him. He backed away from her even more rapidly. As unmanly as it was, he was practically running from her.

"Thank you," she called after him, as he went through the door to the hallway.

Her voice sounded as if it had laughter in it. Minx. She *liked* making him uncomfortable.

And he liked making her laugh. In fact, Brand was very aware that a man could live to make her laugh, to wipe the worry lines from her forehead, to erase the sorrow from her eyes...

A better man than him, he reminded himself. One without baggage, a ragtag excuse for a family, a number of failed forays into the relationship department, his only serious one, Wendy, having failed quite colossally.

Bali, he told himself. That should take his mind off her. Sand and surf and work. Lots and lots of work.

Work. It had always been the place he escaped. It was a world where a person could apply their mind to problems and make them dissolve. It was a world where the challenges were not personal, where they had no emotion attached to them. It was a world he could lose himself in, shut out any little thing that bothered him or caused him distress or discomfort.

The only thing was, he'd never been aware before that he used it to escape the nebulous unsolvable kind of problems that popped up when you became attached to another person.

He waited until he was out of the house to slide his phone from his pocket. He punched in the familiar number. He got her answering message.

"Hi, Mom, I'm going to be away for a couple of days. I'll video-call you tonight on your phone."

His mother loved that feature on her phone. "It's just like being on *The Jetsons*," she'd say with wonder every single time he called.

CHAPTER EIGHT

BREE CAME AWAKE with a start and a little shriek.

"Sorry, I didn't mean to startle you."

His voice wrapped around her in the darkness and made her feel safe.

"Brand?" she asked sleepily. In what context would she be waking up to Brand? It was a dream, obviously, a delightful dream that she never wanted to end.

"I had no idea you were in here," he said, softly, his voice like the touch of a silk scarf across the back of her neck.

She remembered, slowly, she was in one of the deep recliner chairs in his media room. She had helped herself to one of the Icelandic wool blankets artfully placed in a huge basket in one of the corners.

"What time is it?" You could never tell in the media room, because, unlike the kitchen, which was saturated in light from the banks of windows, light had been deliberately blocked out of this room.

"Eight."

"In the morning?" she asked, shocked.

"Yeah."

"Are you just getting home?"

"Yeah. I was going to unwind from the trip in here for a bit, but I'll—"

"No—no, of course you can unwind in your own home. Chelsea and I finished late. It was about two in the morning. I should have gone home," she said, suddenly embarrassed. "I was just going to sit here for a moment, but I made the mistake of reclining the chair. So comfy! I hope I didn't leave the ovens on." She sniffed the air. "I wouldn't want to burn down two kitchens."

"There's nothing burning. The house smells incredible, though. You could bottle that smell. Make a fortune."

Her eyes were adjusting to the dark. He was still dressed for the tropics in light pants and a sports shirt. He looked so yummy, ever so slightly travel-rumpled, his hair not quite as crisply groomed as normal, his cheeks and chin dark with whisker stubble.

She remembered she had on the white-net baking cap, and she tried to remove it as surreptitiously as possible and stuff it in the pocket of her chef's jacket. Why did he always have to catch her at her worst?

"How was Bali?"

He didn't answer.

"Not what you hoped?" she asked. "Did something go wrong?"

"No, not really. I'm just a bit off. Time difference." He moved by her, took the deep chair next to hers and pushed it back into full recline. "Anything new in the fire investigation?"

Bree cast Brand a glance out of the corner of her eye. His hands were folded over his stomach and he was looking at the ceiling. It had been a week since she'd seen him. Was he deliberately avoiding talking about himself?

"Chelsea's a mess. She's been interviewed twice, and they've intimidated her horribly."

"Does she have a lawyer?"

"On what I pay her?"

"Would you let me look after it?"

A terrible tenderness unfolded in her at the weariness etched into the lines of his handsome face.

Of course she felt tender toward him! He had saved her business. He had given her a place to work that was beyond her wildest dreams. Now he was offering to help Chelsea.

"Thank you," she said, feeling any defenses she had left against him crumbling as she accepted his gift with the graciousness it deserved. "You should go to bed."

"You should, too."

Together. She knew the renegade thought proved she was not just feeling tender toward him because of her business or his offer to help Chelsea.

"I think I'm awake for the day," she said hastily, to move the talk and her still dream-weakened thoughts away from the topic of beds.

"Yes, me, too. The worst thing I could do this morning is indulge my desire to sleep. I need to force myself back on to this time."

It reminded her, no matter how tender she felt toward him, that her feelings had to remain her closely guarded secret. They were from different worlds. He was a man accustomed to dealing with jet lag, business trips to Bali and beyond. She made cookies for a living.

"How did the cookies go?" he asked, as if he could read her mind. He asked it as though he really cared, damn him, and as if there was not a huge gap in their socioeconomic circumstances.

"We're completely caught up. All my regular orders are done. Perks got their first order. Chelsea took the

Crystal Silvers order to the airport last night when we finished."

"You've been busy," he said.

"Yes, my poor cat has been feeling neglected." Now why had she said that? Add crazy cat lady to cookie maker! Besides, it wasn't true. Her neighbor, an elderly lady, loved Oliver and had liked nothing more than taking the cat while Bree put in these long hours.

"I guess you probably feel the same about Beau? Will you pick him up and bring him home today?"

"I'll probably banish him while the baking is going on. I think your health standard would be compromised by his presence."

"Aw, poor guy."

"Not really. He's used to me being away. He's got a pretty nice setup at the office, too. There's people working there all the time."

"Your office runs all the time?"

"It's that creative-brain thing. Lots of my people say they work best at night. I just go with it. The office is open twenty-four hours. I let them keep track of their own time."

"You need more cookies if you're running twenty-four hours," she said. "Your office is next on the list. I've been filling orders in between the Crystal Silvers special order, and I'm caught up. Your office will be going into the rotation starting on Monday."

"You haven't sent me a contract yet," he said. His voice was husky with sleepiness.

She wouldn't tell him this just yet, because he was sure to reject it, but she wasn't sending him a contract. She was baking his office cookies for free, for the rest of her life. And cookies for Beau, too, as soon as she figured out a dog-friendly recipe.

His chest was starting to rise and fall.

"You can bring Beau home," she said. "I'll be taking the next two days off."

She realized she wanted to stay here forever, feeling warm and safe and oddly happy. She forced herself to throw back the blanket and get up. "Can I bring you anything before I leave?"

"Sure. A Love Bite and a Decadent."

He remembered things. That was the nature of being a businessman, remembering details about people and their businesses. Still, she felt inordinately pleased that he remembered the names of her cookies.

Then he added, "And with anyone else, a decadent love bite would mean something quite different than it does with you. Just saying."

She laughed, a bit uneasily. There it was again, between them, teasing, which was wonderful, but it was teasing with some finely held tension, like a shiver when you went outside on a cold day. "I'll be right back."

But he got up and followed her into the kitchen.

"I don't want to go to sleep," Brand insisted. "I know from past experience what giving in to that temptation does. It can take weeks to get back to normal if you don't force yourself back into a regular daily schedule right away."

Morning light was streaming in the kitchen windows. In the brightness, he still looked tired, and also sexily roguish with that hint of whisker shadow on his face. She could see his skin had picked up a faint golden glow from the sun.

She felt something tingle along her spine. There was something about the way he was looking at her that could give that expression, about giving in to temptation, many meanings. They had been apart for a week. It had not cooled the way she felt about him. It had intensified it.

Did he feel the same way? Or was it all just banter to him? He would be good at flirting, probably with no awareness of how good he was at it. In one sentence of that *City* article they had called him Vancouver's most eligible bachelor.

"Wow," he said, looking around. "If there's a heaven this is what it looks and smells like."

She looked around and saw what he saw. His kitchen was, indeed, a beautiful sight. It was bright and clean, with clearly defined workstations. But the best sight of all—well, besides him—was those big clearly labeled rectangular bakery boxes, stacked up on racks in the center island. Cookies all boxed up and ready to go to their various destinations and drop-off points.

"I'm interested in what brought you to filling up your life with cookies," he said as she handed him the two flavors he had requested. Their fingertips brushed. Something electrical, like static, leaped between them.

It was probably from the Icelandic wool!

"I don't usually recommend these for breakfast," she said, as if she could chase away the electricity, and the helpless feeling it gave her, with stern words.

"Ah, well, its suppertime in Bali." He popped a whole cookie in his mouth—no easy task—then closed his eyes and chewed contentedly.

"They aren't healthy for supper, either!"

Though watching him, a memory tickled the back of her mind.

"My dad used to eat them for supper sometimes," she said softly, then added thoughtfully, "I guess that's the *why* of cookies. I got an Easy-Bake Oven for Christmas when I was six, and was soon tired of the limitations of it. I graduated to the big-girl oven and started baking cookies for my dad. If there were cookies, warm out of the oven, when he got home, he'd get so excited. He'd gobble them down for supper. He'd do impressions of the Cookie Monster until my mother and I were in hysterics, rolling on the floor, begging him to stop. Of course, it just egged him on.

"The base dough for those cookies you are eating right now is the recipe I kept working on as a kid. It still changes slightly from time to time. For instance, last year, I started adding a bit of coffee to it."

"Good business," Brand said, opening his eyes and regarding her. "Coffee and chocolate, highly addictive."

"I never gave that a thought."

"You wouldn't," he said.

If he was going to insist on seeing her as an innocent, she was going to have to kiss him again.

No! She could never kiss him again. Because it made her long for things she could not have.

He was so far out of her league it wasn't even funny.

"I haven't just been making cookies. I've been looking for another kitchen. I can't impose on you forever. I think I've got a line on one. It sounds as if it might be available for the beginning of the month. Beau can come home."

"Sheesh, stop feeling guilty about Beau."

"I've displaced him. And you, too."

"This is pretty normal for me. To travel. To be away for long periods."

"Do you ever stay still?" she asked quietly. "Do you ever just kick back and enjoy your beautiful home?"

"Oh, sure," he said. "I wind down here. You've seen the media room. It's perfect for football and a beer."

"That's not actually what I meant," she said.

"Oh? What did you mean?"

"I meant…" She tried to think of how to put it. "I meant a fire in the fireplace. And a turkey in the oven. A Christmas tree."

"It's May!" he said.

"I'm not explaining it very well." She was *not* explaining it very well, but she also suspected he was being deliberately obtuse.

"No, you're not."

"It's not about Christmas. It's about a feeling. Of being *home*."

"Cue the *Little House on the Prairie* music," he said sarcastically.

But, in actual fact, she already knew this about him: his space lacked a sense of being a home. It was as if the house had spoken to her while he'd been away, divulged some of his secrets.

It was a beautiful house, like the houses you saw in magazines. She had taken advantage of his invitation and in his absence she had napped in one of the gorgeous upstairs bedrooms. She had found excuses to inspect all the powder rooms.

Everything was perfect, as perfect and as high-end as the kitchen would have you predict it would be. There were beautiful original art pieces, priceless hand-knotted rugs, painted silk wallpapers, incredible one-of-a-kind light fixtures and the aforementioned hand-knitted Icelandic throws. There were collectibles from many different countries, artfully worked into the décor. The furniture was all stunning. There were gorgeous scenes all over the house, as if they were waiting for a photographer. A desk with a leather-bound journal open and a pen beside it in an alcove under an upstairs window. A fireplace in the formal living room with the fire laid, as if all you had to do was strike a match. There were two vases of spring fresh tulips on a long dining room table that looked as if it had never been eaten at. There were fresh rosebuds in all the guest bedrooms, and a bucket full of delicately blushing pink peonies in the landing of the grand staircase.

And yet, as almost overwhelmingly beautiful as everything was, and despite how busy and how exhausted Bree was, she thought that his house felt empty. Staff came in, to clean and change flowers, but that just made it feel even more like a house that was being beautifully staged to sell, rather than a house anyone lived in.

There was no sign of his entertaining female guests, either. There was no second toothbrush, no tubes of mascara left out, no feminine shoes in the front coat closet, no chick flicks in his enormous collection of movies, no yogurt or diet soda in his fridge.

She felt as if the house cried for the feminine touches that would have made it a home and for children screaming and running up and down the halls and leaving messes everywhere. It felt as if the house longed for laughter, love, energy. It felt as if the house wanted to be filled up with the smells of people living in it: roast beef in the oven, crisp Yorkshire puddings erupting out of baking tins.

It was the saddest thing she could think of: a house that had never had cookies baked in it, or at least not while he had lived here. She could tell none of the three ovens had ever been used. The state-of-the-art appliances all sparkled prettily, but, like the stoves, she would put money on whether or not they had ever been turned on until she came along.

And even now, it was the scent of cookie *production*, not cookies, that had welcomed him back from his trip.

That is what she was very aware of. It was a house.

Not a home. A place to crash and watch a football game and drink a beer.

Instead of making her feel awed by his success, the house had made her feel the acute loneliness of it. She understood perfectly why he would not spend a great deal of time here, or be eager to come "home" to it.

The only room she truly liked was the media room, with its deep, ugly chairs, and its stinky dog bed, and its gaudy Elvis posters and its faint smell of old popcorn.

Underneath Brand's sarcastic tone—"cue the *Little House on the Prairie* music"—Bree heard the faintest thing: a longing, a wistfulness.

All of a sudden she knew she wasn't leaving right away, even though that would be the smartest thing to do, even though her cat had suffered enough neglect this week.

If she wanted to protect her poor heart, and she did, she should already be halfway out that door.

But suddenly, it was not all about her. Suddenly, she was aware that was not how she had been raised. She was almost ashamed of the self-centeredness that wanted her to protect herself when she had the most precious gift to give this man who had done so much for her.

She had discovered what she could give him. This man who had saved her business, casually, as if it meant nothing, as if life was a game of Monopoly and he had a pocket full of save-a-business-for-free cards.

She wanted to repay him. But how did you repay a man who had everything? You gave him the one thing he had never had.

She could give him something he had missed. She knew from the small snippets of his childhood that he had confided in her about—living in a car for three days, for goodness sake—that it was unlikely his home had held normal activities, like baking cookies.

Giving him cookies for life was not enough. Besides, they were material. He could buy warehouses full of cookies. Her cookies, or someone else's. She'd been in this business long enough to know competition was stiff and rapidly growing. Hers was not the only company that produced a delicious, meticulously made product.

So, she could give Brand the experience of *making* cookies. A piece of a missing childhood. A magic piece. A sense of what that place called *home* could feel like.

"Have you ever made cookies?" she asked him.

"No, never." He confirmed what she had already guessed, but he looked wary.

"Let's change that. Right now."

"No, you're tired. Go home."

But she wasn't going to go home. Now that she had figured out the gift she could give him, it felt imperative to do it now. Maybe because he was tired, his defenses were down a little bit.

Because really? Under normal circumstances what billionaire was going to spend a morning baking cookies?

But he cocked his head at her, reluctantly interested. He lifted a shoulder in assent.

"Do I need one of those?" he asked, gesturing at her chef's jacket.

"Only if you're worried about your shirt." She shrugged out of her own. "We're not baking commercially right now. We're making a single batch of my original-recipe chocolate-chip cookies. For you."

"Do they have magic in them?" he asked softly.

"Oh, I hope so," she responded, just as softly. And then, she moved away from the intensity building between them. She moved, instead, over to her iPod station.

"Want some music?" she asked.

"Sure."

She found an Elvis Presley hits playlist and started it, then glanced back at him. "What?"

"Maybe not Elvis this morning."

There was something in his face, guarded and yet vulnerable. There was some secret about him and Elvis he was not yet willing to divulge.

Yet. The word suggested her subconscious was already looking to a future her rational mind knew was not possible.

She changed the setting to random. She supposed, if he listened, her music selection was going to say as much about her as his house did about him.

Romantic. Hope-filled. Longing for love.

"Okay," she said brightly, hoping to distract him from the telling messages of her music choices. "Let's start. Cookies 101."

"Do I have to touch HAL? I don't think I can touch HAL."

She giggled at his pretended fear of the mixer. "I was thinking something a little more old-fashioned. A big bowl. A wooden spoon, some basic ingredients. And my secrets."

"I want to know your secrets," he said huskily, "especially if they involve a wooden spoon."

He was tired. She was tired. They had to tread very carefully here, so she ignored his playful, suggestive innuendo, even as she filed it away. *He's seeing me as a grown-up. You don't say things like that to someone you think of as a kid.*

"Secret number one, coming right up." She went to the fridge, reached in and held the tinfoil packet out to him with showmanship.

"Butter," he said. He lifted his eyebrows at her. How could a man say so much without saying a single word?

"Stop it!"

"I never said anything."

"I know. That's a special talent, being so bad without saying a word."

One eyebrow stayed up as the other went down. It was a very sexy look.

"You're being very wicked," she said sternly.

"Yes, I am," he said, not a bit contrite. "I think people usually use oil, but butter might—"

"You need to stop it." The protest was token. Again, she felt a little tingle. He was definitely seeing her as a woman! That decision to show him some magic was having consequences much more dangerous than she could have imagined. She didn't feel anything like a Girl Guide doing a good deed!

She wondered exactly what she had let herself in for.

And the truth was she couldn't wait to find out!

"There is no wickedness in cookie making," she told him sternly.

"Yes, ma'am, no wickedness in cookie making." He repeated it dutifully. The way he said *wickedness*, with so much heat, could melt an iceberg!

"Butter, real butter, no imitations, is the number-one secret to making good cookies," she said primly, as if his teasing was not making her feel alive and happy. She could feel the laughter bubbling up inside of her. Of course, if she laughed, there would be no stopping him. She had not anticipated this particular problem when she had thought of giving the gift of some childhood magic to a fully grown man.

She had to ignore his sexiness. If she didn't, she would teach him nothing about home, and underscore his ability to distract. She had wanted it to be fun, yes, but she could not succumb to his charm, or fun was going to take an unexpected turn that had nothing to do with her original motivation in extending this invitation.

"You need to pay attention." She said it out loud to herself, a reminder to stay focused on cookies and not the dark tangle of his lashes, the sensual curve of his bottom lip, the way his light pants clung to the large muscles of his thighs.

"Will there be a test?" he asked solemnly.

Focusing hard, she unwrapped the butter from its tinfoil and put it in a small bowl. Her fingers felt clumsy under his gaze, as if she had dipped them in glue that had hardened. She turned from him and softened the butter in the microwave. "Thirty seconds," she told him, "just enough for it to slide out."

"Slide out," he repeated as if he was being an obedient student, which he was not! He made the words sound like something out of the *Kama Sutra*!

She shoved the two-cup measure at him. "One of white sugar, two of brown."

She cast a glance at him a minute later after the room had descended into total silence. His tongue was caught between his teeth. His focus was intense.

"You're not measuring gunpowder."

"You're the one who stripped all the fun out of it already."

"I did not."

"I'm surprised you didn't tell me I can't use the word *stripped*. As well as not speaking of anything wicked."

"For heaven's sake, I am not a complete stick-in-the-mud!"

"Okay. When's the last time you had fun, since you brought it up?"

"This *is* fun for me."

"But you are not a complete stick-in-the-mud," he said sadly. "An example of fun that has nothing to do with cookies. Tell me the last thing that made you laugh."

The last things that had made her laugh all involved him. Nearly. "I bought a laser pointer. My cat chases the red dot."

He was silent.

"Obsessively."

He remained silent.

"It's much funnier than you think."

"You need to get out more."

Her sense of deep gratitude to him, and of wanting to give him a gift, was dissipating quite rapidly.

"We can't all spend our lives frolicking on beaches, turning that lovely shade of gold that you are right now."

"You do look a little pale," he said, regarding her solemnly. "Jailhouse pallor. Chained to the kitchen too long. You need to get outside."

"Thank you. If you could measure the brown—"

"If you did frolic on a beach, would it be in a bikini or a one-piece?"

CHAPTER NINE

SHOOT, BRAND THOUGHT. There it was, out of his mouth.
The whole time he'd been in Bali he'd wondered that.
Bikini or one-piece? Bali had not been quite the escape that he had hoped for. Now, here he was in the
kitchen with Bree, being as wicked as baking cookies
allowed, and somehow the question had just popped
out of his mouth.

Bree's mouth fell open. She looked flustered.

Well, who could blame her? He was tired. He should
have never agreed to the cookie-making session.

He knew what it was really about. She had seen
something in him, sensed something in this house. A
longing. A vulnerability. He was going to distract her
from her quest.

Which was what? To know the real him?

That, yes, but more. She was determined to show
him something he had missed.

Her motivations, he was one-hundred-percent positive, were nothing but altruistic. He should have never
let it slip about living in the car, about his childhood
being less than ideal, because she was busy filling in the
gaps now. The problem was, once you had been shown
something like that, didn't you then ache for it forever?

He did not want to be thinking of the word *forever* anywhere in the vicinity of her.

"Why don't you guess?" she suggested, her cheeks pink.

His distractions, he was pleased to see, were working. He had entirely removed the focus from himself.

"I'm going to guess a one-piece—"

"That's correct."

"When it should be a bikini."

"Four eggs," she said, a little too loudly. She held up a device in her hand. "This is a handheld electric mixer. Think of it as HAL's little sister. We're going to whip the butter."

"Look, if you don't want any wickedness you can't talk about whips."

She put her hands on her hips. "I hope you aren't that kind of guy, Brand Wallace." Sternly, she handed him the electric beaters. "Put them in the butter and sugar and turn them on. That should drown out the sound of your voice."

"I'm offended," he said, though he was not. In the least.

"Aside from butter, this is the secret to making really, really good cookies."

"Good whipping?" he said innocently.

She pinched her lips together. It didn't help one little bit. The laughter gurgled out past her closed lips.

He'd totally succeeded in distracting her from the topic of himself.

And he had totally failed to protect himself.

Because her laughter was a balm to a life that suddenly came face-to-face with the emptiness of all his accomplishments and all his stuff. He had somehow missed the most important thing of all.

Connection.

She laughed until she doubled over, until tears ran down her face.

It made him realize he knew secrets about her, too, that she probably did not want him to know.

Despite her laughter right now, there was some sadness in her that would not let her go, that had not been in her when he had escorted her to her prom. She had been shy, yes, and awkward, yes, but almost filled to the brim with an innocent confidence life would be good to her. He wondered, not for the first time, what might have happened to her.

Don't go there, he ordered himself. *Keep it light. You don't want to go deep with her. You'll be drowning in the pools of light that are her incredible eyes before you even know you're in trouble.*

That was the whole problem, wasn't it? He wasn't that kind of guy, there was nothing twisted or kinky about him. Not even close. But he was not the kind of guy that a girl like her needed, either. As long as both of them were playing by the same rules, as long as both of them remembered that.

"All I am is the kind of guy who likes to make a pretty girl blush."

"I'm not blushing." She was trying to stop laughing. She was blushing with the intensity of a house on fire. She had unbent herself and was cracking eggs into the cookie mixture as if her life depended on it. "Keep, er, mixing it."

As he mixed, she slowly added flour and other ingredients. She was standing close to him, and he could look down on her hair, her gorgeous sunshine-on-sand hair. Would it get lighter if she frolicked on a beach?

The dough began to take on the texture of thick peanut butter.

It was such a blatant lie, about her blushing, that he laughed. Her face, from laughter and racy undertones to the conversation, was nearly as red as the stand mixer.

"And I'm not that pretty, either," she said quietly.

"What? What the hell?" His own laughter died. So did his resolution not to go there, to her secrets, to her sadness, to some place that had stolen the confidence that had just begun to bloom in her when he had taken her to her prom, a lifetime ago.

"I'm not," she said firmly.

"What would make you say something like that?"

"Maybe I'm adorable, like a Yorkie," she said. "But I know I'm not the greatest. All those guys—the ones I meet on e-Us? They never call me back. Not even the Elvis look-alike."

"That's impossible," he said grimly.

"I have an affliction."

Good grief! "An affliction? Like you're dying or something?" He could not believe how his heart stopped in his chest.

"Oh, for Pete's sake," she said. She actually flicked a piece of cookie batter at him. "Of course I'm not dying."

He tried not to let his relief show. He scraped the dough off his shirt and licked his finger. He was aware of her eyes on him. He took his time licking his finger. The dough was delicious.

"The affliction?" he reminded her, not allowing himself to be distracted by the deliciousness of the dough, as difficult as that was.

"Even growing up," she said slowly, "I knew exactly what I wanted. It was so ordinary and old-fashioned. My girlfriends wanted to be doctors and lawyers, writers and scientists. Oh, sure, they wanted to get married, and have families, but it was like an afterthought. I'll win the Pulitzer Prize, *then* I'll have a baby.

"But my happiest moments were when my family was together, raking leaves, or sitting beside the fire on a cold night, all reading our books. I loved plain moments— arguing over whether it was really a word in Scrabble, or my dad trying to explain football to me, yet again."

It was that *thing* that he had worried about. That she was painting pictures of all the things he had never had, and it could create an ache in him that would never ease.

"I felt safe and cherished—"

Things he had never felt, except maybe with Beau. He was pretty sure that made him, the guy who had been named businessman of the decade, and who had just returned to his beautiful home from a business trip in Bali, pathetic. But this was not about him.

"And that's all I ever wanted for my future. To feel that way, forever."

"And?" He had to force himself to ask the question, because she was taking him on a journey that he did not have a map for. He did not like journeys without maps.

"When my dad died I wanted it even *more*."

"That seems pretty natural."

"I can't *make* it happen." Now that she had started, it felt like the floodgates were wide open. "I'm plagued by first-date anxiety so strong I never get a second one."

"You're getting a terrifying look on your face," he told her, and it was true.

"A terrifying look?" she asked, all innocence.

"As in you want a first date that leads to a second date, and then a third one."

"And?"

"And then wedding bells and babies."

He hadn't thought she could blush any deeper than when he'd been teasing her while whipping the cookies, but she could.

"I had no idea I was so transparent!"

"Believe me, on the transparency scale? You are a perfect ten."

"My only perfect ten," she said glumly.

"That's not true."

"Anyway, I can't help it if my dreams are written all over me. It seems deceitful to not let it be known upfront what your end goal is. I mean why lead someone to believe I'm into casual—"

The fiery burn moving up her cheeks increased, if that was possible. No wonder her kitchens caught fire. She managed to avoid using the word *sex*.

"Casual relationships when nothing could be further from the truth."

"It seems to me if that dream is what you really wanted, you'd already have it because not all guys are as terrified by such dreams as me."

"Well, as I told you, I have an affliction."

"That wasn't it?" he asked. "Wanting babies and weddings and forever?"

She scowled at him. "No."

"Okay, give. About the affliction."

"I get nervous," she confessed.

"Who doesn't get nervous on a first date? That's hardly an affliction."

She sighed.

"I guess you better give me an example."

"I blurt out dumb things. I sweat in my dress. I've steamed up my glasses, and gotten dust under my contact lenses. I've spilled my wine. And dribbled food down my front. Once, I broke a tooth and I had to find an emergency dental clinic. And he didn't even help me.

"It's like I have that terrible affliction like the one golfers get. Where they start whiffing or flubbing or whatever it's called, and once they start thinking about it, they can't get over it. It just gets worse and worse and worse."

She had been focusing hard on the cookie dough. She looked up at him. Her eyes were wide and earnest.

He could feel his lips twitching. Anyone who did business with him, or worked with him on a regular basis, knew it was not a good thing.

But she, innocent that she was, looked puzzled. "Are you laughing at me?"

"Laughing? No! I'm feeling really annoyed with you." The truth was, he wanted to kiss the living daylights out of her, because she had so badly lost who she really was and had painted herself into such a corner of self-deceit.

"What? Why?"

"Because you are believing this line of crap that you are telling yourself. And you know what I'd like to know? What's really going on? What's really made you so afraid of your own happiness?"

He inserted a word between *your* and *happiness* that was the universal song of displeasure and that meant "I am dead serious. Do not try and snow me."

CHAPTER TEN

BREE STARED AT BRAND. How had things gone so terribly off the rails? She was supposed to be helping *him*. She had entered his kitchen with the naivety of a Girl Guide thinking she was doing her good deed for the day.

How had he turned things around like this?

And how could it possibly feel as if she *had* to tell him, as if to carry this burden alone for one more second would be to be crushed under the weight of it?

How could it possibly feel as if he had unlocked some secret that she had hidden, even from herself? That somehow she was so afraid she was sabotaging her own dreams?

Could that be true? She grabbed a bag of chocolate chips and began to dump them in the bowl. She should have passed him the wooden spoon, but she felt the need to blow off the energy building in her. She started to mash those chips into the cookie dough, when really it should have been a nice, gentle blending motion.

"It was a man," Brand said softly.

She risked a glance at him. He was regarding her with narrowed eyes, flashing dangerously now, with something that was not mischief. He took the spoon from her and began to pummel the cookie dough with barely leashed aggravation.

"How could you know that?" she whispered.

"I can tell by looking at you," he said. "Some evil bastard broke your heart."

You could never, ever forget this about Brand, not even when you were baking cookies, that he was a keen observer, that he saw things that would remain hidden to those not quite as astute.

Don't tell him, she begged herself. And yet, it felt that if she told him, if she finally said these dreadful things out loud, she would be free in some way. She would solve a puzzle that had mystified her. He already knew anyway. He had guessed it.

"As you know, my dad died shortly after my prom," she said tiredly. "I had already been accepted at college, and I knew he would want me to go.

"But I was extremely vulnerable. I was grieving. My mom had already moved on, already made a decision to sell our house, all of which shocked me and left me with a sense of my whole world disintegrating. I had never spent time away from home before, or lived on my own. One of my professors took an interest in me. It doesn't take a psychiatrist to know I was trying desperately to replace my father's love with the affection of this older man.

"I actually was so naive that I thought my father was in heaven looking after me, that he had sent me this man to ease my broken heart."

Bree had been focusing intently on the cookie dough, but some small sound coming from Brand made her glance up.

The fury in his face might have been a frightening thing if it was directed at her. But it was not.

"Go on," Brand said tersely.

"I found out how much I really meant to him when I discovered I was pregnant."

Brand groaned, a growl of fury and frustration so pure it was almost animal-like. But his voice was soft when he said, "Aw, Bree."

"Even though the pregnancy was the end of my love affair, and I felt I had to leave school so as never to see Paul again, I was happy about the baby. It made me feel not quite so alone in the world. It made me feel as if I had purpose and meaning.

"And then," she whispered, "the baby was gone, too. I miscarried."

She felt his arms go around her. Ever so gently, Brand turned her into his chest. He held her hard and tight. He held her as if there was one solid thing in the world for her to hold onto. He held her in a way that made her finally let go.

At first it was a small hiccup. And then a sob. And then the floodgates opened, and she leaned hard into his strength and his warmth and his acceptance.

"When you told me you knew a thing or two about unforgivable, that day Beau knocked you over, you were right. Really right. And I'm so sorry you had to experience something like that."

That he remembered something she had said, almost casually, days and days ago, released something more in her.

Brand stroked her hair and her back, and whispered to her over and over again, gentle words of pure compassion.

"Let it go, sweetheart. That's my girl. Get it all out."

And she did. She cried until she was exhausted from it, until there was not a tear left, until surely a different man would have given up holding her a long time ago.

But, no, Brand Wallace stood there like a rock—her rock, immovable in his utter strength.

And when the tears finally did stop, Bree felt something she had not felt for a long, long time.

She felt utterly at peace with herself.

"Thank you for listening," she said. "You've given me some things to think about, self-sabotage for one."

She pulled away from him. His summer shirt had a big splotch on the front of it. She turned to the big bowl of cookie dough. "I think we should just throw this out. I don't think tears make a good secret ingredient."

"I disagree completely," he said. "I think healing is the secret ingredient. Let's bake them and see what happens."

And so, side by side, they scooped dough onto the sheets. She had done it millions of times, and so her cookies were uniform and all the same size.

His were haphazard heaps that made her smile. He made big cookies and small ones and lopsided ones, and she found herself loving all those imperfections. And loving being with him. Was it because she had shared her most secret of secrets that she felt so connected to him? So safe? So comfortable?

But not just comfortable. Aware. Maybe even aware in a way she had not allowed herself to be aware since Paul.

Of Brand's masculinity, in contrast to her femininity. Of his physical size and strength in comparison to herself, of how she had fit against him, of how he smelled, and of his energy.

They put in the cookies to bake, and there was quiet between them as they cleaned up the kitchen, but it was in no way uncomfortable. In fact it was quite lovely, something Bree was aware she had not felt for a long, long time.

It was exactly the gift she had intended to give him, but as was the way with most gifts, she received it herself. Bree had a sense of being home after a long journey away.

The timer rang on the cookies, and she pulled them out of the oven and then she and Brand filled a plate with cookies so warm that chocolate was oozing out of them. Without speaking about it, they both knew where to go, and they retreated to side-by-side chairs in his media room.

She nibbled on one cookie, aware it was his enjoyment that made it the best batch of cookies she had ever made. He ate every one of those cookies they had put on the plate.

And she hoped he was right, that the strange ingredient—tears—had put healing in them. Because just as he had seen so clearly that there was something broken in her, she also saw that in him.

Maybe what had just happened had strengthened some bond between them. Maybe he would share confidences with her, too.

But he fell asleep with crumbs from the last cookie still in his hand. She brushed them away from him and placed the soft wool blanket, the one that she had used earlier, on him.

She tucked it around him, and took advantage of the

fact he was sleeping to study him: the sweep of thick lashes on his cheek, the strong nose, the full lips gently parted, his hair, dark as those melted chocolate chips, just touching his forehead. There was something soft in his face that made her realize how guarded he was most of the time.

All that boyish charm hid something deeper. Something he didn't want anyone to see.

But she had seen it. And as he had said in her apartment that day, it was impossible to "unsee" it now.

He was a man who had absolutely everything. Every material gift that it was possible to own, he owned.

He owned cars, and art pieces and a beautiful house in one of the most exclusive neighborhoods in the world.

And yet, the most precious things of all had evaded him. Children screaming up the staircases, and the Scrabble board open on a table, with a misspelled word on it. Heaps of leaves to leap in, and tying the Christmas tree to the roof with string so it wouldn't fall off. The smell of dinner in the oven, or cookies, the little arguments over whether the toilet-paper roll should unroll over or under. All the simple, complex, wonderful things that went into a home and a family he had missed.

Knowing this with her soul, Bree felt something for him so deep and so stirring that it made her want to weep all over again.

She bent over him, touched his warm, rough cheek, and then followed where her fingertips had been with her lips.

She knew exactly what was happening to her.

It was like the words of that tender Elvis song had crept around her from the first moment she had walked in this house and seen the kitchen where he used the microwave and didn't even know he had a stand mixer, or steam oven or what either of them were, for that matter.

"What exactly does that song say?" she whispered, "That only a fool would rush in?"

She laughed at herself. That's exactly what it was. Foolishness. Foolish to feel the posters staring down at her. She wasn't rushing at all.

Still, she couldn't stop herself from finishing the first line of the beautiful, haunting song.

Her voice a husky whisper, she sang the words softly, as if it was a lullaby to the sleeping man.

Her voice fell into utter stillness.

And she recognized the truth of it. She was falling in love with him. Or maybe, more accurately, had never fallen out.

She had loved him as a girl. Oh, it had been an innocent love, based on his looks and his physique, and his charm, but still, that wild crush on him had been her first experience with love outside of her family. That night that he had walked into the gala, and she had tried to leave before he even saw her, hadn't she sensed the danger of him?

Hadn't some part of her known that despite the dating sites, despite going through the motions of wanting love, she hadn't really? She hadn't felt brave enough for it. Hadn't she known as soon as she'd laid eyes on him, he would be the one that would call it from her, that need to be brave, to engage love again, to risk its slings and arrows?

She gazed at him a little longer, and then turned rapidly on her heel, and nearly ran from the room and from his house, and from the hard hammering of her own heart.

Once home, Bree busied herself with laundry and the multitude of other things that had gotten stacked up while she had been trying to get her cookie orders caught up. She was also trying, unsuccessfully, to win back the affection of her neglected cat with his favorite game, but his chasing of the red light seemed desolate at best.

Her phone rang. She stared at the caller ID. There was that hammering in her heart again!

"Hello?" She hoped she didn't sound breathless.

"You sound out of breath. What am I getting you from?"

She tucked the laser pointer behind a plant, as if he could see it, as if it was evidence of a life that had gotten too staid, too safe.

"I was just coming up from the apartment-building laundry room with a basket," she said. Okay. Fifteen minutes ago. She was *not* still out of breath from that. "I take the stairs. My version of a StairMaster."

She was talking to a billionaire about basement-laundry facilities and stairs. He probably hadn't done his own laundry in years.

"You weren't supposed to let me fall asleep," Brand chided her. His voice was so natural, as if this was the most natural thing in the world, his calling her.

She felt something in her relax, just a bit. She thought of baking cookies with him, and the way his face had looked when he was sleeping.

Okay. He was a brilliant businessman. He was a billionaire. He was also still just Brand.

"I know you have your own formula for dealing with

jet lag, but you just looked so tired. I didn't have the heart to wake you up."

"I have chocolate around my lips."

She giggled, even though she did not want to be thinking about his lips.

"I was thinking about what you said about taking a couple of days off," Brand said. "Are you going to spend them doing laundry?"

"Possibly," she said cautiously. She tried to think of something more exciting that she could tell him she was doing with her days off, but she was coming up blank. The sound of his voice was having that effect on her.

"Look, when I've been under a lot of stress, or I've been really busy—or if I'm fighting jet lag—I like to go kayaking. It grounds me."

"Oh," she said. Just when she was thinking she could dismiss his billionaire status, he had to show her the difference in their worlds. Basement laundry. Trying to get your cat to play. Jet lag. Kayaking.

"Have you ever done it?" he asked.

"No," she said, a little tightly.

"Would you like to?"

She had to sit down. Was Brand Wallace asking her on a date? And then it hit her. No, not a date.

More of the same. Poor girl. Had an affair. Ended up pregnant. Left school. Life in ruins. Needs looking after. Needs bolstering. It was so far from how she wanted him to feel that she could have screamed. Instead she bit down hard on her lip.

"Are you there?" he asked.

"Are you asking me because you feel sorry for me?" she finally asked.

"Yeah," he said, "I am."

She didn't know what to say to that. Well, besides no, she couldn't go on a date with him on that basis, because it wasn't really a date. She wasn't even sure what it was.

"There I was in Bali while you were slaving away over cookies. I've been thinking about your jailhouse pallor."

"Oh, brother," she said. She had been so far off the mark it wasn't even funny. He wasn't thinking about her confidence at all. Well, maybe it was still a little funny. Or maybe not. Here she was thinking she was falling in love, and he was thinking about jailhouse pallor.

"It's making me feel guilty about the trip to Bali. I hate feeling guilty."

"I thought maybe you were asking me because you felt sorry for me," she said. "After I confided in you about what happened to me in college."

"Weird," he said.

"In what way?"

"That you would think I would perceive you as weak, because of that. The opposite is true. I find you very brave."

"Me?"

"Yes, you. You don't see yourself as brave?"

"No, not really." Bree had never, not even once, thought of herself as brave. Though she supposed maybe it did take a certain amount of bravery to wear that silly cookie beret and her quilted apron!

"That's how I see you," he said firmly. "It takes a lot of guts to start a business, especially after your dreams have pretty much had the crap kicked out of them. You picked yourself up, you dusted yourself off, you started again."

So, he had heard everything she had said to him, and

instead of making him see her as weak and foolish, a girl who had let her heart get her in a world of trouble, he saw it in a completely different light.

"You have what it takes, Bree, you have what it takes to make your business whatever you want it to be."

"Thanks."

"But you have to take care of yourself, too. You have to know how to intersperse hard work with fun and time away from your business."

So, it wasn't really a date then. More like a mentorship. She should say no, shouldn't she? Just on principle? Just because, in their minds, it was obvious they were moving the relationship in different directions?

"Hey, I don't ask just anybody to go sea kayaking. It's not for the faint of heart."

Another very good reason to say no. She was not sure Brand had mentioned the *sea* part of kayaking when he had first mentioned it. Kayaks were very small boats, weren't they? In a sea that could roil up, cold and dangerous, in a second? In channels shared with huge ships and creatures of the deep?

"In fact," Brand said, "I've never asked anyone to go with me before."

"You haven't?"

"It's kind of my sanctuary out there. A deep and private pleasure. But also, amazing stress relief. Which is why I'm asking you. I know you've been under enormous stress, with the fire, and catching up on those orders."

Bree listened to what he wasn't saying.

It struck her that, despite the "mentorship" spin on this, he was nervous about asking her. She was almost positive about that: the gorgeous, self-confident, successful Brand Wallace was nervous about asking her to do something with him.

Suddenly, the whole "unknown" of it, the adventure of it—not just of sea kayaking, but of getting to know Brand better—was completely irresistible.

Something had been healed in her when she told him her most completely guarded secrets, when her tears had fallen like a secret ingredient into those cookies.

And this is what it was: for a long time, despite going through the motions, despite going on the dating sites, despite saying something different, she had been saying no to life instead of yes.

And suddenly she just wanted to say yes, even though it sounded faintly terrifying. But she wanted to be brave again, even if it ended in heartache, to embrace whatever life, in all its magnificence, offered her.

More, she wanted to trust someone again.

None of which she said to him. To Brand, as casually as she could, as if a billionaire invited her to go kayaking with him every day, Bree said, "That sounds fun. Sure."

CHAPTER ELEVEN

BREE HAD TO look up online what to wear for kayaking
and it was only then that she realized she knew nothing about what she had let herself in for. Was she going
to be paddling her own kayak? She hoped not! Most
sites recommended a few lessons before you went out
on your own, particularly so you would know what to
do if you capsized.

Capsized? In ocean water in May? She checked what
the temperature of the water would be. Forty-six degrees Fahrenheit. Not a death sentence, but still, even if
you were wearing the recommended clothing it would
be simply awful. Wouldn't it? Unless Brand saved her...

Given her investment in the cloak, she couldn't really justify buying an outfit made specifically for kayaking, so she was pleased with the look she managed
to assemble: cotton leggings, a T-shirt topped with an
oversize wool sweater and a light jacket.

Brand was already at the English Bay parking lot
they had agreed to meet at when she got there. He was
single-handedly sliding a slender kayak from the roof
rack of the vehicle.

Bree paused for a moment, just watching him, the
play of muscle, the ease with which he handled himself,

before she got out of her vehicle. He was gorgeous and rugged-looking in multi-pocketed outdoor pants and a hooded jacket.

As she approached him, she was welcomed with a smile that made her feel like her heart was a flower opening up to the sun after a long rain.

After they greeted each other, she studied the kayak.

"It has two holes in it," she noted. "I thought you said you usually go by yourself?"

He slid her a look. "I didn't figure you for the jealous type."

"It's dating the Elvis guy," she admitted. "It's given me a suspicious mind."

He threw back his head and laughed. She knew, with sudden delight, it was going to be that kind of day—laughter-filled and fun. His laughter was a sound that eased some of the nervousness in her, caused both by trying something new and more one-on-one time with the billionaire.

"By myself is relative, I guess," Brand said, answering her question. "Beau usually takes the front hole, which, by the way, is generally referred to as a cockpit."

The idea of that big dog in the kayak with him made her laugh, too. She'd been nervous, but now with the sun on her face, and the smell of the sea in the air, and Brand smiling at her, and handling the kayak with easy strength, she could feel her confidence rising.

He took her cell phone and keys and put them in a waterproof bag.

"We aren't going to get wet, are we?" she said, and her confidence dipped a little.

"It's Vancouver. It could start raining anytime."

"I didn't mean that."

"I know you didn't. I am seriously hoping we are not going to get wet. But we'll put these on just in case."

Bree was glad she had not purchased an expensive outfit when he handed her an ugly yellow life vest, which made about as much fashion statement as wearing a neon marshmallow!

He came and helped her when her zipper stuck.

"Is this Beau's, too?" she said, blinking up at him as he leaned in close to her to unstick the zipper.

"Believe me, you'd smell it if it was."

And they were laughing again, even as she became aware that what she smelled was him: a delicious scent, deeply masculine, outdoorsy, clean.

He picked up the kayak and swung it up over his head, part of it resting on his back.

"I can help," she offered.

"Don't worry. I'm used to doing it by myself." She took the paddles and followed him down to the water's edge, admiring his strength and the broadness of his shoulders, the ease of long practice that made what he was doing seem natural to him.

He set down the kayak and pushed it into the water, but just a bit.

"Okay, get in. Straddle it, feet on both sides, paddle in the middle, push it along until you can step in to that front cockpit."

Before she knew it, she was in the kayak, and she hadn't even gotten her feet wet, though she had worn light canvas sneakers just in case. When she wiggled a bit to get comfortable, the kayak rocked, despite him steadying the back of it.

But then he shoved it hard, and got in the back cockpit in one easy motion. The vessel seemed to stabilize with his weight, and they glided off the beach.

"We'll do a fairly short paddle today," he said, "Just to get you used of it."

He was saying that as if there might be more excursions!

"Don't feel like you have to paddle with me. Rest if you start getting tired. And don't be shy to tell me if you've had enough."

And then he went over some of the rudiments of steering and paddling together. They practiced stopping, turning and reversing direction a few times. It was fun! She hated to admit how right he had been about her life not having enough fun in it.

Maybe this wasn't a date. She wasn't quite sure about how to define this outing, but whatever it was it was so much better than anything that had ever happened on e-Us. Going for coffee suddenly seemed like the most ridiculous way to get to know a person! And meeting someone at the bookstore hardly seemed better.

Because this was getting to know a person: learning to paddle together, watching in awe as eagles soared and fish jumped, laughing when she accidentally splashed him and then laughing harder when she did it again on purpose.

The setting was glorious and kayaking seemed very simple, but she suspected he was doing most of the work. Before she knew it, they were gliding effortlessly through the stillness of the dark water toward the mouth of the bay.

Tell him when she had had enough? Really, it felt as if she could never get enough of this.

It occurred to her, once they were way out in the water, that she had him exactly where she wanted him.

Because she could finally ask him questions he could not get away from. She could, maybe, find out where all this was going. Was this a date? Was this delightful little outing going to lead to something else?

Don't be terrifying, Bree warned herself. *No wedding bells or babies.*

They paused to rest off the shore by Stanley Park. She was breathing hard, and her arms and shoulders ached, but in the nicest way. Not too far off was the hum of traffic, and she could see people walking and biking the Seawall, but she had a sense of it being deeply quiet. The kayak rocked ever so gently on the sea. He passed her a bottle of water.

"Do you like it?" he asked. "Kayaking?"

"Love it." She took a deep sip of her water. "Brand, why don't you have friends who are, um, women?"

He took a sudden interest in something on the shoreline. "Is that a deer?"

She squinted where he was pointing. "I think it's a branch."

"Oh."

"How come?" she said, refusing to be distracted. She might never have him in a boat again!

"What makes you think I don't?" he said, raising an eyebrow at her.

"Your house told me."

"What? How?"

"A million ways. No forgotten umbrella. No makeup around. No *The Lucky One* or *Dirty Dancing* or *The Notebook* in your movie collection."

"Did you go in my bedroom?"

"Of course not! I didn't have to to know you basically live out of three rooms. I bet your bedroom is a man cave, too."

"You're right," he said with a shrug. "The house is a masculine haven inhabited by Beau and me."

"I'm trying to get the *why* no significant other." *When you're obviously so irresistible.*

"I'm busy," he said uncomfortably.

She waited, not commenting. As she had hoped, there was no place to run from the question.

"I had a girlfriend. We saw each other for two years. We weren't engaged, though I think she wanted to be. We actually, ah, tried living together. She moved in. And she moved out again. Three days later."

"What happened?" she asked in horror. Three days? Was something horribly wrong with him? Three days?

"Beau."

"What?"

"He ate some of her stuff. Like her sofa. She gave me an ultimatum. Dog or me."

She knew she shouldn't laugh. She knew she shouldn't. But she giggled. "She knew you had a dog, obviously, before she moved in."

"Yeah, she just hadn't had to live with him before."

"Fantasy meets reality?" She would do well to remember this. He was the kind of man a woman might build a fantasy around.

But for two years? His ex hadn't known after two years how much that dog meant to him? She could actually say to him "dog or me" and think she was going to win that one?

Bree felt she knew Brand better than that after just this tiny bit of time!

"She took down the Elvis posters. She didn't even ask."

"Actually, since you mention it, I'm curious about the Elvis thing. I don't get the impression you like Elvis much."

"Actually, I know it really wasn't about Beau or the Elvis posters," he said carefully.

She was looking over her shoulder at him. Unless she was mistaken, he was deliberately not telling her how he felt about Elvis. He had the cookie jar, yes, and the posters, but when she had put on Elvis music that morning he had arrived home from Bali, she was almost positive he had flinched.

"So what's it really about then?"

"I'm not cut out for it. The whole domestic-bliss thing. I wanted to be, but I'm not. We'd been dating two years. It was fine when we both had our own spaces, but as soon as she moved in I felt suffocated by her. A two-year relationship in ruins, and I was so happy to see her marching out of my house, I was practically dancing. I don't know what that says about me."

"That she wasn't the right woman?" Bree suggested mildly.

"I don't think that's it. I think it's more that I'm not the right guy. Maybe I'm just like my old man. No staying power. When the fun stops, I'm gone."

This brutal self-assessment surprised her so much it put her off the trail of how he really felt about Elvis.

"I don't believe that," she said firmly. "I've seen how you treat people. Not just me, but your employees. Chelsea told me your lawyer who called her has hired his own fire investigator. She's practically a stranger to you, and you did that for her. You're a good, good man, Brand Wallace."

"Aw, shucks," he said with mild sarcasm, clearly trying to brush off the compliment.

"No, I mean it."

"Does this mean you've forgiven me for not kissing you at your senior prom?"

"That was part of being a good man, wasn't it?"

"Yeah, I guess."

"I think we should have a do-over."

"What?"

She could not believe this was her, but one thing she was learning was you only came this way once. Why not take chances? Why not go after what you wanted? Why not take a risk?

She was falling in love with him. She knew that. Even today, it felt as if it was deepening around them. The level of comfort, of connection, of companionship.

And something was definitely brewing on a deeper level, too.

Awareness.

A wanting.

To taste him again. To know him in a different way.

In a way, his choosing kayaking was the safest thing he could have done. There was a whole boat in between them! No cuddling was possible. No physical contact. The closest she could come to touching him was splashing him!

Was she just going to let him relegate her to friend-I-can-decompress-with position? Was she constantly going to be the one *helped*? No, for once in her life she was taking a chance. She was going to put it all on the line.

"Your company's charity ball is coming up," she said.

"Did the organizer get in touch? Are you making cookies for it?"

"Yes, for the midnight lunch, plus four-cookie boxes for party favors, though that's not why I mentioned it."

He waited. She glanced over his shoulder at him.

She took a deep breath. "I'd like to go."

He dipped his paddle in, setting them in motion, trying to move away from it. "Of course you are welcome to go!"

"Not as the cookie caterer."

The strength of his stroke carried them a long ways out into the stillness of the water.

"With you," she told him firmly.

She could feel the bravery in her. She could feel a shift in her perception. She wasn't the hapless, heartbroken woman pleading for people to choose her on the internet, desperate for a first date, never mind a second one.

She just wasn't that person anymore. Maybe just speaking about what had happened to her with Brand had clarified something in her.

Helped her make a vow.

No more being a victim. Not of men. Not of life. Not of circumstances.

She was going to take the helm. She was going to steer. She was going to move in the direction she wanted to, not wait for someone else to move her. Instead of waiting passively for something to happen, she was going to take charge of her own life,

She wasn't waiting, hope-filled, for something to happen to her. She was making it happen.

He didn't answer. His paddle entered the water and pulled the kayak forward with such force Bree wondered if she had ever been helping paddle at all. He looked wary of her invitation.

As well he should, she thought happily, as well he should! Because she was changing right before his eyes. It might not have hit him yet, but what she was really asking him was did he want to explore what was going on between them in a new way? Did he want to move forward?

Yes or no.

As simple as that.

But, of course, she should know by now, nothing in her life was ever simple. Because as that question hung there in the air between them, as she explored the meaning of bravery in this brand-new and infinitely exciting way, out of the corner of her eye, she caught a movement.

She swung her head toward the ripple in the water maybe a hundred feet to the left of the bow of the kayak.

The ripple became larger. A huge round back, black and shiny as a freshly tarred road, rose out of the water.

Her heart felt as if it might beat out of her chest. A mountain was shoving its way out of the gray endlessness of the ocean, way, way too close to them. The powerful movement was rocking the kayak. They were in very real danger of being capsized by a whale!

CHAPTER TWELVE

THE KILLER WHALE swam beside them, its ripples rocking the small kayak. Thankfully, it quickly outdistanced them. It blew out its top spout, a geyser of water droplets making a rainbow in the air. And then the whale's terrific bulk lifted out of the water. The grace, in a creature so large, was astounding. It shot up in the air, a cork released from a bottle. And then it crashed back down with such force that they were sprayed with water, and the kayak rocked more violently, before settling into stillness.

Brand had never seen a whale that close, not in all his years of being on the water.

Bree turned and looked at him. When the whale had first begun to surface, she had gone dead quiet and utterly still. He had been able to read the tension in her posture.

But now, all of that was gone. She was radiant as she turned her wide eyes to him.

"Oh!" she breathed. "Oh! That was the most amazing thing I have ever experienced."

His male ego wanted to remind her that she had just kissed him, only days ago. Certainly for him that kiss had been as earth-rocking as the breaching of the whale.

The whale had distracted her from her invitation to him. On the surface, it seemed as if maybe she was asking him to go to the charity ball. With him.

But, of course, with her, there was another layer to it.

Bree was asking him to define what was going on between them. He'd known, as soon as he had to escape to Bali to get away from her pull, what it was.

He was in the danger zone.

And maybe it was already too late to fix that, to escape it, to change it to something else.

The way she was looking at him now, her face so radiant, a person so capable of wonder, after all that had happened to her, it asked him about the nature of bravery.

It asked him if he could be a better man.

It asked him if he could stand the loneliness of going back to a life that didn't have her in it.

He was not a man used to being terrified, and yet really, he was aware that had been there since the moment he had rescued her from under that cascade of her own cookies at the Stars Come Out at Night gala.

That she would ask more of him. That she would require more of him than anyone had ever required before.

That she would hold out to him the most enticing gift of all: an ability to hope for things he had given up on a long time ago.

There was a possibility he was constitutionally unsuited to the world he saw shining in her eyes like a beacon calling a weary soldier home.

But he had warned her of that. He had tried to tell her.

And this was what she was trying to tell him: she

was not the innocent girl he'd escorted to her prom any longer.

She was a woman, capable of making her own choices, capable of embracing all the risks of the unknown.

Love. The greatest unknown of all.

Love, that capricious vixen who called you in, then shattered you on the rocks.

Somehow, he could not see being shattered on the rocks with Bree. Her eyes were warm, everything about her was genuine.

She wasn't going to hurt him.

And so he said, "Sure, let's go to my charity ball together."

He said it casually, as if it was not every bit as thrilling and as terrifying as that whale breaching the water beside them had been. Saying it was a lift of his shoulder that said "no big deal," as if he had not just stepped off a cliff, and was waiting to see if the parachute would open.

And the parachute was her.

Despite a paddle against a slight current coming back in to English Bay, Bree was brimming over with energy. Life felt the way it had not felt in so long.

Exciting and ripe with potential.

"I'm famished," she said, when they had pulled the kayak up the beach and hoisted it onto his roof rack. "Should we go grab a bite?"

This was the new bold her! Taking chances. Asking Brand to spend yet more time with her. He was going to say—

"Sure. What did you have in mind?"

"I love that Hot Diggity food truck."

"Hot Diggity?"

"Hot dogs. If you give me back my phone, I'll check their schedule and see where they are today."

He was smirking as he handed her the phone. "You know, I can afford a little better than a hot dog."

"You probably can. I'm buying."

"No, you're not."

"Look, Brand, if it's going to be a relationship of equals, you have to let me do my bit, too."

The word *relationship* word wavered in the air between them, like a wave of heat shimmering off hot pavement.

"Did you actually get stiffed for the coffee with the e-Us loser, or did you offer to buy it?" he asked.

"Different lifetime," she said, scrolling through her phone. "I've moved on. You should, too. He's on Robson Street today, by the art gallery."

"The guy who stiffed you for coffee?" Brand asked, surprised.

She glanced at him and saw he was teasing her. Warmth unfurled in her like a flag. "Parking won't be fun."

"My office has some spots down there, if you don't object to that on some principle of equality. We could travel together."

She certainly wasn't going to object to that part.

And so Bree found herself in the deep and luxurious leather passenger seat, enjoying his confidence as he maneuvered his oversize vehicle through downtown traffic. He turned on his CD player. No Elvis. Light classical.

He parked in a private stall in a private lot and they walked the short distance to Hot Diggity. He didn't put up too much of a fight about letting her pay, and just as she had hoped, he fell in love with the hot dogs.

By the time he drove her back out to English Bay, the sun was setting, and both conversation and silence felt comfortable between them. He had an old blanket in the car, and they sat together on it, shoulders touching, until there was no light left.

"My turn to supply food tomorrow night," he said as he walked her to her car. "Meet me at my office around six?"

"Okay."

For a moment he hesitated. For a moment she hesitated.

And then his arms were around her, and he pulled her into him, kissed her soundly on the lips and let her go. They stood there, studying each other with a kind of wonder.

"I don't remember when I've had such a perfect day," she confessed.

"I don't know when I have, either."

"Are you scared?" she asked softly.

"Terrified," he answered.

"Me, too."

"The good kind of terrified, like when a very large whale breaches beside a very small vessel."

And then he kissed her again, harder this time. "Get in your car," he said huskily, "before I invite you home with me. And it wouldn't be to make cookies."

She got in her car. She felt so intoxicated with lust she didn't know how she would drive. Somehow she managed to get home. And somehow she managed to get through the next day until it was time to be at his office.

* * *

It was much emptier than the last time she had seen it, but just the same, Beau came barreling through the door. This time she wasn't so shocked to see him. In fact, she felt delighted. And glad she had opted for slender-fitting jeans that could stand up to him. The rose-colored silk blouse, however, didn't fare so well!

Brand came through the door. "Beau! I don't know what it is about him and you. He managed to give me the slip and was through that door before I knew you'd arrived."

"What did you have planned for dinner? Do I have to change?" she asked.

Brand's eyes moved to the wet splotch on her breast. "Uh—"

"That's a yes."

"Well, we're eating in."

"Here?" she said, surprised.

"Yeah, I thought we'd have dinner and then I'd show you the climbing wall. And the ball pit."

She giggled.

"I have extra shirts here."

"Why not?" she said.

His office was dark, except for candles that burned on the coffee table between the love seats. As the sun went down, the Vancouver skyline was lighting up outside his windows.

She could see the table had been set. And that food was already there. For a guy who claimed to be hopeless at relationships, he seemed to be doing just fine at romance!

"Here," he said. He went into a large cabinet that

turned out to be a wardrobe and passed her a shirt. "Powder room is through there."

The powder room was exquisite and luxurious. She put on the men's shirt. It was clean and crisp, way too large, and for some absurd reason it made her feel sexier than hell.

She came out, his shirt to her knees, with her own soiled shirt balled up in her hand.

"Give that to me. I'll put it in the basket that gets sent out to the cleaners."

"Don't be sil—"

He gave her a look. She passed him her blouse.

"In any other context, me getting you out of your blouse might be kind of fun." He raised that delightfully wicked eyebrow. Then her smile died. She had the feeling he found her as sexy in his shirt as she felt!

"Have a seat," he said. "I took the liberty of ordering from one of my favorite places."

He poured her a glass of wine, and she looked at the plate before her. It held a salad, and she took her fork and took a tentative taste. The salad had greens, but also tomatoes, avocado and crab. It was exquisite, of course!

"Well?" he asked.

It was so endearing that he was anxious that she be pleased. Really, it was like something out of a dream.

"It's not Hot Diggity," she said thoughtfully, "but it's passably good. The bouquet of the balsamic vinegar is lovely."

And then they were laughing together, and as always, when they laughed together everything else fell away.

The rest of the menu was just as exquisite as the salad, as they dined on grilled quail, served with tiny roasted potatoes, and fresh green beans in a lime butter sauce.

"This is so good," Bree said.

"This is what happens when a man doesn't use his own kitchen," Brand told her. "He figures out where to get the best takeout in the city."

The dog, who had been sitting quietly, moaned softly.

"He knows we're done. I won't let him beg at the table, but I always give him a little something after."

Brand opened a bag from the same restaurant, removed a container and went over to a huge bowl.

"What's he getting?" Bree said as she came over and stood beside him.

"Same thing as us. Deboned."

For a moment, she felt extremely awkward and out of place. She was with a man who thought nothing of feeding his dog deboned quail from one of Vancouver's finest restaurants.

He turned back to her. "You want dessert now? Or do you want to try the climbing wall?"

"Definitely the climbing wall!"

There seemed to be no other people in the office tonight, and they had the "play" equipment to themselves. Beau came with them, and Brand threw one of his toys in the ball pit. The big dog leaped in and soon balls were flying everywhere as he searched joyously for his toy.

The awkwardness was gone, just like that. Brand knew how to have fun!

He helped her strap on a harness, and gave her a few tips for her first attempt at the wall. He put on his own harness, though it was obvious he did not need one. With the confidence and agility of a billy goat he topped the wall in about twenty seconds. From his perch up there, he called tips down to her.

"Oh," she cried as, just when she thought she had gotten the hang of it, she fell. But the harness took her weight easily. He was beside her in a second, showing her how to get back onto the wall, or lower herself to the floor and start again. She lost her hold several times, which was good, because she also totally lost her fear. The harness caught her and swung her gently each time.

They spent the rest of the evening finding different ways up the wall. Like the kayaking, it proved to be a terrific way to get to know each other. It involved communication, but not that interview-style intensity that Brand had pointed out was a flaw of the online dating world.

Beau finally captured his toy and abandoned the pit to go chew on it.

Since muscles she did not even know she had were aching, Bree was glad when Brand suggested they take over the pit. Following his example, she let herself fall in over the side, arms spread wide. The balls caught her and cushioned her, and she shrieked with delight, just lying there. Brand swam the backstroke and then dove into the colorful sea of balls. Bree joined him, until she was laughing so hard her stomach ached from it.

They retreated back to his office and had coffee and crème brûlée for dessert.

And then he walked her home, through quiet Vancouver streets, one hand in hers and the other holding Beau's leash.

Bree felt so happy. She thought they probably looked just like one of those couples she had always envied, out with their dog on an evening walk.

He insisted on seeing her right to her apartment door.

"I'd invite you in," she said, "but I don't think Oliver is ready to meet Beau."

"I'm sure he's quite jealous of all the time you've spent away. And now, after arriving with the scent of a strange dog on you, the slathering beast is right on his doorstep."

"I'm not worried. Oliver's forgiveness can be purchased with a new toy," Bree said, and pulled a bright purple mouse from her purse. "Voilà!"

They both laughed when Beau made a try for the toy.

"Plus, Oliver has selected my neighbor as a suitable slave in my absence. She spoils him atrociously. She's recently lost her husband, and I think she and the cat are both loving the relationship."

Of course, Oliver was not ready to meet Beau, but really that was just a convenient excuse not to invite Brand in. It wasn't the real reason, and she suspected he knew it, too. There was something lovely unfolding between them. It felt new and fragile. To move things to a physical plane too soon would bring a layer of complication to what was going on between them that she knew she was not ready for.

He seemed to feel the same way. He kissed her on the lips. It was a beautiful kiss. Welcoming and tender. Brand seemed to recognize exactly where she was at, because he pulled away and looked at her with a kind of respect and reverence that she had never experienced before.

"I usually take Beau for a really long walk in the morning," he said. "Are you game?"

"Absolutely."

And so they began to tangle their lives together in lovely ways: walking the dog, grabbing a bite to eat, watching a movie at his place, cooking dinner at hers. One memorable afternoon, they opened the Klingon-dictionary app on her phone, and they sat out in his backyard in the spring sunshine trying out phrases until they were both rolling on the ground laughing, with Beau leaping joyously between them.

A commercial kitchen space opened up for her, and she moved out of his kitchen. In a way she was sad to be leaving it, because it was so beautiful and she had felt so at home there, but in a way she was happy that their business interests were separating.

They did such ordinary things, but they did things that reflected his wealth and status as well. He took her on a helicopter tour of Vancouver, he rented a yacht for a day, complete with a chef, and he flew them on a private jet one night for a play in San Francisco, where they met Bree's mother and her husband.

It was a beautiful evening.

Her mother looked at her, when they had a moment alone together in the theater powder room, and hugged her hard.

"I know you thought I moved on too quickly from your dad," she said. "But when you love someone the way I loved him, the thought of not having love in your life is unbearable. Of course, every love is different. What Mike and I have is not the same as what your father and I shared. And yet, it is lovely, too. So lovely."

And then she added softly, "But you know that now, don't you, my dear Bree? That a life without love is unbearable?"

Bree thought, just as her mother, she had probably known that all along. Life without love was unbear-

able. It had made her such easy prey for a bad person.
And then it had made her back off of love altogether.

But her mother was so right, that life without love
was like crossing an endless desert, thirsty for water
you could not find.

Her mother confirmed what Bree already knew in
her heart. She was not going down that road again. She
felt like a completely different person than the girl she
had been before.

"Brand is such a good man," her mother said. "Your
father always knew that about him. I have a feeling he'd
be extraordinarily pleased right now."

But, for all that, for all that Bree got to experience
lifestyles of the rich and famous, it seemed to be the
small and ordinary things that had taken on a shine,
that made Bree feel alive and engaged and as if happiness was a ball of light in her stomach that glowed ever
more strongly outward.

Everyone noticed it. Her clients, Chelsea, her neighbors, her girlfriends.

When Brand went away on business trips, she stayed
at his place and looked after Beau, who had completely
stolen her heart. Oliver began to come along, and soon
ruled Beau with an iron paw.

Brand would always bring her back small, enchanting gifts—a crystal butterfly from Sweden, an exquisite
wooden carving from Thailand, a soapstone polar bear
from the Canadian north. They even had a tradition:
as soon as he came home, they baked cookies together,
sometimes in her tiny apartment kitchen, sometimes in
his state-of-the-art kitchen.

By the time of the charity ball, they had been seeing
each other for a month. Bree was certain of how she

felt. She was certain it was not an infatuation, certain where she wanted it to go, certain of Brand's place in her future.

Everything she had known the night she had heard that song in her head—"Can't Help Falling in Love"—was confirmed.

And so Bree decided to find a dress for that charity ball that would tell him all that as much as words ever could.

That would tell him beyond a shadow of a doubt that she was ready for whatever came next.

CHAPTER THIRTEEN

"I CAN'T FIND the right dress," Bree wailed to Chelsea a week later as they were locking up the new kitchen for the day. "Time's running out. I can't go to Brand's charity ball looking like the very same person I was at my high-school prom. And yet everything I've tried on does exactly that. It makes me feel as if I'm a kid pretending to be a grown-up."

"We could remake one of my salsa costumes," Chelsea said. "It would be easy."

Bree had attended a number of Chelsea's dance competitions. She made all her own outfits. "Chelsea, I don't know. Your outfits are gorgeous, but kind of over-the-top sexy."

"You just said you wanted to be sexy."

"Yes, but—"

"I have a red one. Red always makes men sit up and take notice. It's short, but I could add some layers to it. We're almost the same size. I think it would look phenomenal on you. Come home with me right now, we'll try it. You have nothing to lose."

That was true. She had nothing to lose. It was not as if she had found the right dress anywhere else. Plus, the price was right.

Chelsea lived in a cute little basement suite not very far from the new kitchen. It was an easy walk, and they went in.

Bree stopped. There was a large pair of men's sneakers at the door.

"Oh," Chelsea said with a blush, "Reed left those here."

"Reed?" Bree asked. She looked at her young assistant closely. She had been so wrapped up in herself that she hadn't notice a different kind of sparkle about Chelsea. Who was now blushing pink.

"He's the fire investigator our side hired."

Meaning the one *Brand* had hired.

"Don't look at me like that. Of course, he can't get involved with me while he's doing an investigation."

Which, of course, begged the question, why his shoes would be there, but Chelsea looked so pretty and so flustered that Bree didn't have the heart to pursue it.

Chelsea, eager to change the subject, brought out the dress, still in its dry-cleaning wrapper.

Bree took off the wrapper. The dress slid into her hands, surprisingly cool, since it looked so hot, like flames.

"Put it on," Chelsea insisted, and Bree went through to her tiny bathroom.

"No underwear," Chelsea shouted.

Good grief! Still, Bree put the dress on, then turned to face herself in the full-length mirror on the back of the door.

"Cripes," she said, astounded.

The dress fit her like a glove. The top was pure red, with tiny spaghetti straps at the shoulders. The neckline plunged to a narrow waist, where it took on the color of flame, leaf-like layers of fabric in colors of orange and yellow and several shades of red.

"Come out," Chelsea said.

"I'm scared to," Bree answered back, but then opened the door and stepped out. Chelsea's eyes widened.

"It's all wrong," Bree said at the very same time Chelsea said, "It's so right."

"It's too short."

"I knew that. But I've got lots of that fabric, and an idea how I can make it floor-length."

"And the neckline is too—"

"Shush. One little stitch. Here, I'll get a pin and show you."

That single pin changed everything.

And then Chelsea was at her feet, pinning and tucking and pinning some more. "This is just to give you an idea. It will be way more sophisticated. Fall leaves, until you move, and then each piece of fabric will move differently and catch the light differently. It will change from fall leaves to flame."

Finally, Chelsea was satisfied and told Bree she could go back into the bathroom, the location of the only full-length mirror in her tiny apartment.

Bree was almost afraid to look. She turned to the mirror with her eyes closed. Slowly, she opened them, and when she did, her heart beat double time. The dress was incredible, with its beautiful silk leaves falling to the floor, dancing around her. Just as Chelsea had promised, when she moved, the light caught the fabric and turned it to flame.

Chelsea managed to squeeze through the door to join Bree. "These outfits are made to celebrate the female form," she said, "and to move all on their own. It's really a seduction."

A seduction? Bree gulped. Was she ready for that?

She realized it wasn't Brand who had looked at her like a child pretending to be an adult, but that that was the role she had cast herself in.

And suddenly she felt so completely adult, she could feel herself stepping over some imaginary line that separated a girl from a woman.

Oh, yeah, she felt so ready for that! These weeks of keeping each other at arm's length, of only sharing chaste kisses, the longing building to something almost unbearable...

Chelsea moved in behind her and scooped up her hair. It made Bree's neck look long and elegant, and her eyes look huge, dark and startled, like those of a doe.

"I don't know how I can thank you," Bree said.

"Oh, Bree, you already have. You have had faith in me in the face of evidence you should not have. I know you think there's a possibility I set the kitchen on fire. Thank you for not suing me."

"That's ridiculous. The suing part."

"But not the catching-the-kitchen-on-fire part?" Chelsea said with wry self-recognition. And then they were laughing, and Bree felt as if she had been given many gifts.

A man she loved, and the sister she never had.

"It will be ready before the ball," Chelsea promised. "And you will be the most ravishing woman Mr. Brand Wallace has ever laid eyes on."

Bree slipped out of the dress and came back into the main area in her ordinary-girl clothes. But Chelsea wasn't finished with her yet.

"I'm just going to show you a few moves," she said. "Subtle, but sexy as hell."

Bree's eyes got very wide as Chelsea demonstrated exactly what she meant!

* * *

The night of the ball arrived and if Bree had had another outfit suitable to go change into before Brand arrived, she probably would have. She felt nervous and naked. Who did she think she was? she wondered. Julia Roberts?

She, indeed, looked like a movie star—red-carpet ready, which was, as Chelsea had assured her, a very good thing.

Tonight was as close as Vancouver got to a red-carpet event!

But as soon as Bree opened the door, and saw the look on Brand's face, she was happy—almost deliriously so—that she had not lost her nerve about the dress.

Because Brand looked like a man slain. His mouth fell open, and his eyes darkened with heady desire and drank her in with a kind of thirst that could never be quenched.

"You look absolutely stunning," he said, his voice hoarse.

He reached for her and kissed her on the cheek, put her away from himself and stared. "It seems not so long ago you were telling me how ordinary you were," he said.

She realized, with a shiver of pure appreciation, this was true. Being with him, feeling cherished by him, had made her feel beautiful and confident in a way she never, ever had before. He took her hand and walked her outside her building.

A long, sleek, white limo waited, the uniformed driver holding open the door for them. He tipped his hat to her, and called her "Miss."

Sinking into the luxurious leather and having Brand pour her some champagne into a flute was the beginning of a night out of a fairy tale. She floated through every minute of it. The entrance, chatting with people, nursing a drink and, finally, what she had been waiting for her whole life.

The thing she had got the tiniest taste of the night of her prom, a taste that had left her wanting. She danced with Brand.

Not as a child, dancing with the man who had been talked into escorting her to her prom.

But as a woman who knew exactly what she wanted. It was an evening out of a dream. His eyes never left her. Every move he made was subtly sensual, welcoming her in a different way. Brand was so comfortable with himself, and with his body, and it made her more comfortable with her own newfound sexy side.

She demonstrated some of the moves Chelsea had shown her. They had exactly the right effect on him, making his eyes darken and his hands linger on the curves of her back and hip.

They laughed. They teased each other. They danced and their hands touched each other, as if they could not get enough.

Despite the fact there were so many beautiful people there, in gorgeous clothes and jewelry, moving in amazing ways, it felt as if the ballroom belonged to them and them alone. Their eyes rarely left each other. Even when they spoke to other people, it was as if they were in a bubble that really held only them.

Bree had that first glass of champagne, and then one more, not enough to be making her feel as intoxicated as she did.

The evening went both too quickly and too slowly, because she was anticipating the moment they were alone.

So, here they were, seemingly only a breath after he had picked her up, facing the last dance of the evening.

Bree was stunned when she heard the opening notes of the Elvis song "Can't Help Falling in Love." Had he requested it? She didn't think so.

It was the universe conspiring.

His hand found the small of her back and he pulled him in to her. They might have been the only two people in the room.

She put her head back so that she could look up into his beautiful face, so beloved to her now.

The last bars of the song melted over top of them and then the music ended, but what was flowing between them did not. He lowered his head. He took her lips. She reached up, almost on tiptoes, and returned his kiss. It was as if they were in the room alone together.

The heat was scorching.

"Do you mind taking a miss on the midnight buffet?" he whispered in her ear.

"No," she said, trembling.

His hand found the small of her back. Nodding here and there, he propelled her through the crowd. Suddenly they were out on a wet street, the rain refreshingly cool on her scorching skin.

And then they were in the back of the limo.

He stared straight ahead. So did she. She knew if they even glanced at one another, the chauffer was going to get much more of a show than he'd bargained for.

They tumbled out of the limo when it stopped at her apartment, almost running to the building's entrance.

To a passerby it might have seemed they did not want to get wet.

But there was urgency between them now. To open the last chapter, to go to the place between them that had not yet been mapped.

That exquisite new country of pure discovery.

"Security cameras?" he whispered in the elevator.

"No."

He was on her. He had her backed against the wall of the elevator, his hands around her back, crushing her to him, her hands twined around his neck, pulling his lips to her own.

By the time the elevator door opened, they were both gasping with need, with red-hot desire. They tumbled from the elevator. Thank God, at this time of night, her hallway was abandoned.

With great effort, nearly dumping the contents of her tiny evening bag on the floor, she found her key. Her hands were shaking so badly she could not make the lock work.

He reached by her and took the key, inserted and twisted it.

The door fell open.

She stared at him.

He stared at her.

"Are you sure?" he growled.

"Yes," she whispered, and then stronger, because she had never been more sure of anything, she repeated, "Yes!"

CHAPTER FOURTEEN

THEY WERE IN the kitchen, their coats wet puddles of fabric on the floor. He lifted her onto the counter and, with her legs wrapped around him, she tasted him as if she could never get enough. Hungry. Starving.

All grown up. So filled with passion she was trembling with it. She could feel him trembling, too. He rubbed his whisker-roughened cheek down the delicate skin of her neck, as her nails dug into the broadness of his back.

His lips found hers again, no gentleness in them now, no tenderness.

He was a warrior conquering, he was taking what he wanted. But she was no captive, except maybe of her own heart's longings, because she met his savage taking of her lips with an answer of her own that was bold and uninhibited.

The woman in her explored the man in him—she tasted it, and touched it, and rode the enormous energy of it. It sizzled and hissed between them like a fire out of control. She was pulled toward the heat of it, helpless as a moth to a flame, sure to be scorched and yet unable to move away from what was happening between them.

His hands went to her hair. It tumbled out of its knot

and scattered wildly around her shoulders. He kissed the low-cut space in her dress, between her breasts, and she moaned with desire, lifted his questing lips to her own and took them again.

And then a sound.

An insistent sound.

The quacking of a duck.

Stunned, she realized it was coming from him. She realized it was some kind of ringtone. Bree was even more stunned when Brand took his phone out of his pocket and answered it.

Bree had never heard that ringtone come from his phone before. In fact, he rarely answered or looked at his phone when they were together.

But now he took it, his features set in grim lines. He held up a finger to her, answered and went out the door of her apartment.

He came back in seconds later. "I'm sorry," he said, running a hand through his hair. "I've got an emergency. I have to leave."

"An emergency?" she whispered, feeling shattered by her own longing, by the fact what was happening between them had not been so sacred that the phone could be ignored.

"An urgent family matter."

She stared at him, trying to figure out the incongruity of using a quack tone for an emergency. And yet, there was no doubting the gravity of the situation. His face, so familiar to her, was completely closed, set in the ferocious, impenetrable lines of a warrior called to action.

"What family?" she stuttered.

"My mother."

She tried to absorb that. All this time together, and except for the odd reference to a bad childhood, she had not even been aware his mother was still alive. In fact, the afternoon that he had arrived at her apartment shortly after the kitchen fire, she was positive he had *implied* his mother was deceased. She felt the shock of him blocking that part of his life from her.

"I have to go."

But her sense of loss and recrimination needed to be put aside for the time being. He looked so shattered. He looked as if, whatever this was, he should not be alone with it.

"I'm coming with you."

He started to shake his head, but she could see he was rattled, that he both wanted her support and didn't. She scrambled off the counter and went and changed quickly, her evening as a princess as over as if she was Cinderella, midnight had come and she had turned back into the ordinary girl she really was.

His steps were long and urgent as he shepherded Bree outside. In their rush to get into her apartment, he had forgotten to dismiss the limo, and it idled at the curb waiting for him. Now, they got in and he gave his own address. There they switched to one of his own cars, ignoring the soulful sounds of Beau, from inside the house, crying that he knew they were home.

The car Brand chose from his six-bay garage was an Italian four-door Maserati, but it might as well have been a pumpkin for how the magic had drained from the evening. He was silent and grim, barely acknowledging her as he scrolled through his phone, looking something up with urgency.

And then they were driving through the seediest part

of Vancouver, streets lined with dilapidated buildings with people huddled in the doorways.

He stopped in front of one. It was a no-parking zone, but he ignored that. A sandwich board announced Tonight and Tonight Only, Elvis Impersonations.

He was storming through the door, Bree hard on his heels.

The room was dark, and had only a smattering of people sitting at tables. It smelled bad, of smoke and spilled beer.

The stage was illuminated, though, and an Elvis gyrated across it, belting out "Hound Dog."

He *did* remind Bree of that horrible man she had met on e-Us.

She looked at Brand, arms folded across his chest, as he scanned the tables. The performance, the club and the Elvis impersonators sitting around waiting for their turns might have been funny in an absurd way, particularly coming from the ball to this, but it was not funny. Bree glanced at Brand's face. She was not sure she had ever seen such terrible torment in one person's expression before in her life.

He spotted something and moved across the dark room. Bree, not sure what to do, or what exactly was going on, followed.

Brand slid into a chair at a table occupied by a lovely woman with gray hair. She turned and smiled at him, put her arm on his sleeve, then turned back to the music, rapt. Brand, though he hardly seemed to know Bree was there, pulled out the chair beside him and nodded at it. Bree took it.

The song ended with blessed abruptness, as if someone, having suffered quite enough, had pulled the plug on the karaoke machine.

"I'm glad you called me, Mom," Brand said quietly into the sudden silence.

Mom.

"I was trying to get up my nerve to go on," his mother said, and then, her voice sad, she added, "But it's not me anymore, is it?"

"Maybe not," he said gently.

"But don't throw out my posters just yet!"

Her posters. All this time, Brand could have told Bree, but nothing. Not a single word, even though there had been opportunities.

"Hello," his mother said softly, noticing Bree. "I'm Diana. I used to do a great Elvis impression."

Almost shyly she took a bag out from under the table and spilled its contents out for Bree to see. She fingered the white, metal-studded fabric almost lovingly.

"I was good, wasn't I, Brand?" she asked, her tone wistful.

"Yeah, Mom," he said. "You were good."

Bree's mind felt tumultuous as snippets of conversations came back to her. *Somehow I didn't figure you for an Elvis kind of guy. What's your favorite Elvis song? Must I pick only one? Impossible.*

"Bree," Brand said, his flinty eyes intent on her face, "meet my mother."

Bree looked to him, and then to the woman. She extended her hand. "Mrs. Wallace?" she said uncertainly. "My pleasure. Bree Evans."

"Diana."

Lively eyes, dark like his, scanned her face, a certain shrewdness in them. "I suppose I should go home now?"

"I think that's a good idea, Mom."

They left and he put his mother in the front seat, and Bree took the back. They drove through the city in complete silence to a lovely building, which, even in all its loveliness, was clearly some sort of institution.

"I'll call you a cab," Brand said grimly.

"I'll wait," Bree said, just as grimly.

He looked as if he might argue, but his mother got out of the car, and looked as if she might be considering going anywhere but in. The weariness on his face was heartbreaking, and he just lifted a shoulder, got out, put his hand on his mother's shoulder and guided her to the main door.

It was nearly an hour before he came out.

His face was gray with exhaustion. He slid into the seat beside her.

"I'm sorry I took so long," he said. "She was quite agitated. I stayed with her for a while until she settled. It's an assisted-living place, not a jail. My mother's bipolar, with schizophrenic tendencies."

He sounded like a doctor, clinical, rhyming off facts.

"The medication takes away her upswing, and the voices. She misses both. She can be very good at hiding the fact she isn't taking her medication. I probably should have picked up on it."

Bree heard self-recrimination there. He'd been too involved with her. It had distracted him.

"I'll drive you home now. There was no need for you to wait." They drove away.

She knew he had no intention of coming in, that the moment was gone, possibly forever.

She knew he was tired. But it still had to be said. "You don't think we have things to discuss?"

"Must we?"

"Yes. Why didn't you tell me, Brand? Why didn't you trust me with this?"

He was silent. They pulled up in front of her building. He nodded to the door, as if he expected her just to get out!

"You let me believe your mother was dead."

He looked truly astonished by that. "What?"

"That day at my apartment, when we were drinking the cheap wine, you said she would have considered it champagne. *Would have*. Past tense."

"Because she doesn't drink anymore, not because she's dead!"

"All this time you could have said something. Anything. That day in the kayak, I asked you about you and Elvis, I said I got the impression you didn't like Elvis that much. Some might say a perfect segue for you to tell me about your mom. But no. Nothing. Not a word."

"Pardon me for not revealing all my secrets to you." His voice was cold.

"But I revealed all mine to you, Brand," she reminded him softly. "I told you about my baby. I shared my deepest loss with you. I trusted you with it."

She thought this reminder of her own vulnerability would soften him, but his silence was cold. It made her more grimly determined to have her say.

"It's not that your mother is ill that hurts," she told him. Her tone was quiet, but she was not sure she had ever felt so angry. "It's that you didn't trust me to do the right thing with it. To be the right person."

Again, he was silent for a long time, and when he turned to her, her heart stopped beating, and her breath stopped the steady rise and fall of life. What she saw in his eyes was an unfathomable coldness. Cruelty.

She saw everything had changed. She saw he would not see her again.

"No," he said harshly, "I didn't trust you with it. Goodbye, Bree."

Stunned, she got out of the car. In a moment of fury, she slammed the door so hard his car rocked. Still, he did not squeal away. She wished he would have. Instead, he waited to make sure she got to the door. She kept her shoulders straight, her spine proud, as she put in her door code. It was as he drove away that she dissolved, and let the first tears fall.

All this time, she realized, she had given more and more and more trust to him.

And he had given her none in return. He had not even trusted her to be understanding about his mother's fragile, broken condition.

Had he not known her at all?

"All men are rotten," she decided furiously. "All of them!"

Brand drove away after he saw Bree was safely inside her building. He felt sick for what he had just said to her, that he didn't trust her with it.

The truth was, he had not trusted himself with it.

He had allowed himself to be distracted from the truth of his life, to pretend that he could have what other people had.

He had allowed that dangerous thing called hope to creep into his world.

This is what Brand had managed to avoid facing after the enchantment of the last month—that he brought a long and horrible history with him, running down his line from two sides. A selfish man who had such a cold heart he had abandoned his wife and, worse, his son.

And then his mother, his poor long-suffering mother, who would sometimes get better for long periods of time, only to fall back into her delusions, an intensifying of her obsession with Elvis usually providing the first red flag that she had abandoned her medication, that she missed the "ups" and missed the "voices."

But this time, he hadn't noticed. He'd been too busy. Selfish and cold, just like his father.

This is what he knew for sure.

He loved Bree Evans with a love that nearly took his breath away. He loved how funny she was and how brave. He loved how she made the most ordinary of things shine as if they were lit from within. He loved the wonder in her face when he invited her into a world where money could buy anything, and her equal wonder over a dog romping joyously through a mud puddle. He loved her loyalty and her creativity and how smart and how inventive she was. He loved how she had hope.

This is what he'd forgotten that day he had decided that she could not hurt him. This is what he had so selfishly put aside: that he could hurt her. That's what he had forgotten in that totally self-centered moment of *wanting* what he had seen shining in her.

All the things he had never had: a safe harbor, future children laughing.

She deserved those things. The truth was this: both conditions his mother had could be inherited. If he had either, they would have shown up by now. But that did not make his children safe.

Is that what his father had thought, when he walked

away and never come back? That he could barely deal with one person with mental-health issues? What if his son had those issues, too?

Brand could not bear it if he was the one who crushed in Bree, for all time, those things that mattered so much to her. How could he create the kind of home she'd enjoyed as a child? How would he learn those skills when he had never experienced the security and stability of a good home? Nothing in living in a car, and stealing creamers from fast-food restaurants, and walking in the door, listening to see what Elvis song his mother had on so he could judge her mood, had prepared him for the kind of life Bree desired so desperately and deserved so richly.

Really, the most loving thing he could ever do for her?

He had just done it.

He had said goodbye. Not just for tonight. Forever. It had felt as if he was ripping his own heart out saying that to her, keeping his face cold and cruel in the light of her hurt and her wanting and her hope. Especially her hope.

As he drove away through the rain-filled night, it felt as if he had entered a pit of impenetrable blackness such as he had never known before, and in a way he welcomed it, like a man facing his absolute reality and coming home to the place he'd always known that he belonged.

CHAPTER FIFTEEN

BREE WOKE UP the morning after the ball knowing exactly how Cinderella had felt. She had *almost* had it all. And then, at the ring of a clock at midnight—or the quack of a phone, as the case might be—it had been snatched away from her. She was lying in her bed waiting for that familiar despair to creep over her, to steal her breath and her strength and her desire to get up.

Instead, as she was lying there, scanning her feelings, she was pleasantly surprised that she didn't feel despair at all. She felt really, really angry.

"All men are rotten," she repeated to herself. She liked it. It would be her new mantra!

She got up and looked in the mirror in her bathroom. Her eyes were ringed with black from last night's cry, but as she washed up, she was aware she was done crying, and that she had something very important to do.

She dressed in slim-fitting jeans and a plain cotton blouse, and then threw her beautiful new cloak over top. She filled up Oliver's water and food dishes, then she put on sneakers to drive, but put her red stilettos in the backseat.

And then she drove. She thought she would have second thoughts on the long drive, lose her courage or her nerve, but neither happened. If anything, her confidence grew. She had a sense that this was something she should have done a long, long time ago.

She drove through the familiar campus. It was summer session, but there was still lots of life. She noticed the girls, in particular, looking so carefree, so filled with hope for their futures.

She had been that girl once. She had *allowed* Paul Weston to steal that from her. But here was the part that filled her with shame: had her silence allowed him to steal it from other young women, as well?

The new her parked in the spot reserved for visiting VIPs, and she changed shoes. The new Bree walked right by the president of the university's stammering secretary, knocked briefly on his door and went in.

He looked up, surprised, and she let the door swing shut behind her.

Twenty minutes later, with assurances of a complete investigation, she strode across the campus in her heels. She felt like a warrior: she could feel the absolute confidence shimmering around her, like a crackle of electricity in the air before a coming storm.

Men stopped and stared at her as if she was the most ravishing woman they had ever seen. Some of them ventured a smile. Women seemed to know she was on a mission for all of them, because they smiled at her as though they recognized her, or recognized something in her that they liked.

She didn't even hesitate at the familiar steps of the culinary arts building. The heels did not even slow her down.

She went in and stopped by the lecture hall.

And there he was. She could see him through the small rectangular glass frame that looked in to the hall.

He was dressed as he always had been: a tweedy jacket and rumpled pants. Today he was sporting an ascot. She could clearly see he was wearing the costume of a distracted, artsy college professor.

She took a deep breath and opened the door. All eyes were on her as she went down the sloping aisle, past the rows of theater-style seats, up the three stairs to the raised dais he stood on.

"Paul, do you remember me?" she asked, her voice loud and clear.

His eyes wide, the man who had haunted her nightmares looked at her. His mouth opened, then closed, opened again.

"Bree," he said, "I'm in the middle of—"

She saw what she had never seen as his eyes shifted away from hers. The weakness and the cowardice, a man who had used his position and power to feed his own sick needs.

"I don't care what you're in the middle of," she said, and she turned to face his students. She took a deep breath, and began.

"I want to tell you about a young girl, who sat right where you are sitting now," she said. There was no hesitation and no fear. "Her father had just died."

"Bree." His voice was plaintive.

"Paul, sit down and shut up."

He stared at her. He scuttled over to a chair and sat down.

She finished her story. For a moment, there was shocked silence. For a moment, she wondered if she had done the right thing. And then one lone, brave young woman stood. Bree could see tears running down her face. She began to clap. And then another rose, and another. The young women were the first, but the young men followed. She turned to look at Paul. His chair was empty.

And then she was surrounded in a sea of caring.

Strangers who felt as if they were not strangers at all were hugging her, some of the girls were telling her about the creepy moves Paul had put on them.

Bree realized she felt as if she was leaving her body, as if she had floated way up above herself and was looking down at the woman in the stiletto heels and the red cape, and seeing her for what she was.

Brave enough, finally, to be worthy of the gift called love.

Days later, she did not feel quite so brave. She felt worn down from emotion, and her devastating sense of loss. Her mantra was not strong enough to carry her, and didn't even seem true anymore.

How did "all men are rotten" fit into being worthy of the gift that was love? It didn't. Her father had not been rotten. And Brand was not rotten, either.

He was human.

She thought of the look in Brand's eyes the last night she had seen him. She had mistaken it for coldness and cruelty and rejection.

But now, having seen Paul Weston again, she was very aware of what those things looked like. And Brand had none of them in him. None.

What she had seen in his eyes was the lonely bleakness of a man who thought he had to protect her, even if that meant from himself.

Bree realized she had to use all this newfound bravery to go into his dark world and bring him to safety. She had to be brave enough to go after him. To go after Brand, a man who had only ever used his position and his power for good. A man who was as worthy of her as she was of him.

He just didn't know it yet.

But when she called his cell, there was no answer. When she called his office, she was told he was not available.

The new Bree put on her bravery cloak, and went downtown. She had a cookie contract after all. There was no reason not to drop by his office!

For once, there was a receptionist at the front desk in that luxurious front foyer. No joyous dog came bounding out the door.

"I need to see Mr. Wallace," Bree said.

The receptionist looked at her, and obviously recognized her. Bree had been a bit of a fixture for the past month. Was there the faint pity of one not unfamiliar with the heartsick trying to get through to her boss in her tone?

"I'm afraid he's out of the country at the moment. I'll tell him you called by?"

"Out of the country? But when will he be back?"

"I'm not at liberty to say that."

Bree wanted to leap across the desk, place her hands around that skinny throat and squeeze an answer from her. What country? How long would he be gone?

"I think he's going to be away for some time," the receptionist said, and now she looked genuinely sad.

"Where's Beau?"

"He's out of the country, too."

Bree felt a wave of relief. "Thank goodness," she murmured. Beau, the only one he trusted completely with his heart, was with him.

She turned to leave. The door that separated the office space from the front entrance swung open.

A young man walked out. She recognized him from his beard, and from her first day here, when he had been swinging on that hammock, throwing a beanbag in the air.

It niggled her memory. *He is one guy I make sure to talk to every single day.*

"Kevin?" she said.

He turned and looked at her absently.

She racked her memory for the afternoon that she and Brand had practiced phrases out of the Klingon language, laughing until they could laugh no more.

Klingons, Brand had told her gravely, did not have greetings per se, but still she drew a phrase from her memory.

She tentatively tried out the crazy sounding mix of consonants and vowels. She must have done something right.

Kevin brightened instantly. He responded with the same mix.

Literally, it meant "what do you want?"

"I want to take you for coffee," she said. The receptionist had been watching the whole interchange. When Bree glanced back at her, she had ducked her head, but she was smiling.

CHAPTER SIXTEEN

IT WAS A life out of a dream, Brand told himself, as he shook seawater from his hair and tucked his surfboard under his arm.

He had his dog, he had the ocean. He had spectacular sunsets, and day after day of sunshine. The palm trees were swaying gently in a tropical breeze. Up the beach was a cottage, completely open-air, with state-of-the-art electronics, so he could check in with the office and talk to his mother.

Unfortunately, the sand was everywhere, golden and unending.

And it was the very same color as Bree's hair.

Unfortunately, even though he was having the life out of a dream, it was not a dream he would wish on anyone.

He had never been plagued with loneliness before, and now he awoke with it as his companion and slept with it at night.

Even Beau was aware something was amiss. Instead of following him exuberantly into the water, snapping at waves he could never catch, he laid on shore, watching, lethargic, sadness coming out of every pore and stinky wrinkle.

Except right now, Beau's ears were perked up. His great head was lifted off his paws, and he was staring at the line of palm trees along the edge of the beach.

Suddenly he gave a woof, heaved himself up and began to gallop along the beach toward the trees.

Someone was coming. A woman.

As she got closer, he saw her hair. It couldn't be. But he had thought no one else in the world had hair like that.

He wasn't tormented enough? Out in the middle of nowhere a woman with the same hair was coming toward him? A woman with a colorful wraparound skirt knotted at a slender waist, wearing a black bikini top.

His heart rose as she got closer.

It couldn't be. It was a mirage, a man dying of thirst in the desert imagining the only thing that could save him.

The dog reached her, and she went down on one knee.

There was only one person his dog greeted like that. Brand wanted to run to her, just like the dog, to throw himself in a delirious pile of joy at her feet.

But he could not.

He needed to be strong. Stronger than he had ever been in his life.

For the love of her, for the love of Bree Evans, he needed to be strong.

He forced himself not to go to her. Instead, he wrapped a towel around his waist, dropped down into his hammock, put on his sunglasses and picked up a book.

"Brand?"

He lowered his sunglasses and peered at her over the rim. He pretended surprise, and then irritation.

"What are you doing here? Nobody knows I'm here."

"Kevin does."

"No, he doesn't."

"Well, he's a geek. He traced a telephone ping or something."

"Why would he do that?"

"He'd do anything for a woman who speaks Klingon."

"Which you don't," Brand said with a snort.

"You'd be surprised what love is willing to do to find its way."

Love. He snapped his sunglasses back over his eyes, nestled deeper in his hammock, looked intently at his book. He hoped it wasn't upside down.

"You've wasted your time," he said. "I don't want to see you. Go away."

"I'm not going away."

He hazarded a look at her, frowned and looked away hastily. There was something new in her. A strength, a self-certainty that she had not had before.

He contemplated that. He was falling to pieces here on his desert-island dream world with his dog. And she was…what? Blossoming? Coming into herself?

She was more gorgeous than she had ever been and she'd been plenty gorgeous.

A bikini! That said it all, really. Over a month ago, she'd been a one-piece kind of girl. He glanced at her again. He wanted to touch her hair. It was the *exact* color of the sand. He glared at the book.

"Do you want to know what I've learned over the past few weeks, Brand?"

"Not particularly," he said. He deliberately licked his finger and turned a page of the book.

She shoved the hammock. It rocked wildly and he

thought he was going to get dumped in the sand. He managed to extricate himself and find his feet.

He stood looking down at her. She gazed up at him with those soulful, earnest eyes. Those soulful earnest eyes that had a new layer to them.

Bravery.

The kind of bravery a man who did not feel brave could cling to, like a life raft was going by just as he had resigned himself to drowning.

"Humph," he said, annoyed with himself.

She lifted an eyebrow, as if she could *see* right through him.

"This is what I learned about myself," she said with that quiet new confidence. "I thought love had broken me once. After Paul, after the baby."

Did she have to mention that? It made it hard to be mean to her, to do what needed to be done to drive her away. No, not hard—impossible.

"But now I see that's not true at all. What broke me was an imitation of love. Real love is different."

He stared at her. He could feel himself swimming toward the paddle she was holding out, even as he ordered himself to swim away from her, to choose the loneliness of an endless sea.

"Real love doesn't break people," she said. "Real love is like the love I received from my family. It filled me with hope and it made me a promise that good would always outweigh bad."

"Naive," he growled. But she put her fingers on his lips. Her touch was a balm to his tormented soul. He could not do anything now but listen, even though he knew he was touching the paddle she was holding out.

"Love, genuine love, makes you stronger. It gives you

a belief in yourself and the world. It makes you more authentic, not less."

He was silent, but inwardly he could feel the slow tremble of complete surrender.

"You think," she said softly, "that you will be like your father, but you have already shown in every way that you are in the world that you are not. He ran away from your mother, and responsibility.

"You have embraced those things."

"Speaking of my mother, there's a chance it's genetic—"

"Shh," she said. "You think I don't know that's the fear you've wrestled with your whole life? Brand, you already know so much more about love than you have ever given yourself credit for.

"Love—the kind that sticks with it through the hard stuff—you already know that. That's what has made you who you are. That's what has made me love you so helplessly. So hopelessly."

"Look, I tried this. The love stuff. It's not for me. I warned you. Wendy. Lasted three days, I—"

"Shh." There it was again. Gentle. But a command.

"I'm not saying you aren't scared of love," Bree said. "I'm not saying that at all. Why else would such a smart man pick such a perfectly ill-matched person as Wendy?

"You're scared of it. You've seen the power it has to wound.

"But what I've seen? I've seen the power it has to make a man like you, who is so *good*, so decent, so courageous, despite the wound."

In his mind, he could see himself heaving himself into her lifeboat.

She felt his absolute surrender the moment it happened. Her arms went around him. She held him with astonishing strength. He could feel the strong beat of her heart, and the tenderness of her skin.

"I love you," she said. "And I'm going to love you until my very last breath. I am never, as long as I live, going to stop."

He let those words ease into him, ease past all his defenses, ease over his walls, something warm and fluid, that could not be stopped by something so small as one man's desire to shield others from the possible pain of this force.

"What about my children?" he asked, and he could hear the anguish in his own voice.

And she could hear it, too.

"What blessings they will be to the world," she said quietly. "What blessings our children—loved and accepted for all their strengths and all their flaws—will be to the world."

He took her face between both his hands and searched it for any trace of fear, for any trace of a lie.

But he saw what he had always seen in her face, even when she was a young girl going to her senior prom.

He saw that her gift to the world was hope.

Belief.

A tremendous unshakable conviction.

And that conviction was that love would always win. It was even stronger in her now than it had been then, when she was a young girl who had never had one bad thing happen to her.

Now, she had had bad things happen to her. She had suffered tremendous losses.

And still, she stood before him, unshakable in her faith, stronger than ever.

The word came from somewhere deep within him. It was his soul recognizing what she had held out to him. It was his soul yearning for a place to rest, for a place he had never had.

It was his soul, his heart, his mind, his whole being accepting the invitation she had held out to him.

To be brave.

To step into the unknown.

To have hope.

To believe.

To embrace the greatest force in the entire universe—love.

"Yes," he whispered to each of those things, and then, his voice stronger, to her he said, "Yes."

And then stronger still, even though this time it was just within himself, it felt as if he was shouting it to the earth and the waves and the trees, and the stars, shouting it with all the joy and strength it deserved—yes.

CHAPTER SEVENTEEN

THE GARDEN LOOKED the way it had always meant to look. Pails of white flowers—begonias, Brand vaguely thought—flanked the back steps, and peeked out from every shaded corner of his backyard.

The house looked different. Every window was open and so were the French doors. Analytically, he knew the house had not changed. It was the same color, there had been no renovations.

And yet, everything felt different, as if the house was happy, and as if its happiness was spilling out those open doors and windows.

The clatter of people busy in the kitchen and a shout of laughter reached him.

His back garden was filled with chairs with white satin bows on them, and people milled around, filling the space with color and energy and laughter and a shared belief in happy endings.

Given Vancouver's weather, it was a miracle it was not raining today, but there you had it.

Brand was a man who had come to believe in miracles.

Bree could have had the wedding anywhere. In a different country, on a beach, in the best hotel in Vancouver, but she had looked surprised when he had asked her where she would like to become his wife.

"At home, of course," she said. "That's where your mom will be most comfortable, and then Beau can be part of our celebration, too. Even Oliver can be part of our day."

Sure enough, Oliver was peeping sourly out from under one of those pails of begonias. They had been adjusting the cat to his new home for several weeks now. He had taken to it—and to bossing around Beau—with a kind of regal disdain that Brand had learned meant he was almost deliriously happy.

He considered that word. Home. In the last few months, his house had been transformed into a home. Bree had not moved in. She had wanted to. He had refused her. And he had refused her desire to seal their relationship physically as well.

He had almost given in to that temptation the night of his company's charity ball. Now, he sometimes wondered about that. If the intervention hadn't been divine.

Because that was not what he wanted with Bree.

He wanted to be the man she deserved, the man her father had always expected he would be. A man who would cherish her and treat her with complete honor, always.

So, here he was, minutes before his wedding, contemplating the nature of miracles and divine intervention. He was a changed man from what he had been just a few months ago.

Then, he had mistakenly thought he had everything. Then, he had thought he was wealthy.

"Time to go, buddy."

Chelsea's man, Reed, tapped him on the shoulder.

He and Bree had become so close to the other couple, who had begun dating almost as soon as Reed submitted his findings on the fire to the investigating team.

An electrical fire.

No one to blame.

A faulty circuit.

Or a miracle. One that had brought this young couple, obviously made for each other, together.

Just as a last-minute decision to go to that gala had reunited Brand with Bree.

Brand walked up the aisle of chairs to the back of his yard, where a flower-bedecked trellis had been erected. Reed flanked him on his right and Beau padded along beside him, looking as pleased as his wrinkly face would allow. Beau's white ribbon was already somewhat bedraggled.

People began to drift to the chairs.

Brand's mother took her seat in the front row, looking beautiful in a pink two-piece suit that Bree had helped her choose. She radiated the soft glow of wellness. Elvis was banished, for now. Brand dared not hope forever, but there was something about watching Bree with his mother that made his throat close and his eyes sting.

Bree treated his mother with an unfathomable tenderness that his mother reacted to like a parched plant that had needed rain. Brand knew love couldn't heal her, or else his already would have, and yet there was something about the steadiness of Bree's love that brought out the best in his mother, that brought out a side of her he had never seen.

He'd asked Bree once how she loved his mother so completely, and she had seemed so genuinely surprised by the question.

"She's part of you," she had said. "She's part of everything that is best about you—your strength and your decency and your drive. I love her for what she gave you, and I love her for her innate bravery. And I love her for the way she sees the world."

Bree's own mother, came and sat by his, and their hands found each other, two women who knew there was a certain kind of bitter sweetness to saying goodbye to one kind of relationship with their children, and hello to another one.

The music started. No Elvis, there was no sense testing his mother's newfound equilibrium with that.

No, it was the soaring and falling notes of Pachelbel's Canon.

The chatter quieted, and a hush fell over the filled seats, letting the music fill the garden area of the yard.

First, Chelsea came out. She was beautiful in a short aquamarine dress. Brand glanced at Reed beside him, and saw everything he felt for Bree in that other man's face.

Chelsea, like Bree, had come in to herself, and she radiated the quiet confidence of a woman well-loved.

A hush fell over the back garden as Bree stepped out of the house and slowly came down the steps. At her side was her stepfather, Mike.

Brand had to swallow, and then swallow hard again.

He had never seen a woman as beautiful as his soon-to-be wife.

The dress, of course, was exquisite. Her sunshine-on-sand hair was up, and threaded with flowers, her shoulders were bare, and the dress fit tight to her slender form, and then flared out at her waist in a cloud of white that floated around her and behind her.

But it was not the dress that stole the breath from him. Bree was so radiant she put the sun to shame. Everything in the garden faded: the music, the flowers, the guests, their mothers, her stepfather on her arm. Everything faded, until it was just her. Until the whole world was just her.

Coming toward him, with the entire future shining in her clear eyes.

* * * * *

SWEPT AWAY BY THE ENIGMATIC TYCOON

ROSANNA BATTIGELLI

To Nic, who has always believed in me as a writer, read every draft, made delicious meals, and gone along with my dreams.

Here's to a new chapter in our lives, Nic! xo

CHAPTER ONE

JUSTINE SURVEYED THE peaceful tableau lazily. The waters of Georgian Bay were calmer today, and she watched the gentle undulations with pleasure, letting her senses revel in the rugged beauty before her.

The clear blue water, shimmering with pinpoints of reflected sunlight, was dazzling—mesmerizing, really. The water lilies clustered along the water's edge looked like they were straight out of a Monet painting, their crisp white petals and yellow centers resting among dozens of flat, round, overlapping green pads. Occasionally the seagulls announced their monopoly on the sky with their shrill, almost human-like cries as they swooped and glided, tail feathers outspread, but even that wasn't enough to disrupt Justine from her contemplative mood.

She breathed in the fresh July air and congratulated herself again for exchanging the smog and humidity of the big city for *this*…this nature lover's paradise on Georgian Bay. She had made the right decision in accepting her parents' offer, Justine assured herself again as she rubbed sunscreen over her legs. Their proposal had come at the perfect time.

Working in the Toronto law office of attorney Robert Morrell had become too stressful—she'd had no choice but to resign. The memory of how she had trusted him in the first place still caused her pangs of remorse. Her mouth twisted cynically. How naïve she had been, falling for a man who was going through a turbulent divorce.

After leaving her resignation notice on his desk she had immediately headed home to Winter's Haven. As she'd pulled into the driveway, seeing her parents sitting together on the porch swing holding hands had made her burst into tears. *Why couldn't she have been so lucky?* In all her years at home she had never doubted her parents' trust, respect and devotion to each other. And to *her*. With such loving role models how could she settle for anything less?

Their love and support had cushioned her for the next four days, and then the morning she had thought herself ready to drive back to Toronto, eyes still puffy and shadowed, they'd made her an offer that took her breath away.

They had talked extensively, they'd said, and had decided that the time had come for them to retire from managing their cottage resort and to enjoy their golden years. They wanted to travel around the world while they still had their health and energy. If Justine were willing, they would sign Winter's Haven over to her and move into the smallest of the twelve cottages there. Justine could enjoy her inheritance early, and they would be delighted that the business would stay in the family.

"Take your time to think it over, sweetheart," her father had said, hugging her tightly. "But we have every confidence in your skills—business or otherwise."

Her mother had nodded and joined in the embrace, her eyes misting, and after kissing them both Justine had left, her own eyes starting to well up.

A month later the lease on her apartment had been up and she'd headed home to Winter's Haven for good.

The sting of Robert's deceit had begun to subside, and although she still had down days, feeling alternately embarrassed and angry for letting herself be fooled, she had come to terms with the end of their relationship. Taking over from her parents would occupy her time and her energy, and Justine was looking forward to exploring new ideas for the business while enjoying the more relaxed pace of the area.

Now, two months after her return, Justine could flick away any thought involving Robert almost nonchalantly. Usually followed by any number of silent declarations.

I am so over it! I'm done being a bleeding heart! Done with men and their games!

Justine closed her eyes and listened to the gentle lapping of the waves. She allowed herself to be soothed by the rhythmic sounds, enjoying the touch of the sun over her body as she settled back on the chaise longue. Tilting her sunhat to protect her face, Justine felt the familiar magic of Winter's Haven ease the stress out of her, and with a contented sigh she allowed herself to drift into a peaceful nap.

The sound of typewriter keys and a telephone ring jolted her awake. She fumbled for her cell phone, by her side on the chaise. Squinting, she read the text.

Good God, Justine! Where the heck are you? Did you forget the two o'clock appointment I arranged for you?

Justine sat up, her heart skipping a beat. It was one fifty-five. She'd never make it in time.

She leapt up and ran the short distance from the beach to her house, not stopping until she reached the washroom on the second floor. She usually enjoyed taking leisurely showers after a soak in the sun, but on this occasion she was in and out in less than five minutes. Her shoulder-length hair would have to dry on the way there. And there was no time for make-up.

She hastily put on a flowered wrap-around skirt and a white cotton eyelet top, and made a dash to her car. She usually walked to the main office, but she wanted to avoid any further delay.

She had managed this place efficiently since her parents had turned over the business to her two months earlier. "I'll run this place as smoothly as you did," she'd promised them before they left for their retirement travels, and she had done just that—except for today.

Justine had never been late for anything in her life. She'd have to make sure it didn't happen again. It didn't make her look very responsible. She should have never given in to Mandy, who had uncharacteristically scheduled an appointment on her day off.

The sight of a sleek silver-green Mustang convertible in the parking lot dashed her hopes that her visitor might be late.

She took the steps to the office two at a time and entered the building, taking deep breaths. Mandy Holliday, her friend since high school and her assistant and office receptionist, smirked at her from behind the wooden desk, cocking an eyebrow toward the double doors leading to the diner.

"He's been waiting there thirty minutes. The last time I checked he was talking to the Elliots in Cottage Number One."

"Of all the times to doze off on the beach..." Justine grimaced. "I wonder why this Forrest man has insisted on seeing *me*. If he wants to rent a cottage, you could have dealt with him. I wish you had been able to squeeze some information out of him."

She adjusted the tie belt on her wrap-around skirt.

"I hope he's not one of those pompous business types. You know—the punctuality nuts, the arrogant *'you must be as perfect as I am'* professionals who—" She stopped at the sudden furrowing of Mandy's eyebrows.

"Perhaps you should reserve your judgment until after our meeting," a cool voice suggested directly behind her.

"I'll be in the diner if you need me," Mandy murmured, before retreating hastily.

Justine turned around stiffly to face her visitor. He was not at all what she'd expected. But what *had* she expected after hearing that ice-tinged drawl?

She tried not to reveal her surprise as her gaze smacked into the chest of his impeccably tailored gray suit before moving slowly upward to his face. His height topped hers by at least a foot. Her pulse quickened as her eyes took him in. A five o'clock shadow she suspected he wore permanently. Dark brown hair with burnished bits, styled like someone out of *GQ*. Chestnut eyes with flecks of gold.

She felt sweat on her upper lip. To her horror, she ran her tongue over her lips without thinking. She felt like combusting.

How could he look so cool in that suit? She almost felt like suggesting he remove his jacket or tie… And then her mouth crinkled slightly, nervously, at the thought of how such a suggestion would sound to him.

He caught the crooked smile, but didn't return it. He looked down at her imperiously, his jaw tense.

He's angry, Justine thought, unable to tear her gaze from his face. It was so *male* and rugged, with a straight nose and firm, sensual lips clearly visible under the meticulously groomed shadow. At second glance she caught a slight curl in his hair, and his eyes, unwavering, were disturbingly hypnotizing.

"I'm sorry," she said quickly. "I didn't mean to offend you. I was irritated at myself for being late. It's not like me." She extended her hand, forcing herself to offer him an apologetic smile. "I'm Justine Winter."

For a moment, he just stared at her, and Justine was about to withdraw her hand in embarrassment when he finally took it, his long fingers closing around hers completely in a firm clasp.

"Apology accepted," he replied, motioning abruptly for Justine to sit down.

She did so and he pulled up a nearby chair.

"What can I do for you, Mr. Forrest?"

"Forrester. Casson Forrester."

Her eyebrows shot up at his name. "Yes, of course. You made an appointment with Mandy to see me, but you didn't state your reasons. Are you interested in renting a cottage? Did you want a tour of the grounds and facilities before making a reservation? We may have an opening, depending when it is you want to stay." She paused, realizing she was babbling.

His lips curved slightly. "Yes, I'm very interested in the cottages. You see, I've just purchased the adjoining land on both sides of your property."

Justine frowned. "I can't believe the Russells have sold their properties—" She broke off, stunned. The Russells' ancestors had been among the original homesteaders in the area.

"I made them a convincing offer." He was unable to conceal the satisfaction in his voice. "Our transaction was mutually profitable."

Justine looked at him warily. "I don't suppose you arranged this appointment just for the sake of meeting your new neighbor…?"

He laughed curtly. "You're perceptive, if nothing else."

Justine flushed, her mouth narrowing. She didn't like the negative implication of "if nothing else." "Why don't you come right to the point?" she suggested sweetly, trying not to clench her teeth.

His eyebrows arched slightly at her directness. "I have development plans for both lakefront properties," he explained brusquely. "However, *your* property, being in the center, poses a number of problems for me. It would seem that the ideal solution would be for me to purchase this property in order to maximize the success of my venture." His eyes narrowed. "Just name your price. You'll have it in your bank account first thing tomorrow morning."

Justine couldn't prevent the gasp from her lips. "You can't be serious!"

"I'm not the joking type," he countered sharply. "Nor do I intend to play any money games with you, Miss Winter. Negotiations aren't necessary here. I'm willing to pay whatever you feel is an optimum price for this place."

Justine felt her eyes fluttering in disbelief. "I'm not interested in selling—no matter what you offer, Mr. Forrester," she stated as firmly as she could muster. "It's not a matter of money; it's a question of principle."

She stood up, both palms on the table, willing him to leave.

A muscle flicked at his jaw. He made no move to stand, let alone leave. "Kindly explain yourself, Miss Winter," he said evenly.

Justine took a deep breath. "I would not want to see the natural beauty and seclusion of this area spoiled by a commercial venture. That's what you have in mind, don't you?" She put her hands on her hips, her blue-gray eyes piercing his accusingly.

"Let me clarify my intentions."

He leaned forward, resting both elbows on Justine's desk. His face was disturbingly close to her chest. She was mortified as she noticed her black bra peeking from under the white eyelet blouse. She hadn't even thought about the selection of her bra in her after-shower haste. She sat down and crossed her arms in front of her.

"I think the rugged beauty of this stretch of Georgian Bay shoreline should be fully enjoyed—not kept a secret. I am contemplating the construction of a luxury waterfront resort and a restaurant that will enhance the experience of visitors. Nothing like high-rise condominiums; that would be unnatural in these surroundings."

He rubbed his jaw with long, manicured fingers.

"I like the thought of luxury cottages nestled privately among the pines and spruces, each overlooking the bay." He paused briefly, but as she opened her mouth to reply, added coolly, "Let me make one thing clear, Miss Winter. Even if you refuse to accept my offer, I intend to go ahead with my plans for the Russell properties."

Justine had listened with growing trepidation as she thought of the repercussions his commercial venture would have—not only on her property, but on the surrounding area. She had no intention of giving in to him. His plans would *not* enhance the existing atmosphere of this stretch of the bay—she was certain of it. The seclusion and quiet ambiance her customers depended on would definitely be compromised with all the construction and traffic his venture would generate.

She felt her jaw clenching. No, she did not intend to let him bully her into selling.

"I cannot accept your offer," she told him coldly. "*Someone* has to cater to common folk with regular incomes who want a holiday away from it all. I cannot, in all good conscience, agree to a proposal that would not only deprive my regular customers of a quiet, restful vacation retreat, but also exploit the natural wilderness of the area."

She was unable to control a slight grimace.

"Have you even thought of looking into the Georgian Bay Biosphere Reserve? Or the Provincial Endangered Species Act? Obviously, Mr. Forrester, personal financial gain is higher on your list of priorities than the preservation of nature."

Justine stood up again, hoping he would take the hint and leave.

Instead he leaned back in his chair and continued to gaze directly at her, an unfathomable gleam in his chestnut eyes. She cleared her throat uncomfortably, wondering what she could say to get him out of the office without resorting to being rude.

Stroking his jaw thoughtfully, he murmured, "Why don't I just make you an offer anyway? How does this sound to you…?"

Justine only just stopped herself from swaying. Even half the amount he was offering would be exorbitant. No wonder the Russells had sold out to him if this was the way he conducted his business transactions. For a moment her mind swarmed with thoughts of what she could do with that kind of money, and she couldn't deny that she felt the stirrings of temptation to consider his offer.

She looked at him, sitting back comfortably with his arms crossed, and the hint of smugness on his face gave her the impression that he knew exactly what she was feeling. He was counting on it that she would abandon her principles if the price were right.

Well, he was *wrong*. She might have been tempted in a moment of weakness, but she would never sell Winter's Haven. It represented a lot of things for a lot of people, but for her it was *home*. Her special healing place. Even her hurt over Robert had lessened since she had come back. There was an atmosphere here that she had never felt in the city—or anywhere else for that matter. She had an affinity for this kind of natural lifestyle, and after leaving it once she had no intentions of ever leaving it again.

Her blue-gray eyes were defiant as she looked across at him. "I'm sorry, Mr. Forrest…"

"Forrester."

"Mr. *Forrester*. I can imagine that your offer might be tempting to some, but nothing would make me sell my home and property. I belong here."

Surprise flickered briefly in the depths of his eyes. "Bad timing."

"What do you mean?" she demanded defensively.

"Your parents were almost ready to accept an offer I made on this place three months ago, then changed their minds when you showed up. It's too bad for me that you didn't time your arrival for a week later. The deal would have gone through by then," he continued bluntly, "and I wouldn't have had to waste my valuable time talking to you."

He rose fluidly from the chair.

Justine could feel her cheeks flaming. She remembered her parents mentioning an offer somebody had made— it hadn't been the first time—but that they had turned it down.

"What's *really* too bad, *Mr. Forrester*," she shot back indignantly, "is the fact that you've become my neighbor."

He smiled, but the smile didn't reach his eyes. "Not for long, perhaps," he replied coolly. "I will come up with another offer soon—one you may not be able to resist, despite your lofty principles."

"Don't count on it," she snapped.

"We'll see," he replied softly. "Any woman can eventually be bought. I don't imagine you're any different." He turned to leave with a cynical smile. "Except maybe a little higher-priced," he said, his tone cold as he opened the door and clicked it shut.

Justine stared at the door speechlessly. She slammed one palm down on the desk, furious that he had had the last word—and the last insult.

"Ouch," she moaned, slumping into her chair.

She felt emotionally drained. The last thing she had expected from her visitor today was an offer to buy Winter's Haven. *And what an offer,* she mused.

Casson Forrester obviously meant business, and money

was no object. She didn't imagine he would stop at anything until ultimately he got what he wanted. And he wanted Winter's Haven. He hardly seemed the type to back away from any venture once he had made up his mind.

Justine recalled the set of his jaw and the steely determination in his eyes. Those dangerous tawny eyes. Tiger eyes, she thought suddenly, eyes that made her feel like the hunted in a quest for territorial supremacy.

How long would he stalk her? she wondered nervously, rubbing at her sore palm. What means would he use to try to break down her resolve and get her to give in to him?

It doesn't matter what he tries, an inner voice reasoned. *There's nothing he can do to make you change your mind.*

"Nothing!" She rose to leave.

At that moment Mandy returned to the office, unconcealed curiosity on her face. "What do you mean, *'Nothing'*? Tell me what that hunk of a man wanted... Please say he's booked a cottage for a month. I'll be more than happy to forego my vacation and tend to his every need—"

"He's not worth getting excited about," Justine sniffed. "He's an assuming, boorish snob who thinks money can buy anything or anyone." She felt her cheeks ignite with renewed anger. "He's got a lot of nerve."

"I take it you didn't quite hit it off?" Mandy said, sitting on the edge of the desk. "What on earth did he say—or do—to get you so riled up? I've never seen this side of you."

"That's because no one has ever infuriated me so much," Justine huffed.

She told Mandy the purpose of Casson Forrester's visit.

"I'll never sell, though," she concluded adamantly. "To him or to anyone else."

"Hmm...it doesn't sound like we've heard the last of him, though, since he *is* our new neighbor." A dreamy look came into her eyes. "I wonder if he's married..."

"I pity his wife if he is," Justine retorted. "Having to live with such an overbearing, narrow-minded brute!"

"I'd like to see what your idea of a hunk is if you consider this man a brute!" Mandy laughed.

Justine gave an indelicate snort. "All that glitters isn't gold, you know. He may look...*attractive*—"

"Gorgeous," Mandy corrected.

"But it's the inside that counts. Trust me, Mandy, he has a *terrible* personality. No, it's not even terrible. It's non-existent."

Mandy eyed her speculatively. "Not your kind of man?"

"Not at all," Justine replied decisively, turning to leave. "If he calls again, think up any excuse you can; just tell him I'm not available. Whatever you do, *do not* set up another appointment. I've had enough personal contact with Casson Forrest... Forrester—whatever his name is—to last me a lifetime. All I want to do is forget him."

Easier said than done, she thought, driving the short distance back to her house. How could she forget those tiger eyes? His entire face, for that matter... It was not a face one could easily forget. Not that *she* was interested, but she had to admit grudgingly to herself that Casson Forrester probably never lacked for female companionship.

Or lovers, she mused, stepping out of her car. She felt a warm rush as she imagined him in an intimate embrace, then immediately berated herself for even allowing herself to conjure such thoughts.

Justine sprinted up the stairs to her bedroom, changed into her turquoise swimsuit, grabbed a towel, and headed to her private beach.

The first invigorating splash into the bay immediately took some of her tension away. And as Justine floated on the bay's mirrored surface, absorbed in interpreting the images in the clouds, the threat that Casson Forrester posed to Winter's Haven already seemed less imposing.

What vacationers liked most about the place was the seclusion of each of the twelve rustic cottages tucked amidst the canopy of trees, only a short walk to their own stretch of private beach. They also appreciated the extra conveniences that Justine's parents had added to enhance their stay. Along with the popular diner—which featured freshly caught pickerel, bass or whitefish—over seventeen years her parents had added a convenience store, a small-scale laundromat, and boat and motor facilities with optional guiding services.

Many of their guests came back year after year during their favorite season. Justine hoped that Casson Forrester's plans wouldn't change that.

She swam back to shore, towel-dried her hair, patted down her body quickly and decided she would change and eat at the diner instead of cooking. She liked to mingle with the guests, many of whom had become friends of the family.

Justine put on her flip-flop sandals, hung up her towel on the outside clothesline, and walked up the wide flagstone path. On either side myriad flowers bloomed among Dusty Millers and variegated hostas.

Ordinarily Justine entered through the back entrance after going for a swim, but the sound of tires crunching slowly up toward the front of her house made her change her mind. A new guest, she thought, mistaking her driveway for the office entrance.

She rounded the corner with a welcoming smile. The car sitting in her driveway had tinted windows, so she couldn't make out the driver. But she didn't have to. Her smile faded and she stopped walking. She knew who the silver-green Mustang convertible belonged to.

With the windows up he had full advantage, seeing her with her swimsuit plastered to her body, hair tousled and tangled. She wished she had wrapped her towel around her.

She felt her insides churn with annoyance. Frustration.
*Was he going to come out of his car, or did he actually
expect her to walk up to his window?*

She stood there awkwardly, her arms at her sides, feeling ridiculous. Just when she thought she couldn't stand it
anymore, the convertible top started to glide down. Spanish guitar music was playing.

He had shades on, which annoyed her even further. He
had taken off his jacket and tossed it on the seat beside
him. His shirt was short-sleeved, and even from where she
stood Justine could tell it was of high quality, the color
of cantaloupe with vertical lime stripes. His arms were
tanned, and she watched him reach over to grab a large
brown envelope, turn down the music slightly and step out
of his car. Without taking his gaze off her.

"I wanted you to have a glance at this, Miss Winter."
He held out the envelope.

Justine crossed her arms and frowned.

"It's a development proposal drafted by an architect
friend of mine. I would be happy to go over it with you."
When she didn't respond, he added, "I would appreciate
it if you at least gave the plan and the drawings a glance.
They might help dispel some of your doubts about my
venture."

Justine stared at him coldly. "I'm not interested, Mr.
Forrest. You're wasting your time." Her entire face felt
flushed, the refreshed feeling after her swim completely
dissipated.

He stood there for a moment, his mouth curving into
a half-smile. He held the envelope in front of her for a
few moments, then turned and tossed it into the Mustang.
"Very well, Miss *Wintry*. Perhaps you need some time to
think about it."

"Not at all," she returned curtly. "And my last name
is *Winter*."

"So sorry, Miss *Winter.*" He took off his sunglasses. "And mine's *Forrester.*"

Justine's knees felt weak. His dark eyes blazed at her in the sunlight. She knew she should apologize as well, but when she opened her mouth no words came out. She watched him get behind the wheel and put on his sunglasses.

"But you can call me Casson," he said, and grinned before turning on the ignition.

He cranked up the music and with a few swift turns was out of her driveway and out of sight.

Now that he could no longer see Justine Winter in his rearview mirror, Casson concentrated on the road ahead. He loved this area. His family—which had included him and his younger brother Franklin—had always spent part of the summer at their friends' cottage on Georgian Bay, and the tradition had continued even after they'd lost Franklin to leukemia when he was only seven years old.

Even after his parents and their friends had passed away, and the cottage had been sold, Casson had felt compelled to return regularly to the area. There would always be twinges of grief at his memories, but Casson didn't want the memories to fade, and the familiar landscape brought him serenity and healing as well.

Determined to find a location for what would be "Franklin's Resort," he had spent months searching for the right spot. After finding out that the Russell properties were for sale, he'd hired a pilot to fly him over Georgian Bay's 30,000 Islands area to scope out the parcels of land, which were on either side of Winter's Haven.

The seductive curve of sandy beach, with the surf foaming along its edge, and the cottages set back among the thickly wooded terrain had given him a thrill. The bay, with its undulating waves of blue and indigo, sparkling like an endless motherlode of diamonds, had made his heartbeat quicken.

The sudden feeling that Franklin was somehow with him had sent shivers along his arms. Casson had always sensed that the spirit of Franklin was in Georgian Bay, and he'd had an overwhelming feeling that his search was over. He'd made the Russells an offer he was sure they couldn't refuse and had then turned his attention to Winter's Haven.

Now, as he sped past the mixed forest of white pine, birch and cedar, he caught glimpses of Georgian Bay, its surface glittering with pinpoints of sunlight. A mesmerizing blue.

Just like Justine Winter's eyes.

The thought came before he could stop it. His lips curved into a smile. He hadn't expected the new owner of Winter's Haven to be so…*striking.* So outspoken. From the way her father had spoken he had expected someone a little more shy and reticent, someone more *fragile.*

"I've decided not to sell after all," Thomas Winter had said, when he'd phoned him a few months earlier. "My daughter Justine has had enough of the big city—and a bad relationship—and she needs a new direction in life. A new venture that will lift her spirits. My wife and I have decided to offer the business to her and finally do some travelling. Winter's Haven will be a good place for Justine to recover…"

Recover?

Casson had wondered if Mr. Winter's daughter was emotionally healthy enough to maintain a business that had obviously thrived for years under her parents' management. Which was why he'd decided to wait a couple of months before approaching her with his offer. With any luck the place would be in a shambles and she'd be ready to unload it. And even if that wasn't the case, he'd come to learn that most people had their price…

At first glance Justine Winter had seemed anything but fragile. She had dashed into the office with damp hair, flushed cheeks, tanned arms and shapely legs under a flowered skirt that swayed with the movement of her hips. And as he'd sauntered toward her his eyes hadn't been able to help sweeping over that peekaboo top, glimpsing the black bra underneath...

He had felt a sudden jolt. He had come to Winter's Haven expecting a depressed young woman who had needed her parents to save her by offering her a lifeline. *Not a woman whose firm curves and just-out-of-the-shower freshness had caused his body to stir uncontrollably...*

And then she had turned to face him, her blue-gray eyes striking him like a cresting wave. And, no, it *hadn't* looked like the place was anywhere near in a shambles, with her pining away for her former lover.

He had watched her expression flit from disbelief about his purchase of the adjoining Russell properties to wide-eyed amazement at his offer. And he had felt a momentary smugness when her gaze shifted and became dreamy.

She had been thinking about what she could do with the money. He'd been sure of it.

And then her gaze had snapped back to meet his, and the ice-blue hardness of her eyes and her flat-out refusal of his money had caused something within him to strike back with the prediction that she would eventually cave at a higher price.

He had almost been able to feel the flinty sparks from her eyes searing his back as he'd left...

Casson drove into the larger of the Russell properties— *his* properties now—and after greeting his dog, Luna, he grabbed a cold beer and plunked himself down into one of the Muskoka chairs on the wraparound porch.

Luna ran around the property for a while and then settled down beside him. Casson stared out at the flickering waters of the bay. It already felt like he had been there for years.

This really was a slice of heaven. Prime Group of Seven country.

Casson had grown up hearing about the Group of Seven as if they were actual members of his family. His grandfather's friendship with A. J. Casson—who had been his neighbor for years—and the collection of Casson paintings he had eventually bequeathed to his only daughter, had resulted in Casson's childhood being steeped in art knowledge and appreciation. Not only of A. J. Casson's work, but the work of all the Group of Seven artists.

And now here he was as an adult, just days away from sponsoring and hosting Franklin & Casson on the Bay— an exhibition of the paintings of Franklin Carmichael and A. J. Casson at the Charles W. Stockey Centre for the Performing Arts in Parry Sound. The center was renowned for its annual Festival of the Sound summer classical music festival, as well as for housing the Bobby Orr Hall of Fame—a sports museum celebrating Parry Sound's ice hockey legend.

It was all close to falling into place. This exhibition was the first step in making his resort a reality. Franklin's Resort would be a non-profit venture, to honor the memory of its namesake and to provide a much-needed safe haven for families.

At the exhibition Casson would outline his plan to create a luxury haven for children after cancer treatment— a place to restore their strength and their spirit with their families, who would all have experienced trauma. The families would enjoy a week's stay at the resort at no cost.

He had no doubt that the Carmichael/Casson exhibition would be successful in raising awareness and backing for his venture. And the *pièce de résistance* was a painting from his own personal collection. It was one of A.J. Casson's early pieces, *Storm on the Bay*, and had been given to Casson's grandfather when A.J. had been his neighbor. It was the prize in a silent auction, and Casson hoped it would attract a collector's eye and boost the development of the resort.

A lump formed in his throat. He had been only ten when Franklin had died, and although he had not been able to articulate his feelings at the time, he knew now that he had coped with his feeling of helplessness by overcompensating in other ways. Helping with chores; learning to make meals as a teen and excelling at school, in sport and at university. Subconsciously he had done everything he could not to add to his parents' misery.

After pursuing a Business and Commerce degree in Toronto, Casson had returned home to Huntsville—an hour away from Parry Sound—to purchase a struggling hardware store downtown. He had been grateful for the money his grandfather had left him in his will, which had enabled him to put a down payment on the business, and he'd vowed that he would make his grandpa proud.

Within a couple of years the store had been thriving, and Casson had set his sights on developing a chain. Six more years and he'd had stores in Gravenhurst, Bracebridge, Port Carling and—his most recent acquisition—a hardware store in Parry Sound, just outside the Muskoka area.

Casson had revived each store with innovative changes and promotions that would appeal both to the locals and the seasonal property-owners. The Forrest Hardware chain had made him a multi-millionaire by the time he was thirty-four.

Losing his brother at such a young age had affected Casson deeply; he hadn't been able to control what happened to Franklin, so he had learned to take control of his own life early. He was still in control now, steering his expanding hardware chain, and yet he had no control over Justine Winter. Not that he wanted to control *her*; he simply wanted control of Winter's Haven. Her property was the last piece of the puzzle that he needed to fit into his plan.

Earlier, the thought had flashed into his mind to invite Justine to go with him to the Stockey Centre the following day—to show her that his motive when it came to the Russell properties and Winter's Haven was not one of financial gain, as she had immediately assumed. However, the fact that he'd even considered telling Justine the truth shocked him... He *never* talked about Franklin. He'd learned to keep those feelings hidden.

Why had he nearly told her?

It might have had something to do with those initial sparks between them...

Anyway, he hadn't wanted to show his vulnerability or how much this venture meant to him as a tribute to his brother. So instead he had thrust his offer upon Justine with the arrogant expectation that she would be so dazzled by the amount she'd agree to it, no questions asked.

And if she *had* asked questions he wouldn't have been prepared to open up his soul to her. Tell her that he was doing this not only for Franklin, but for himself. For all the lonely years he had spent after his brother's death, unable to share his grief with his mother, whose pain at losing Franklin had created an emotional barrier that even Casson could not penetrate. His father had thrown himself into his work, and when he was at home had seemed to have only enough energy to provide a comforting shoulder for his wife.

It was only in later years that Casson had contemplated going to a few sessions of grief counselling. It had been emotionally wrenching to relive the past, but Casson had eventually forgiven his parents. It had been during that time that his idea for a resort to help kids like Franklin had begun to take root. What he hadn't been able to do for Franklin at ten years of age, he could now do for many kids like him—including his godson Andy, his cousin Veronica's only child.

Andy's cancer diagnosis a year earlier had shocked Casson, and triggered memories and feelings of the past. Supporting Andy and Veronica during subsequent treatment had made him all the more determined to see his venture become a reality. Casson just wished his parents were still alive to witness it as well...

Franklin & Casson on the Bay was only a few days away. His plan was on target. There was one key missing.

And Justine had it.

Casson took a gulp of his beer. *Damn*, it was hot. He loosened his tie. As he contemplated changing and going for a swim, a vision of Justine Winter standing with wet hair in her bathing suit flashed in his memory. That turquoise one-piece had molded to the heady curves of her body, and her tanned thighs and legs had been sugared with white beach sand that sparkled in the sun. Her hair, straight and dripping water over her cleavage... An enchanting sea creature...

He had sensed her discomfort, knew how exposed she'd felt. If only she knew what the sight of her body had done to *him*.

Casson unbuttoned his shirt and went inside to change. A dip in the refreshing waters of Georgian Bay would cool him down—inside and out...

Casson stretched out on the edge of the dock to let the sun heat his body. There was nothing like that first dive into the bay when your body was sizzling hot. He closed his eyes for a few moments, and when he opened them, wondered if he had dozed off. Although he had slapped on some sunscreen earlier, his skin felt slightly more burnished.

He scrambled to his feet and Luna shuffled excitedly

around him. Casson heard a faint voice calling him, but when he turned there was nobody there. There was some rustling in the trees and a flash of blue, followed by the shrill call of a blue jay.

Casson looked down at the water, anticipating the bracing pleasure awaiting him. A hint of a breeze tickled his nose, followed by the faint smell of fish. He blinked at his reflection, wiping at the sweat prickling his eyes. In the gently lapping bay he imagined Franklin beside him, wearing his faded Toronto Blue Jays cap, his skinny arms holding a fishing rod with its catch of pickerel and his toothy grin. And the sparkle in his eyes...

And then the sparkle was lost in the sun's glittering reflection and the image was swallowed up by the waves. Casson dropped down to sit at the edge of the dock, his original intention forgotten. He continued to peer intensely into the water, and it was only moments later, when Luna pressed against him to lick his face, that Casson realized she was licking the salty tears on his cheeks.

CHAPTER TWO

THE RAIN DRUMMING on the roof woke Justine an hour before she'd intended. She didn't mind at all, though. Rainy days were good for doing odd jobs, renovating an empty cottage, or just relaxing with a good book in the window seat in her room. It was one of her favorite reading spots, with its plush flowery cushions and magnificent view of the bay.

Justine changed into jeans and a nautical-style T-shirt, brushed her hair back into a ponytail, and went downstairs. After having a quick coffee and one of the banana yogurt muffins she had made last night, she grabbed her umbrella and dashed to her car.

Despite the fact that she had always liked this kind of weather, Justine couldn't help but feel a twist in her stomach, remembering the rainy day she'd walked into Robert Morrell's law office for an interview. She'd been twenty-four, and had graduated *summa cum laude* in Law and Justice from the University of Toronto. That and her business electives had impressed Robert and Clare, his senior administrative assistant, who would be retiring in six months, and Robert had offered her the job the following day.

As time had progressed the initial rapport between them had developed into an easy friendship. Justine had sometimes stayed at the office during lunchtime, catching up on paperwork between bites of her sandwich or salad. And

Robert, to her surprise, had often done the same, claiming he wanted to go home at a decent hour so his wife wouldn't complain that he was "married to the job."

Shared conversations had begun to take on a more personal note during Justine's second year at the office, and when Robert had started to hint at his marriage breakdown she had felt compelled to listen and comfort him as he'd revealed more and more.

The underlying spark of attraction between them had not come to the forefront until after his divorce had almost become final. Then, with nothing and nobody to hold them back, Justine and Robert had begun dating...

Justine forced Robert out of her thoughts as she turned the corner and drove into the parking lot of the hardware store, finding a spot near the front doors. Something looked vaguely different about the place, and then she realized the signage had changed. New ownership, she had heard.

Without bothering to get her umbrella, she dashed into the store and toward the wood department.

"May I help you?"

Justine turned to find a middle-aged employee smiling at her.

"Yes, thank you, Mr. Blake," she said, smiling back. "Glad to see you're still here. I'd like to order some cedar paneling for one of the cottages."

"I thought it was you. Back from Toronto, I hear. Your dad told me you'd be taking over Winter's Haven."

Justine nodded. "I'm glad to be back."

As she handed him a piece of paper with the measurements a feeling of contentedness came over her. She *had* made the right decision, coming back home.

This was what she loved about living in a small town— knowing the names of local merchants, dealing with people who knew her parents.

She had felt the call of the big city, and had enjoyed it for

a time, but the breakup with Robert and the lonely month
that had followed had made her realize how truly *alone*
she was. With no job and no meaningful friendships—the
people Robert had introduced her to didn't qualify—she'd
yearned for the small-town connections of Parry Sound.
Home. The place she had always felt safe in, nurtured and
supported by family, friends and community.

"Are you thinking of running the business on a perma-
nent basis?" Mr. Blake glanced at her curiously.

"I sure am." She beamed. "I can't imagine ever leaving
Winter's Haven again."

Mr. Blake glanced over her shoulder, as if he were looking for someone, and then gave her a hesitant smile. "Well,
good luck to you. When your order is ready I'll give you
a call. You can let me know then when you want the job
done."

"Sounds good!" Justine leafed through her bag and took
out her car keys. "Thanks, Mr. Blake, and have a great
day."

Justine strode toward the exit, wondering why the expression on his face had seemed to change after her saying she couldn't imagine ever leaving Winter's Haven.
She grimaced when she came to the door. The rain was
coming down in torrents now, and she regretted leaving
her umbrella in the car. She would get drenched despite
the short distance.

She made a run for it, giving a yelp as she stepped in
a sizeable puddle.

"Damn," she muttered as she inserted the wrong key
in the lock. She should have brought a rain jacket, she berated herself, slamming the door at last.

Her top was plastered against her, and although she had
planned to do some further shopping she was not about to
go anywhere in this condition. Her jeans were soaked as

well—front and back—and she couldn't wait to get back home, strip everything off and take a shower.

She backed out carefully and drove out of the parking lot. Although it was barely mid-morning the sky had darkened, and she could hear ominous rumbles of thunder. Her wipers were going at full-tilt, but the rain was pelting the windshield so hard that she could barely see through it.

As Justine drove slowly out of the town limits and toward the long country road that would take her home she tried to ignore the clammy feeling of her wet clothes against her skin.

A sudden beeping noise behind her startled her, and she glanced immediately in the rearview mirror. She could see a burgundy pickup truck, but it was impossible to see the driver.

To Justine's consternation the honking became more persistent. The truck didn't have its indicators on, so the driver couldn't be in any kind of trouble. And she didn't imagine it was an admirer. She wasn't unused to appreciative smiles from male drivers once in a while, along with the occasional whistle or honk of their horn, but she doubted that this was the case today.

The rain was subsiding—thank goodness. And as she looked in the rearview mirror again she saw that the driver had his arm out the window, signaling for her to pull over. Now she felt alarmed. Was it a cop? No, not in a pickup truck. And it wouldn't be for speeding...

He honked again and she looked back, but a sudden rush of oncoming cars made her concentrate on the road. She cautiously pressed on the gas pedal. *Too many weirdos on the road,* she thought. She swerved around a bend, and a quick look reassured her that the creep was gone.

She reached the turnoff to Winter's Haven. The rain had stopped and the sun was breaking through the clouds. She clicked off her wipers, headed directly past the office building and turned into the road through a lengthy wooded stretch that led to her driveway. She sighed, but had barely turned off the ignition when she heard the crunch of an approaching vehicle.

A moment later the burgundy pickup truck she'd thought she had seen the last of pulled up right next to her.

She was more angry than worried now. *How dare he?* Without a thought to any potential danger, she flung the car door open and got out, her cheeks flaming. The man had gotten out of his truck and was leaning against it, casually silent, as he watched Justine march stormily up to him.

"Why are you following me?" she demanded, stopping a few feet away from him. "It was bad enough trying to drive with you tailgating and honking incessantly. Can't you find a more civilized way of pursuing a woman? Highway dramatics don't do anything for me."

The man's mouth twisted and he continued to stare at her through dark sunglasses. A few seconds passed. Why wasn't he answering her? Maybe she should have stayed in the car. He might have a knife. She could scream, but nobody was close enough to hear her.

She looked at him closely. She might need to file a report if she managed to get away from him. His faded jeans and jacket seemed ordinary enough, but his bearded face, dark glasses and baseball cap might very well be concealing the face of an escaped criminal. Would she be able to run back to her car? No, she'd never make it if he intended to pursue her.

She shivered and said shakily, "What do you want?"

Another twist of his lips. "Your hubcap flew off a few miles back," he drawled. "So you can relax. I'm not about to attack you."

Justine let out an audible sigh. And then she felt her cheeks start to burn. She had accused him of *pursuing* her.

"I'm usually more civilized when it comes to pursuing women," he said, and laughed, as if he had read her thoughts. "And 'highway dramatics,' as I believe you put it, are not my style."

Justine's discomfiture grew. "I apologize for jumping to the wrong conclusion, but you can hardly blame me, can you?" Her eyes narrowed. "Your voice sounds familiar..."

For some reason, the realization bothered her.

A suspicion suddenly struck her in a way that made her knees want to buckle.

"Haven't figured it out yet?" he said, removing his sunglasses.

Tiger eyes. Damn!

With the cap, sunglasses, casual clothes and truck, and two weeks' growth of beard, she hadn't even suspected.

"It's...*you!*" she sputtered, wide-eyed.

"Nice to see you again, too," Casson Forrester murmured, with the slightest hint of sarcasm. "Actually, I spotted you in the hardware store, but you left before I could reach you. There are a few things I want to discuss with you."

"You didn't have to follow me."

"I didn't think you'd accept my call." His eyes narrowed. "Among other things, I was going to suggest you don't bother paneling or doing any other kind of work if you're going to end up selling the place..."

Justine's eyes flashed their annoyance. "That's your mistaken presumption," she retorted. "And were you eavesdropping on my conversation?"

"I didn't have to. Mr. Blake happened to mention it when I called a staff meeting."

"You *own* Forrest Hardware?" she said slowly. "And Forrest Construction...."

Of course. Forrest was simply an abbreviated form of his name, and an appropriate choice for his chain of stores in the Muskoka area—including the latest one in Parry

Sound. She had briefly noticed the new sign, but the name hadn't registered in her consciousness—least of all the connection with its owner.

She gave a curt laugh. "No wonder you can buy practically anything—or anybody—you want."

"Not always," his tiger eyes glinted. "Although it's not for lack of trying."

She shivered. And at the sudden clap of thunder they both looked up to the sky. The clouds had blocked out the sun again, and a few errant raindrops had started coming down. Realizing she had been standing there in her wet T-shirt and jeans, her hair flattened against her head except for the few strands that were now curling with the humidity, she crossed her arms in front of her.

"Excuse me," she said icily, "I'm going to have to leave." She turned away, then glanced back. "I'll look for the hubcap later."

She retrieved her keys and bag from her car and strode toward the house. When she was halfway there the rain intensified, making her curse indelicately as she ran the rest of the way. Breathing a sigh of relief as she reached the door of the porch, she closed it behind her as another clap of thunder reverberated around her.

Hearing the porch door creak open again, she turned around to close it tightly. But it wasn't the wind that had forced it open. It was Casson Forrester. And a big dog.

"I hope you don't mind if we wait out the storm in your house." He closed the porch door firmly. "Driving would be foolish in almost zero visibility. And Luna is terrified of storms." He took off his cap and grinned at Justine. "Would you be so kind as to hand me a towel? I'd hate for us to drip all over your house."

Justine blinked at the sight before her. Casson Forrester and his big panting dog, both dripping wet.

Casson took off his baseball cap and flung it toward

the hook on the wall opposite him. It landed perfectly. He looked at her expectantly, one hand in a pocket of his jeans, the other patting Luna on the head. Both pant legs were soaked, along with his jean jacket.

She tore her gaze away from his formfitting jeans and looked at Luna. She'd make a mess in her house, for sure. She sighed inwardly. Did she have any choice but to supply this dripping duo with towels? She couldn't very well let them stand there.

Anther clap of thunder caused Luna to give a sharp yelp, and she rose from her sitting position, looking like she wanted to bolt.

Justine blurted, "I'll just be a minute," and hurried inside, closing the door with a firm click. She wasn't going to let either of them inside until they were relatively drip-free.

She scrambled up the stairs to the hall closet near her room, fished out a couple of the largest towels she could find and then, as an afterthought, rifled through another section to find a pair of oversized painting overalls. He could get out of his jeans and wear these while his clothes dried.

Unable to stop the image of his bare legs invading her thoughts, she flushed, and hoped her cheeks wouldn't betray her.

She walked slowly down the stairs, and after taking a steadying breath re-entered the porch.

"I found a pair of painting overalls. You can get out of your wet clothes and throw them into the dryer," she said coolly. "There's a washroom just inside this door, next to the laundry room. If you want, I can pat down your dog."

She handed him the overalls and one of the towels.

He reached out for them and the towel fell open. His eyebrows rose and he glanced at her with a quirky half-smile. "I like the color, but I'm afraid they're a tad too small for me. But thanks."

Justine wanted the floor to split open and swallow her up. She snatched the hot pink bikini panties from where they clung to the towel and shoved them in her pocket. They must have been in the dryer together. She bent down to dry Luna, not wanting Casson to see how mortified she felt.

She let out her breath when she heard him enter the house.

Luna whimpered at the next rumble of thunder and started skittering around the porch. "Come here, Luna, you big scaredy-cat," she said. "Come on." To her surprise the dog gave a short bark and came to her, tail wagging. "Good dog. Now, lie down so I can dry you."

Luna obeyed, and Justine patted her head and dark coat with the towel. She was a mixed breed—Labrador Retriever, for sure, and maybe some German Shepherd. Her doleful eyes and the coloring around the face and head—tan and white, with a black peak in the middle of her forehead— made Justine wonder if there were some beagle ancestry as well.

"Don't you have pretty eyes?" she murmured, chuckling as Luna rewarded her with a lick on the hand.

They looked as if someone had taken eyeliner to them. And the brown of her coat tapered off to tan before ending in white paws, making it seem as if she had dipped them in white paint.

"You're such a pretty girl—you know that?" Justine gave her a final patting and set down the towel. "Even if you've left your fur all over my towel."

Justine crouched forward and scratched behind Luna's ears. Before Justine could stop her Luna had sprung forward to lick her on the cheek. Unprepared for the considerable weight of the furry bundle, Justine lost her balance and fell back awkwardly on the floor.

"Luna, come!"

Casson's voice was firm, displeased. She hadn't heard him come back.

"It's all right, she was just being affectionate," Justine hurried to explain. "I lost my footing."

She scrambled to get up, and her embarrassment dissipated when she saw him standing there in a T-shirt and the white overalls. It wasn't the T-shirt that made her want to burst out laughing. Under different circumstances those muscled arms would certainly have elicited emotions other than laughter. It was the overalls—the not-so-oversized overalls.

They fit him snugly, and only came down to just above his ankles. How could someone so ruggedly handsome look so…so *dorky* at the same time? She covered her mouth with her hand, but couldn't help her shoulders from quaking as she laughed silently. Here was Mr. Perfect—the stylish, wealthy entrepreneur Casson Forrester—wearing something that looked like it belonged to Mr. Bean.

Casson's eyes glinted. "What? You find this fashion statement humorous? Hmm… I suppose it does detract from your previous impression of me, however—"

The boom of thunder drowned out his words, and as the rain pelted down even harder Justine motioned toward the door. Once they were inside she ran to make sure all the windows were closed. The rain lashed against the panes, obliterating any view at all. She turned on a lamp in the living room.

"Have a seat." She gestured toward the couch. "I need to check the windows upstairs and change my clothes too." She glanced at Luna, who was whimpering. "You might want to turn on the TV to drown out the thunder."

After Justine had left, Casson smirked at the memory of her face when she'd turned to find him and Luna inside her porch. Her eyes had almost doubled in size, with blinking lashes that had reminded him of delicate hummingbird wings. Peach lips had fallen open and then immediately pursed. It had taken him everything not to burst out laughing.

Although laughing was not what he'd wanted to do when her pink panties had emerged from that towel… Her cheeks had immediately turned almost the same intense color, and he'd felt glad he hadn't given in to the impulse to hand them to her.

It had been her turn to smirk, though, when he'd appeared in these painting overalls. Casson knew he looked ridiculous—but, given the situation, beggars couldn't be choosers.

He grabbed the remote and found a classical music channel that would diffuse some of the thunder noise. Sitting back on the couch, he looked around with interest. The stone fireplace across from him was the focal point of the room, with its rustic slab of oak as mantel, and the Parry Sound stone continued upward to the pine-lined cathedral ceiling.

He drew a quick intake of breath as his gaze fell on the Group of Seven print above the mantel. *Mirror Lake*, by Franklin Carmichael. His eyes followed the curves of the multi-colored hills, the bands of varying hues of red, blue, purple, turquoise, green and gold and the perfect stillness of the lake, its surface a gleaming mirror.

This piece always tugged at his emotions and brought back so many memories—memories he didn't want to conjure up right now, with Justine set to return at any moment.

Casson's gaze shifted to the oversized recliners flanking the fireplace, one with a matching ottoman. Their colors, along with the couch and love seat, were an assortment of burnt sienna, brown and sage-green, with contrasting cushions. The wide-plank maple flooring, enhanced by a large forest green rug with a border of pine cones and branches, gave the place an authentic cottage feel, and the rustic coffee table and end tables complemented the décor.

The far wall behind the love seat featured huge windows of varying sizes, the top ones arching toward the peak of the ceiling and the largest one in the middle a huge bay window, providing what must be a spectacular view of the bay when the rain wasn't pounding against the panes.

A well-stocked bookshelf against one wall, eclectic lighting, and a vase containing a mix of wildflowers enhanced what Casson considered to be the ideal Georgian Bay cottage. He sat back, nodding, making mental notes for his future resort cottages.

After making a few investigative circles around the room Luna plunked down at his feet, panting slightly, her ears perked, as if she were expecting the next clap of thunder. Casson leaned forward to give her a reassuring pat and she grumbled contentedly and settled into a more relaxed position.

Casson wished *he* could feel more relaxed, but the painting overalls were compressing him in too many places. He wondered what Miss *Wintry*'s reaction would be if he stretched out on the couch. At least then he wouldn't feel like his masculinity was being compromised, he thought wryly. He checked the time on his watch. Sighing, he lay back and rested his head on one cushion.

Ah, relief.

He closed his eyes and listened to the classical music, accompanied by the rain pelting against the windows. A picture of Justine changing into dry clothes popped into his head.

Would she be slipping on those pink panties?

What was he doing?

He was here to wait for his clothes to dry and the storm to pass, not to imagine her naked...

* * *

Upstairs in her room, Justine peeled off her clothes, dried herself vigorously, and wished she could jump into a hot shower. But that would have to wait until Casson was gone. She didn't want to be thinking about him while she was... undressed. She changed quickly into white leggings and a long, brightly flowered shirt.

As an afterthought she opened her closet and moved a few boxes until she found the one she was looking for. Although Christmas was months away, she stashed away presents whenever she could instead of waiting for the last minute. The box she opened contained a dressing robe she had picked out for her dad. It was forest green, with burgundy trim at the wrists and collar, and she had embroidered the letters 'WH', for Winter's Haven, on one side. She had wanted to surprise her dad with this as a new idea—providing a robe in each cottage, like they did in hotels.

She lifted it out of the box and its tissue wrapping and hooked it over her arm. At the door she hesitated, feeling a sudden twinge of guilt, and then, before she could change her mind, she strode downstairs.

The TV was on and Luna was lying at Casson's feet. Justine held out the robe. "I thought you might appreciate this instead," she said.

He stood up and took it from her, before tossing the cushion he was holding back on the couch. "Indeed I do," he said, his jaw twitching. "Now I know you're not all flint and arrows."

Justine opened her mouth to voice a retort but his hand came up.

"No offence intended," he said. "I realize we didn't start off on exactly a positive note but, given the present circumstances, could we perhaps call a truce of some sort?"

Justine was taken aback. "We're not in a battle, Mr. Forrester. So there's no need for a truce. Excuse me. I'm going to put on some fresh coffee. Care for a cup?" She turned toward the open-concept kitchen/dining room.

"Love some coffee," he replied. "Just milk or cream, no sugar. And you'll have to excuse *me* as well. I'm dying to get out of these overalls."

He smirked and headed toward the washroom. Luna lifted her head quizzically, gave a contented grumble, and promptly settled back into her nap.

When Casson came back into the living room he had the overalls neatly folded. He placed them on a side chair and then sat down on the couch. The robe fit him well, which meant it would have been a size or two too big for her dad.

"That coffee smells great," he drawled, tightening the sash on the robe before crossing his legs.

Justine came out of the kitchen with a tray holding two mugs, a small container of cream and a plate of muffins. She caught her breath at seeing him there, one leg partially exposed. She felt a warm rush infuse her body. It was such an *intimate* scenario: Casson leaning back against the couch, totally relaxed, as if he were the owner of the place.

She saw his gaze flicker over her body as she approached. She wanted to squirm. Her jaw tensed. This was *her* place. Why did she suddenly feel like she was at a disadvantage?

She would *not* let him know that his presence was affecting her. She would treat him like any other cottage guest. Politely, respectfully. And hopefully the heavens would soon clam up and she could send him on his way. His clothes shouldn't take too long to dry.

She set the tray down on the coffee table and, picking up the plate of four muffins, held it out to him. "Banana yogurt. Homemade."

"Thank you, Miss Winter."

He reached forward and took one. At the same time

Luna lifted her head, sniffing excitedly. Before Justine had a chance to move the plate Luna had a muffin in her jaws. Startled, Justine tipped the plate and stumbled over Casson's foot. She felt herself falling backward, and a moment later landed in the last place she'd ever want to land. A steaming volcano would have been preferable.

She felt his arms closing around her. The muffin was still in his hand.

"Now that you've fallen right into my lap," he murmured huskily in her right ear, "would you like to share my muffin?"

CHAPTER THREE

JUSTINE COULD FEEL Casson's breath on the side of her neck. She shivered involuntarily. His left arm was around her waist and his right arm was elevated, holding the muffin. His robe had opened slightly in the commotion and, glancing downward, she saw to her consternation that one bare leg was under her.

She was sitting on his bare leg.

Her head snapped up. She was glad he couldn't see her face. She needed to get off him. But to do so would mean pushing down against him to get some leverage. She bit her lip. Why didn't he just give her a push? That would avoid her needing to grind into him.

She cleared her throat. Luna had downed one muffin and was eyeing the two that had flipped onto the coffee table.

"Oh, no, you don't." Casson's voice was firm. "Luna, lie down."

His tone brooked no argument. With a doleful look at the muffins, and then at her master, Luna obeyed with a mournful growl. And then Casson gave Justine a gentle push and she was out of his lap.

He set down his muffin and crouched down to face Luna. "Dogs don't eat muffins," he said emphatically, before giving Luna a low growl.

Justine knew that Casson was emphasizing his alpha male status. Luna responded with a look of shame at being reprimanded, and Justine couldn't help chuckling—which caused Luna to begin wagging her tail, her doggy enthusiasm restored.

Casson lifted an eyebrow and Justine wondered if he was going to growl at *her* for interrupting his disciplinary moment. She saw his mouth twitch and he rose, grabbed his mug and muffin and sat down again.

"And no whining!" he reproached Luna, who flopped back on her side.

Flustered, and trying not to show it, Justine sat down on the love seat. She sipped her coffee and turned to glance out the big bay window. Through the sheets of rain battering the pane she could glimpse patches of sky and bloated gray-black clouds. The water in the bay would be churning, the whitecaps foaming.

"Good muffin." Casson reached for the two still on the coffee table and handed one to her. "I hope these are for sale in the diner."

Justine took it from him and broke off a piece from the top. He seemed totally comfortable sitting in her living room, lounging with nothing on but a robe. She concentrated on pulling the paper back from the muffin and forced herself to avoid glancing at his well-muscled calves and bare feet. And the slight patch of hair in the V below his neck.

She hoped the rain would abate soon. She nibbled at her muffin and took long sips of her coffee, and then realized she hadn't responded.

"Um…yes, we do have muffins for sale in the diner. I usually make a fresh batch every morning…"

The thought of being alone with Casson for much longer was disturbing—mostly because her body was betraying her physically, reacting in a way that was not in sync with her mental perception of Casson Forrester. Her mind had reacted coolly to him from his first arrogant appearance; however, her body was becoming increasingly warm...in ways that made her want to squirm.

"What made you want to return here?" Casson asked with a note of genuine curiosity.

Justine looked up from her muffin and stared blankly at him, her mind scrambling to come up with an alternative explanation, since she had no intention of revealing the truth to him. Her involvement with Robert was none of Casson's business.

"It really doesn't matter," she said, making her voice light. "I'm just glad I returned when I did...to save our humble property from certain demise." She finished her muffin and folded the paper muffin cup several times, before setting it down on the table. "But I'm willing to forget our first negative meeting if you are. We might as well be civil to each other, since you own the Russell properties now."

She picked up her mug and sipped while gazing at him, wondering how he would reply.

Casson stood up and walked to the bay window. He drank his coffee and stared out at the storm. Justine wondered if he intended to ignore her peace offering. Her heart thudded against her chest as she watched him, standing there in the robe. The dark green suited him. His hair was thick, and slightly longer than when she had first seen him, and his short beard did not detract from his good looks. In fact, she was having a hard time deciding if he was more handsome with or without it.

Casson turned then and she started, realizing how intently she had been staring at him.

"Of course we can be civil."

He eyed her for a moment, then left his position at the window to sit down next to her on the love seat. Justine drummed a quiet beat on the arm of the seat, wondering why his eyes were glittering so devilishly. Was the room getting darker, or was it just her imagination?

What they needed was more illumination, she decided, and was about to turn on the other table lamp when a deafening series of thunderclaps shattered her thoughts. Instinctively she swiveled toward Casson, both palms landing flat against his chest. Luna yelped and scampered around the room, barking and panting.

Casson clasped her shoulders. Simultaneously horrified and shocked at her reaction—and his—she stared at him wordlessly, unable to wrench herself away. The rise and fall of his chest as he breathed made her shiver. While his eyes remained fixed on hers, his arms slid around to encircle her back.

Casson's face was suddenly closer, his eyes intense, and Justine felt herself quiver. His lips made contact with hers and involuntarily she closed her eyes. His arms tightened around her and his kiss deepened. Justine felt her lips open as if they had a mind of their own. His gentle exploration ignited sparks of desire along her nerve-endings.

As if he could sense her powerlessness to tear herself away, Casson guided her hands from his chest to the back of his neck. He pressed Justine tightly to him. She responded hungrily, caught in the moment. When she felt the intensity of his kiss diminish she opened her eyes. He pulled slightly away from her, his eyes searing hers, and with a muffled groan lowered his face to nuzzle her neck.

Justine froze, her pulse pounding as erratically as the raindrops beating relentlessly against the window panes. *What were they doing?* How could she have allowed her emotions to get out of control like that? She didn't even *like* this man, nor what he intended to do with his properties, and yet here she was, allowing him to be so *intimate* with her—as if they were a *couple*.

Casson must have felt her stiffening. He straightened and let her arms fall from around his neck. "That was a mistake," she said as steadily as she could, avoiding his gaze. "You'd better go."

She shifted away from him and crossed her arms and legs.

"Don't you want to know what I had to tell you?"

Justine looked at him in bewilderment, and then recalled his earlier words.

"After checking in on my store, I was about to officially start my holidays and head out to Winter's Haven when I spotted you in the paneling department."

Justine frowned. "Why *were* you heading out to Winter's Haven?" She looked at him pointedly. "You didn't actually think there was a chance that I'd change my mind about selling, did you? I told you before—I'm not interested in any proposal you have to make."

Casson's mouth lifted at one corner. "Perhaps you'll change your mind before my stay here is over," he said calmly, stroking his beard.

"That will never happen, believe—" She broke off, her eyes narrowing warily. "What do you mean, your stay *here*?"

"I plan to spend a week of my holiday at Winter's Haven. I'd like to see first-hand how things are run here."

"That's impossible." She gave him a frosty smile. "All twelve cottages are booked to the end of the summer."

Casson stood up lithely. "Just wait here a minute. I'll go check my clothes."

Justine watched him leave the room. Luna bolted after him and he turned, caught Justine's eye, and said, "Go back, Luna. Go lie down."

He winked at Justine and left the room.

Luna padded back and plunked herself down by Justine's feet. Despite her annoyance with Casson, Justine couldn't help being charmed by his big, friendly, generally well-behaved dog.

"Did you enjoy my muffin, you big cutie?" She laughed, patting Luna on the head, and Luna responded with a noisy yawn and rolled to one side. "Oh, now you want a belly rub, do you?" She smiled, leaning forward. "It's obvious your master spoils you."

"She deserves spoiling."

Casson's voice was behind her.

"Her original owner wasn't so nice to her. He left her on the side of the road and took off. Before I could drive up to the spot she was gone. I found her wandering in the woods. Fur all covered with burrs. She was barely a year old."

"Oh...poor baby."

Justine felt tears stinging her eyes. She blinked rapidly, but a few slipped down. Luna sat up and immediately licked her on the cheek.

Not wanting Casson to know how emotional she felt, Justine laughed and said, "Well, maybe I might just give you another muffin, Miss Luna."

"You'd better not," Casson advised. "Muffins are *not* part of her diet."

He stood across from her. He had changed back into his jeans and T-shirt, but his jacket was in his hands. He flung it on the arm of the couch and then reached into the pocket of his jeans. He held out a key that looked all too familiar to Justine.

She blinked. "Where did you get that?" she demanded. She could see the number engraved on it. The number one. For Cottage Number One—the cottage closest to her house. Justine stood up and reached for it. Casson's reaction was quick. He drew back his arm, leaving Justine grasping at thin air.

"How did you get that key? The Elliots are renting that cottage."

"They *were*," he corrected.

"But—"

"Let me explain," he interjected smoothly. "While I was waiting in the restaurant for you a couple of weeks ago I met the Elliots. Talking to them gave me the idea of renting one of your cottages. I made them an offer they couldn't refuse—an all-expenses-paid round-trip anywhere in the world in exchange for their cottage for a week." He smiled. "My timing was perfect. They had recently received an invitation from friends in Greece and declined, since they couldn't afford it. Needless to say, they jumped at my offer."

Justine gaped at him. "I can't *believe* this. They would have said something to me about it. It's against the rules to let someone else stay in their cottage without asking me or Mandy first. And *I* make the final decision."

Another infuriatingly smug smile. "I made them promise not to say anything. I told them I wanted to surprise my *very good friend* with a visit…and a *proposal*."

Justine's stomach muscles tightened. Her anger had been growing with his every word, and at this revelation she exploded. "A *proposal*? You had them believe you were going to *propose* to me?" She glared at him, her hands on her hips. "You had it all planned, didn't you? How dare you manipulate my customers to get what you want? You had no right to use the Elliots that way, for your own advantage."

"Would you have rented out a cottage to me if I had consulted you first?"

His voice was calm, which infuriated her all the more.

"Certainly not! I don't rent out to devious, untrustworthy, manipulative… Oh, what's the use?" She threw her hands up in the air. "You can't teach an old dog new tricks."

Casson chuckled. "I've been called many things by

women—mostly positive, I might add—but 'old dog' is a new one for me." His eyes blazed down at her. "Could you be more specific as to the breed?"

"Don't try to be funny, Mr. Forrester, and make light of this. I'm not amused." She stuck out her hand. "The only decent thing for you to do is to give me back the key. Besides, you now own the properties on either side of me. Why don't you stay on one of *them* to carry out your surveillance tactics?"

"You make me sound like a spy," he countered wryly. "I admit you have a good point, Miss Winter, but although I now *own* the properties I can't really observe the way things are run at Winter's Haven unless I'm actually *here*. Day and night. I thought it fair to at least tell you before settling in."

"Fair?" She filled her lungs with air and let it out in a rush.

"Look, all I want is a week to see how this place operates." His eyes narrowed speculatively. "You never know— the experience might even change my mind about going ahead with a large-scale venture. I may find that a smaller operation is more in keeping with the balance of nature in this area..."

"I have no guarantee that you will change your mind," Justine retorted, "and I refuse to be subjected to your scrutiny for any length of time. Your tactics are futile. I have no intentions of selling to you. *Ever.* Now, give me the key, please. My hand is getting tired." She glowered at him. "What you did may have negative legal implications— which, I assure you, I will look into if you do not return my key."

"There's nothing illegal about what I did and you know it," he said, putting the key back in his jeans pocket. He glanced out the bay window. "I see the rain has stopped for the time being so, if you'll excuse me, I'd like to take advantage of your dining facilities…"

He turned to leave.

"Won't you join me, Miss Winter?"

Justine was sure her face was aflame. "No, thank you," she replied icily, her blue-gray eyes flashing a warning at him. He was pushing her too far. If he didn't soon leave she would throw…throw the remaining muffin or a cushion at him.

"See you later then," he said with a slight nod. "Come on, Luna, I'll take you to your new digs. I don't believe you're allowed in the diner." When he opened the door to the porch, he called out, "Thank you for taking us in. Luna and I enjoyed the muffins…and your company."

Justine swiveled around with a retort on the tip of her tongue, but he was already out the door. Deflated, she sank back down on the love seat.

Casson felt like letting out a boyish cheer as he left Justine's place. *Step one, accomplished!* The rain had diminished to a soft drizzle, which he barely noticed as he opened the side door of his pickup truck. Luna jumped in happily, turning several times in her spot until sinking down, her big brown eyes looking at him expectantly.

Casson grinned and gave her several pats on her rump. "I suppose I should thank you for your part in this, Luna Lu."

Luna gave a soft bark. Casson laughed and reached into his pocket.

"I may not have Miss Winter in the palm of my hand, but it sure felt good having her in my lap."

And tasting her lips.

It was the last thing he'd expected to happen between them. He hadn't planned it, but he couldn't say he regretted it. How could he regret the feel of those soft, pliant lips against his? The way they'd opened to him, let him in deeper? The feel of her under that thin T-shirt, pressed against him so tightly? A mistake, she'd called it. But he had felt the electricity between them as she withdrew.

He wondered if she suspected he was using his masculine wiles to influence her and weaken her resolve about refusing to sell. That was not his intention, but he doubted she would believe him if he attempted to explain. So of course he had feigned indifference at her withdrawal, and proceeded to explain why he wanted to stay at Winter's Haven.

He drove back to the Russell house—*his* house now—and set down his briefcase on the kitchen table. He pulled out a thick folder containing the deeds to his new properties. Now that he was actually on the main property he wanted to examine the maps and surveyors' documents again. He wanted to become familiar with every curve, corner and contour of his land and shoreline.

Even on paper, the Russell and Winter properties occupied an impressive stretch of the Georgian Bay shoreline. The Russells had cleared very little of this property—just enough to snake a path through the dense forest and construct their home on the main parcel and a small cottage on the second one.

Casson peered closely at the map showing the zoning of the adjoining properties. He examined the boundaries of Winter's Haven. It was obvious the Winters had also endeavored to maintain the rugged features of their property. Even though they had eventually added twelve cottages to the land, and an office/diner, they, too, were built with minimal clearing and, like the Russell property, sat further back from the shoreline.

Casson stared at one of the more detailed zoning maps. He shuffled through the folder and pulled out an older document. He rubbed his jaw thoughtfully as he compared them. He was no zoning expert, but he was certain there was a discrepancy in the documents. The older one showed the adjoining properties before any structures had been built. The document showing the addition of the properties revealed something that made him start.

Why hadn't this been brought to his attention? Had the realtor even been aware of it?

Casson knew that both structures had been built in the fifties, and evidently had been beautifully maintained, with occasional renovations, but one thing he hadn't known was the way a section of the Winter home had been erected on a slice of land that clearly belonged to the Russells.

Casson let out a deep breath. Justine's place was sitting partially on *his* property.

He was certain she had absolutely no knowledge of this. Her parents probably didn't either. Or if they did they hadn't revealed it to Justine. It might have been an oversight that the Russells had dismissed, given that they owned so much land. *And* they had been the best of friends with the Winters. Mr. Winter had said as much, when he and Casson had first discussed the potential sale of Winter's Haven.

Casson drummed his fingers on the smooth surface of the table. He wasn't sure he wanted to share his findings with his new neighbor. Not just yet. But he would write a letter to Justine and wait for the appropriate time to give it to her.

He pulled out his laptop and quickly typed it up, ending with an invitation to meet him and discuss options. He was glad he had brought his portable printer with him—a habit, since he did so much travelling. After printing out a copy, he placed the letter and the other documents in an envelope and into his briefcase, along with his laptop.

Casson looked around. There would be time enough to enjoy his new place after a week at Winter's Haven.

With a feeling of anticipation for the week ahead, Casson grabbed his briefcase and the one piece of luggage that he had packed the night before. Heading out to his truck with Luna, he began to whistle.

He couldn't wait to settle in to Cottage Number One.

CHAPTER FOUR

NONE OF THE cottagers were in the diner yet. Justine glanced at the board indicating the special of the day—turkey cranberry burgers with arugula salad—and helped herself to a cup of coffee before sitting at one of the tables by the window. Mandy was still in the office, on the phone with a booking. Justine had waited for a bit, anxious to tell her what Casson Forrester had had the nerve to do, but Mandy had waved her away, indicating she would join her when she was done.

Justine sipped her coffee and looked out at the bay. The sky was a slate of gray, ruffled with layers of low cloud. She thought about Casson Forrester settling in to Cottage Number One and felt a shiver run through her body.

She replayed earlier events in her mind—from her realization that the jerk following her was Casson, to his barging into her home with Luna and the deafening series of thunderclaps that had caused her to end up in Casson's arms. The last thing she had ever imagined when he'd first strode into the office was that she'd be thoroughly kissed by him in her own home...*and that she'd thoroughly enjoy it.*

She wasn't sure how long she had sat frozen on the love seat after Casson had left. She'd felt like she had been tossed about in a whirlwind, and had had to let her brain and body restore its calm and balance. Her feelings had alternated between fury at being manipulated and help-lessness. She'd pondered calling a local police officer she knew, who had breakfast regularly in the diner. But what could he do, really? Perhaps she needed to consult a law-yer to see if there was a way of getting Casson Forrester off her property...

Do you really want him off your property?

Justine started at the tiny inner voice that had popped into her mind. To be honest with herself, if Casson had been renting a cottage for a week or more, without any in-tention to take over, she would have been happy—*thrilled* would be more accurate. After all, who *wouldn't* want to have the pleasure of looking at such a fine specimen of a man for any length of time? Despite the fact that she had been duped by Robert, she wasn't so jaded that she could ignore the presence of someone as handsome as Casson.

But the fact of the matter was that Casson had an ul-terior motive in staying at Winter's Haven. And even if he *had* kissed her it was her property he wanted, not *her.*

"Hey, Justine. What are you dreaming about?" Mandy smiled and sat down across from her.

Justine snapped out of her thoughts and took a deep breath. "Remember Casson Forrester, who was here last week?"

Mandy's eyes widened. "Mr. Gorgeous, you mean? The hunk I wish they'd name an ice cream flavor after?"

"Mandy! You're *engaged*, remember?" Justine couldn't help laughing.

"I'm engaged—not blind!"

"Well, Mr. Forrester has just finagled his way into stay-ing at Winter's Haven. He wants to observe how things are run up close. I guess he figures he'll find a way to convince me to sell. He's staying in Cottage Number One for a week."

Justine paused, watching Mandy's face wrinkle in confusion. She clearly had no idea of the transaction between Casson and the Elliots.

"*What?* How can that be? The Elliots are in there!"

Justine explained, then sat back, crossing her arms. "Now, what should we do? Call Constable Phil? A lawyer?"

"Geez…" Mandy's brows furrowed. "Do we want to complicate things? Other than being hot, Casson Forrester seems pretty harmless. Ambitious, maybe, but not dangerous. Look, you're not going to sell, so why don't you just let him enjoy the cottage and in a week's time you can kiss him goodbye!"

Justine knew Mandy was speaking figuratively, but the thought of kissing Casson again gave her a rush. She felt her cheeks burn, and saw Mandy looking at her speculatively, but she wasn't ready to share what had happened…

"I hate to spring another surprise on you, Justine, but the call I just took…" Mandy sighed. "It was *Robert*. He wants to see you. He tried to book a cottage."

Justine just about dropped her coffee mug. She set it down and stared at Mandy. "What for?"

Mandy took a deep breath. "He told me that he knows he made mistakes but that he hopes you'll give him a chance to apologize."

"He's the *last* person I want to see," Justine moaned, covering her face with her hands.

"I hope you're not talking about *me,* Miss Winter."

Justine slowly let her hands slip from her face.

"And I hope you don't mind if I join you for lunch." Casson looked at her directly. "I haven't picked up any supplies for my stay yet, and I hear the locals come to eat here a lot, which convinces me I should try it." He glanced over at Mandy. "Hello, Miss Holliday. Nice to see you again." He offered his hand.

"My pleasure." Mandy beamed. "And, yes—please join us."

Justine wanted to scowl at her, but Casson had turned to look at her again.

"Only if the Boss Lady agrees," he said, amusement tinging his voice.

"That's fine," Justine said, trying to keep from clenching her teeth.

Casson pulled out a chair to sit next to Mandy.

"Actually, I'm not staying for lunch," Mandy said. "My fiancé's taking me out." She waved at Justine and Casson. "See you later."

She glanced slyly at Justine, and Justine shot her a *Just wait 'till you get back* glare.

When a waitress walked over and set down two glasses of water for them Casson thanked her and looked over at Justine expectantly.

Justine flushed. "Hi, Mel. Casson Forrester—meet Melody Green, our wonderful waitress."

After Melody had taken their orders—turkey burger for her and fish and chips for him—Casson flashed Justine a smile. "I can see why people want to stay at Winter's Haven," he smiled. "The cottage is perfect. Luna has already found her favorite spot." As Justine's eyebrows went up, he said, "Couch in the living room. She's curled up on it right now." He chuckled. "But I don't doubt she'll find a way to join me on the bed tonight."

Casson saw something flicker in Justine's eyes. He might be totally out in left field, but was that a spark of—?

"She's a nice dog," Justine said grudgingly.

"And she's very protective of her owner." Casson grinned.

"I can't imagine *you'd* need protecting."

Casson gave a hearty laugh. "I might—if the owner of

this place becomes aggressive with me." He gazed quizzically at Justine. "But, then again, Luna likes you. If you tried to tackle me she'd probably do nothing. Or think we were playing and try to join in." He gazed at her for a few seconds.

Justine's face wrinkled into a frown. "There would be no reason for me to tackle you, Mr. Forrester."

"*Please.* Call me Casson. After all, we'll be neighbors for the next week. By the way—I have a couple of guests coming to spend the weekend with me. I figured it was okay, since the cottage has a loft and a pull-out couch. But I did want to mention it in case there's an extra charge."

He looked expectantly at Justine. She was slightly taken aback, judging by her hesitation in responding and the sudden tapping of her foot against the table leg, which she seemed unaware of.

"Yes, a limited number of guests are allowed. There is a minimal charge."

"Great—just add it to my bill." Casson nodded in satisfaction.

"Here are your orders," Melody announced cheerfully. "Enjoy." She placed a platter in front of each of them. "Is there anything else you'd like to drink, Mr. Forrester?"

"Water will be fine, thanks." He slipped her a couple of bills. "No change needed." He smiled at Melody's look of appreciation, and then picked up one of his fries. *"Bon appétit."* He winked at Justine.

They ate silently for a couple of minutes, and even though Casson tried not to make it obvious he couldn't help glancing occasionally at Justine. While he enjoyed his fresh-cut fries and battered whitefish, Justine was trying to eat a massive burger delicately. When she set her bun down in frustration he saw a smear of ketchup on her cheek and chin. He had a crazy desire to lean over and lick it off her face.

But of course he wouldn't.

Casson watched as she ran her tongue over her lips and just outside her mouth. His heart did a flip. He picked up a clean napkin and, rising slightly, reached over and gently wiped at the two spots of ketchup, his eyes locking with hers.

It was like looking into the bay. *Deep blue. A blue that could swallow you up.*

He didn't know how long he stayed in that position, half out of his seat, but when he sat down he felt like something had knocked him out temporarily. Justine's face was flushed, and she immediately looked down and concentrated on finishing her burger.

"By the way, it seems that one of your prospective guests couldn't book a cottage here, so he asked around and was told about the Russell properties being under new ownership. He came looking for me and asked if he could rent the small cottage." Casson shrugged. "I hadn't even thought about renting it, but what the heck? Might as well let someone enjoy the place."

He saw Justine stiffen. "Who did you rent it out to?" Her voice trembled slightly.

"A lawyer called Robert Morrell."

CHAPTER FIVE

JUSTINE WANTED THE floor to open up and swallow her. It was bad enough that she had an issue with Casson. Having to deal with Robert now was just too much. She had spent the last couple of months convinced she was finished with him, and had never imagined he would come to see her here at Winter's Haven. Not knowing what he was planning to do jangled her nerves. She couldn't believe he had called the office and tried to rent a cottage... He could walk into the diner at any moment...

She realized Casson had asked her a question...asked if she knew Robert. "Yes, I know him." She tried to respond in a neutral tone, so Casson wouldn't ask any more questions, but she heard her voice crack.

She saw Casson looking at her thoughtfully. The sun had nudged its way through the clouds, shining through the window, and it was reflected in his deep brown eyes. His suntanned face with its dark beard, his plaid shirt with its rolled-up sleeves and his jeans made him look like a muscled hiking guide. She felt her heartbeat accelerating.

"Old boyfriend?"

Justine stared at him. "How did you—?"

"Know? You're not that hard to read. You know that expression *'wearing your heart on your sleeve'*? Well, with you, your feelings show on your face."

Justine cocked her head at him and frowned.

He nodded. "Yup. Eyelashes fluttering. Blue eyes darkening. Cheeks flushing. All the classic signs." His eyes narrowed and he leaned forward. "Did you dump *him* or was it the other way around?"

Justine wanted to squirm. Casson wasn't her *friend*, for goodness' sakes. She wasn't about to reveal anything about her past to him, and nor did she intend to enlighten him as to who had dumped whom.

While she grappled with an appropriate response Casson leaned back again and took a long drink of his water. Afterward he stood up, and with a nod said, "Sorry. I was being nosy. Nice doing lunch. I'll see you later..." He turned away and then glanced back at her. "If he let you go, he was a fool..."

Not waiting for her to reply, he walked out of the diner.

Justine followed him with her eyes until the last inch of him was out of sight. Reaching for her handbag, she shuffled through it for her keys. She left the diner and got into her car. She was glad she had already planned to go into Parry Sound to pick up her order of bread for the diner. Now, with the disheartening news about Robert, she decided she'd stay away even longer.

Justine headed first to *West Lake Cosmetics*. She loved owner Wendy's natural handmade soaps, skincare products and bath treats. She also stocked the cottages with products having names like *Muskoka Mimosa*, *Rose Rapture* and *Georgian Bay Linen*. After today's stress, she needed *something* to help her relax.

She chose a *Rose Rapture* soap and a *Citrus Wave* bath pod, and looked forward to pampering herself later with a long, soothing bath. But first she'd have to relieve Mandy for the afternoon shift.

Justine left the shop and moments later stepped into *The Country Gourmet Café and Gallery* to pick up the loaves she had ordered for the diner and two walnut loaves for herself. She thanked Chris, the friendly owner, then headed back to Winter's Haven and tried not to think about Robert.

Everything looked fresh and clean after the earlier downpour. Justine rolled down her windows, lifted her face to the warm breeze and thought about Casson's last words. *If he let you go, he was a fool...* Her heart catapulted at the memory, just as it had done when he had uttered the words.

She replayed the conversation in her head as she drove, and wondered why Casson had wanted to know who was responsible for the ending of her relationship with Robert.

Robert!

He was the one who had decided to break things off. Unable to face working with him every day, Justine had resigned immediately and fled to Winter's Haven for a few days, needing the support of her parents. She had been stunned when they'd made her the offer...

She'd gone back to Toronto and fortunately had only had to wait a month for the end of the lease on her apartment. But it had been the hardest month to get through. She'd had lots of time to process the failed relationship. To go over every painful detail of how Robert had taken advantage of her trust, her naiveté. She winced at the memories, and a rash of anger ignited and spread under her skin.

She *had* been naïve. She had allowed Robert to draw her in, letting her care for him while his marriage deteriorated. Robert had used her, milking her genuine concern and thoughtfulness until she had been practically frothing over him. She had believed his intentions to be honorable, and his betrayal had hit her like a winter gale from Georgian Bay.

By the end of the month she'd accepted that it was over and had become determined not to allow anyone to use her again. She'd realized it was a godsend that her parents had offered her the opportunity of taking over the business.

It had been time to leave the city and go home.

When she'd driven into Winter's Haven two months ago, and breathed in the fresh scent of the woods and the bay, she'd known she had made the right decision. The chapter of her life with Robert Morrell in it was finished.

Until now.

Justine took a deep breath and let it out slowly. She dropped off the loaves to Melody, took over the office from Mandy, and tried to focus on business tasks. Every once in a while she looked up, wondering anxiously if Robert would suddenly appear.

Justine was relieved when the time came to close up the office. When she got home she kicked off her shoes, put away the bread, and eagerly reached for the bag inside her purse. She was more than ready for a relaxing Citrus Wave bath. And, although it was not yet eight, she started to fill up the tub. She began to undress—then heard the doorbell ring.

Her heart skipped a beat. Was Casson here with another strategy to entice her to sell? He *had* said, "I'll see you later..."

Justine slipped her T-shirt back on and flew down the stairs to the front door. Through the window curtain she could make out a profile.

Wrong man.

When Casson entered his cottage he made a pot of coffee and satisfied himself that the place was ready for his guests' stay. His cousin Veronica would be arriving around noon the following day, along with her son Andy.

Casson smiled. Andy was such a good kid. When he was born, five years ago, Ronnie had asked Casson to be his godfather and he had been thrilled. Ronnie was like a sister to him—the sister he'd never had.

Casson's jaw tightened. She had separated from her husband Peter over a year ago. Peter had been unable to deal with the day-to-day challenges of his son's illness, and had found solace in the comforting arms of a woman who was "there" for him.

But Ronnie had rallied and Andy was now in his second year of his treatment. He had recently finished another round of maintenance chemotherapy, and when Ronnie had texted Casson with this news he had immediately invited them to spend a weekend with him at Winter's Haven. To his delight, Ronnie had called to accept.

Casson poured himself a big mug of coffee before going out to sit on the back deck. Watching the blue waves, he found his thoughts returning to Justine, and the alarm he had glimpsed in her eyes when she'd found out Robert Morrell was renting his cottage.

His jaws clenched. Had the creep hurt her in some way?

He'd find an excuse to check on Robert tonight. And Justine, just to make sure she was okay. Whether it was his business or not, and despite the fact that he might very well be wrong in his suspicions, Casson needed to know what Robert Morrell wanted with Justine.

CHAPTER SIX

JUSTINE HESITATED. WHY had Robert waited until this evening to come and find her? She jumped as Robert tapped the door knocker. She could ignore him...but he probably would have seen her approaching through the lace curtain.

He knocked again. She bit her lip and opened the door slightly, the chain still in place. She didn't offer a greeting; she just gave him a cold stare.

"Justine... Look, I wouldn't blame you if you slammed the door in my face. I just... I just had to try to make things right with you." His voice had a slight tremor. "Even if we never see each other again."

Justine pursed her lips, unconvinced. She wasn't sure if he expected her to let him in, but she felt reluctant to let him step foot in her house. After all, she had never invited him to Winter's Haven before they'd split up—no, before he'd dumped her—so why should she allow him into her private space *now*?

And besides, did she really want to hear what he had to say?

Justine shivered, even though the evening air was warm and still.

She cleared her throat. "Why would you want to do that now, Robert?" She hoped her voice was cool, uncaring—

unlike the way she had responded when he'd told her it was over.

Robert cringed visibly at her tone, as if she had just struck him across the face. "I want to apologize, Justine. Please—just let me try to make amends. I made a mistake in the way I treated you. You deserve more than an apology…"

He looked like a puppy dog, Justine thought, with doleful eyes that were begging for a little mercy. Justine felt herself waver. Robert sounded genuinely sorry. Maybe she needed to hear him explain his less than cavalier behavior toward her…

Nodding, she slid the door chain off. "I don't have a lot of time," she lied.

Relief flooded Robert's face. He stood hesitantly as Justine opened the door wider and then offered a grateful smile as he entered her home. He looked around appreciatively. "Nice place," he said, eyebrows lifting as his gaze settled on the bay window. "Beautiful view."

She gestured toward a recliner, away from the love seat…

Robert nodded and passed in front of her. And then she heard the water still flowing into the bathtub.

"Good heavens!" She threw him a panicked look. "I forgot to turn off the water."

She bolted up the stairs two at a time. She drew out a long breath of relief as she turned both taps off. The water level was an inch below the top of the tub. With jangled nerves she returned to the living room. She wanted to get this apology thing over with, see Robert out, and then have that relaxing bath she had planned.

She sat in the recliner opposite Robert and glanced at him pointedly.

He shifted in his seat, his forehead glistening with beads of perspiration. "Look, Justine, it was never my intention to hurt you. I—I was in a dark place emotionally with my wife, and you were like a ray of sunshine." He smiled at her crookedly. "Sorry, I know that's an overused cliché But after spending my evenings arguing with Katie, and my nights on a couch, I came to appreciate your positive, funny and charming personality...and I *wanted* that. I—I wanted *you*."

He paused, waiting for her to reply, but she had nothing to say—*yet*.

"I was all mixed up. I admit it." He looked away and gazed at the view of the bay. "It was exciting to be with you, and yet once I'd tasted some freedom I started wanting even more. More freedom, more fun, more adventure."

Justine felt a jab in the pit of her stomach. "And that's when you decided to break up with me?" she said, as steadily as she could. "You said the whole divorce thing had depleted you and that you didn't have the energy to carry on with a serious relationship. Only I found out the *real* reason you were 'depleted' when I came to the office early the next morning to pack my things and leave my letter of resignation on your desk... That's when I spotted your lover's panty hose on the couch in your office."

He cringed again. "I'm sorry, Justine. I was screwed up. I know I crossed the line." He gazed at her helplessly. "I hope you can find it in your heart to forgive me. I was so mixed up. Afraid of another commitment but hungry for love. I played with fire and you were the one that got burned." His eyes glistened. "I was the loser, letting you go." His voice broke. "I'll do *anything* to have you back."

Justine let out a deep breath. She hadn't expected *this*.

"I've rented the cottage on the property next to yours for a few days, hoping I can eventually convince you to forgive me and give me another chance."

He stood up and began walking toward her. When he was a foot away, he got down on one knee.

"I—I'm not seeing that other woman, Justine. I swear it didn't mean anything." He placed a hand over hers. "Tell me what I can do to get you to come back to me."

Justine's heart began to hammer. But not because she was overcome with joy at Robert's words, she realized. And his touch left her cold. She tried to slide her hand out from under his but he tightened his grip. She frowned and, meeting his gaze, saw his dilated pupils. She caught the unmistakable smell of alcohol.

"Robert, please let go of my hand." She said it quietly, trying to keep the alarm out of her voice.

He swayed a bit and moved closer, ignoring her request. And then she saw it over his shoulder—the bottle cap he had left on the base of the fireplace.

He had brought a bottle with him.

She had never seen him in this state, and tried not to think about what might happen if he was not in his right mind. She had to think of something to get him out of her house.

"Look, Robert, I forgive you."

To her relief, he loosened his hold.

"You do?"

He gazed at her wonderingly, and Justine knew then that the alcohol he had consumed had started to take effect. While he still had that dazed expression Justine managed to get up and start ambling away from him. Her gaze fell on the bottle that peeked out of his back pocket.

"Yes, Robert." She gestured toward the door. "But now you need to get back to your cottage."

He scrambled to his feet. Justine bit her lip. His senses might be dulled, but otherwise—

"*Please* let me stay, Just—Justine."

In a flash, he had reached her, encircled her waist with both arms and was brushing his cheek against hers.

Justine inhaled the heavy scent of alcohol on his breath.

Her stomach twisted, but before she could even think of breaking free he had pushed her back onto the couch and pinned her arms down. She tried to lift a knee but he flattened it with his own. She stared at his foggy eyes, and at the mouth that was looming over hers. She was strong, but he was a dead weight.

She closed her eyes, cringing at those lips about to touch hers...

"Luna—tackle!"

Sharp barks filled the room.

"Go get him!"

Robert Morrell backed away from Justine, only to be tackled by Luna. He was soon sprawled on the carpet, with Luna's paws and body over him, his face a mask of terror as she emitted low growls.

Casson strode over to help Justine up. Her eyes were wide as she took in the scene before her, her face blanched, her hair messed up. He gave her a tight hug, then with one hand swept her hair away from her face, something inside him melting as she met his gaze, her eyes glistening with relief and gratitude.

He turned away and, taking his phone out, proceeded to take several photos of Robert with Luna. "These are all I need to prove that you were trespassing." His jaw clenched. He shot an icy glare at Robert. "I hope you have a good lawyer. I'm calling the police."

"No, *pl-please*." Robert attempted to sit up, but promptly lay back as Luna growled and pushed her face into his. "I wasn't going to— Justine, I'm really sorry." Tears glazed his eyes. "I'll be ruined..." he moaned.

"You should have thought about the consequences of your actions," Casson ground out. "Luna—sit back."

In the pathetic state Robert was in, it was unlikely he

would attempt anything. Luna obeyed, but stayed close to Robert, eyeing him warily.

Robert sat up, his head slumping in his hands. "Please..." He lifted his head and looked at Justine and then at Casson. "I promise I'll leave and never come back."

He had a resigned look in his eyes as his gaze returned to Justine, and Casson caught Justine's ambivalent expression. He started to dial for the police, but she placed a hand on his arm.

It took everything he had to put his phone back in his pocket. His eyes bored into Robert's. "You're one lucky snake," he rasped. "I won't call the police, but if you ever try to come near Justine again I'll file charges immediately. Not only for trespassing, but for attempted sexual assault. And, trust me, I'm on the best of terms with Attorney Joseph Brandis." He saw Robert's eyes widen. "Yes, *the* Joseph Brandis."

He watched as Robert slowly got to his feet.

"I don't expect you to drive, in your condition, but I want you out of the cottage first thing in the morning. Give me your car keys. You can walk back; it'll clear your head. Tomorrow you can walk over to my place and get your car—understand?"

Robert nodded.

"I didn't hear you." Casson took a step toward him.

Robert flinched. "Yes, sir." He dug his keys out of his pocket and handed them to Casson.

"Luna, follow him out."

Luna gave a short bark and leapt up to obey.

Robert stopped at the door to look back at Justine. "I'm s-sorry." Shoulders slumped, he left, with Luna and Casson close behind.

Casson waited until Robert was out of sight. He gave a whistle and Luna came racing back, her tail wagging furiously. Casson crouched down and scratched behind her ears. "Good girl," he said, emotion catching in his voice. He reached in his pocket and gave her a treat before opening the door.

Justine was sitting down on the couch. Luna bounded toward her and nuzzled into her hands. She seemed to snap out of her stupor and leaned forward to caress her.

"Thank you, Luna Lu," she murmured.

Casson's heart constricted at her use of Luna's nickname. He watched Justine plant a kiss on Luna's forehead, then bury her face in the soft fur around Luna's neck. When he saw Justine's shoulders shaking, and Luna attempting to lick her cheeks, Casson realized Justine was crying.

In two strides he was crouched next to her and had her in his arms. He let her sob on his shoulder, her chest heaving against him.

"It's over," he said huskily, caressing the back of Justine's head. Then, slowly, his hand slipped to her cheek and he turned her face toward him. "You're safe now."

Justine's breath caught on a sob. "But what if you hadn't shown up with Luna?"

He took her chin in his hand and with his other hand stroked away her tears. "We showed up. That's all that counts."

He looked into her eyes, more gray than blue now. Her lashes were laced with teardrops, and he was overcome with a feeling of tenderness.

"Come and sit here," he murmured, leading her to the love seat. "I'll make you a hot drink."

He took the soft throw that was on the arm of the love seat and draped it around her shoulders. Luna jumped up beside her, but before he could reprimand her, Justine smiled weakly at him.

"Let her," she said. "I don't mind."

Casson strode to the kitchen. He needed a drink himself.

Justine's words played over in his head. *What if you hadn't shown up with Luna?* He didn't want to think of what might have happened. If Robert had— No! He wasn't going there. It would just torment him. It was bad enough that he still had a picture in his mind of Robert bending over Justine, restraining her, about to put his mouth on hers.

Casson felt his stomach turn. He needed something stronger than milk. Brandy, maybe. He found a bottle, poured himself a shot, and put a lesser amount in Justine's milk.

"Okay, Luna—skedaddle." Casson sat next to Justine and handed her the cup of milk.

She took a tentative sip, then wrinkled her nose.

"Drink it all up," he ordered. "It'll help you sleep."

"Casson?" She looked at him with eyes that were starting to flutter in exhaustion. "Can you and Luna stay tonight?" She shuddered. "What if he comes back?"

Casson set down his glass, his heart jolting. He saw the fear in her eyes. "He won't come back," he assured her, squeezing her hand. "But, yes...we'll stay."

CHAPTER SEVEN

JUSTINE COULD BARELY keep her eyes open. She peered at Casson drowsily. "Thank you for staying. You can take the spare room…"

She stood up and headed for the stairs. Luna followed her with Casson close behind. At her doorway, she turned and pointed to the room across from hers. Casson nodded but didn't move.

"Goodnight," she murmured. "Oh, just a minute…"

She entered her room and grabbed the robe that hung behind her door. The one she had given him earlier.

Casson's mouth lifted at one corner. "Thanks. Goodnight, Justine." His hand brushed hers as he took the robe.

She saw something flicker in his eyes and wished she could tell him how much she yearned for his protective arms around her again, but she didn't trust herself in the hazy state she was in. Inviting his embrace could only complicate things.

She needed to sleep. Put the traumatic encounter with Robert out of her mind. She'd have a clearer head in the morning, and maybe then she might be able to make sense of her feelings about Casson. *For* Casson.

She realized he was waiting for her to turn in before heading to his room.

"You might want to close your door, Justine, or you

could find yourself sharing your bed tonight," he said huskily.

Justine felt something electric swirl inside her at the thought of him—

"With Luna."

Justine felt her cheeks burn. She lowered her gaze.

Of course. How ridiculous to think that he would—

"And then I would have to come in and get her off…"

Her head snapped up. There *was* something in his expression. She swayed suddenly and in a moment Casson was there, supporting her. She breathed in his pine scent, felt the strength of his bare arms. Her lips brushed against his neck, and she gasped when he suddenly scooped her up and carried her to her bed.

For timeless moments she felt she was suspended in paradise, with Casson's expression of concern spreading heat to every inch of her body. His eyes were fathomless, heady, and she wished the fog in her head would dissipate so she could—

"You've had a shock tonight, Justine. You need to sleep," he murmured against her ear as he set her down softly on top of the flowered quilt.

Luna nudged her way past him to place her head on the bed and he gave a soft chuckle.

"Don't even think about it, Luna Lu. You're sleeping with *me*, remember? Come on—let's go…"

Justine watched them disappear, and when she heard the click of the door she sighed and turned down the bedcovers. She undressed and slid into bed, too exhausted to find her nightie.

Within moments she felt herself drifting into sleep.

Leaving his door open a crack, Casson switched on a lamp on the night table and Luna settled down on the rug. He undressed and put on the robe, before stretching out on the bed.

He couldn't deny that Justine ignited something within him. Seeing her so vulnerable, unable to defend herself against Robert, had aroused something primeval in him. Maybe if Luna hadn't been there Casson might have given in to his baser instincts and pounded the guy. With no hesitation. But he had to admit he was glad that *that* scenario hadn't taken place. It wouldn't have been pretty.

Tonight had been an ordeal Justine wouldn't soon forget. He found himself wondering what exactly had happened in her relationship with Robert...how long they had been together...if she had enjoyed Robert's touch before their breakup...

Why did it bother him so much?

He hardly knew Justine. Yet when he had held her tight against him it had felt...*timeless*. Things had shifted, whether he liked it or not. She had managed to throw him off course. Made him question his motives. He had to regroup and think of a strategy that would give them both what they wanted. Surely they could find common ground and come to a compromise?

Somehow he didn't think it would be as easy as it sounded.

Listening to the raindrops batting softly against the window, he closed his eyes—although he wasn't sure how much sleep he'd get tonight, listening in case Justine called out...

Justine was awakened by a moan, and then realized it was coming from *her*. For a moment she felt confused, not sure where she was. Her head throbbed. She opened her eyes and instinctively squinted at the clock radio on her night table. *Almost five a.m.* She must have been dreaming, but she had no recollection of any details—and then she remembered the events of the night before. How Robert had come to ask for forgiveness, and how he had lost control. She felt her stomach constrict at the memory of how helpless she had felt, and how Casson and Luna had arrived just in time...

Why had they come to her house anyway?

She had been too shaken even to formulate this question last night, let alone ask Casson.

A warm rush permeated her body as she recalled how he had hugged her so tightly, prepared her a hot drink, scooped her up so effortlessly when she'd felt her knees give out... She had felt as safe as if she were snuggled within a silky cocoon. Even the effects of the brandy hadn't stifled the desire that had overcome her while suspended within those muscled arms. Nor the stab of disappointment when he'd set her down and left moments later.

Don't be silly, she chided herself. What had she *expected* him to do? She didn't know much about Casson Forrester, but one thing she instinctively knew was that he wasn't the type to take advantage of someone in such a compromised state.

And, despite her disappointment that he hadn't gone any further, she was relieved that he hadn't. If Casson took her in his arms again—and she had no reason to believe that he would even do such a thing—she wanted to have all her senses functioning at an optimal level, not depressed by alcohol or trauma...or a headache like the one she was experiencing now. She needed to take something quickly, before it escalated into a migraine.

She slipped out of bed and padded to the door. She started to turn the handle and suddenly froze.

She was naked, and Casson was in the room across from hers.

She shivered and retraced her steps to get her nightie from the plush chair by her bed. She stepped out of her room, glanced toward the room where Casson was sleeping, and tiptoed to the washroom, cringing when she heard the maple floor creaking on the way.

She closed the bathroom door gently and her gaze fell on the tub, still full of water. So much for her plans for a relaxing bath... She was about to drain it, then decided against it. It was still too early to make so much noise.

She found the bottle of pills and took two with water. She needed to have this headache gone before heading into the office. It was still too early to stay up, though. She'd be a wreck if she didn't catch a few more hours of sleep. She paused for a moment.

What day is this? Relief flooded her. *Friday. Her day off this week.*

But what if Robert came back?

She froze, and then reminded herself that Casson was with her. He would make sure Robert didn't come near her...

As she stepped gingerly into the hallway she heard a snuffle and looked across to see Luna's nose edging the door open. Before Justine could even think of dashing into her room Luna had bounded toward her.

Casson soon appeared, his hair disheveled, his robe obviously thrown on without thinking. It was inside out and he had tied the sash loosely. Justine felt her gaze settle on his muscled chest, the fine line of hair swooping downwards, and then she started to shiver...and giggle.

Casson's brow creased. "Do I look that funny?" He looked down at his robe.

Justine shifted. "No, it's your dog; she's tickling my feet."

She tried to back away from Luna, who was intent on giving her feet and calves a thorough licking. And then she realized how skimpy her nightie was. It was barely mid-thigh, with spaghetti straps and an eyelet trim around the sweetheart neckline. It wasn't transparent, but the fine cotton draped over her breasts accentuated their peaks.

Mortified, she started to edge toward her room, all too aware of Casson's gaze. Luna began to follow her.

"Luna—*stay*. Are you okay, Justine?"

His husky tone made her quiver inside, and she prayed her legs wouldn't buckle under her again. Although Casson was trying not to make it obvious, his eyes were flickering over her body, from her neck and shoulders all the way down to her thighs and calves. And then back to her eyes.

It couldn't have taken more than a couple of seconds, but to Justine it had felt like an eternity.

"Oh… Other than a dull headache, I'm okay." She crossed her arms over her chest. *"Stop, Luna."*

The dog had inched forward to start licking her feet again. Her tone had no effect on Luna, but in a flash, Casson was striding toward them both.

"Luna—stop." His voice was deep, authoritative, and he didn't have to put a hand on his dog. Luna snapped to attention and immediately assumed a sitting position, her chocolate-colored eyes never wavering from her master.

"You have to show who's Alpha," he said in a soft tone to Justine, his tawny eyes blazing, and she felt like melting on the spot.

CHAPTER EIGHT

IF JUSTINE DIDN'T soon go into her room he didn't think he could continue to maintain his composure. Standing there in that...that kerchief-sized nightie, she had *no* idea how she was affecting him.

His heartbeat had accelerated with every shift of his gaze. It had started with her tousled hair, sleep-flushed face and the graceful curve of her neck, then revved up as it descended to the compact but curvy areas covered by her nightie. Areas that he could only imagine cupping, squeezing, *kissing.* And the sight of those shapely tanned legs, and the way Justine had wriggled them away from Luna's attempts to lick them, had almost done him in.

Casson had had several relationships—all short-term, since he was determined to focus on building his business— but none of them had caused him the inner commotion he was feeling right now. He practically vibrated with the primeval impulse to gather his woman in his arms, lay her down and make her yield to him. *Willingly.*

But she was not his woman.

He felt a jab in his gut. He had to put a stop to this.

"I don't know about you, but I doubt I'll be able to fall back to sleep." He tried to keep his gaze fixed on her eyes and not her body. "How about I make some coffee?"

"Sure," she said lightly, letting her arms drop to her side. "I'll just have a quick shower."

She pivoted slightly and rushed into her room—but not before Casson had caught a glimpse of her bareness under the nightie. He let out a long, long breath and went to get dressed.

His mission was getting harder by the minute.

When Casson went downstairs, he turned on the light switch in the kitchen and put on the coffee maker. While the coffee was brewing he took Luna outside. It was still dusky, and the grass was wet. He scowled when he saw Robert's car. Robert would no doubt be sleeping for a while yet.

Out of the corner of his eye he saw Justine's turquoise retro-style bicycle. An idea popped into his head and he grinned. In less than a minute he had the bike and Luna in Robert's car and was on his way to giving the creep his early-morning wake-up call.

No point making Robert walk back to his place. No, *he* would take his car to him, and personally see Robert off his property. The bike-ride back to Justine's would take no time at all, and Luna would enjoy the run.

Justine towel-dried her hair and went downstairs. Casson was pouring coffee into two mugs. He looked up and smiled. Justine's pulse quickened. He looked so at home, standing behind the island…

"Let's take our coffee into the living room," he suggested. "We can catch the sun rise over the bay."

Justine's heart thrummed. The way he said it made it sound so *intimate*. She felt her cheeks burn as she started to follow him, and then, remembering Robert, walked tentatively toward the window and glanced out.

"He's gone," Casson said gruffly, "and he won't be back. I promise you."

Justine nodded, picked up her mug, and headed to the living room. She didn't need the details.

She started as Luna bounded in front of her and leapt onto the couch next to Casson. Seeing that he was about to order her off, Justine quickly said, "She's fine. She deserves special treatment after saving me last night."

She sat down on the love seat and bit her lip, the memory of Robert's face looming over hers making her stomach twinge.

Casson picked up his mug and strode to the fireplace. He stared at the painting while drinking his coffee. "I love this one," he murmured. *"Mirror Lake."*

"Oh? You're familiar with Franklin Carmichael's work?"

Casson smiled at her as if what she'd asked were amusing. "His and his buddy A. J.'s—and the rest of the Group of Seven."

Justine's eyes widened. "A. J. *Casson*," she said slowly. "So, what *is* the connection between your name and his?"

"My grandparents lived on the same street as the Cassons in north Toronto. They became friends. They loved his work, and by the time they passed away, they had quite a collection. My mother inherited it. She *loved* the Group of Seven. Casson and Carmichael were her favorites. And I inherited everything when she died."

Something flickered in his eyes and his brows furrowed. Justine wondered if it was sadness at his mother's passing, but she didn't have the courage to ask.

"Which is why," he said lightly, "she named me and my brother after them."

"Casson and Carmichael?"

"Yes and no. Casson and Franklin." He set down his mug on the mantel. He turned away to face the painting squarely. "Franklin was my little brother."

Justine caught the slight waver in Casson's voice. *Was*, he'd said. She felt her heart sinking.

"My father bought a limited edition print of *Mirror Lake* for my mom when Franklin was born. After he died they donated it to the Hospital for Sick Children in Toronto."

CHAPTER NINE

CASSON TOOK A deep breath and turned to face Justine. She had a stricken look, and her eyes had misted.

"I'm sorry," he said, returning to sit at one corner of the couch—the corner nearest the love seat where Justine was sitting. "It wasn't my intention to bring up my past." He set down his mug and glanced back at the painting. "It's just that that particular painting brings back so many memories."

And pain.

"Please, don't apologize," Justine said, her voice husky. "I'm very sorry for your loss. I—I can't even imagine…"

Casson felt a warm rush shoot through him as he met Justine's gaze. Her blue-gray eyes had cleared and were as luminous as the lake in the painting. He didn't make a habit of bringing up the death of his brother, but something in her expression made him willing to talk about it.

"It happened a long time ago," he said, patting Luna absentmindedly. "I was ten. Frankie was seven." He paused, his mind racing back to his childhood. "They found out he had a rare form of leukemia when he was six. He was rushed to SickKids and they started treatment immediately. Mom stayed with him there, and Dad stayed home with me."

Casson looked out beyond the bay window. The sky was

beginning to lighten, with intersecting bands of pink and pale blue. His stomach contracted at the memories of that year: his father becoming increasingly moody and agitated; the empty house when he got home from school; no welcoming hug and snacks from his mother; no little brother to play hockey or baseball with; his bad dreams and the nagging worry that Franklin would die…

"That must have been so tough…"

Casson's gaze shifted back to Justine. He breathed deeply. "What was really tough was visiting him at Sick-Kids. Seeing him with no hair, covered with bruises. Seeing him attached to tubes and hooked up to machines." His jaw clenched. "He was so small." Casson shook his head and averted his gaze. "Sorry. Didn't mean to put a damper on things…"

"No worries," Justine said, placing a hand on his arm.

His head jerked at the unexpected touch and his heart did a flip at the genuine caring in her voice. And in her gaze. She looked so sweet and natural, with her hair in that ponytail. Cheeks that looked as soft and rosy as a peach. Eyes that he could swim in.

He found himself drawing closer. She blinked but didn't move away.

He wanted nothing more than to kiss her. And, he could be wrong, but he thought she looked like she wouldn't have a problem with it. But he had a feeling that kissing Justine Winter now would not be wise. He had tasted those lips before, and he knew that once their lips touched it would be sheer torture to break away.

"I have to go," he murmured, looking deep into her eyes.

He wished he didn't, but he had a few things to do before his guests arrived. He saw the warmth in her eyes fading, and she withdrew her hand from his arm. He stood up and Luna, who had fallen asleep, stirred and jumped

off the couch. Casson went back into the kitchen to get his
hoodie and his keys, and then, nodding to Justine, headed
for the door.

"Casson…"

He stopped and turned around. She was steps away,
the fingers of both hands tucked into the front pockets of
her Capri pants. "Thank you for…for staying the night."

He smiled. "My pleasure."

He opened the door and Luna bounded off.

Justine watched Casson and Luna get into Casson's truck,
then returned to the kitchen, her thoughts turning to Robert. She had been such a bleeding heart, letting him in.
But he had looked so tormented…and his apology *had*
seemed genuine.

It was now obvious that in the time since she had resigned Robert had come apart. She had never known him
to drink to excess, but last night he had revealed a different side to him. His alcohol-tinged breath, his unrelenting
hold on her… She felt a shudder go through her again at
the thought of what might have happened.

His divorce must have been harder for him to deal with
than she had realized. Perhaps losing his wife and trying
to adjust to all the changes afterward had been too much,
inducing him to seek solace in the bottle.

Justine sighed. Robert was a fine lawyer, but even the
finest lawyers were not immune to emotional collapse.

She inhaled and exhaled deeply. Could she believe he
meant what he had said? He would leave and never come
back? Justine had caught so many emotions in that look
he'd given her at the door: regret, shame, embarrassment,
despair. And fear. Most likely fear that Casson would press
charges. Which meant that Robert wasn't so far gone that
he no longer cared about his work, his livelihood.

Maybe what had happened last night would be his

wake-up call and he'd get help before his life spun completely out of control.

Justine bit on her lower lip. Countless times after she had resigned she'd wished she had explained to Robert how devastated she had felt at his infidelity. Betrayed. *Used*. How she had cried herself to sleep for days. How she'd half hoped he'd come after her and beg for forgiveness. And how, in her darkest moments, she'd thought that when he did she'd forgive him and they would start fresh...

But a month had passed, and then two more after her return to Winter's Haven, and Robert had never once attempted to call, let alone ask for forgiveness.

Seeing him last night had been *her* wake-up call, and she realized that deep down she had never known the true Robert. How could she ever put her trust in him again? No, she had no illusions about starting over with him, or of him being any part of her 'happy-ever-after.' And after the merry-go-round of emotions she had been through she wasn't ready to trust anyone else...

Justine started as she heard a knock on the door. Her stomach gave a lurch, and then she saw that it was Casson. Relieved, she opened the door.

"Luna sent me back," he said, a twinkle in his eye. "She'd like you to join us."

Her eyebrows lifted and she just blinked at him wordlessly.

"I need to drive to Huntsville to pick up a couple of things. Why don't you join me? *Us*. Luna says she's getting bored with my company. And with Spanish guitar music," he added with a deep chuckle. "Besides...you might just discover I'm not the man you think I am."

Justine's pulse had quickened at Casson's very first words. She was tempted to accept his offer, to let a fresh country drive distract her from what had happened with Robert, but... But was it wise to spend time with Casson, given the reason why he was here at Winter's Haven in the first place?

And given her undeniable attraction to him?

Luna barked from the open window and she couldn't help her mouth quirking into a smile.

Although she was well aware that her heart and mind were battling over her decision, she threw caution to the wind. "Tell Luna I'm in," she said, wondering why she sounded so breathless. "I'll just grab my handbag."

Casson had his window partially rolled down. Every once in a while he snuck a glance in Justine's direction. Luna had graciously given up her spot for her and was now in the back seat, head uplifted to enjoy the breeze. Justine alternated between looking out at the scenery and resting back against the leather headrest, her eyes closed and her lips curved in a relaxed smile.

His intuition had been right. She needed to get away from Winter's Haven—even if only for a few hours.

He was all too aware of her proximity: the curve of her peachy cheekbones tapering to her glossy lips, her fitted pink T-shirt rising and falling with her every breath, and her shapely legs so tantalizingly close to his own that every time he manipulated the stick-shift his hand came close to skimming her thigh. He didn't know what was louder: the thrum of the engine or the thrum in his chest.

Casson had to force himself to concentrate on the road several times, and after a stretch on the main highway southbound to Toronto, took Exit Ramp 213 toward Highway 141 to Huntsville. He felt a sense of contentedness with Justine sitting so close to him, even without music or conversation.

This highway had far less traffic, and Casson maneuvered the truck deftly through the winding turns and up and down the hillsides.

"I'll get us some breakfast when we get to my place."

"Your place?" Justine turned her head sharply to stare at him.

"We won't be long," he said casually. "I just have to pick up a couple of things."

He turned on a radio channel of classic rock tunes.

"Are you okay with this?"

At her nod, he cranked it up a bit and, grinning, pressed on the gas pedal.

CHAPTER TEN

JUSTINE'S PULSE POUNDED along with the bass of the stereo. She had enjoyed the quiet, but now welcomed the distraction of music and the kind of songs that she would ordinarily sing to while driving. Her feet and fingers tapped along automatically, and she had to consciously restrain herself from swaying to the music.

She stole a glance at him. The sun beaming down through the windshield and into his truck highlighted the soft golden-brown fuzz on Casson's forearms. His fingers tapped a beat on the steering wheel, and as the muscles in his arms flexed Justine's pulse quickened at the memory of those strong hands and arms carrying her to bed…

Justine was familiar with this route from when she had business in Huntsville, and always loved the views of the myriad sparkling lakes in the Muskokas, but somehow on this trip she barely noticed Lake Rosseau, Horseshoe Lake and Skeleton Lake, among others, and was surprised when Casson turned off the radio to announce that they were coming to Fairy Lake.

Soon Casson was driving through a winding stretch of woodland, with pinpoints of light sparkling through crowns of maple, birch, and pine. Eventually he turned into a long, paved driveway that she thought would never end. But when it finally did Justine couldn't help letting out a gasp. The house—no, *the estate*—was massive, with four dormer windows on the upper level, a wrap-around deck that seemed to equal the circumference of a football field, a four-car garage, and a view that could only be described as heaven, with Fairy Lake a brilliant blue reflecting millions of sun specks.

Justine was still gawking when Casson held the door open for her, and she climbed out, with Luna bounding after her. Two vehicles were sparkling in the sun: the silver-green Mustang convertible she had first seen Casson drive, and a heart-stopping red Ferrari Testarossa.

So Casson Forrester liked his toys. And flaunting his success... But did anyone really need four vehicles? She wondered what luxury model was behind the fourth door...

"Welcome to my place," he said.

Justine's eyes widened as she entered the marble foyer that was connected to a massive living area with gleaming maple hardwood floors and floor-to-ceiling windows. The Muskoka stone fireplace was the focal point, around which several luxurious leather couches were arranged. Hanging on the wall above the polished mantel were two paintings, and as Justine approached she saw that she had guessed correctly: one was a Casson and the other a Carmichael. Both depicted stunning Georgian Bay views. On the mantel itself there was a small baseball cap and a miniature red racing car.

So he was sentimental, too.

"Things from your childhood that you couldn't bear to part with?" she said casually.

She turned to see something flicker across Casson's face.

He stared at her wordlessly for a moment. "Those belonged to Franklin," he said finally, his voice breaking at the end.

He picked up the car and Justine bit her lip as she watched him.

"I came back to get his cap; I always take it with me when I return to Georgian Bay—especially when I go fishing... As for the car..." He picked it up and made the wheels spin. "Frankie loved his toy cars, and this was his favorite. Said he was going to get one when he grew up." His jaw muscles flicked. "Well, I got one for him..."

Justine felt something deflate inside her and her heart felt heavy. He hadn't bought the Ferrari as a status symbol, but as a way of honoring his brother's dream. Guilt washed over her. She wanted to apologize to Casson for being so judgmental, and then she remembered she hadn't voiced her feelings about him flaunting his success.

She gulped. Maybe she shouldn't let her feelings about Robert cloud her judgment about Casson. Maybe she should stop lumping them into the same box...

"Okay..." Casson pressed his lips together. "Let's lighten things up. How about I make you a light and fluffy omelet?"

His mouth curved into a smile and he motioned for her to continue into the kitchen at the other end of the room.

Justine nodded, and was instantly wowed by the chef's kitchen with its stunning curved granite island the color of sapphire, plush stools, and at least double the amount of cupboards she had, with a sturdy harvest table in the dining area that she was sure could comfortably sit twenty.

She sat on a stool and watched Casson in T-shirt and jeans, the muscles in his arms flexing with his every movement. Her heartbeat did an erratic dance...

Had he just said something to her? She stared at him blankly.

His mouth quirked, an eyebrow lifted, and he waved the spatula in his hand. "Wanna get the toast?"

"Sure."

Avoiding his gaze, she slid off the stool and put the toast on. *He must lift weights*, she thought, edging a glance at his arms as he flipped the omelets. *Or else he regularly lifts two-by-fours at his hardware stores.*

The sudden image of him wearing nothing but jeans and steel-toed boots, pumping a stack of wood, made her insides blaze.

Casson slid the omelets onto two plates, and Justine buttered the toast. He poured coffee into two mugs and sat down next to her.

"Bon appétit," he said, his eyes crinkling at her as he tasted the omelet. "Not bad."

"Delicious," she agreed.

"I'll believe it after you've had a bite." He looked pointedly at her untouched portion.

Justine could have kicked herself. *Good one.*

"I mean it *looks* delicious," she said lightly, gazing down at her plate.

His leg was almost touching hers, and she tried not to think about it, or about the way his jeans fit, and the way his arms looked, so smooth and bronzed.

Like a sculpture that you just wanted to stroke...

"More coffee?" His voice melded with her thoughts.

She turned her head, her stomach tightening at how close his face was to hers. His eyes were like shiny chestnuts, with flecks of gold around his dark pupils.

"Yes...please..." she managed, and then concentrated on eating her omelet.

Casson waited until Justine was finished and then offered to take her on a tour of the rest of the house. He started with his study on the main floor, and he could see that she loved it, unconsciously stroking the gleaming surface of his mahogany desk and pausing to peruse the volumes in his floor-to-ceiling bookshelves.

She turned to fix him with a crooked smile. "Is this a lending library?" she said, a teasing glint in her eye.

"Only for—"

"Oh!"

She had caught sight of the mahogany spiral staircase in one corner.

"That leads up to my bedroom," he said, as casually as he could. "When I can't sleep I like to spend time down here with my literary friends." He gestured toward the bookshelves.

Casson had a sudden vision of Justine in a silk robe, reading a book in his Italian leather recliner and then gliding up the staircase...

He gave himself a mental shake and suggested they go to the upper level. He ordered Luna to stay, and then walked out of the room and up another flight of stairs. He led Justine through two luxurious guest bedrooms, and then the guest bathroom, repressing his desire to smile as her eyes popped at the sight of the transparent walls of his shower stall, with its back wall designed to be the center part of a larger window overlooking the lake and hills. The enormous claw-foot bathtub looked out at the same view.

He proceeded toward the huge double doors leading to his bedroom. "Don't worry," he said in a conspiratorial tone, "I don't have any nefarious intentions. It's just that this room has one of the best views of the lake."

If Justine had been impressed by his study and bathroom, he could tell she was blown away by his bedroom, with its rustic four-poster king-sized bed, cottage-style dressers, pine-green and forest-themed linens, the huge walk-in closet, massive custom-built windows and a set of sliding doors. They opened on to a semi-circular deck that spanned from one end of the house to the other, with a hot tub in one corner and a screened-in sunroom with lounging chairs and a bar. And a pull-out couch.

"For those summer nights when I'd rather sleep outside," he murmured.

"Oh…my…" Justine looked out at the sparkling waters of Fairy Lake. "I… I have never seen anything like this. You must hate to leave this place," she said, glancing back at him.

He gave her a measured look. "It serves its purpose…" He hesitated, and wondered if he should tell Justine that, much as he loved his home, he felt that something was missing. Or maybe a special *someone*. But, no, there was no reason for him to go there.

He had learned to keep his thoughts and feelings in check since his childhood. Maybe he even shied away from serious relationships, from love, because of the trauma of losing his brother, and in some ways his parents as well.

Why would he do anything differently now and suddenly open up to Justine? Reveal all his thoughts, hopes and dreams to her? Share the real reason for his resort venture? Although he may have cracked a bit, telling her about Franklin's cap and toy car, he had no intention of ending up like Humpty Dumpty.

She walked to the edge of the deck and, looking over, gasped again.

He caught up to her and followed her gaze to the ground level, beyond the salmon-colored interlocking patio to a huge kidney-shaped swimming pool. Around it the lush landscaped lawns and gardens featured flowering bushes, working fountains and lounging areas. A white gazebo stood close to the waterfront, along with a half-dozen Muskoka chairs around a fire-pit.

A man trimming the hedges by the gazebo looked up at them and waved before leaving the grounds.

"That's Phillip, my gardener, groundskeeper, car maintenance man and all-around good guy," he said, waving back. "I lucked out when I found him. And his wife Sue.

She does the housekeeping and provides me with an occasional dinner when I don't want to batch it," he said, grinning at Justine.

"With a place like this, I'm surprised you have to *batch it* at all…"

The words were out before Justine could stop them. She felt her face igniting at her implication that women would seek his company only for his material possessions.

"I'm sorry. I didn't mean to imply—"

"That the ladies are all over me just for my hot tub and my pool?" He laughed. "I generally don't have time to do a lot of *that kind* of entertaining. My business ventures keep my hands tied. Although…" he raised his eyebrows and his tawny eyes pierced hers "… I occasionally *un*tie my hands…"

Justine's heart began to palpitate and she looked away. How could she even begin to respond? And what was this sharp twist in her stomach at the thought of his hands on another woman? In the hot tub and sharing his bed?

She felt pinned under Casson's gaze. Sensed he had moved closer. She couldn't help but breathe in his fresh pine scent, and when she tentatively looked back at him his lips were suddenly on hers, his arms bracing her against him. She gasped, and felt all her muscles slacken. Closing her eyes, she surrendered to the desire pumping through her. Pressing her hand against the back of his head, she responded hungrily as he deepened his kiss.

And then she felt him break away from her, so suddenly that she almost lost her balance.

"I'm sorry," he said gruffly. "I didn't intend to—"

"Neither did I," she said in a rush. "We should go in…"

When they were back on the main floor, Casson strode over to the fireplace and took Franklin's cap.

"This is what I came for," he said lightly. "And the Mustang. I won't be needing my truck for a while."

Justine was glad Casson had slipped in a Spanish guitar CD. Luna didn't seem to mind it at all, and had fallen asleep in the back seat. Justine closed her eyes, wishing she could fall asleep herself. It was so awkward now... especially in the more intimate confines of his Mustang.

She looked out her window, forcing herself not to steal glances at Casson. When he swerved slightly to avoid a porcupine she found herself pinned against him for a moment, and her heart flipped at the proximity of his firm lips...

Her thoughts tumbled about during the rest of the drive. And when Casson switched the music to Pachelbel's *Canon in D*, Justine felt herself swept up by the sensual strains of the violins and *basso continuo*, closing her eyes as the wind ruffled her hair.

As the Mustang started to slow down before turning in to Winter's Haven, Justine realized she must have dozed off. She asked Casson to drop her off by the office, and when he did, scrambled out of the car before he could get the door for her. He shrugged and got back into his seat.

"Thanks for the drive and breakfast." She managed a weak smile.

Two teenagers from one of the cottages rode by on their bikes and waved.

"Hey, mister," one called out, coming to a stop not far from the Mustang, its silver-green exterior and chrome sparkling in the sun. "She's a beauty!"

Casson removed his sunglasses and met Justine's gaze. "She sure is," he said softly. And then he turned and gave a thumbs-up to the boy.

Something swirled inside of Justine and spiraled up to her chest.

Had he just paid her a compliment? Or was the sunlight addling her brain?

Casson's car thrummed as he started the ignition, made a sleek turn and drove away. When he was out of sight Justine walked back to her place, needing the time to replay the events of the morning with Casson. She caught sight of the coffee mugs, and as she filled the sink with soapy water Justine felt herself burning with curiosity about his guests.

Well, she'd find out soon enough.

She dried her hands and walked over to look at *Mirror Lake*. She had always loved it, with its undulating hills, their stunning colors reflected in the glassy surface of the lake. Hues of green, purple, gold, red and blue, blending in sensuous curves and prismatic streaks across the hilly landscape. A feast for the eyes.

Looking at it now, she felt a lump in her throat, thinking of Casson's brother Franklin suffering at such a young age, and of his family, suffering along with him, all in their different ways. *Poor Casson.* He had been nine when Franklin was diagnosed and ten when Franklin died. *Ten!* Her heart ached when she thought of how Franklin's passing must have changed their lives. And how Casson was still honoring his brother's memory all these years later.

She had witnessed a hint of Casson's vulnerability when he'd told her about Franklin's cap and toy car, and she felt renewed remorse at her earlier thought that he had bought the Ferrari as a status symbol. Maybe Casson had been right… *He wasn't the man she'd thought he was.*

Justine had sensed that Casson was unwilling to open up any further and share more details of his past to her. *And why should he?* She didn't trust his motives when it came to Winter's Haven—and Casson was well aware of this—so why should *he* trust *her?*

She tore her gaze away from the painting and went upstairs.

By the time she'd got out of the shower and let her hair dry naturally outside on the deck, it was almost noon. She biked over to the office and while she waited for Mandy to finish a call, quickly checked the register and saw the names "Ronnie and Andy Walsh" listed as Casson's guests.

Mandy got off the phone, and Justine briefly told her what had happened with Robert.

Mandy's mouth dropped. "Thank goodness Casson came to your rescue," she said, her eyes wide. "And Luna! Talk about great timing!" She gave Justine a tight hug. "I'm so glad you're okay."

Mandy shot a glance toward the diner entrance.

"Your hero is in there," she said in a conspiratorial tone. "Having lunch with his guests. Oh, here they come!"

Justine looked casually over her shoulder. Casson was laughing, with a guest on either side of him. Not two brothers, as she had expected. A good-looking woman and a boy of no more than five or six. *'Ronnie' was a woman.* And the boy—it had to be her son—must be Andy.

The three of them looked like a family. As they approached, Justine tried to ignore the sinking sensation in the pit of her stomach, and she hoped her smile didn't appear as fake as it felt.

CHAPTER ELEVEN

CASSON HAD HIS arm around Ronnie's shoulder and was holding Andy's hand. Ronnie was a petite brunette, with a perky haircut that emphasized the fine bone structure of her face. She wore faded jeans and a retro-style cotton top with short gathered sleeves and a splashy flower print. Her running shoes were lime-green.

Tiny but not afraid to roar, Justine couldn't help thinking, unable to prevent a blistering sensation from coursing through her. *Was it jealousy?* She wished she could hide, but it was too late.

The little boy—Andy—was small, too. He wore a Toronto Blue Jays cap and a red and white T-shirt and jean shorts, and his skinny little legs moved quickly to keep up with the adults. He kept smiling up at Casson, and occasionally tugged at his hand.

Justine couldn't make out their conversation, but as they approached heard Andy saying something about catching a big fish. Casson threw back his head and let out a deep laugh, and Justine felt her stomach twist at the intimate scene the trio presented.

Mandy went back to her desk to accept a delivery, and Justine stood there awkwardly, knowing how strange it would look if she suddenly left.

She wished she had never decided to come to the diner for lunch. Somehow, her appetite was gone.

Casson was still smiling when they reached Justine, but his arm was no longer encircling Ronnie's waist. "Let me introduce my guests," he said. "Justine Winter, this is Veronica Walsh and her little fisherman Andy." He grinned down at the boy. "He says he wants to catch a *big* one while he's here."

Although he was pale, with dark shadows under his green eyes, Andy's elfin grin made his freckled face light up.

"Nice to meet you, Andy." She held out her hand and was pleased when he shook it and nodded.

"Nice to meet you too, Miss Winter," he said, looking up directly at her.

Justine smiled, impressed at his communication skills. She turned to Veronica. "I hope you enjoy Winter's Haven, Veronica."

What else could she say?

Veronica held out her hand, and for a tiny person her handshake was surprisingly strong.

"Please call me Ronnie." She smiled, her eyes crinkling warmly. "Everyone does—except for Casson, when he wants to be formal. Or when he's scolding me." She laughed. "You have a lovely place, Justine," she said, waving her arm in an arc. "Casson was right. He told me it was enchanting."

Justine avoided looking at Casson.

Of course he finds it enchanting; that's why he wants to take it off my hands.

Justine hoped her cynicism didn't show through in her smile, which was starting to waver.

"Hey, Cass," Andy pulled at Casson's hand. "When can we go fishing?"

Cass? It was obvious this was no ordinary relationship

for Andy to be using this nickname. Justine watched as Casson's eyes lit up again as he looked down on the boy.

"You've just barely arrived and you're hounding me already!" He chuckled. "Speaking of hounds—there's one waiting for you in Cottage Number One."

"Luna!" Andy tugged at Casson's hand. "Let's go, Cass. I can't wait to play tag with her! We can go fishing after that!"

"Bossy little thing, eh?" Casson's smile took in Ronnie and Justine. "I have a feeling I won't have a moment's peace while this munchkin is here. Hey, there, Andrew Michael Walsh." He feigned a stern glance at Andy. "If you pull my hand any harder it'll fall off—and I won't be able to fish with one hand."

Andy giggled. "Then we'll have to take *her* with us, since Mommy doesn't like to fish."

Justine flushed, not knowing what to say.

Ronnie burst out laughing. "Andy's right. All I want to catch while I'm here are some rays." She looked up at Casson and winked. "We'll settle into the cottage while you go and get Luna's food at the vet's." She turned to Justine. "Nice meeting you!"

As Ronnie's car turned the bend and disappeared Justine's mind launched a battle inside her brain's hemispheres of reason and judgment. Casson obviously had no scruples—kissing *her* during the storm, and again at his house, when all along he had a significant other.

How uncouth of him! Despicable, really, when the relationship involved a child.

A child who obviously adored him.

The more she thought about it, the more her stomach twisted at the thought of Casson deceiving Ronnie and continuing to allow Andy to become attached to him. If he and Ronnie broke up Andy would undoubtedly be heartbroken. Casson's underhandedness, his toying with the emotions of both Ronnie and Andy, was reprehensible.

He was toying with you, too...

She cringed.

And you enjoyed his charms...

"Are you all right?" Casson had turned to face her. "You looked like you were in pain..."

Justine caught a whiff of his cologne, its now familiar woodsy scent. She so wanted to give him a blast for being a cad, but the concern in his voice made her hesitate. And then she recalled the look of trust in Andy's eyes, the hero-worship...

"I'm fine," she heard herself reply coldly as his hand cupped her under one elbow.

She stepped away from him, trying not to make it obvious that she didn't welcome his touch. She swayed slightly and he reached out again. The pressure of both his hands on her bare arms sent a shiver rippling through her.

"Maybe the heat is getting to you," he murmured. "I'll grab you a bottle of water from the diner—"

"I can get it myself," she said curtly, and then, more politely, "Thanks."

Casson let go of her, gazed at her for what seemed longer than necessary, and then strode to his car. Afraid that he would turn around and see the conflicting emotions on her face, she fled into the office.

Mandy was preoccupied with a jam in the printer, and Justine was glad she had a few moments to compose herself.

She glanced out the window and watched Casson drive off, an ache blooming in her chest. Ronnie and Andy were only here for the weekend, but it sounded like they were going to have a great time with Casson.

"I'm not surprised he's taken," Mandy murmured. "But they're not engaged; I didn't notice any ring on her finger." She came around from the printer to look at Justine thoughtfully. "Hey, girl, this is your day off. Get thee to a beach. I hear there's a great one right here at Winter's Haven. And after all you've been through you need some serious relaxation."

Justine avoided looking directly at Mandy. The last thing she wanted was to show how emotional she felt, especially with some of the other cottagers now coming out of the diner.

"Yeah, I think I'll do just that," she said lightly.

Leaving the office, Justine got on her bike and pedaled furiously back to her place. Sweating, she peeled off her clothes in the upstairs washroom and got into a one-piece coral swimsuit. After slapping on some sunscreen, she grabbed a beach bag and threw in a book, an oversized beach towel, a small cushion and a bottle of water. With sunglasses and a floppy beach hat, she headed to the beach.

With any luck the cool waters of the bay would extinguish the blaze consuming her, body and soul.

On his drive to and from the town, Casson couldn't stop thinking about Justine's aloofness. And the way she had recoiled from his touch. If he had imagined it the first time he had extended his hand to her elbow, her reaction the second time around had left no doubt in his mind about her feelings. Yet she hadn't resisted his touch during the storm and after he'd kicked Robert out of her house last night...or this morning at his place...

Something twisted in his gut. Maybe Justine was only just beginning to process the traumatic impact of Robert's intrusion and attempted sexual assault. And was transferring her feelings of fear and distrust to *him*.

He had felt his own stomach muscles tighten when he'd gone to return Robert's car to him earlier. Robert had come to the door, his face pale and his eyes puffy, with dark shadows. After ascertaining that he was sober, Casson had handed him his car keys with a terse reminder of the promise he had made to Justine. Robert had apologized for the trouble he had caused, and with a look of resignation driven away.

Casson frowned. Justine hadn't trusted him to begin with. How on earth could he make that change now?

He strode into the cottage and plunked Luna's bag of dog kibble in a corner of the entrance. He couldn't help grinning at the sight of Andy and Luna in the living room, Andy giggling every time Luna licked his cheek. He ducked and feigned trying to escape, Luna skittering around him.

While Ronnie got Andy settled upstairs in the loft Casson prepared a couple of wine spritzers and brought them into the living room. His thoughts turned to Justine again. The feel of her in his arms... The look of her in her nightie...and in the turquoise swimsuit he had first seen her in.

He felt a swirl of heat radiate throughout his body and took a long gulp of his spritzer. He wanted her property, yes—but, like it or not, his body was telling him that he wanted *her*, too. There was absolutely no chance of *that* happening, though. He couldn't imagine that Justine would allow herself to trust him enough to share his bed.

Despite his attraction to Justine—no, he had to be honest with himself and call it what it was: his almost constant torturous desire that was aching for release—he had business to take care of. Contractors waiting. Timelines and deadlines. He had to find the opportune moment to bring up the property issue, and to convince Justine to sell.

If things went his way, he anticipated sealing the deal by the end of his "holiday" at Winter's Haven. But for now his plan would have to wait, until after Ronnie and Andy left.

While he waited for Ronnie to join him he tried to justify to himself why he couldn't tell Justine the real reason he wanted the Russell properties and Winter's Haven.

Maybe because that would make him vulnerable... And maybe he wasn't quite ready to reveal that side of himself to her...yet.

CHAPTER TWELVE

JUSTINE COULDN'T STOP thinking about Casson's guests.
They were obviously very good friends, judging from his
use of their nicknames. Veronica—Justine couldn't bring
herself to call her Ronnie—was very pretty, confident,
and seemed the type to say what she wanted to say. And
from what she could see Andy was a polite little boy who
had been taught good social skills.

It was obvious he loved "Cass." And for him to have developed a relationship with Casson they must have spent a
lot of time together. Which meant Casson had spent even
more time with his mother.

Justine felt something jab at her insides. She stopped
and brushed the remnants of beach sand from her legs.
What did she expect? That a gorgeous, successful entrepreneur like Casson Forrester would be unattached? *And
why should she care?*

His intentions were not on par with hers when it came to
Winter's Haven. She shouldn't even be trusting him, given
his manipulative way of getting himself onto her property.
And after Robert's infidelity she'd vowed she wouldn't
offer her trust to any other man so easily in the future.

*But you trusted Casson to stay over in case Robert
came back...*

Yes, she had. And he had comforted her too. Made her

breakfast at his place. *Kissed her.* And while he had been doing all those things Justine had forgotten what Casson was really here for.

Justine reached the house and went up to shower. She had spent more time than she'd originally planned on the beach. After a refreshing swim in the bay she had dried off on the chaise lounge and drifted to sleep, listening to the waves lap against the shore.

Now she towel-dried her hair and slipped into a pair of white denim shorts and a flowered halter top. She went down to the kitchen and grabbed a lemon-lime soda, and decided to make herself a tuna and tomato sandwich on walnut bread.

She checked the clock. She had a feeling it was going to be a long evening and night.

After finishing her sandwich, she went out to water her vegetable and flower gardens with the hose that was connected to a pump in the bay. Ordinarily she loved doing this—it was part of her morning and evening routine—but tonight she did it perfunctorily, lost in her thoughts.

A sudden bark startled her and she turned. Casson jumped back and Luna skittered away, barking at the offending spray of water. Justine dropped the hose and stared at Casson helplessly as he pinched his drenched shirt and pulled it away from his chest.

"I'm *so* sorry," she told him.

Luna came bounding toward her, now that she had relinquished her water weapon, and Justine patted her and glanced edgewise at Casson.

"I can get you a towel…" she offered contritely.

"If you insist," he drawled. "The funny thing is, I was coming to see you about getting a couple of extra towels for Ronnie and Andy. I was supposed to go back to the office earlier for some, but Ronnie and I got to talking, and then once Andy had a rest we spent the rest of the afternoon on the beach. It wasn't until after supper that I realized I had forgotten. By that time the office was closed."

His eyes narrowed as he spoke, and Justine could feel his gaze lowering over her body.

"I see that you were out on the beach as well," he said, starting to undo the top buttons of his shirt.

Justine frowned. *How would he know that?*

"You're more tanned than the last time I saw you," he said dryly.

He finished undoing all his buttons and flapped the wet panels of his shirt away from his body. Justine's gaze slid down and she caught a glimpse of his chest and sculpted abs. She felt her pulse accelerating, sparking an invigorating trail along her nerve-endings. When her glance moved upward she was mortified to find that Casson was well aware of her visual exploration.

"Yes, it was a perfect day to relax on the beach," she said, a little too brightly. "I hope your guests enjoyed it also?"

"Oh, they did. Andy and Luna had fun kicking a ball around before splashing about in the bay, and Ronnie enjoyed lying in the sun before her swim."

Justine wished he hadn't gone into detail. She didn't *want* to picture Veronica lying there in a bikini while Casson spread sunscreen all over her. But her mind had a will of its own, and she began to think of what he and Veronica might have been doing while Andy and Luna were playing…

Kissing, maybe. She'd have run her hands over the soft fuzz on his chest…

"I'd appreciate you lending us some extra towels."

His voice nudged her back to the present, and she nodded. "I'll only be a minute. You can wait in the porch if you'd like."

"Oh, by the way," Casson added as she opened the inner door. "I had another reason for coming by..."

Justine turned, and there was something in his voice that made her wonder if it had to do with Robert's departure. Or selling Winter's Haven.

She looked at him suspiciously, her guard up.

"If you haven't made other plans, you're welcome to join us for a campfire. I picked up a bag of marshmallows for Andy." He grinned and his gaze swept over her. "But you might want to change into something more substantial," he said, his gaze lingering on her exposed shoulders. "I don't want the mosquitoes to attack you when it gets dark."

Justine first thought was to decline. She couldn't imagine being the fourth wheel around the campfire.

What would they talk about? And did Veronica know that he was inviting her?

And then she heard her own traitorous voice murmuring casually, "Sure, why not?" before she flew in to get some towels, her heart a jackhammer.

Justine's acceptance took Casson by complete surprise. He'd been sure Justine was going to turn down his invitation. Earlier, she had been courteous enough to Ronnie and Andy, but Casson had detected a slight resistance on her part to over-extend herself.

He'd thought about it on the beach this afternoon while Ronnie had sunbathed and Andy had played with Luna. He'd tried to put himself in her shoes, having to put up with someone who had manipulated—though he would say *masterminded*—his way into Winter's Haven.

Of course Justine would be on the defensive—not only with *him*, but maybe even with his guests. Or rather *guest*. He wasn't an expert on female psychology, but he had sensed a bit of tension from Justine. Maybe it was the way she had glanced edgewise at Ronnie and stood there a little awkwardly, her cheeks like pink blossoms.

Luna flopped down on Justine's entrance mat. "Make yourself at home." Casson chuckled. "Although I might as well do the same."

He made himself comfortable on a padded wicker chair—or as comfortable as he could be with a wet shirt that kept sticking to him—and a minute later Justine re-emerged. She had changed into a red T-shirt and a navy hoodie and sweat pants. Her lipstick was the same shade as her top—a cherry-red that activated his pulse. She handed him a towel and placed a big nautical-style beach bag on the wicker chair next to him before bending down to put on her running shoes.

Luna ambled over to lick her face, making Justine lose her balance. Casson dropped his towel and leaped forward to help her straighten up. He heard her quick intake of breath and wanted nothing more than to lean forward and seal those lips with his own.

Taste their fruity nectar.

Unable to stop himself, he began to move his face toward hers...

Justine pulled away as if she had been jolted by an electric current. Something shifted in his expression and he gave her a curt smile.

"We'd better be going. Andy gets tired quickly, and usually has an early bedtime, but he won't leave me in peace until I make him a campfire and we have a marshmallow roast."

Justine nodded and saw his gaze drop to her beach bag. "A flashlight for when I walk back home," she said. "And the extra towels you asked for."

As they started walking Justine diverted her thoughts to what Casson had said about Andy getting tired and having a rest earlier. Most little boys his age had boundless energy. Many of the cottagers at Winter's Haven had kids staying, and they tore around like little hellions—often to the consternation of their parents.

"I noticed that Andy seems a little...fragile," she said, trying to break the awkward silence. "He must have had a late night before the drive here this morning; he has such dark shadows under his eyes."

Casson didn't respond. Justine bit her lip, wondering if she had sounded judgmental.

They continued to walk in silence along the road, Luna beside Casson. Justine kept her eyes on the sun-dappled shadows of the pines.

Suddenly Casson slowed his steps and turned to look at her. "It wasn't because he had a late night," he said, an edge creeping into his voice. "It's because he has cancer."

Justine felt waves of shock rippling through her body. For a few moments she couldn't move. Or speak. She stared up at Casson and knew her face must reveal the questions she wanted to ask but couldn't bring herself to for fear of sounding insensitive.

"He's in remission and undergoing maintenance chemo," Casson said. "His treatment has taken a lot out of him—*and* Ronnie—but he's a tough little guy, despite the impression he may give with those skinny little legs and body. He's got a lot of spirit..."

His voice wavered and Justine felt her heart breaking.

Casson looked away and continued walking. "He had some dizzy spells and nosebleeds when he was four," he said as Justine caught up to him. "And he was getting headaches. When he had a seizure with a high fever they did some tests and he was brought immediately to Toronto's Hospital for Sick Children, where they started chemotherapy—which took months. Once Andy was in remission they started maintenance chemo. He's now in his second year of that."

"Poor child..." Jasmine squeezed her eyes so she wouldn't cry, but felt a teardrop trickle down anyway. "And his poor parents." She shook her head. "I can't even imagine what they must have been going through..."

Casson didn't offer any further details, and Justine didn't feel it was appropriate to ply him with questions, so they walked in silence again.

No wonder Andy looked so gaunt beneath his baseball cap.

She didn't remember seeing any hair around his temples, but had just assumed that he had gotten a summer buzz cut.

Justine felt sorry for Veronica. How heart-wrenching it must have been for her to hear that her only child was afflicted with a disease that could take his life.

And what about Andy's father? Where was he? And what exactly was the relationship between Veronica and Casson?

It must have been devastating for Casson to learn of Andy's diagnosis as well—especially after having lost his brother to leukemia.

These thoughts and more kept swirling in her mind. She had been able to tell from that first meeting this morning that Casson had a special relationship with Andy. And with Andy's mother. They looked like a happy family, vacationing together and doing all the things that families did.

So why was *she* being invited to take part in their evening? If Casson and Veronica were more than just friends, wouldn't he want to spend the evening alone with her? Okay, Andy was with them, but he'd eventually go to bed...

Justine had no intention of asking Casson to enlighten her about any of these questions. They had arrived at the cottage and Andy was opening the screen door in excitement, holding the bag of marshmallows.

Casson's face lit up immediately. Seeing him like that

made Justine choke up. She hoped she could keep it together now that she knew about Andy's condition. She smiled at Andy and he smiled back and waved before attempting to open up the bag.

"Hey, hold on a minute, kid!" Casson chuckled. "Let me get the fire going. If you open the bag now there won't be any left to roast."

"Aw, Cass, I promise I'll just have one..." Andy grinned.

"And I'll be watching him like a hawk to make sure," his mother said, emerging from the cottage. She greeted Justine with a smile. "So nice you could join us, Justine."

"Hi, Veronica." Justine returned the smile, not wanting to reveal how uncomfortable she was.

"Please." Veronica grinned at her as she came down the cottage steps. "It's Ronnie, remember? Only my mother calls me by my full name."

Justine laughed. "Okay—Ronnie. By the way, here are the towels." She pulled them out of her beach bag.

"Great—thank you." Ronnie took them and before opening the door said, "Can I get you a drink before we head down to the beach? I'm having white wine, but I can mix you a margarita, if you like, or a martini. I make a wicked chocolate martini!"

"Oh...um...a little white wine would be fine..."

"Great. How about you, Cass? A margarita?" she said teasingly.

Casson made a face. "I'll have a nice cold beer, thank you. A good Canadian lager for a good Canadian boy."

Ronnie let out a belly laugh. *"Andy's* a good Canadian boy. *You*—I'm not so sure." She turned to her son. "What can I get you, sweetie? How about some lemonade?"

"Sure, Mom," Andy replied distractedly, busy helping Casson gather twigs from the bushes nearby and putting them in a large canvas bag.

"Hey, Ronnie!" Casson grinned. "Would you mind

grabbing me a T-shirt and my hoodie? I don't want to get eaten alive by mosquitoes down by the water."

"Is there anything *I* can do?" Justine said after Ronnie had gone to get the drinks.

Casson turned and looked at her. *For a little too long.*

"You can help Ronnie bring down the drinks," he said finally, a gleam in his eyes. "Andy and I will head down to the beach and get the fire started. Ready, partner?" he asked the boy.

"Ready!" Andy nodded excitedly.

His baseball cap fell off, and Justine felt a twinge in her heart at the sight of Andy's shaved head. She watched them walking away, Casson's muscular frame next to Andy's little body, Luna bounding ahead of them. She could see that Casson was deliberately walking slowly so Andy could keep up with him.

He's a good guy, an inner voice whispered.

Justine shivered, even though the night air was balmy. She remembered how upset she had been after their first meeting in the office, and how rattled when he'd let himself into her house with Luna. And when she'd stumbled and fallen into his lap…

But she couldn't deny that he had some good qualities. He had stayed the night in case Robert came back, hadn't he? And the way he interacted with Andy, you'd swear he was the boy's father. *That's how a father should be,* she mused.

Another thought occurred to her. Could it be that Ronnie was divorced and Casson was potentially her next husband?

"Hey, Justine, can you give me a hand with this wine and the glasses? I'll bring the beer and the pitcher of lemonade. And Casson's clothes."

"Sure."

Justine stepped up to the door. She took the tray and held the door open for Ronnie.

As they walked down the path to the beach Ronnie said softly, "Isn't Casson something? He goes above and beyond when it comes to Andy... He's told you about Andy's condition?" She glanced at Justine.

"Yes." Justine felt Ronnie's gaze and turned to meet it. "I was so sorry to hear about that," she said simply. "I can't imagine what you and Andy have been through."

Ronnie's pace slowed. "I couldn't have done it without Cass. He's not only a great cousin, but an even greater godfather to Andy." Her voice quivered. "We're so blessed to have him in our lives."

Justine's heart was racing. *Cousin? Godfather?*

"He's like a brother—the brother I never had." Ronnie's eyes welled up. "Here I go, getting all weepy again." She blinked the tears away. "Casson's going to be a great dad someday. And an awesome husband for one lucky lady..."

Casson had the fire started by the time Ronnie and Justine got down to the beach. The dry kindling was crackling over crumpled up newspaper. He looked up briefly and nodded at them before arranging thicker branches in a spoke-like configuration. Andy threw in some small twigs occasionally, watching in fascination as the fire crackled and sent out sparks.

There were four Muskoka chairs arranged in a semicircle behind the fire-pit, and in the middle a huge tree stump served as a tabletop. Justine set down the wine and glasses, and Ronnie followed suit with the beer and lemonade.

Casson took off his damp shirt and tossed it onto one of the chairs, before reaching for the T-shirt and hoodie that Ronnie had hooked over her arm and was now holding out to him. Justine was just steps away, and he could tell that she was trying not to glance at his bare torso.

Feeling a rush suffuse his body, he turned away to check the fire.

When the fire was robust, Casson stacked half-logs over the branches and in no time at all the fire was roaring. Feeling the sweat trickling down his face, Casson thanked Ronnie for the beer, and helped himself to a long swig. Ronnie poured Andy a glass of lemonade before filling the wine glasses.

"Here's to summer fun." Ronnie lifted her glass. "Cheers, guys."

Casson tipped his beer bottle to clink with Ronnie's glass. They laughed when Andy clinked his glass with them. When Casson turned to do the same with Justine their gazes locked. Something swirled in the pit of his stomach. Justine's face was mesmerizing in the light and shadows cast by the fire. Her eyes looked like blue ice, and standing so close to her beside the spiraling flames he felt desire flicking through his body.

He wanted her.

With a yearning that stunned him.

Out of the corner of his eye he saw Ronnie and Andy putting marshmallows on the branches Casson had collected and sharpened earlier. He was glad their attention was diverted, and even more glad that Justine's eyes seemed to be reflecting something he hadn't seen before. In her or in any other woman he had dated.

Maybe it was the romance of a campfire on a starry night, with the dark, silky waters of Georgian Bay just steps away, the soft gushing of their ebb and flow joining with the crackling of the fire. Maybe it was just the fact that Justine was one helluva beautiful woman, and that having already kissed those lips once, he felt the urge to kiss them again.

And again.

It was a good thing, perhaps, that Ronnie and Andy were there, or right now he'd be—

"Hey, Cass!" Andy called. "Come and roast some marshmallows. You too, Justine. Mom went to get me my hoodie."

Casson watched the expression in Justine's eyes change instantly. She gave Andy a bright smile and strode over to pick up a stick and a marshmallow. She laughed at the sight of Andy's sticky face.

A warm feeling came over Casson at the picture they made. Justine seemed so comfortable around Andy. *Natural.* Not stiff, like some of his past dates when he'd introduced them to his godson. Justine was chatting with Andy as if she had always known him. And he was responding in a spirited fashion, bursting into giggles at one point.

She would make a great mother.

A sudden mental image of Justine pregnant, her hands resting gently over her belly, followed almost immediately by a picture of him feeling the mound as well, startled him.

Where were these thoughts coming from?

Casson felt his heartbeat quicken and the sweat start to slide down his temples. He wiped his face with his sleeve and had another gulp of beer before rising.

As the four of them twirled their sticks over the flames Casson stole a glance at Justine. She was the first to be done. She stepped back and, after waving her stick to cool off her perfectly roasted marshmallow, bit into its golden-brown exterior and got to the warm, gooey white center.

"Mmm…heaven…" she said between bites.

She'd got some of the caramel center stuck around her mouth, and Casson found himself wishing he could lick the stickiness off…

"Hey, Cass, you need to concentrate a little better than that!"

Ronnie's laughing voice reached his ears and, looking away from Justine, he groaned when he realized that his marshmallow had blackened. Shrugging, he set down his stick.

"Here, let me show you how it's done." Justine grinned. She prepared a new stick and twirled it slowly, until the marshmallow reached a toffee-like color, and then handed it to him. He bit into it, savoring its caramel sweetness, his eyes never leaving her face.

"That," he said, after finishing it off, "was the best marshmallow I've ever had. What do you say, Andy? Should we give Justine the prize for Best Marshmallow?"

Andy nodded vigorously. "But what do we *give* her, Cass?" He cocked his head in puzzlement.

Casson stroked his chin, pretending to look thoughtful. "How about we take her fishing tomorrow?"

"Yeah! Can you come, Justine?" Andy's face lit up. "You won the prize!"

Justine gazed from Andy to Casson and then to Ronnie, who was nodding approvingly.

"Yes—go! I don't fish." Ronnie chuckled. "I just eat."

Casson met Justine's gaze. "You can take us to the hot spots…"

He watched Justine's eyes flicker and her mouth twitch ever so slightly. Her gaze shifted to Andy, who had his little hands in a prayer position and was looking up at her beseechingly.

Her face broke into a big grin. "I guess I can't turn down first prize," she said, reaching down to give Andy a hug.

After they'd feasted on another round of marshmallows Casson walked to the water's edge and filled a couple of large pails. While he extinguished the fire Ronnie and Justine finished what was left of their wine and started gathering up the glasses, bottles and the pitcher of lemonade.

They returned to the cottage, and Andy said goodnight to Justine before going inside.

"Well, I'll say goodnight too," Justine said brightly, slinging her beach bag over her arm. "Thank you for a nice evening. It's been a long time since I roasted marshmallows."

"Goodnight, Justine," Ronnie said, waving. "Andy had fun with you."

"I won't say goodnight just yet," Casson said to Justine when they were alone. "I'm walking you home after I read Andy a story. *And it'll be a short one*," he added huskily.

CHAPTER THIRTEEN

CASSON HAD INVITED her to wait inside the cottage, but Justine had said she'd be fine outside. The night air was warm and the half-moon provided some illumination. She sat on a lawn chair by the front door of the cottage with Luna at her feet. The screen on the door was partially up, and she could faintly hear Casson's voice.

Barely a few minutes had passed when Casson re-emerged. "The little guy was wiped," he said. "Couldn't keep his eyes open. By the third page he was out." Casson shrugged. "Come on, Luna." He ruffled her fur briskly. "Time to take Miss *Wintry* home." He flashed Justine a grin.

Justine rose and put up her hand in protest. "I'm a big girl and I can take myself home. Really." She looked at him pointedly. "I won't get lost; it *is* my property." She made herself smile in case she had sounded abrupt. "But, thank you; I appreciate your offer."

Casson's eyes glinted. "I'm not offering. You may know your way around, but I won't be able to sleep wondering if a big, bad wolf is following you. Or the three little bears."

Justine couldn't help laughing. "You've been reading too many kids' books, Mr. *Forrest*. Your imagination is running wild."

"Indeed."

The way Casson was looking at her made her heart do a flip. Taking a deep breath, she started walking.

If he wanted to walk with her she couldn't very well stop him. And, to be honest, she didn't really want to.

But having him walk so closely beside her was unnerving.

Why did he have to look so gorgeous, even in the moonlight?

Justine shivered, and before she knew it Casson had zipped down his hoodie and taken it off to put it around her shoulders.

Even though she had her own hoodie on, Justine could feel the warmth from his. She couldn't very well take it off and tell him the *real* cause of her shivering.

The fact that her attraction to him was alarming her, especially since the only reason he was at Winter's Haven in the first place was to find a way to convince her to sell.

But, although she might dislike Casson's intentions when it came to her property, she had to admit that there were things about him that she did like. *A lot.* The way he looked, for one. And the way he sounded. The way he cared for Andy.

The way he had come to her rescue and made her feel safe...

Her acknowledgement of liking Casson worried her. How could she even *think* of encouraging any of those feelings? What possible outcome could come from acting on them? After all, Casson would be leaving after his little holiday at Winter's Haven. And she'd still be holding the keys.

"If you're not doing anything tomorrow night..." Casson slackened his pace and waited until she turned to glance at him. "I'd really like to talk to you about my proposal."

Justine's heart plummeted. For a moment it had sounded like he was going to ask her for a date.

Get with it, an inner voice ridiculed. *He wants Winter's Haven, not you. And don't forget it.*

She gave a tired sigh. "I don't really see the purpose of a meeting. There's nothing that would make me contemplate selling. To you or to anyone else."

She picked up her pace, anxious to get home and away from any further discussion around Winter's Haven.

He stepped into place with her. "There are…things I haven't told you," he said softly. "Things that might just change your perspective."

Could he be anymore cryptic?

"If it has to do with offering more money, I'll save you the energy of making the offer." She smiled cynically and tossed her head back. "Not *everyone* can be bought."

"I realize that." He nodded. "I can see how much this place means to you." He reached over as they walked and shifted the hoodie on Justine's shoulders to prevent it from slipping off.

She felt his fingers pause momentarily, and her pulse drummed wildly. And then his hand was off her shoulder. He slowed his pace, and Justine felt like the path leading to her house was an eternity away.

Other than the tread of their footsteps, the chirping of the crickets was the only sound breaking the silence. Justine inhaled the sweet scent of a nearby linden tree.

This is all too much, she thought.

Having Casson walk her home was doing things to her that confused her. She was prepared to battle him verbally, whatever he proposed, and yet her body seemed to want to surrender to him…

Justine stopped walking and frowned. "Why can't you tell me *now*?"

Casson's mouth twisted. "There are things I need to show you as well, and I don't have them with me. Tomorrow we're fishing during the day, so I thought the evening would be a perfect time to—"

Justine practically jumped as Casson's cell phone rang. He reached into his back pocket and a frown appeared on his face.

"Hey, Ronnie, what's up?"

Ronnie's voice came loud and clear. "It's Andy, Cass. His temperature is way up and I'm worried he's going to have a seizure. I need to take him to the hospital…"

"I'm on my way," Casson told her, and stuck his phone back in his pocket. "We'll talk tomorrow," he said to Justine, his hand reaching out to squeeze her arm.

He whistled to Luna, who was investigating a scuttling sound in some bushes. Luna bounded after him and Justine watched with a sick feeling in her stomach as they ran down the driveway and disappeared around the bend.

Casson raced back to the cottage, every footstep matching the beat of his heart. Andy's face and arms were flaming hot. He was moaning, and couldn't keep his eyes open. Ronnie had placed a cool cloth over his forehead and pulled back his top blanket. Casson's heart twisted at the sight of him, and of Ronnie's pale face and wide eyes.

Casson picked Andy up and carefully made his way down the stairs. He set him down gently in the back seat of Ronnie's car while Ronnie sat next to him and fastened his seatbelt before placing a light shawl over him. After a dash inside to make sure there was water in Luna's bowl, Casson drove to the hospital in Parry Sound, hoping he wouldn't get stopped for speeding.

Andy was checked in and seen by midnight. But by the time the doctors had inserted an IV, run some standard tests, and the Emergency Room doctor had examined the results, it was close to four a.m.

Andy was transferred to a room. Although his fever had

dropped, the doctors wanted to continue to monitor him, given his condition and recent treatment.

Casson and Ronnie kept vigil by his bedside, taking turns to shut their eyes, and at seven a.m. a doctor came to explain that, although Andy was unlikely to have a seizure, he recommended that a follow-up appointment be made with Andy's specialist at SickKids.

Ronnie decided it was best to take Andy back home and make the appointment.

Casson wanted to drive them home to Gravenhurst, but Ronnie reassured him that she had caught enough sleep to handle the drive alone.

With her reassurance that she would call him if she needed him, Casson brushed a kiss on Andy's forehead and they left the hospital.

By the time he drove her car back to the cottage, and she returned to the hospital they would be ready to discharge Andy.

When Casson got out of Ronnie's car and she switched to the driver's seat he reached down to give her a hug. "Drive safely, Ronnie. And call me when you get home."

Casson watched her drive away, then entered the cottage to Luna's welcome. He opened the door to let her run out, and when they were both inside again took off his shoes and, without bothering to undress, fell on top of his bed and crashed.

Casson woke up three hours later. He felt pretty ragged, and could only imagine how Ronnie felt. He checked his phone and saw that Ronnie had texted to say they were home and she would let him know of any developments with Andy. He sent her a quick message, apologizing for sleeping through the text and sending them hugs.

He not only felt rough, he looked it, too, he thought a few moments later, staring at his reflection in the bathroom mirror. He stroked his jaw and chin. He had let his usual five o'clock shadow grow for over two weeks, and now he decided the scruff had to go.

After shaving he had a hot shower, letting the pulsating jets ease the tension in his muscles. He lathered himself with the shower gel provided, his nose wrinkling at the scent. It reminded him of something...of *Justine,* he realized.

He glanced at the label. Rose Rapture. Wonderful, he thought wryly, rinsing off, he'd always wanted to come out smelling like a rose. Stepping out of the shower, he grabbed a towel and briskly dried himself. Wrapping it around his hips, and stepping into flip-flops, he padded into the kitchen and put the coffee on.

Casson reached into the cupboard to get a mug, and then a movement at the screen door caught his eye. He stood there, mug in hand, towel around his hips, and met Justine's embarrassed gaze through the glass of the door.

CHAPTER FOURTEEN

JUSTINE HAD BEEN on the verge of turning away, but now it was too late. Casson had already seen her. She let her hand drop, wishing she had thought to call first. He didn't seem too perturbed over the fact that he was wearing nothing but a towel, though, and she tried to keep her eyes from wandering as he walked to the door. She focused on his face, now clean-shaven, and couldn't help but gulp.

Shadow or no shadow, Casson was gorgeous. Drop-dead gorgeous.

He opened the door and she blurted, "Is Andy okay? Is he back from the hospital? I made some chicken soup for him and some lemon blueberry muffins..." She stopped, and looked down at the stainless steel pot she was holding on to for dear life, aware that she was blabbering.

"That's very kind of you, Justine." Casson smiled. "His fever dropped, thank goodness. They checked him out... did some tests. He might just have been overtired, and with his compromised immune system it doesn't take much to knock him down. The doctor suggested Ronnie do a follow-up at SickKids. They're home now. Come in," he added, taking the pot and container.

The sight of his sculpted torso sent a ripple of pure desire through her body. As he set the items down on the kitchen counter she felt her cheeks burning. She patted

Luna and then turned around slowly, hoping Casson had gone to change, but he was still standing across from her, one hand on the back of a chair and the other on his hip.

"I suppose I should go and get decent," he said, the corners of his mouth lifting. "I'll be right back."

"Um…well, since Ronnie and Andy aren't here you can have the soup and muffins yourself…" Justine said, trying hard to keep her eyes on his face.

"I don't think so," he drawled, his eyes crinkling at the corners. "We can have the muffins with coffee. As for the soup—we can share it later. If you haven't already made supper plans."

He started to walk away, and then paused to look back at her.

"Since you're here now, we might as well have that meeting I was talking about yesterday. But I think you'll be much more receptive to what I have to tell you if I put some clothes on." He grinned. "It's so much more professional than just wearing a towel and Rose Rapture."

Justine felt her cheeks flaming. She couldn't tear her gaze away from him as he strode away, and her eyes took in every detail from his damp, curling dark hair to his muscled neck and sculpted arms and shoulders. And the firm slope to the small of his back…

As the door clicked shut Justine snapped out of her stupor and took a deep breath. She wiped her brow. It was a hot one today, but she felt even hotter inside—especially after seeing Casson half naked. Again, she wished she had thought to phone him instead of just showing up at his door…

She wondered what exactly he had to show her. He seemed to think it could sway her in some way. She couldn't help feeling apprehensive. Too much had happened since Casson had set foot at Winter's Haven, and somehow she had an uneasy feeling that he had something up his sleeve. Something that might tip the scales in his favor.

Justine braced herself. She had no intention of letting him weaken her resolve. No matter what he presented her with, she would turn it down.

"Hey, make yourself at home." Casson chuckled, coming out of his room with a large brown envelope in his hand. He had changed into a black T-shirt and a pair of faded jeans with a couple of worn-through spots above the knees.

Justine wished he didn't have to look so damned sexy. She pulled out a chair at the kitchen table and sat down while Casson poured coffee into two mugs. He set out the milk and then, sitting down across from her, helped himself to a muffin.

"Mmm." He nodded. "Thanks for breakfast." He pushed the container toward her.

"I had one earlier, thanks."

She stared pointedly at the envelope beside him. Casson had tried to hand her this very envelope before, when he had first come to her house. He had said it was a development proposal drafted by an architect friend of his, and had suggested that she at least give the plan and drawings a glance. He obviously thought that whatever was in the envelope might dispel her doubts about his venture.

Well, she still had doubts. Only she supposed she could let him at least show her his plans.

Casson set his mug down. "Look, Justine, do you have plans this afternoon?"

"Wh-why?" Justine shifted uncomfortably.

"It might take some time to go over the details."

"I can't imagine there will be much to discuss," she said, "so don't get your hopes up." She didn't want Casson to think that there was even the *slightest* chance she would change her mind about selling.

His eyes blazed into hers and his mouth curved slightly. "A man can always hope," he drawled. "Well?"

"Well, what?" She tossed her head.

"*Are* you free this afternoon?"

"I will be after you show me what's in the envelope. I'll have a few minutes. But then I have to run a quick errand before relieving Mandy. She's off early today to go to a wedding."

"Mmm…" Casson rubbed his chin. "I need more than a few minutes." He tapped his fingers on the table top. "Why don't we leave the envelope till later this evening? Do you have time to go out for lunch? My treat." He smiled crookedly. "To thank you for your kindness to Andy."

Justine felt a slow flush creep over her cheeks. "That's not necessary."

"Look, Justine…" He set his elbows on the table and leaned closer, his gaze becoming serious. "A lot has happened for both of us in the last couple of days. Let's forget about the sale and everything else for a while and just enjoy an hour. Away from work, away from worry. What do you say?" His eyebrows lifted.

Justine examined his face for the slightest sign of insincerity and couldn't find one. She glanced at the time on her phone. "I'm sorry. I don't even have an hour."

Darn, if only she had brought the soup over earlier…

"Thanks for the offer, though."

Flushing, Justine averted her gaze and patted Luna before leaving. She resisted the temptation of looking back as she walked toward her car.

As she pulled out of the driveway she glanced in her rearview mirror. Casson was in the doorway, watching her…

Casson rubbed his chin as Justine drove off. He was disappointed that his impromptu offer hadn't worked out, but there was still tonight to look forward to.

Justine's expression when she'd told him not to get his hopes up had been so different from when she'd had first arrived at the door, when she'd tried not to show that she was glancing at his body... He had caught a spark of *something* in those blue-gray depths then. Something that made him wonder if there was a current below the surface, a fuse that just needed to be lit.

No matter how much Justine tried to show otherwise, Casson felt deep in his gut that she wasn't immune to him. Maybe at first, when she'd fallen into his lap and they'd kissed, it might have been just physical for both of them, but after their evening around the campfire he'd sensed there was something *deeper*. He had *felt* it. It had been as if she were seeing him with new eyes.

He had caught her expression when he was with Andy, too; it had seemed softer, relaxed, approving. But of course there was a limit to her approval. She was far from approving of his intentions regarding Winter's Haven.

But maybe that would change tonight.

His initial plan was to show her the architect's drawings and then suggest she sell him Winter's Haven with the proviso that she would manage his new resort. If she accepted his offer he would agree to delay renovations or construction until he had a deeper understanding of the unique features of the huge parcel of land that comprised both the Russell properties and Winter's Haven.

Justine would be a great asset, and he was sure that eventually she would see that what he was planning would not be to the detriment of the landscape, but an enhancement— with the most important consequence being its benefit to kids like Andy, and their parent or parents, who deserved some pampering after dealing with the heartbreak of a cancer diagnosis and treatment for their child.

And then he would show her the deed.

She would be shocked, perhaps even angry, but it had

to be done. Justine had the right to know. And maybe the knowledge that he owned part of Winter's Haven already might just sway her into considering selling...

If Justine still balked after that he would pull out his ace: a considerable increase in his initial price offer and, if she agreed to it, an offer for her to continue to live in the house rent-free for as long as she was managing Franklin's Resort.

Casson closed the door. It was too bad their fishing trip today was a bust. Andy would have loved it. He checked the time on his cell phone and wondered how Andy was doing. His stomach twisted at the memory of Andy moaning, his face contorted and pale.

Grabbing his phone, he sent Ronnie a text.

Ronnie responded quickly, saying that Andy was resting and his temperature had stabilized. She thanked him for everything and promised to visit him again when Andy got the go-ahead from his specialist in Toronto.

The pot sitting on the counter caught his eye. The chicken soup Justine had made for a sick little boy she hardly knew.

His heart swelled.

She's a keeper, an inner voice told him as he placed the pot in the fridge.

"Time for a swim," he called out to Luna, and she bounded after him.

He could do with a splash in the bay.

Afterwards, Casson stretched out on a chaise lounge, and Luna plunked herself down next to him. He reached out and stroked her back. Much as he loved his dog, he thought about how nice it would be to have Justine lying next to him...

He propped himself on his side and looked out at the bay, a blue sheet twinkling with diamonds under the sunny sky. He could hardly believe that in two days his Franklin & Casson on the Bay exhibition would open.

Before he'd left home to take possession of the Russells' properties he had checked with all his contacts to ensure that everything was in place for the event. The paintings would be kept in a secure depository until the day before the opening. Lighting was adjusted. Security was arranged. Responses from the invited patrons verified. Media presence confirmed. An adjoining room had been prepared for the silent auction. The banquet courses were finalized.

All this had been delegated to a committee he had carefully chosen almost a year earlier. They were all prepared, as was he.

There was only one thing he hadn't planned or even considered up to now...and that was bringing a date.

CHAPTER FIFTEEN

JUSTINE LOOKED UP to see Mandy walking toward her. She hadn't even heard her car in the driveway.

"Nice cut and style," she said. "But what are you doing back here?"

"I left the wedding card on the desk. Here it is." Mandy peered at her with a slight frown. "Hey, why did you look so glum when I first walked in? Like you lost your best friend…"

Justine sighed and told her about Andy and his illness, and how Casson and Ronnie had rushed him to the hospital…

"Poor little fellow," Mandy said. "I hope it turns out to be nothing serious…" She sat on a corner of the desk. "My goodness, there seems to be a lot of drama around Casson Forrester. And not only at Winter's Haven."

"What do you mean?" Justine frowned.

"While I was waiting for my hairdresser to call me over I checked out the public bulletin board. There was a poster about an event that Casson's putting on at the Stockey Centre. It's being sponsored by his company, Forrest Hardware. I can't believe neither of us heard about it before."

"What kind of event? A home show?"

Mandy chuckled. "No, it has nothing to do with lumber or building. It's an art exhibition—two of the Group of Seven artists. Some of their most famous works will be on display for a week, and there's also a silent auction for one of the paintings on opening night, and an invitation-only fund-raising banquet."

Justine's mind raced.

Casson had never mentioned an exhibition when he was telling her about the Franklin painting...or had she forgotten?

No, she wouldn't have forgotten something like that.

And why hadn't he mentioned it at all today?

"When is this happening?" Justine tried to keep her voice steady, thinking about Casson's brother and his connection with *Mirror Lake.*

"All next week. Why? Do you want to go?" Mandy raised her eyebrows. "It starts on Monday night. Two days from now." She sighed dramatically. "I can't believe this guy. Not only is he gorgeous and successful—oh, and did I mention gorgeous?" She laughed. "He's also a devoted godfather *and* a patron of the arts. I've checked all the boxes under 'Man of Your Dreams.' She glanced slyly at Justine. "Except maybe the categories of 'great cook' and 'even better lover.'"

Justine's mouth dropped open. "Are you *kidding* me?"

"I'm serious. He's single, you're single, and now that you've found out that Ronnie's his cousin you should grab your chance while he's on your property, for heaven's sakes." She gave Justine's shoulder a gentle punch. "I think you'd make a great couple."

"I think it takes a little more than *that* to make a couple, Mandy," she scoffed, returning the soft punch. "And, besides, he wants my property—not *me.*"

Mandy walked away, shrugging.

Before the door closed behind her Justine called out sheepishly, "What did you say the name of the event was?"

"Franklin & Casson on the Bay."

* * *

Later, after closing the office, Justine went home and changed into a sky blue bikini. It was too humid to do anything but go for a refreshing swim.

Walking down to the beach, Justine couldn't stop thinking about Casson. About his exhibition and what he had told her about his brother Franklin, and what he *hadn't* told her. The fact that he was a patron of the arts just added to the data she had been unconsciously accumulating about him from the time he had stepped foot on her property.

There was quite an accumulation of physical data. She had to admit that when she wasn't involved with desk matters or the cottagers at Winter's Haven her brain kept summoning up images of Casson. They flicked through her memory as if she were looking through a photo gallery online: Casson in a tailored suit, his dark chestnut eyes glinting at her; Casson sitting in his Mustang convertible; Casson by the campfire and Casson walking through the door with a towel around his hips. Images that circulated constantly in her head.

The emotional data took up just as much space. The knowledge of his relationship with his brother. His congenial manner with Mandy and Melody and the cottagers in the diner. His kindness and caring toward Andy and Ronnie. His love for his dog. His appreciation for art. His entrepreneurial drive and success in building the Forrest Hardware chain.

But there was so much more that she wanted to know...

What had she filled her thoughts with before Casson walked into her life?

Whoa, there, she chided herself. He had walked onto her property, not into her *life.*

That realization sobered her. Besides his showing a typical male physical reaction to her on occasion, she couldn't delude herself into thinking that Casson Forrester had any emotional intentions or feelings toward her. Sure, he had shown some consideration, even kindness and concern, but...

But what? an inner voice prompted.

But she wanted more.

Justine bit her lip. Yes, she couldn't deny it to herself any longer. Casson had sparked something within her, and she couldn't control what it was igniting throughout her entire being—not only physically, but emotionally as well. She wanted *him.* Despite all her conflicting feelings about his ploys to get her to sell, she wanted Casson to want *her* more than he wanted Winter's Haven.

But it wasn't that simple.

Or was it?

The sudden urge to go and see Casson stopped Justine in her tracks. He *had* mentioned something about sharing the chicken soup...

She ran back up to the house, slipped on a pair of yellow cotton shorts and a shirt patterned with yellow daisies over her bikini.

Maybe she needed to *show* Casson Forrester that she was interested. Besides throwing herself into his arms— which was what she wished she could do—she had to come up with *something* to see if he was interested too.

And then maybe eventually she'd have the nerve to reveal the fact that she was falling in love with him.

Casson thought about going to the diner before supper. The swim in the bay had revitalized him, and he wanted to chat with the other cottagers and get a feel for what they liked about Winter's Haven and the area. This was his opportunity to discover what features to keep and what could be changed or added in future.

If Justine sold to him.

This last thought jolted him. Before, he had always thought in terms of *when* Justine sold to him.

Why the sudden uncertainty?

He brushed off any remaining beach sand from his feet and Luna's fur, hung his towel to dry on the outside line and entered the cottage. His gaze settled on the pot on the counter. Maybe he should scrap his idea about going to the diner now in case Justine decided to come over a little early...

While Luna was happily devouring her supper Casson went to his room and changed into a white T-shirt and khaki shorts. Whistling, he returned to the kitchen to check the soup, the aroma making his mouth water. He heard his phone ring from his bedroom and sprinted to get it, expecting it to be Ronnie.

His stomach twisted with the thought that Andy's condition might have worsened. But his phone didn't show any caller ID. He frowned.

"Hello?"

"Hello, this is Justine..."

Casson's stomach did a flip. "Hi."

"I—I thought I'd give you a call before coming to knock at your door," she said. "I have some time if you want to show me whatever it is you have to show me..."

Yes!

"Oh, well, a call wasn't necessary. You could have just come to the door."

He heard her clearing her throat. "Well... I just wanted to make sure you were...you weren't..."

He suddenly got it. She didn't want to come unannounced to the door and find him half-undressed again. The thought made him want to laugh, but he restrained himself.

"I'm fully clothed and I'm just heating up your soup," he said. "I was hoping you'd join me."

"Okay... I wouldn't want it to go to waste. And then we can talk."

"Are you at the office? When can you get away?"

"I'm at the end of your driveway," Justine said, and Casson detected a note of sheepishness in her voice. "I'll be there in a minute."

Casson looked out the kitchen window and there she was, straddling her bike as she paused to phone him. He saw her putting her phone in her pocket and start to pedal toward the cottage.

His smile turned into a grin before he burst out laughing.

Casson was holding the door open for her. Justine smiled her thanks and started to walk by him, but Luna's rush to the door stopped her in her tracks. She was penned in between Luna and Casson, who had now shut the door and was standing directly behind her.

"Hey, girl." Justine bent to pat Luna and then immediately regretted it, when her backside brushed against Casson's body. She straightened instantly, her face flaming, and was glad she couldn't see Casson's expression.

"Luna,—couch," Casson's amused voice drawled behind her, and Luna gave a plaintive howl but proceeded to obey.

Justine wiped her brow with her forearm. The humidity outside was high, but it was stifling in the cottage. She wished she could just strip off her clothes and remain in her bikini, like she did in her own house.

She glanced at him edgewise as he set the table. If he'd looked gorgeous in a black T-shirt, he looked magnificent in the white one he was wearing now. It emphasized his broad shoulders, and the firm contours of his chest and stomach. And his khaki shorts fit him oh, so well...

Justine couldn't help thinking that he looked like a hunky model out of a magazine.

Casson put a bottle of white wine in the fridge and then set the platter of cheese and crackers on the table.

"I suppose I should have thought of bringing something a little cooler," Justine said as Casson filled two bowls with soup, "but I thought if Andy was sick chicken soup would do him good."

"Your intentions were honorable," Casson said, and smiled, "and that's what counts."

Justine felt her insides quiver as she met his warm gaze.

They ate in silence for a few minutes and then Casson suddenly rose from his chair. "What am I thinking?" His eyes glinted. "There's cheese, but no wine on the table. Forgive me, my lady."

He gave a mock bow. A spiral of pleasure danced through Justine's body at his words. If only he knew how much she wanted to be *his lady.*

He poured white wine into two glasses and offered her one. "Let's toast our little Andy's health."

They clinked glasses and Justine's gaze locked with Casson's as she tasted the wine—a Pinot Grigio from Niagara-on-the-Lake. With its peachy bouquet and hint of vanilla, it complemented the Oka and the other cheeses Casson had selected.

"Let's take it down to the beach," he said suddenly, when they had each finished their first glass. "It's too hot in the cottage. I'll bring the wine and the glasses, and you can bring the cheese tray." He laughed. "Luna can bring herself."

Justine couldn't quite believe what was happening. Earlier she had decided to show Casson that she was interested. Now here she was, following this gorgeous man to a private beach where they would be sharing wine and cheese on the most sultry night of the summer.

She shivered in anticipation, the wine in her system already starting to loosen her up.

They sat side by side in the Muskoka chairs, nibbling on cheese and crackers and cooling themselves with wine. There was no breeze whatsoever, and the surface of the bay was mirror-still. In minutes it would be dusk, and Justine's pulse quickened at the thought of being with Casson in the darkness.

The sky was a magnificent palette in the twilight, with streaks of vermillion, orange, magenta and gold. She turned to Casson, exclaiming at the beauty of it, and met his intense gaze.

He held out his glass. "Here's to another beauty," he said huskily, and leaned over so that his face was close to hers.

Their glasses clinked but neither of them drank. Casson moved closer, and with a pulsating in her chest that spread down her body Justine felt herself tilting her face so his lips could meet hers. When they made contact, ever so lightly, Justine closed her eyes with the wonder of it. And when Casson's lips pressed against hers, and then moved over her bottom lip, she thought her limbs would melt.

She let out a small gasp, giving Casson the opportunity to deepen the kiss. She was sure her heart would explode as she reciprocated, tasting the wine on his tongue.

Justine lost all sense of time and space, and when he finally released her the glorious colors of the sky had faded to dusky gray and indigo. He took her hand and helped her stand up. Pulling her to him, he lifted his hands to cup the back of her head and kissed her again.

Justine wrapped her arms around his waist, then slid them up his back and around his neck. She trembled when his hands began their descent down her back and around her waist, before finding the edge of her cotton top. And then his hands were on her bare waist, searing her already heated skin.

"Let's go for a dip," he said, his breath ragged.

He pulled off his shirt and tossed it on a chair. He left his khaki shorts on. She let him help her pull off her top and shorts, and was thrilled at the way his eyes blazed when his fingers brushed against her bikini top and bottom.

Somewhere in the distance a loon gave its haunting call, and as they splashed their way into the still but bracingly cold depths of the bay, with Luna following, Justine felt freer than she had ever felt in her life.

After the initial shock of the water on their heated skin they automatically came together. The water was up to Justine's chest. Justine tilted her head back as Casson's lips traced a path up her neck to her mouth. He pulled her in even closer, and their bodies fit together in a way that sent a series of jolts through her.

As Casson's hands began to wander over the thin material of her bikini Justine gasped in pleasure at the sensation under water. She let her hands wander as well, sliding over the firm expanse of his back, exploring his contours. She kissed the base of his neck and his mouth, giving in to the desires that had been simmering within her and needing release for days.

Casson was in another world, with Justine pressed against him in the water, his senses filled with the sight and feel of her. He wanted to stroke every part of her with his hands and his lips, to make her gasp with pleasure. She looked like a sea nymph, with those smoldering blue eyes and silky skin. She was looking up at him now, their bodies locked together, their arms encircling each other.

The dark sky was suddenly lit up with a flash of lightning and the effect was surreal, the light reflecting in each other's eyes.

Luna started barking. She had already dashed out of

the water after a quick dip, and had been waiting for them on the beach, but now she was running about in a panic from the electricity in the air. When the rolls of thunder followed she started yelping even more, and ran frantically in and out of the water.

The rain started seconds later.

Casson took Justine's hand, and by the time they got out of the water and onto the beach the rain was pelting down on them. It was warm rain, but heavy, falling down in sheets. They quickly gathered their clothes, and the items they had left by the Muskoka chairs and table, and dashed to the cottage.

Once inside, they stood in the entrance, the rain dripping off their bodies onto the linoleum floor.

"Luna—stay." Casson patted her, trying to calm her. "Lie down, girl."

He turned to Justine and his heart thumped at the sight of her standing there, barefoot in her bikini, her drenched hair clinging to her cheeks, her dusky blue eyes wide and fluttering, her eyelashes beaded with raindrops. Despite the warmth inside the cottage, she had started to shiver.

He put his hands on her shoulders. "Don't move," he murmured. "I'm going to grab some towels."

He leaned over and planted a kiss on her lips. He had to tear himself away then, before his prehistoric instincts took over and he picked her up, dripping and all, and carried her straight into his man cave.

He brought back three bath towels. He placed one over Justine's shoulders and set one aside while he ran the third towel over Luna and wiped the beach sand from her paws.

"Okay, Luna, go on your mat."

He turned to Justine. She was towel-drying her hair. Gently he took the towel out of her hands and continued to pat her hair dry. Then he proceeded to dry her neck, her shoulders and back, before moving to the front of her body.

He held her gaze with his as he patted her chest and moved downward. By the time he reached her thighs and calves he could feel shivers running through him—although he suspected it had nothing to do with being cold.

"Here…" Justine took the towel from him and hung it on a hook behind the door. She reached for the remaining dry towel and wrapped it around his head. "My turn." She smiled shyly and started drying his hair. And then she followed his lead, slowly patting him dry, lingering in some areas more than others…

She made him catch his breath, and her eyes seemed to flash in delight at his reaction to her touch. When she was done they stood there, staring into each other's eyes, and he suddenly knew, without a doubt, that Justine had completely snagged him.

Hook, line and sinker.

CHAPTER SIXTEEN

JUSTINE PRACTICALLY JUMPED into Casson's arms at the next crack of thunder. Luna gave a howl and started to tear around the cottage, panting and giving low growls.

"You can't go home in this weather," Casson said, drawing Justine closer.

"You could drive me," she murmured, sounding unconvincing even to herself.

"I couldn't leave Luna alone; she'd be terrified," Casson said, sounding relieved that he had come up with an excuse. "You can have my room. I'll sleep on the couch. Luna will want me near her tonight."

Justine stopped herself from blurting out, *So will I.*

She took a deep breath. Things were spinning away too fast for her. *She* was spinning. She needed some space, some distance to make sense of what was happening between her and Casson. And spending the night in the same cottage with him, even if they were in separate rooms, would provide her with neither enough space nor distance.

"You should get out of your wet bikini," Casson said "I'll go get you some of my clothes." He chuckled. "I'll see what I can find in your size."

While he went to his room Justine went to comfort Luna. It felt so strange, walking around barefoot in a bikini *here*. Her stomach fluttered with the prospect of sleeping in Casson's bed. Could she trust him to stay on the couch?

Could she trust herself...?

Casson came out of the bedroom with a navy T-shirt. "This will have to do," he said, and held it out to Justine. "You can change in here."

Justine felt herself flushing. The T-shirt was large, and would probably reach her knees. *But she wouldn't be wearing anything underneath.* And of course it wouldn't cross Casson's mind to offer her a pair of his shorts.

She took the T-shirt from him and went into his room, shutting the door firmly behind her. She took deep breaths to slow down the beating of her heart. Scanning the room, she wasn't surprised to see how neat and orderly it was. Bed made, clothes hung up in the partially open wardrobe, and a suitcase in one corner of the room. Her eyes fell on the open laptop on the desk, and she saw the brown envelope he had brought out earlier.

She walked over to the bed and set the T-shirt on it while she took off her bikini. She caught sight of herself in the dresser mirror and felt her pulse leaping at the thought of Casson seeing her this way. She shivered and slipped the T-shirt on. It came to just above her knees, and it was baggy, but at least it was dry.

She still felt vulnerable, though, and had the crazy thought of searching through the drawers in the night table for a pair of his underwear. She sat on the bed, considering it, and saw a bottle of Casson's cologne on the night table.

Unable to resist, she picked it up. She uncapped it and inhaled the scent she had come to recognize: a blend of bamboo, pine and musk. An expensive Italian brand she had seen advertised in magazines.

A sudden thumping noise at the bedroom door startled her, and she fumbled with the bottle. She caught it before it could fall and break on the plank floor, but in grabbing it she accidentally sprayed herself.

Cursing inwardly, she set the bottle back on the night table. *Explain that to Casson...*

"Luna, get away from that door," she heard Casson say, chuckling. "Your friend is coming out any minute."

When Justine opened the door she saw Casson's eyes scanning over her appreciatively. He walked toward her and stopped, his nose wrinkling.

Justine smiled sheepishly. "Accident," she murmured, shrugging.

He leaned over and sniffed deeply, his nose and lips grazing her neck. She couldn't help shivering as he released his breath, and the sensation on her skin made her heart begin to pound.

"I guess I won't have to put any cologne on, then," he said huskily. "I'll go and change, too." He gazed at the bikini top and bottom in her hand, and then back at her. "You can hang those and your other clothes in the washroom."

When Justine returned to the living room she sat on the edge of the couch, her stomach in knots as she waited for Casson to come. She would tell him she was exhausted and would be going to bed right away, she decided.

A moment later he emerged, wearing blue-striped pajama bottoms and a beige T-shirt, holding a pillow in one hand and a change of clothes in the other. Justine's heart flipped. She stood up, knowing she'd better get to his room before...before her resolve started to weaken.

"I'm beat," she said. "I'll say goodnight."

She gave him a half-smile and quickly averted her gaze. She patted Luna, then gingerly stepped past Casson. To her relief he didn't stop her, and as she closed the bedroom door with a click she let out her breath.

She left the wooden shutters in his room partially open, so the morning light would wake her, and then turned off the light switch. As she slipped into bed she began to have second doubts.

Was she crazy? Passing up an opportunity to spend the night with Casson in this bed?

He would be beside her right now had she given him the slightest indication of wanting that.

Justine bit her lip. She had come to his cottage with the intention of showing him that she was interested and seeing if he felt the same. Well, she had no doubts that he was interested in her body—neither of them could deny the chemistry between them. But she wanted—no, *needed*—more than that. She needed to know that Casson Forrester wanted her heart and soul as well. When she knew that for sure, *then* she would be his.

She snuggled under the covers, savoring the feeling of intimacy in just lying on the sheet Casson slept on. She breathed in his scent on the pillow, and let it and the rhythm of the rain, and the muted grumbling of thunder, soothe her to sleep.

Casson stared at the door for a few moments after Justine had closed it. Tonight was going to be sweet torture, lying on the couch. How could he possibly sleep, knowing that Justine was only steps away? Especially after the intimacy they had shared?

He groaned softly and, turning off the kitchen light, made his way to the couch. He plunked down his pillow and stretched out. It was too humid in the cottage to cover up. And too hot for pajamas. He pulled them off impatiently, leaving his boxers on. With any luck he'd get a breeze coming through the screened-in windows during the night.

Good luck falling asleep.

Casson felt so frustrated. And deflated. Justine had relayed her intentions loud and clear after he had given her his T-shirt. *I'm beat. I'll say goodnight.* He couldn't deny it: if he had seen even a spark in Justine's eye to invite him to follow her into the bedroom he wouldn't have thought twice. But she had deliberately avoided looking at him.

Although he had seen her blue eyes darken with desire in the bay, and when they were drying each other, something had caused Justine to pull back. Could she still have feelings for Robert? *No!* He didn't want to believe that. His jaw tensed. Or maybe Justine's suspicions about his intentions had resurfaced, making her keep any attraction she felt for him in check, especially after her experience with Robert. Maybe she believed he was using her, trying to use sex to influence her decision not to sell.

She didn't trust him.

Casson felt as if someone had kicked him in the gut. He breathed in deeply and exhaled slowly. He wanted Justine to trust him, to believe that he wasn't using her.

But how could he convince her of that? Convince her that it wasn't just her body he had fallen in love with, but her gentle spirit?

Yes, he thought in wonder, *he had fallen in love with her.*

She was kind and considerate…making soup for a little boy she hardly knew. And it wasn't because she had some ulterior motive to get Casson to like her. No, it was simply a thoughtful and sensitive gesture. And she was kind to Luna. Casson had seen a flash of real sorrow in her eyes when he'd told her about how Luna had been abandoned and left at the side of the road. And what about her concern that Robert would be ruined if they'd called the police? It was only because of her that Casson hadn't gone down that route. *He* would have been much harder on Robert. And he really hadn't expected Justine to demonstrate that kind of compassion after Robert's behavior.

But Justine was soft. *Softer.* And that was what he loved about her. She had a gentleness and a generosity that his previous dates had lacked. He might have been too focused on building his business to spend time searching for the right person in his life, but now Casson realized that a search was not necessary.

He closed his eyes and turned onto one side. He felt drained. So much had happened since that first meeting with Justine. He let some of the memories play in his mind for a while, but then, remembering that tomorrow evening was the opening of the Franklin & Casson on the Bay exhibition, he pushed those thoughts back.

He had checked his email earlier, and everything was ready to go at the Stockey Centre. The banner stands were in place, the paintings were arranged, the lighting adjusted. And the A. J. Casson painting was sitting regally on an antique brass easel next to the mahogany desk in the silent auction room.

The media would arrive at five-thirty p.m. to interview Casson and local dignitaries. The doors would open to the public at six. Casson would make a formal address at six-thirty, sharing his vision of Franklin's Resort before unveiling the A. J. Casson painting.

He had arranged the hiring of two notable gallery owners, who were experts on the Group of Seven—especially the two featured artists—to interact with the public and enlighten them about the individual paintings on display. Casson would also mingle with the invited patrons and the public.

At seven, the invited guests would make their way to the banquet room, where they would enjoy a fabulous five-course meal. The event would close at nine o'clock.

Casson felt a twinge in his heart. The three banner stands he had ordered showed an enlarged photo of him and Franklin at their parents' friends' cottage in Georgian Bay. The title was at the top: Franklin & Casson on the Bay. One would be placed in the entrance of the Stockey Centre, another would be in the exhibition room, and the third would be in the room displaying the A. J. Casson painting for the silent auction.

The photo had been taken by his mother, in the summer two months before Franklin's diagnosis. He and Franklin were standing on the dock, the bay a brilliant blue behind them, and he was helping Franklin hold up his fishing rod. The fish—a pickerel—wasn't big, but it was a keeper.

The backs of Casson's eyes started to sting. He squeezed them shut and turned his pillow over.

Okay, Franklin, tomorrow evening's the big event. Get some sleep up there in heaven, buddy, 'cause you're coming with me, and it'll be past your bedtime when we're done.

CHAPTER SEVENTEEN

JUSTINE SCREAMED, AND seconds later her eyes fluttered open. She sat up, her back against the headboard, and then, her heart thudding, she heard the door clicking open. The light came on to reveal that it was Casson.

He turned the dimmer switch on low and closed the door behind him. He strode to the foot of the bed. "Are you okay? Did you have a bad dream?"

Justine felt her lip quivering.

The nightmare had seemed so real.

Casson had been walking her home, and they had arrived at the edge of her property when she'd caught sight of a wrecking ball, advancing toward her house. She'd started to scream, and Casson had tried to silence her with a kiss. She'd managed to pull away and had screamed again as one side of her house had caved in.

And then she'd woken up.

Justine blinked. The genuine concern in Casson's eyes pushed her emotions over the edge. She felt her eyes filling up and, biting her lip, nodded. "I—I was dreaming that—that you were starting to have my house torn down so you could build your resort…"

She shivered and burst into tears, covering her face with her hands. Then sucked in her breath when she felt a shift in the mattress and Casson's arms around her. She didn't have the strength to move away from the warmth of his embrace. She felt herself sinking against his chest, and as he held her tightly she let the tears flow.

How could she have such conflicting feelings about Casson? Her wariness about his motives concerning Winter's Haven was manifesting itself even in her dreams, and yet she couldn't deny or resist his magnetic pull.

"It's okay, Justine," he murmured, gently stroking the back of her head. "I would never have your home demolished; I can promise you that."

His heartbeat seemed to leap up to her ear, and for a few seconds she just concentrated on its rhythm while inhaling the heady pine scent of his cologne.

"I'm sorry," she whispered, moving her face away from the wet spot on his T-shirt. "I—I didn't mean to slobber all over you."

She looked up and met his gaze tremulously. His expression made her heart flip.

Slowly his hand slid from the back of her head to cup her chin. He held it there, and with his other hand slowly wiped the tears from her cheeks. His fingers fanned her face gently, and she felt an exquisite swirling in her stomach at his tenderness. When he leaned closer she stopped breathing, and when his lips kissed her forehead she blew out a long, slow breath and closed her eyes.

"Oh, Cass..."

His lips continued to trace a path over each eye, the bridge of her nose and her cheeks, before finding the lobe of her ear. There his mouth lingered, opening to catch the tip in his mouth. She drew in her breath sharply and a flame of arousal shot through her like the fuse on an explosive. By the time his lips made their way to her mouth her lips were parted and her whole body was trembling in anticipation.

His lips closed over her upper lip and then her lower

one, pressing, tasting, before exploring deeper. Justine let out a small moan and felt herself surrendering, her senses flooded with the taste, smell and feel of him. Her body and his seemed to move in synchronicity, and in seconds the bedcovers were off and they were entwined on the mattress.

Casson pressed her against him and she wrapped her arms around his back, reveling in the heat and hardness of his body.

Justine knew there was no going back when Casson's lips started tracing a path from her neck downward. She shivered when he lifted her T-shirt off, wanting to squirm as his gaze devoured her. Casson shifted to one side and in two quick movements his own clothes were off.

With a searing desire she had never felt before Justine extended her arms and Casson gave himself to her.

At the first light of dawn Casson woke up. He stretched languorously before easing himself off the couch. His body tingled with the memory of his lovemaking with Justine. After they had both been sated they had dozed off. Hours later, when Luna had started pawing at the door and whimpering, Casson had returned to the couch, not wanting to disturb Justine. Besides, he'd needed to be up early to prepare for opening night.

If he hadn't had the exhibition to host this evening he would have been happy to nestle in Justine's arms all day... but the reality was he had to drive back home to Huntsville, get his suit and shoes for the event, and exchange his Mustang for the Ferrari.

There was no way he'd be going to the opening gala without it. and with Franklin's ball cap on the seat next to him. Then he'd go back to the cottage, and hopefully he'd see Justine before heading to the Stockey Centre.

He decided it would be better to leave Luna there, for

when Justine woke up. He glanced at his bedroom door. He had left his laptop in his room but, much as he wanted to, he couldn't bring himself to go in. He checked for new messages on his phone instead and then, satisfied that his committee had everything in place, changed into jeans and a shirt.

Casson started as Luna pawed at the front door. He opened the door as quietly as he could and when they'd returned prepared Luna's dish and set it down.

"Now, you be a good girl until I get back, Luna. Shh... no noise."

He gave her an affectionate scratch behind the ears and then started to walk to the door. Suddenly his footsteps slowed and he abruptly turned around.

What am I doing? I need to let Justine know about the event...

Casson had thought about telling Justine about it a few times before, but had always changed his mind, waiting for the right time to enlighten her as to the real reason for his resort venture.

Well, it was now or never...

Taking a strip of paper off a notepad, Casson scribbled a note to Justine and left it on the table. She might be furious with him for arranging such an event before even securing Winter's Haven, but he was willing to risk her wrath by having her come to the Stockey Centre and learn the real reason behind his actions.

Maybe then she would have a change of heart.

And if she was still absolutely against selling Winter's Haven he would go ahead and make her a new offer.

She could keep Winter's Haven and he would develop only the Russell properties for his venture, with her as manager.

It would be on a much smaller scale than he had originally planned, but he was willing to make some changes if that would keep Justine happy. And *he* would be happy having Justine as manager.

Who was he kidding?

It wasn't just that he wanted a manager. He wanted the love of a woman.

One woman... Justine.

He finished the note, turned the coffee maker on, and then slipped quietly out the door.

CHAPTER EIGHTEEN

THE AROMA OF coffee tingled Justine's nostrils and she opened her eyes, disoriented. It took her a few seconds to realize that she wasn't in her own room. Turning her head to look around, she felt it all come flooding back to her.

She was in Casson's bed.

She had gone to bed in here and he had gone to sleep on the couch.

Her eyes widened at the onrush of memories...

She had screamed, and Casson had come to her immediately. She had been dreaming about her home being demolished... Casson had comforted her, making her forget her dream completely...

She caught her breath as she recalled the way he had ignited her with the gentle exploration of his lips and hands, the way her responses had made him bolder.

And she had done nothing to stop him.

She hadn't wanted to; she had luxuriated in every masterful move he'd made, driving her to reciprocate just as passionately.

She retrieved his T-shirt and put it on, her limbs weak at the thought of Casson being in the kitchen. She wondered if he would be returning to the bedroom...

"Cass?" she said out loud, and then waited, her heartbeat accelerating.

A scuffle at the door seconds later along with a whimper made her smile.

"Good morning, Luna," she called out.

She waited for Casson's good morning, but all she heard was Luna pawing at the door. Justine opened it and Luna barged in, wagging her tail, and promptly jumped on the bed.

"I hope your master gave you permission to do that," Justine said, wagging her finger at Luna.

She peeked out the door, expecting to see Casson, but he wasn't there. She didn't hear the shower, or water running in the washroom, so where *was* he?

Justine walked to the door and looked out. His Mustang was gone. And she hadn't even heard it. Mystified, she walked into the kitchen. He must have only just left; the coffee was still dripping. *But why?*

Had last night meant so little to him that he could just take off like that? Or had something come up with Andy? Had Ronnie called with an emergency?

Her heart began to thud. And then she caught sight of her name on the piece of paper taped on the side of the coffee maker. She peeled it off, and praying it wasn't bad news, began to read...

Good morning, Justine.

I hope you had a good sleep. I'm sorry I couldn't stay, but I have some business to take care of. I'm heading to my home in Huntsville to pick up some things, and then I'll be in and out of the cottage before an event I need to attend tonight.

I meant to tell you about it, and you may have heard about it anyway. The Stockey Centre is holding an exhibition this week of the work of two of the Group of Seven artists. It's called Franklin & Casson on the Bay. It opens this evening. Please come.

I've already taken Luna out this morning, and she's had her breakfast —don't let her tell you otherwise!

Please make yourself at home—I know; it is your home!—and help yourself to coffee and the fabulous lemon blueberry muffins on the counter. A special friend made them.

Casson

P.S. I would have really liked to have had breakfast with you, Justine...

He had added a happy face, and relief flooded her that Casson's leaving had nothing to do with Andy. But she couldn't help feeling disappointed at how impersonal the letter seemed. Until she got to the part where Casson called her "a special friend." Her heart skipped a beat at that. And his last line lifted her spirits tenfold.

It wasn't exactly a declaration of love, or passion, and he had made no reference to the time they had spent together— or *how* they had spent the time—but it told Justine one thing for sure: Casson would have remained at the cottage this morning if he could.

Which meant that he wasn't running away from her, and that the previous evening must have meant *something* to him. That maybe he might be wanting to continue spending time with her...

Feeling a little giddy with happiness, Justine poured herself a cup of coffee. She had already made up her mind; she was definitely going to see Franklin & Casson on the Bay!"

And the man she loved.

Casson rolled down the windows of his Mustang, enjoying the feel of the morning breeze as he exited the main highway and turned on to the country road leading to Huntsville. He smiled at the thought of Justine reading his note in the kitchen. He pictured her in his T-shirt, relaxing with a mug of coffee.

When had he realized that he loved her company, loved everything about her?

Falling in love had not been on his agenda. It hadn't even been on his wish list. But, despite their awkward start, he and Justine had more than made up for it.

His abdomen tightened at the memory of her body, soft and hard in all the right places. It would be sweet torture to be away from her for the entire day. He hoped she would be free to spend some time with him when he drove back to the cottage. And he hoped she would accept his invitation to come to the opening night of the exhibition. It was time she saw for herself what his resort venture was *really* about.

He'd wait until after the event to break the news about the deed, though. He couldn't predict her reaction, but if she felt the same about him as he felt about her—and he was sure that she did—he was confident that they could come up with a solution.

After tonight there would be no more secrets between them. Not that he had kept any information from her with the intention of gaining the upper hand. No, he had simply tried to assess what would be the appropriate time to reveal his real motive in wanting Winter's Haven. And when she would be most receptive to hearing the news about the deed.

It was time for Justine to know the truth. He had seen passion in her eyes, and his body had been rocked with the passion they had shared, but he was certain that what they had experienced was more than just physical. He was confident he had gained her trust.

Realizing that he had increased his speed in anticipation of seeing Justine, he eased his foot on the pedal. Getting a ticket now would just delay his return.

Patience, he told himself. *You're minutes away...*

He had been successful on one count. Now all he needed was Winter's Haven.

And Justine Winter.

Justine finished her muffin and coffee, gave a lazy stretch, and padded back to the bedroom. Luna followed, and Justine ruffled her fur affectionately. She sauntered to the window and opened the blinds fully, letting in the early-morning sun. Turning, she let her eye fall on the brown envelope on the dresser.

She pressed her lips together and picked it up. Casson had wanted to show her the documents inside it from the very beginning. And yesterday as well… She didn't suppose it would bother him if she went ahead and looked through it without him.

She brought the envelope into the living room and curled up on the couch. She took out the contents: a number of files separated by clips. She riffled through them quickly, her eyes registering survey documents and reports, a deed, architectural designs, and a typed letter.

Seeing her name in the salutation startled her, and she pulled the letter from the pile and started to read.

Dear Ms. Winter,

As you know, I have recently purchased the properties on either side of Winter's Haven from Mr. and Mrs. Russell. In perusing the documents I discovered that their ancestors—the pioneers who first owned the acreage that comprises both their and your properties—had partitioned the land and eventually sold the parcel that years later became Winter's Haven.

Well, a few generations have come and gone, and

*it seems that the original papers were misplaced.
After the Russells sold to me, and started packing,
the original deed turned up and they passed it on to
me. I looked it over the other night and compared it
to the surveyor's report I received when my transaction was finalized.*

*To make a long story short, it seems that a sec-
tion of Winter's Haven is actually on the Russells'
property.*

"That's insane!" Justine blurted, letting out a hollow
laugh before continuing to read.

*I have verification that a section of your house
and some of your property is actually sitting on what
is now my property. You are welcome to check with
your lawyer. I already have with mine.*

*The properties passed hands years ago, between
neighbors and friends, and in one of those subsequent transactions a new survey report had to be
drawn up when the original deed couldn't be located.*

Justine clenched her jaw as she rifled through all the
documents and reports. Her cheeks burned. She bit her lip.
This couldn't be true.
After poring over them a second time she sank back
against the couch, the truth turning her body cold.

*I am willing to discuss the ramifications of this
finding with you, and anticipate our working together to discuss options that will result in a mutually satisfying solution.*

*I am prepared to make a substantial offer for Win-
ter's Haven, and would like to meet with you at your*

*earliest convenience to present you with my plans for
a resort development on the properties.*

*My contact information follows. I look forward
to hearing from you.*
Cordially yours,
Casson Forrester

Justine tossed the papers on the coffee table. The ice
that had filled her veins as she read every word of Casson's letter was now changing to a flow of red-hot lava.
She could still feel the burning in her cheeks, the roiling in
her stomach. Her breaths were shallow and her chest was
heaving, her lungs heavy with Casson's deceit.

How could he?

Why hadn't he shown it to her before? Or even mailed
it instead of playing games with her? Instead of manipulating his way into Winter's Haven after weaseling a deal
with the Russells...

The Russells sold willingly.

Justine put her hands over her ears in an attempt to
block that inner voice. Okay, so Casson had been proac-
tive, jumping on an opportunity. The Russells had come
over to her office to say their goodbyes, and had expressed
their excitement at moving south to be with their daughter.
Casson had made a decision that they had been waffling
over very easy. His timing—and his offer—couldn't have
been better, they'd said.

But keeping the deed a secret from her was despicable.

So what exactly did she plan to do about this? Justine
tried to digest the fact that Casson had a claim on part of
Winter's Haven. No wonder he was always so relaxed,
even when she appeared unexpectedly at his door. It was
as if he owned the place already...

Had she known this right from the beginning she
wouldn't have ended up in his bed—that much she knew.

Her stomach tightened as if she had been pummeled. Hot tears slid onto her cheeks and she bit her lip.

Casson had used her—manipulating her to get her under his control, working to soften her up so she would sell...

Her fists clenched. Robert had controlled her in one way—slowly building up their relationship while his marriage withered, and then dropping her when she no longer served his purpose. Justine had vowed never to let another man control her. And yet here she was, caught in the web that Casson had woven so meticulously. She had allowed herself to be manipulated yet again.

She could kick herself for being such a fool. How could she have let her guard down?

And how could she face Casson? He must be gloating inwardly. And what would he be expecting of her now? To give in and turn over the property, seeing how she'd so readily turned herself over to him?

Not a chance in hell.

Wiping the tears from her face, Justine stared blindly out the window. She took no pleasure from the view, her stomach twisting at memories of her and Casson in the bay. And of how thoroughly he had seduced her after her nightmare...

He had been just as bad, if not worse than Robert.

Holding her hand over her mouth, Justine fled to the washroom.

When Casson arrived at his house in Huntsville he wasted no time in gathering what he needed for opening night: suit, shirt, cufflinks, tie and shoes. He had already taken the A. J. Casson painting from his collection to the Stockey Centre when he had taken possession of the Russell properties.

He was anxious to get back to the cottage in time to look

over his opening speech and have a few hours to himself before heading to the center. Well, not really to himself. He smiled. He wanted to see Justine. Invite her properly to the exhibition opening and the banquet.

He had goofed by not mentioning the banquet in his letter, but he hoped she would understand and accept. A surge of excitement shot through his body. He was already feeling high because his dream of a resort for children with cancer was about to kick off, and if Justine accompanied him to the opening event he'd be over the moon.

Casson pulled into a gas station and called the office at Winter's Haven. With any luck Justine would answer, and he'd ask her to meet him at his cottage…

"Hi, Mandy." He tried not to let his disappointment show in his voice. "Would Justine be in the office?"

There was silence, and Casson wondered if there was a problem with the connection.

"Oh…hi, Casson. She…she was in here earlier, but she went back home."

Casson frowned. Mandy's voice wasn't as cheery as usual. "Would you mind giving her a message? I'm on my way back and should be there in half an hour. I'd appreciate it if she could meet me at my cottage when she gets a chance…"

Another pause. Then, "Will do."

"Thanks." Casson turned off his phone.

He shrugged. Mandy must be having a bad day. Oh, well, in a very short time *his* day would be getting even better.

With a roar of his engine, he headed toward Parry Sound.

Justine bit her lip and tried not to cry as Mandy put the phone down. She had already spent an hour crying at home, before splashing cold water on her face and going to the office. She had said nothing to Mandy about spending the night with Casson; she felt too humiliated. The only thing she had shared was the information in Casson's letter about the property.

When Casson had called she had waved her arms frantically, so that Mandy wouldn't reveal that she was in the office. Now Mandy was looking at her worriedly.

"Justine, maybe you *should* go and meet him. He might have come up with a solution..."

Justine gave a bitter laugh. "If I didn't trust him before, I trust him even less now."

"But he said in the letter he wanted to discuss options. Just hear him out. At the very least you can tell him how you feel. I can understand that you're royally ticked off, Justine. But nothing will be resolved without talking to him."

Justine pursed her lips. Maybe she *did* need to tell Casson how she felt. She took a deep breath. Yes, she decided, she would be meeting him at his cottage.

Prepared and ready to do battle.

Casson had let Luna out and was giving her a snack inside when he heard the sharp rap at the door. His heart did a flip when he saw it was Justine, but his smile froze on his way to get the door. There was no returning smile from her. In fact her eyes were puffy and red, her expression cold. She held her arms stiffly behind her back.

He opened the door. "Justine? Has something happened? What's wrong?"

Justine smirked. "Really?" She held up the envelope she had taken with her. "*This* is what's wrong." Her hand trembled. "You deliberately led me on in your scheme to get me to sell Winter's Haven, knowing the whole time that you already owned part of it." She clenched her jaw.

"You could have given me the letter—or mailed it to me—*before*."

Casson glanced at the envelope and then back at her, temporarily stunned. "How…?"

He didn't need to finish.

He had left it on the desk.

"Look, Justine—"

"No, *you* look. What you did was despicable. You and Robert can shake hands. At least he was drunk and not in his right mind. But you knew what you were doing. You *knew*."

Casson's heart twisted.

How could he convince her she had it wrong?

"Justine, I swear I didn't plan it to work out this way—"

"You can't deny you had a plan." Her narrowed eyes shot ice daggers at him.

"Yes, I had a plan—but not the one you think. I planned to come to Winter's Haven, meet you in person, and try to sell you my idea for a resort. I found out about the deed *after* making arrangements to stay at this cottage. I was waiting for the right time to tell you about it."

Justine cringed. "And when *was* that? After getting me to sleep with you?"

A fist in the gut would have been easier to take than the disgust in her voice.

"Justine, I did not sleep with you because I had an ulterior motive. It was not in my 'plan.' What happened between us was not premeditated. I'm not that kind of a guy."

She opened her mouth as if she were ready to fire back a retort, then closed it.

"I never tried to take advantage of you, Justine. My feelings are genuine." He sighed. "But I know now that I should have told you about the deed right from the start."

Justine crossed her arms, her expression grim. "So what exactly are you prepared to do about it?"

"I'm prepared to have a discussion with you about options—"

"*What* options?" Justine said hotly. "I will need to consult a lawyer as to how the deed can be adjusted and… and…" Her jaw clenched, as if she'd realized it wasn't going to be a simple matter to rectify. Especially with part of a structure—her *home*—on his property. "I need to call my parents," she said, throwing her hands up in the air and staring up at the ceiling. "Maybe they'll know what to do."

Something shifted inside of Casson when he heard the hint of despair in her voice.

He didn't want to hurt her; he had never wanted to hurt her.

For the first time he realized how vulnerable she felt when it came to Winter's Haven.

"Look, Justine," he said softly, hoping to reassure her, "I'm not taking or claiming even a corner of your house or your land. Right now, I think the only option is to leave things the way they are." He leaned closer, forcing her to meet his gaze. "When we can come up with a satisfying solution for the both of us, *then* we'll do something about it. And update the deed."

"The only satisfying solution for *you* is to get me to sell you the business." Justine's voice was tinged with bitterness.

"There could be other solutions…and they may come to light before my holiday here comes to an end."

"And what if they don't?" Justine's voice held a challenge.

"We'll figure something out," Casson insisted. "Even if it means locking ourselves in a room together until we do."

Justine shot him a *you're out of your mind* look before handing him the envelope. "I've made a copy of everything to give to my lawyer," she said curtly. "And I've left another copy in the office with Mandy."

She turned to leave.

"Justine." He waited until she'd turned around. "I know you're still upset, and you have every right to be, but I meant every word I said. I'm really sorry I hurt you." His voice wavered. "You might think I'm crazy to even ask… but I'd really like you to come to the exhibition tonight."

Justine's jaw dropped and her eyes narrowed into two beams of fury. "You've *got* to be kidding."

She walked stiffly out the door, letting it slam shut behind her.

CHAPTER NINETEEN

IN THE OFFICE, after giving Mandy a condensed version of the meeting she had had with Casson, Mandy asked if Justine would be going to the opening of the art show. Justine became flustered, and Mandy gave her a comforting hug.

"Just go," she urged. "Give the guy a chance. Let him talk to you when the shock has worn off..."

Back at home, Justine debated for two hours over whether or not she should go. She was still angry and hurt, not to mention bewildered as to what purpose Casson had in asking her to attend the opening.

She wanted to punish him by not accepting, but a tiny voice inside her told her she'd just be punishing herself. She remembered how happy she had been when Casson had suggested she go in his note... Besides, she was not going *with* him; she could stay as little or as long as she wanted. And she had to admit she *was* curious...

So she'd brace her broken heart and show Casson that she hadn't come undone as a result of his deception—that she was strong and capable of standing up to him. *That she wasn't under his control.*

Her mind was too clouded now to think of a solution to the deed issue, but she would contact her parents' lawyer in the morning and book an appointment as soon as possible. There *had* to be a way of voiding Casson's claim to Winter's Haven.

With a defiant toss of her head Justine went upstairs to look through her closet. The warrior in her was *not* defeated, she realized, her jaw clenching. She *would* go to Casson's event.

Dressed to kill.

Justine decided on a sleeveless black dress with a diagonal neckline, accented with filigree silver buttons. After styling her dark hair in soft flowing curls, she put on the dress. It hugged her curves and stopped above her knees. She chose a pair of silver dangling earrings with diamonds and sapphires—her parents' graduation gift. And finally she picked out a black shawl that shimmered with silver threads.

She was pleased when she saw her reflection, liking the way the sapphire stones matched her eyes.

She applied the barest amount of make-up—some delicate touches of blue and silver-gray eyeshadow, and a frosty pink lipstick. Blush wasn't necessary; her cheeks were already flushed.

She stepped into black pumps with silver stiletto heels and, grabbing her silver clutch purse, walked gingerly out to her car.

When Justine arrived at the parking lot of the Stockey Centre many spots were already filled. As she circled around her heart skipped a beat at the sight of a gleaming red car in a far corner.

Casson's Ferrari.

She sat for a moment after turning off the ignition, her hands gripping the wheel.

Did she really want to do this?

People were streaming into the building, being welcomed by a smiling doorman. Women with elegant dresses and glittering shawls, and bling that sparkled in the late-afternoon sun. Men sporting expensive suits and ties, their shoes gleaming.

Justine took a deep breath and climbed out of her car.

The huge foyer was buzzing with chatter. Justine had only taken a few steps when the people in front of her moved on to join their friends. It was then that Justine caught sight of the words Franklin & Casson on the Bay at the top of a huge banner stand. Her gaze dropped to the life-size image of two boys, grinning and holding up a fishing pole with their catch.

And then she froze when she realized that she was eye to eye with Casson. Not Casson the man, but Casson the boy. Her pulse quickened and her eyes flew to the boy next to him, with his two front teeth missing. *Franklin*. Her eyes began to well up. Squeezing them to clear her vision, she stared at the little boy who had passed away a year after this photo was taken.

Justine gulped. She had come to see paintings by Franklin Carmichael and A. J. Casson. The last thing she had expected to see was a huge image of Casson with his brother. It was heartbreaking. *But why had Casson done it?* She knew the connection between the brothers and the artists, but she'd had no idea that Casson would reveal something so personal to the public.

"Mr. Forrester couldn't have picked a better photo for this exhibition."

A guide with the name 'Charlotte' on her tag stood next to Justine. "The brothers on Georgian Bay. And what a beautiful tribute to Franklin—to plan a resort in his name."

"Resort?" Justine said, dazed.

"Yes. You must have heard about it in the news? Franklin's Resort. Mr. Forrester has purchased property in the area and is planning a luxury resort for children with cancer and their families to enjoy for a week after their final chemotherapy and radiation treatments. There will be no charge for them—which is why he is seeking support to augment his very generous contribution and to help keep the project viable."

She pointed to the registration table.

"There's a donation box on the table, and in the adjoining room Mr. Forrester has unveiled an A. J. Casson painting from his own private collection to be auctioned off tonight." She smiled at Justine. "Please sign your name in the guest book—and if you would like to receive information about future fund-raising events for the resort, please include your email address."

"Thank you," Justine managed to reply.

She glanced again at the faces of the brothers and thought of Andy. Feeling her eyes prickling, she quickly signed the guest book, put a few bills in the donation box and then, stifling a sob, turned away and started making her way through the throng to find the washroom, where she could get control of her emotions in private.

Halfway there, the tears started spilling out of her eyes. And then she bumped hard into someone and almost lost her balance, teetering on her stiletto heels.

"Justine."

Two arms came out to stop her from falling.

"I'm so glad you could come."

She recognized the deep voice even before looking up at tiger eyes.

Trembling, she fell against his chest and looked up at him with blurred eyes. *"Why didn't you tell me?"*

"It's complicated," Casson murmured in Justine's ear while helping her regain her balance. "I know where there's a quiet place to talk. *Please,*" he added, seeing her hesitate. "We need to talk."

"Mr. Forrester!" a voice called. "May we have a moment of your time?"

Casson turned and recognized a reporter from the local paper, striding toward him. Jake Ross. Beside him was the paper's photographer—Ken—who had already taken some photos of him next to the banner stand.

Casson smiled and nodded, before turning to Justine to tell her she didn't have to leave while they interviewed him. But she had already walked away and the crowd had closed in around her.

Damn!

Hiding his frustration, he checked his watch and led Jake and Ken to a quieter corner. He'd try his best to hurry things along. He wanted to clear things up with Justine before the banquet and auction.

While Jake interviewed him, asking all the questions Casson had expected to be asked, Casson kept glancing toward the crowd. He couldn't see Justine at first, and then a small group shifted to gather around a series of Casson paintings in order to hear the gallery owner's description of the pieces and he glimpsed her there, her lustrous hair framing her beautiful face.

Casson could hardly concentrate after that, taking in her little black dress from its slanted neckline to where it ended above her knees. Her legs were stunning in silky hose, and those shoes... His pulse couldn't help but race.

He heard Jake ask him a question twice, and forced himself to focus. Casson thanked Jake when the interview was over, and then the photographer asked to take some photos of Casson with the paintings.

"We want Casson next to the Cassons," he joked.

The gallery owner paused as they reached the group, and thanked the guests in advance for graciously waiting while the media did their job. Casson tried to catch Justine's eye, but she was deliberately keeping her gaze on one of the paintings. He stood in the center of the display, with paintings on either side of him, and patiently did what the photographer suggested.

"How about one with some of the guests?" Casson suggested, and placed himself impulsively next to Justine.

She looked up from the painting and raised her eyebrows at him with a *what do you think you're doing?* expression. Just then the photographer began to snap some pictures. Justine turned toward Ken at the first click, and Casson took the split-second opportunity to place his hand around Justine's waist and press her closer to him.

Another *snap* and Ken gave him a wink and a thumbs-up before sauntering off with Jake toward a large group at the Franklin Carmichael display.

Justine strode off in the opposite direction.

Casson quickly caught up.

"Why did you do that?" Justine muttered, glancing from him to all the people who were looking their way, and then back at him.

Even with a frown she was gorgeous. "Because I wanted my photo taken next to a beautiful woman," he said. "You look amazing, Justine." His eyes swept over her and he couldn't help smiling. "I was hoping you would come."

"Why?" Justine stared at him accusingly. "So you could make me feel guilty for not wanting to sell Winter's Haven when it's for such a good cause?"

Casson's smile faded. "I had no intention of making you feel guilty," he said quietly.

"Well, I *do*," Justine said, her voice wavering. "I—I wish you had told me from the beginning that your resort was to be a non-profit venture to help kids with cancer, and not for your own personal gain."

"You were dead-set against my proposal from the beginning," Casson reminded her. "I *wanted* to show you the plans, remember? I drove over to your place, but you weren't ready to see them or to hear me out…"

He moved to let someone go by.

"So I decided I needed to wait for the right time. I wasn't sure how long it would take, but I knew I had to try to find the opportunity to do so. And that's why I booked myself into Winter's Haven."

Casson looked over Justine's head at the crowd.

"Look, we can't talk here. Let's go outside. I know where there's a private exit."

He led Justine through a series of hallways to a door that he made sure stayed open a crack using his car keys. They walked out into a private courtyard with a view of the bay. The water was lapping gently against the rocky shore and a couple of seagulls swooped high above.

Casson stopped and gently took hold of Justine's elbow. "I wanted to tell you I don't know how many times," he said gruffly. "But the idea of talking about Franklin to you made me feel…too vulnerable."

He looked into Justine's eyes and knew he owed her complete honesty.

"I grew up suppressing the truth that my parents—my mother especially—were so devastated with losing Franklin that they forgot…forgot they had another son who was still alive."

He took a deep breath.

"They forgot that *I* was devastated too. I didn't show it, I guess. I tried to be the perfect son for them, so as not to cause them anymore grief, but being perfect wasn't enough to get them to really notice me. Don't get me wrong. I had a nice home, plenty of food, a great education. I didn't want for anything like that. What I wanted most was something that died inside of them when Franklin died."

Casson felt the backs of his eyes prickling.

"And maybe because of that I never knew if I had the capacity to really love somebody other than Franklin."

"You love Andy and Ronnie."

"Yes, I do. And this resort is for Andy's sake, too." He heard his voice waver. "I wasn't able to do anything for Franklin, but I *can* help Andy and other children like him…"

He took Justine's hands and covered them with his.

"I came to Winter's Haven with one thought in mind, and then I found myself falling in love."

"It's not hard to fall in love with Winter's Haven."

"I meant with *you*, Miss Winter."

Casson realized that Justine's eyes were welling up too.

"I was waiting until I felt I could trust you with my feelings, Justine. Until I felt that you wouldn't be indifferent."

"Oh, Cass…" Justine wrapped her arms around him, pressing her head against his chest.

Casson felt something let go inside him. Those two words she had uttered told him everything.

He lifted her chin so she would meet his gaze. "When I found out about the property issue I intended to offer you some options—whether you wanted to sell or not. But something made me hold back. I eventually realized that the better option was to forget about trying to get you to sell, and focus instead on starting with a smaller resort on the Russells' main property. I planned to offer you a position as manager of Franklin's Resort, and then you could still manage Winter's Haven. At least I wouldn't lose *you*."

He gazed at Justine, and what he saw in her eyes made his heart leap.

"You won't lose me, Casson," she replied breathlessly.

Her eyes were shimmering as he pressed her closer to him. He kissed her gently, and as her lips moved to respond he deepened the kiss until they were both enflamed.

With ragged breathing, he pulled away reluctantly. "The

banquet will be starting any minute," he said ruefully. "And I have to get myself under control." He took Justine's hand. "Come and join me. I'll have them add another place setting at my table."

Justine looked at him tenderly and shook her head. "No; this is *your* night, Casson. You need to focus on what you need to say. For Franklin's sake…and for kids like Andy." She planted a soft kiss on his lips. "I'll be waiting for you back home, Cass. With Luna-Lu."

He watched her walk away, his heart bursting, and then, with a lightness he couldn't remember feeling in a long time, he headed to the banquet room.

CHAPTER TWENTY

JUSTINE LEFT THE Stockey Centre with a sensation of wonder that made her whole body feel buoyant. She replayed Casson's words constantly in her head while driving home.

I found myself falling in love... With you, Miss Winter. He loved her.

And his honesty tonight had made her anger and hurt disappear. Her humiliation at being used—gone! Casson loved her, body and soul, and she loved him the same way. And trusted him.

But maybe she hadn't told him in so many words.

Well, she would make up for it tonight.

Her heart had broken when he'd told her about his parents. She could only imagine how lonely he must have felt. Growing up in the shadow of his brother's death. Craving the attention and love of his parents, whose grief had stunted any relationship they could have had with their remaining son.

Thank goodness Casson hadn't taken the dark path to get noticed. Fallen in with the wrong crowd. Justine's heart swelled with pride, thinking of how Casson had studied and worked hard to make something of himself. And if he had gone unnoticed in his youth, he was certainly making up for it now.

How could she have ever lumped Casson and Robert

into the same category? Who they were at their core was as different as dawn from dusk. Robert had acted in ways to satisfy his own ego, to benefit himself. Casson had been driven only by a selfless desire to use the resources he had to help children with cancer and to support their parents as well. And it wasn't a fleeting desire, but a lifelong intention. To honor his brother's memory.

Maybe she would have realized all this earlier, been open to Casson's vulnerability, if Robert's deception and her resulting distrust of him and other men hadn't influenced her judgment...

After leaving Casson, Justine had gone to take a peek at the A. J. Casson painting in the silent auction room. She'd been curious to see what Casson had so generously donated to help boost his venture.

A security guard had stood at the entrance, and Justine had passed him in order to get to the center of the room, where the painting was being displayed. A few other people had been standing around, gazing at the large oil painting on canvas and murmuring to themselves. The other invited patrons must have already left to attend the banquet, she'd thought.

Storm on the Bay was breathtaking. A dark sky was streaked with indigo, gold and red, and the swirling waters reflected the colors like cut glass. On the hilltops, pines swayed in every direction, their distinctive Muskoka shape instantly recognizable.

Justine had almost gasped when she'd read that bidding was set to begin at three hundred and fifty thousand dollars. But this was a prime piece of work by a member of the Group of Seven.

As the guests had bustled about, Justine had heard an elderly woman saying to her husband, "Imagine Casson Forrester doing all this to help children with cancer, in honor of his little brother. Now, *that's* my idea of a true Canadian hero!"

Smiling, Justine had taken her leave. And now here she was, in the driveway of Cottage Number One. With her master key, she let herself in.

Luna's affectionate welcome almost brought her to tears. She took Luna out for a break, made sure she had enough fresh water, and gave her a treat.

"Just for being my BFF," she said, and laughed, giving her a pat.

Justine went into the bedroom. The T-shirt was still on the bed, but it wasn't folded the way she had left it. A flash of electricity surged through her as she imagined Casson picking it up when he got back earlier. Justine shivered as she slipped the T-shirt over her body and breathed in the lingering scent of Casson's cologne. Desire coiled throughout her as she thought about how Casson looked tonight, in a tailored black suit and maroon tie...

With a contentedness and anticipation she had never felt before, Justine snuggled into the bed. She started when Luna suddenly nudged the door open and bounded on top of the bed.

"Okay...for a little while, Luna-Lu." She chuckled, rubbing Luna behind the ears. "Until your papa comes home."

She dimmed the lamp on the night table and closed her eyes, happily imagining everything that might happen after Casson walked in the door...

Justine felt the bed vibrating and blinked in confusion. Luna had jumped off the bed and Justine turned over to see Casson framed in the doorway, gorgeous and grinning, his black suit jacket draped over one arm and his maroon tie loosened.

She positioned herself on her elbows and flashed him a wide smile. "How did it go, Mr. *Forrest?*"

As Casson strode toward her he took off his tie and flung his jacket on top of her clothes on the chair. And then he was sitting next to her, his eyes gleaming.

"A resounding success, Miss *Wintry*. The final bid for *Storm on the Bay* was a whopping nine hundred and fifty thousand dollars."

Justine felt like crying and shouting with joy at the same time. She started to speak, but stopped when she felt her lips tremble. Her brow crinkled and a tear slid down her cheek.

"What's this?" Casson leaned forward and gently wiped her cheek.

He gazed at her so tenderly that Justine wanted to melt in his arms. She shifted to a sitting position and put her hands on his chest.

"I'm just happy for you," she said, fiddling idly with his cufflinks. "And for all the kids who are going to be able to stay at the resort one day. I... I thought about what you said before, Cass, and...and I will gladly accept your offer to manage Franklin's Resort."

Casson took her hand and slipped it underneath his shirt. The feel of his chest muscles and the beating of his heart made her pulse leap. She gazed into his eyes while he undid the rest of his buttons. And then, with a groan, he removed his shirt and wrapped his arms around her, kissing her with a passion that matched hers.

They fell back onto the bed, and Justine savored the firmness of his lips on hers. She ran her fingers through his hair and cupped the back of his head as his kiss deepened. She shivered as he kissed a path down her neck, sending flickers of heat through her. He stopped suddenly, and Justine's eyes flew open.

She watched in bewilderment as he got off the bed and began to kneel down on the rug beside the bed.

"Skedaddle, Luna," he ordered, and with a low grumble Luna got up and padded out of the room.

And there he was, on one knee, bare-chested, hair tousled from her touch, looking at her with those sexy, intense tiger eyes.

"What about my other offer?" he said huskily.

Justine frowned. *What other offer had he made?*

"I don't understand…"

Casson's eyes glinted. "The offer to be my wife."

He brought her hands up to kiss them, his gaze locking with hers.

"I love you, Miss Winter, and I would be honored if you'd accept my proposal to spend the rest of your life with me. I promise I won't pressure you about selling. Winter's Haven is yours, and I respect that. I'd be happy to develop only the Russell properties—*my* properties—for Franklin's Resort."

Justine breathed deeply, her heart ready to burst. "I rather think Winter and Forrester go hand in hand, don't you? Maybe we could change Winter's Haven to Winter's Forrest Haven. As for the offer to be your wife…" Her voice softened. "I accept, Mr. Forrester. And I love *you*."

She pulled at his hands and a smile spread across her face.

"Now, get up here, Cass, and let's seal the deal!"

EPILOGUE

CASSON LEANED BACK on the love seat with his arm around Justine. *His wife.* They had dimmed the lights and were gazing at the twinkling colored lights on the Christmas tree. Tinsel glittered from every tip, and the vintage Christmas ornaments that Justine had bought added to the brilliance.

He sniffed the air appreciatively. Justine had stuffed a turkey, and the aroma of it roasting, along with root vegetables and stuffing, was making his mouth water.

Ronnie and Andy would be arriving soon, to share their Christmas Eve dinner and to stay for a few days. Andy had been given a clean bill of health five months earlier, and had started to look more robust. His hair had grown in nice and thick, too.

Casson smiled. He couldn't wait to take him snowshoeing and ice-fishing. And skating on the bay. He had had a section cleared off for Andy to enjoy, with the new skates and helmet he would be giving him for Christmas, among the other things Ronnie had said Andy was wishing for.

Mandy and her fiancé were also on their way. They had set their wedding date for September, and were happily making plans. Justine's mom and dad were currently enjoying the heat in Australia, but had promised they would return to Winter's Haven in time for the baby's birth.

Casson put one hand on Justine's tummy and suddenly had a feeling of *déjà-vu*.

He had visualized this moment before...

His eyes sought Justine's—as blue-gray as the sky—and he gave a soft laugh.

"What's so funny, Cass?"

"I just remembered that I imagined a moment like this some time ago—when you were roasting marshmallows with Andy..."

She pursed her lips and he couldn't resist leaning forward to kiss her. *Thoroughly.*

When they drew apart, he saw that her eyes had misted.

"You and knowing we are going to have this baby are the best Christmas presents I could have ever hoped for or dreamed of," he murmured, stroking her head. "And when he or she is born in the summer, before the grand opening of Franklin's Resort, I'll be the happiest dad and man alive."

"Whether it's a boy or a girl?" She flashed him a grin.

"Whether it's a boy or a girl," he said solemnly, bringing her hand to his lips.

"We'll have to think about some names..." She cuddled up against him, placing her hand over his heart.

"Look, Justine!" He suddenly pointed toward the bay window. "A blue jay in the closest spruce tree."

He took her hand and led her to the window.

Justine caught her breath. "It's like a snow globe," she murmured. "How magical."

The snowflakes had been drifting down gently since early morning, and the evergreens were now padded with a soft quilt. The blue jay flitted from bough to bough, emitting its shrill cry and scattering snow like fairy dust. Its color was even more brilliant than usual against the dazzling white backdrop.

"How about Jay?" Casson said suddenly.

Justine's brow wrinkled as she gazed up at him.

"Jay…if it's a boy?"

Justine cocked her head at him. "I had a favorite doll called Amy. I was going to suggest Amy if it's a girl…"

The blue jay flew directly past the bay window.

Casson took both her hands, his tawny eyes blazing into hers. "I've got it! How about Amy Jay if it's a girl?"

Justine's heart flipped as she realized what Casson was getting at. *"A. J.,"* she whispered. "Oh, Cass, what a perfect name. I think Franklin would have approved." She placed a hand on her belly. "I have a feeling it'll be a girl…"

"And I have a feeling I'm in heaven," he said, and pulled her into his arms.

* * * * *

HIS MILLION-DOLLAR MARRIAGE PROPOSAL

JENNIFER HAYWARD

CHAPTER ONE

THURSDAY NIGHT DRINKS at Di Fiore's had been a weekly ritual for Lazzero Di Fiore and his brothers ever since Lazzero and his younger brother, Santo, had parlayed a dream of creating the world's hottest athletic wear into a reality at a tiny table near the back as students at Columbia University.

The jagged slash of red fire, the logo they had scratched into the thick mahogany tabletop to represent the high-octane Supersonic brand, now graced the finely tuned bodies of some of the world's highest paid athletes, a visibility which had, in turn, made the brand a household name.

Unfortunately, Lazzero conceded blackly as he wound his way through the crowd in the packed, buzzing, European-style sports bar he and Santo ran in midtown Manhattan, success had also meant their personal lives had become public fodder. A fact of life he normally took in stride. The breech of his inner sanctum, however, had been the final straw.

He absorbed the show of feminine leg on display on what was supposed to be Triple-Play Thursdays—a ritual for Manhattan baseball fans. Inhaled the cloud of expensive perfume in the air, thick enough to take down a lesser man. *This* was all *her* doing. He'd like to strangle her.

"This is turning into a three-ring circus," he muttered, sliding into a chair at the table already occupied by his brothers, Santo and Nico.

"Because the city's most talked-about gossip columnist chose to make us number two on her most-wanted bachelor list?" Santo, elegant in black Hugo Boss, cocked a brow. "If we sue, it'd have to be for finishing behind Barnaby Alexander. He puts his dates to sleep recounting his billions. I find it highly insulting."

"Old money," Nico supplied helpfully. "She had to mix it up a bit."

Lazzero eyed his elder brother, who was probably thanking his lucky stars he'd taken himself off the market with his recent engagement to Chloe, with whom he ran Evolution—one of the world's most successful cosmetic companies. "I'm glad you're finding this amusing," he growled.

Nico shrugged. "You would too if you were in the middle of *my* three-ring circus. Why I ever agreed to a Christmas wedding is beyond me."

Lazzero couldn't muster an ounce of sympathy, because the entire concept of marriage was insanity to him.

"*Show it* to me," he demanded, glaring at Santo.

Santo slid the offending magazine across the table, his attention captured by a glamorous-looking blonde staring unashamedly at him from the bar. Loosening his tie, he sat back in his chair and gave her a thorough once-over. "Not bad at all."

Utterly Santo's type. She looked ready for anything.

Lazzero fixed his smoldering attention on the list of New York's most eligible bachelors as selected by Samara Jones of *Entertainment Buzz*. A follow-up to her earlier piece that had declared the "Summer Lover" the year's hottest trend, the article, cheekily entitled "The Summer Shag" in a nod to Jones's British heritage, featured her top twenty bachelors with which to fulfill that seasonal pursuit.

Lazzero scanned the list, his perusal sliding to a halt at entry number two:

Since they're gorgeous and run the most popular athletic-wear company on the planet—Lazzero and Santo Di Fiore clock in at number two. Young, rich and powerful, they are without a doubt the most delicious double dose of testosterone in Manhattan. Find them at Di Fiore's on Thursday nights, where they still run their weekly strategy sessions from the corner table where it all started.

Lazzero threw the magazine on the table, a look of disgust claiming his face. "You do realize that *this*," he said, waving a hand around them, "is never going to be ours again?"

"Relax," Santo drawled, eyes now locked with the sophisticated blonde who couldn't take her eyes off his equally glamorous profile. "Give it a few weeks and it'll die down."

"Or not."

Santo shifted his attention back to the table. "What's got you so twisted in a knot?" he queried. "It can't be *that*," he said, inclining his head toward the magazine. "You've been off for weeks."

Lazzero blew out a breath and sat back in his chair. "Gianni Casale," he said flatly. "I had a call with him this afternoon. He isn't biting on the licensing deal. He's mired in red ink, knows his brand has lost its luster, knows we're eating his lunch, and still he won't admit he needs this partnership."

Which was a problem given Lazzero had forecast Supersonic would be the number two sportswear company in the world by the end of the following year, a promise his influential backers were banking on. Which meant acquiring Gianni Casale's legendary Fiammata running shoe technology, Volare, was his top priority.

Santo pointed his glass at him. "Let's be honest here. The *real* problem with Casale is that he hates your guts."

Lazzero blinked. "*Hate* is a strong word."

"Not when you used to date his wife. Everyone knows Carolina married Gianni on the rebound from you, his bank balance a salve for her wounded heart. She makes it clear every time you're in a room together. She's still in love with you, Laz, her marriage is on the rocks and Casale is afraid he can't hold her. *That's* our problem."

Guilt gnawed at his insides. He'd told Carolina he would never commit—that he just didn't have it in him. The truth, given his parents' disastrous, toxic wreck of a marriage he'd sworn never to repeat. And she'd been fine with it, until all of a sudden, a couple of months into their relationship, she'd grown far too comfortable with his penthouse key, showing up uninvited to cook him dinner after a trip to Asia—a skill he hadn't even known she'd possessed.

Maybe he'd ignored one too many warning signs, had been so wrapped up in his work and insane travel schedule he hadn't called it off soon enough, but he'd made it a clean break when he had.

"Gianni cannot possibly be making this personal," he grated. "This is a fifty-million-dollar deal. It would be the height of stupidity."

"He wouldn't be the first man to let his pride get in his way," Santo observed drily. He arched a brow. "You want to solve your problem? Come play in La Coppa Estiva next week. Gianni is playing. Bring a beautiful woman with you to convince him you are off the market and use the unfettered access to him to talk him straight."

Lazzero considered his jam-packed schedule. "I don't have time to come to Milan," he dismissed. "While you're off gallivanting around Italy, wooing your celebrities, someone needs to steer the ship."

Santo eyed him. "*Gallivanting?* Do you have any idea

how much work it is to coordinate a charity game at this level? I want to shoot myself by the end of it."

Lazzero held up a hand. "Okay, I take it back. You are brilliant, you know you are."

La Coppa Estiva, a charity soccer game played in football-crazy Milan, was sponsored by a handful of the most popular brands in the world, including both Supersonic and Fiammata. The biggest names in the business played in the game as well as sponsors and their partners, which made for a logistical nightmare of huge egos and impossible demands. It was only because of his skill managing such a circus that Santo had been named chairman for the second year in a row.

Lazzero exhaled. Took a pull of his beer. Santo was right—he should go. La Coppa Estiva was the only event in the foreseeable future he would get any access to Gianni. "I'll make it work," he conceded, "but I have no idea who I'd take."

"Says the man with an address book full of the most beautiful women in New York," Nico countered drily.

Lazzero shrugged. "I'm too damn busy to date."

"How about a *summer shag*?" Santo directed a pointed look at the strategically placed females around the room. "Apparently, they're all the rage. According to Samara Jones, you keep them around until you've finished the last events in the Hamptons, then say arrivederci after Labor Day. It's ideal, *perfect* actually. It might even put you in a better mood."

"Excellent idea," Nico drawled. "I like it a lot. Particularly the part where we recover his good humor."

Lazzero was not amused. Acquiring himself a temporary girlfriend was the last thing he had the bandwidth for right now. But if that's what it took to convince Gianni he was of no threat to him, then that's what he would do.

Making that choice from the flock of ambitious types

presently hunting him and ending up in Samara Jones's column, however, was not an option. What he needed was an utterly discrete, trustworthy woman who would take this on as the business arrangement it would be and wouldn't expect anything more from him when it was done.

Surely that couldn't be too hard to find?

Friday mornings at the Daily Grind on the Upper West Side were a nonstop marathon. Students from nearby Columbia University, attracted by its urban cool vibe, drifted in like sleepy, rumpled sheep, sprawling across the leather sofas with their coffee, while the slick-suited urban warriors who lived in the area dashed in on the way to the office, desperate for a fix before that dreaded early meeting.

Today, however, had tested the limits of even coolheaded barista Chiara Ferrante's even-keeled disposition. It might have been the expensive suit who'd just rolled up to the counter, a set of Porsche keys dangling from his fingertips, a cell phone glued to his ear, and ordered a grande, half-caff soy latte at exactly 120 degrees, *no more, no less*, on the heels of half a dozen such ridiculous orders.

You need this job, Chiara. Now more than ever. Suck it up and just do it.

She took a deep, Zen-inducing breath and cleared the lineup with ruthless efficiency, dispatching the walking Gucci billboard with a 119-degree latte—a minor act of rebellion she couldn't resist. A brief lull ensuing, she turned to take inventory of the coffee bar on the back wall before the next wave hit.

"You okay?" Kat, her fellow barista and roommate asked, as she replenished the stack of take-out cups. "You seem off today."

Chiara gathered up the empty carafes and set them in the sink. "The bank turned down my father's request for a loan. It hasn't been a good morning."

Kat's face fell. "Oh, God. I'm sorry. I know it's been hard for him to make a go of it lately. Are there any other banks he can try?"

"That was the last." Chiara bit her lip. "Maybe Todd can give me some more shifts."

"And turn you into the walking dead? You've been working double shifts for months, Chiara. You're going to fall flat on your face." Kat leaned a hip against the bar. "What you need," she said decisively, "is a rich man. It would solve all your problems. They're constantly propositioning you and yet you never take them up on their offers."

Because the one time she had, he'd shattered her heart into pieces.

"I'm not interested in a rich man," she said flatly. "They come in here in their beautiful suits, drunk on their power, thinking their money gives them license to do anything they like. It's all a big game to them, the way they play with women."

Kat flashed her an amused look. "That's an awfully big generalization don't you think?"

Chiara folded her arms over her chest. "Bonnie, Sivi and Tara went out the other night to Tempesta Di Fuoco, Stefan Bianco's place in Chelsea. They're sitting at the bar when this group of investment bankers starts chatting them up. Bonnie's thrilled when *Phil* asks her out for dinner at Lido. She goes home early because she's opening here in the morning. Sivi and Tara stay." She lifted a brow. "What does *Phil* do? He asks Sivi out to lunch."

"Pig," Kat agreed, making a face. "But you can't paint all men with the same brush."

"Not all men. *Them.* The suit," Chiara declared scathingly, "may change, but the man inside it doesn't."

"I'm afraid I have to disagree," a deep, lightly accented voice intoned, rippling a reactionary path down her spine. "It would be a shame for *Phil* to give us all a bad name."

Chiara froze. Turned around slowly, her hands gripping the marble. Absorbed the tall, dark male leaning indolently against the counter near the silver bell she wished fervently he'd rung. Clad in a silver Tom Ford suit that set off his swarthy skin to perfection, Lazzero Di Fiore was beautiful in a predatory, hawk-like way—oozing an overt sex appeal that short-circuited the synapses in her brain.

The deadpan expression on his striking face indicated he'd heard every last word of her ill-advised speech. "I—" she croaked, utterly unsure of what to say "—you should have rung the bell."

"And missed your fascinatingly candid appraisal of Manhattan's finest?" His sensual mouth twisted. "Not for the world. Although I do wonder if I could have an espresso to fuel my *overinflated ego*? I have a report I need to review for a big hotshot meeting in exactly fifty minutes."

Kat made a sound at the back of her throat. Chiara's cheeks flamed. "Of course," she mumbled. "It's on the house."

On the house. Oh, my God. Chiara unlocked her frozen knees as Lazzero strode off to find a table near the window. Chitchatting with Lazzero when he came in in the mornings was par for the course. Insulting the regulars and losing her job was not.

Amused rather than insulted by the normally composed barista's diatribe, Lazzero ensconced himself at a table near the windows and pulled out his report. Given his cynical attitude of late, it was refreshing to discover not all women in Manhattan were bounty hunters intent on razing his pockets.

It was also, he conceded, fascinating insight into the ultracool Chiara and what lay beneath those impenetrable layers of hers. He'd watched so many men crash and burn in their attempts to scale those defences over the past year he'd been coming here, he could have fashioned a graveyard out of their pitiful efforts. But now, it all made sense. She had been burned and burned badly by a man with power and influence and she wasn't ever going there again.

None of which, he admitted, flipping open the report on the Italian fashion market his team had prepared, was helping him nail his strategy for winning Gianni Casale over at La Coppa Estiva. The fifty-page report he needed to inhale might. As for a woman to take to Milan to satisfy Gianni's territorial nature? He was coming up blank.

He'd gone through his entire contact list last night in an effort to find a woman who would be appropriate for the business arrangement he had in mind, but none of them was right for the job. All of his ex-girlfriends would interpret the invitation in entirely the wrong light. Ask someone new and she would do the same. And since he had no interest of any kind in a relationship—summer shag or otherwise—that was out too.

Chiara broke his train of thought as she arrived with his espresso. Bottom lip caught between her teeth, a frown pleating her brow, she seemed to be searching for something to say. Then, clearly changing her mind, she reached jerkily for one of the cups on her tray. The steaming dark brew sloshed precariously close to the sides, his expensive suit a potential target. Lazzero reached up to take it from her before she dumped it all over him, his fingers brushing against hers as he did.

A sizzling electrical pulse traveled from her fingers through his, unfurling a curl of heat beneath his skin. Their gazes collided. *Held.* He watched her pupils flare in reaction—her beautiful eyes darkening to a deep, lagoon green.

It was nothing new. They'd been dancing around this particular attraction for weeks, *months*. He, because he was a creature of habit, and destroying his morning routine when it all went south hadn't appealed. She, apparently because he was one of the last men on earth she wanted to date.

Teeth sinking deeper into that lush, delectable lower lip, her long, dark lashes came down to veil her expression. "Enjoy your coffee," she murmured, taking a step back and continuing on her way.

Lazzero sat back in his chair, absorbing the pulse of attraction that zigzagged through him. He didn't remember the last time he'd felt it—felt *anything* beyond the adrenaline that came with closing a big deal and even that was losing its effect on him. That it would be the untouchable enigma that was Chiara who inspired it was an irony that didn't escape him.

He watched her deliver an espresso to an old Italian guy a couple of tables away. At least sixty with a shock of white hair and weathered olive skin, the Italian flirted outrageously with her in his native language, making her smile and wiping the pinched, distracted look from her face.

She was more than pretty when she smiled, he acknowledged. The type of woman who needed no makeup at all to look beautiful with her flawless skin and amazing green eyes. Not to mention her very Italian curves presently holding poor Claudio riveted. With the right clothes and the raw edges smoothed out, she might even be stunning.

And she spoke Italian.

She was perfect, it dawned on him. Smart, gorgeous and clearly not interested in him or his money. She did, however, need to help her father. *He* needed a beautiful woman on his arm to take to Italy who would allow him to focus on the job at hand. One who would have no expectations about the relationship when it was over.

For the price of a couple of pieces of expensive jewelry, what he'd undoubtedly have to fork out for any woman he invited to go with him, he could solve both their problems.

He lifted the espresso to his mouth with a satisfied twist

of his lips and took a sip. Nearly spit it out. Chiara looked over at him from where she stood chatting with Claudio. "What's wrong?"

"Sugar." He grimaced and pushed the cup away. "Since when did I ever take sugar?"

"Oh, God." She pressed a hand to her mouth. "It's Claudio that takes sugar." She bustled over to retrieve his cup. "I'm sorry," she murmured. "I'm so distracted today. I'll fix it."

Lazzero waved her into the chair opposite him when she returned. "Sit."

Chiara gave him a wary look. She'd started to apologize a few minutes ago, then stopped because she'd meant every word she'd said and Lazzero Di Fiore was the worst offender of them all when it came to the broken hearts he'd left strewn across Manhattan. Avoiding her attraction to him *was* the right strategy.

She crossed one ankle over the other, her fingers tightening around her tray. "I should get back to work."

"Five minutes," Lazzero countered. "I have something I want to discuss with you."

Something he wanted to discuss with her? A glance at the bar revealed Kat had the couple of customers well in hand. Utterly against her better judgment, she set her tray down and slid into the chair opposite Lazzero.

The silver-gray suit and crisp, tailored white shirt set off his olive skin and toned muscular physique to perfection. He looked so gorgeous every woman in the café was gawking at him. Resolutely, she lifted her gaze to his, refusing to be one of them.

He took a sip of his espresso. Set the cup down, his gaze on her. "Your father is having trouble with the bakery?"

She frowned. "You heard that part too?"

"Sì. I had a phone call to make. I thought I'd let the

lineup die down." He cocked his head to the side. "You once said he makes the best cannoli in the Bronx. Why is business so dire?"

"The rent," she said flatly. "The neighborhood is booming. His landlord has gotten greedy. That, along with some unexpected expenses he's had, are killing him."

"What about a small business loan from the government?"

"We've explored that. They don't want to lend money to someone my father's age. It's too much of a risk."

A flash of something she couldn't read moved through his gaze. "In that case," he murmured, "I have a business proposition for you."

A business proposition?

Lazzero sat back in his chair and rested his cup on his thigh. "I am attending La Coppa Estiva in Milan next week." He lifted a brow. "You've heard of it?"

"Of course."

"Gianni Casale, the CEO of Fiammata, an Italian sportswear company I'm working on a deal with, will be there as will my ex, Carolina, who is married to Gianni. Gianni is very territorial when it comes to his wife. It's making it difficult to convince him he should do this deal with me, because the personal is getting mixed up with the business."

"*Are* you involved with his wife?" The question tumbled out of Chiara's mouth before she could stop it.

"No." He flashed her a dark look. "I am not Phil. It was over with Carolina when I ended it. It will, however, smooth things out considerably if I take a companion with me to Italy to convince Gianni I am of no threat to him."

Her tongue cleaved to the roof of her mouth. "You're suggesting I go to Italy with you and play your *girlfriend*?"

"Yes. I would, of course, compensate you accordingly."

"How?"

"With the money to help your father."

Her jaw dropped. "Why would you do that? Surely a man like you has dozens of women you could take to Italy."

He shook his head. "I don't want to take any of them. It will give them the wrong idea. What I *need* is someone who will be discreet, charming with my business associates and treat this as the business arrangement it would be. I think it could be an advantageous arrangement for us both."

An advantageous arrangement. A bitter taste filled her mouth. Her ex, Antonio, had proposed a *convenient arrangement*. Except in Antonio's case, she had been good enough to share his bed, but not blue-blooded enough to grace his arm in public.

Her stomach curled. Never would she voluntarily walk into that world again. Suffer that kind of humiliation. Be told she *didn't belong*. Not for all the money in the world.

She shook her head. "I'm not the right choice for this. Clearly I'm not after what I said earlier."

"That makes you the perfect choice," Lazzero countered. "This thing with Samara Jones has made my life a circus. I need someone I can trust who has no ulterior motives. Someone I don't have to worry about babysitting while I'm negotiating a multimillion-dollar deal. I just want to know she's going to keep up her end of the bargain."

"No." She waved a hand at him. "It's ridiculous. We don't even know each other. Not really."

"You've known me for over a year. We talk every day."

"Yes," she agreed, skepticism lacing her tone. "I ask you how business is, or 'What's the weather like out there, Lazzero?' Or, 'How about that presidential debate?' We spend five minutes chitchatting, then I make your espresso. End of conversation."

His sensual mouth twisted in a mocking smile. "So we have dinner together. I'm quite sure we can master the pertinent facts over a bottle of wine."

Her stomach muscles coiled. He was disconcerting

enough in his tailored, three-piece suit. She could only imagine what it would be like if he took the jacket off, loosened his tie and focused all that intensity on the woman involved over a bottle of wine. She knew exactly how that scenario went and it was not a mistake she was repeating.

"It would be impossible," she dismissed. "I have my shifts here. I can't afford to lose them."

"Trade them off."

"No," she said firmly. "I don't belong in that world, Lazzero. I have no *desire* to put myself in that world. I would stick out like a sore thumb. Not to mention the fact that I would never be believable as your current love interest."

"I disagree," he murmured, setting his espresso on the table and leaning forward, arms folded in front of him, eyes on hers. "You are beautiful, smart and adept at putting people at ease. With the right wardrobe and a little added… *gloss*, you would easily be the most stunning woman in the room."

Gloss? A slow curl of heat unraveled inside of her, coiling around an ancient wound that had never healed. "A diamond in the rough so to speak," she suggested, her voice pure frost.

His brow furrowed. "I didn't say that."

"But you meant it."

"You know what I mean, Chiara. I was giving you a compliment. La Coppa Estiva is a different world."

She flicked a wrist at him. "Exactly why I have no interest in this proposal of yours. In these high-stakes games you play. I thought I'd made that clear earlier."

His gaze narrowed. "What I *heard* was you on your soapbox making wild generalizations about men of a certain tax bracket."

"Hardly generalizations," she refuted. "You need someone to take to Italy with you because you've left a trail of refuse behind you, Lazzero. Because Gianni Casale doesn't trust you with his wife. I won't be part of aiding and abetting that kind of behavior."

"A trail of refuse?" His gaze chilled to a cool, hard ebony. "I think you're reading too many tabloids."

"I think not. You're exactly the sort of man I want nothing to do with."

"I'm not asking you to get involved with me," he rebutted coolly. "I'm suggesting you get over this personal bias you have against a man with a bank balance and solve your financial problems while you're at it. I have no doubt we can pull this off if you put your mind to it."

"No." She slid to the edge of the chair. "Ask someone else. I'm sure one of the other baristas would jump at the chance."

"I don't want them," he said evenly, "I want you." He threw an exorbitant figure of money at her that made her eyes widen. "It would go a long way toward helping your father."

Chiara's head buzzed. It would *pay* her father's rent for the rest of the year. Would be enough to get him back on his feet after the unexpected expenses he'd incurred having to replace some machinery at the bakery. But surely what Lazzero was proposing *was* insane? She could never pull this off and even if she could, it would put her smack in the middle of a world she wanted nothing to do with.

She got to her feet before she abandoned her common sense completely. "I need to get back to work."

Lazzero pulled a card out of his wallet, scribbled something on the back and handed it to her. "My cell number if you change your mind."

CHAPTER TWO

CHIARA'S HEAD WAS still spinning as she finished up her shift at the café and walked home on a gorgeous summer evening in Manhattan. She was too distracted, however, to take in the vibrant New York she loved, too worried about her father's financial situation to focus.

If he couldn't pay off the new equipment he'd purchased, he was going to lose the bakery—the only thing that seemed to get him up in the morning since her mother died. She couldn't conceive of that prospect happening. Which left Lazzero's shocking business proposition to consider.

She couldn't possibly do it. Would be crazy to even consider it. But how could she not?

Her head no clearer by the time she'd picked up groceries at the corner store for a quiet night in, she carried them up the three flights of stairs of the old brick walk-up she and Kat shared in Spanish Harlem, and let herself in.

They'd done their best to make the tiny, two-bedroom apartment warm and cozy despite its distinct lack of appeal, covering the dingy walls in a cherry-colored paint, adding dark refinished furniture from the antiques store around the corner, and topping it all off with colorful throws and pillows.

It wasn't much, but it was home.

Kat, who was busy getting ready for a date, joined her in the shoebox of a kitchen as Chiara stowed the groceries away. Possessing a much more robust social life than she, her roommate had plans to see a popular play with a new boyfriend she was crazy about. At the moment, however, lounging against the counter in a tomato-red silk dress and impossibly slender black heels, her roommate was hot on the trail of a juicy story.

"So," she said. "What really happened with Lazzero Di Fiore today? And no blowing me off like you did earlier."

Chiara—who thought Kat should've been a lawyer rather than the doctor she was training to be, she was so relentless in the pursuit of the facts—stowed the carton of milk in the fridge and stood up. "You can't say anything to anyone."

Kat lifted her hands. "Who am I going to tell?"

Chiara filled her in on Lazzero's business proposition. Kat's eyes went as big as saucers. "He's always had the hots for you. Maybe he's making his move."

Chiara cut that idea off at the pass. "It is strictly a business arrangement. He made that clear."

"And you said *no*? Are you crazy?" Her friend waved a red tipped hand at her. "He is offering to solve all your financial problems, Chiara, for a *week in Italy*. La Coppa Estiva is the celebrity event of the season. Most women would give their right arm to be in your position. Not to mention the fact that Lazzero Di Fiore is the hottest man on the face of the planet. What's not to like?"

Chiara pressed her lips together. Kat didn't know about her history with Antonio. Why Milan was the last place she'd want to be. It wasn't something you casually dropped into conversation with your new roommate, despite how close she and Kat had been getting.

She pursed her lips. "I have my shifts at the café. I need that job."

"Everyone's looking for extra hours right now. Someone will cover for you." Kat stuck a hand on her silk-clad hip. "When's the last time you had a holiday? Had some *fun*? Your life is boring, Chiara. *Booorrring*. You're a senior citizen at age twenty-six."

A hot warmth tinged her cheeks. Her life *was* boring. It revolved around work and more work. When she wasn't on at the café, she was helping out at the bakery on the weekends. There was no *room* for relaxation.

The downstairs buzzer went off. Kat disappeared in a cloud of perfume. Chiara cranked up the air-conditioning against the deadly heat, which wouldn't seem to go below a certain lukewarm temperature no matter how high she turned it up, and made herself dinner.

She ate while she played with a design of a dress she'd seen a girl wearing at the café today, but hadn't quite had the urban chic she favored. Changing the hemline to an angular cut and adding a touch of beading to the bodice, she sketched it out, getting close to what she'd envisioned, but not quite. The heat oppressive, the blaring sound of the television from the apartment below destroying her concentration, she threw the sketchbook and pencil aside.

What was the point? she thought, heart sinking. She was never going to have the time or money to pursue her career in design. Those university classes she'd taken at Parsons had been a waste of time and money. All she was doing was setting herself up for more disappointment in harboring these dreams of hers, because they were never going to happen.

Cradling her tea between her hands, she fought a bitter wave of loneliness that settled over her, a deep, low throb that never seemed to fade. *This* was the time she'd treasured the most—those cups of tea after dinner with her mother when the bakery was closed.

A seamstress by trade, her mother had been brilliant with a needle. They'd talked while they'd sewed—about anything and everything. About Chiara's schoolwork, about that nasty boy in her class who was giving her trouble, about the latest design she'd sketched at the back of her notebook that day. Until life as she'd known it had ended forever on a Friday evening when she was fifteen when her mother had sat her down to talk—not about boys or clothes—but about the breast cancer she'd been diagnosed with. By the next fall, she'd been gone. There had been no more cups of tea, no more confidences, only a big, scary world to navigate as her father had descended into his grief and anger.

The heavy, pulsing weight encompassing all of her now, she rolled to her feet and walked to the window. Hugging her arms tight around herself, she stared out at the colorful graffiti on the apartment buildings across the street. Usually, she managed to keep the hollow emptiness at bay, convince herself that she liked it better this way, because to engage was to *feel*, and to feel hurt too much. But tonight, imagining the fun, glamorous evening Kat was having, she felt scraped raw inside.

For a brief moment in time, she'd had a taste of that life. The fun and frivolity of it. She'd met Antonio at a party full of glamorous types in Chelsea last summer when a fellow barista who traveled in those circles had invited her along. The newly minted vice president of his family's prestigious global investment firm, Antonio Fabrizio had been gorgeous and worldly, intent on having her from the first moment he'd seen her.

She'd been seduced by the effortless glamour of his world, by the beguiling promises he'd made. By the command and authority he seemed to exert over everything around him. By how grounded he'd made her feel for the first time since her mother had died. Little had she known, she'd only been a diversion. That the woman Antonio was slated to marry was waiting for him at home in Milan. That she'd only been his American plaything, a "last fling" before he married.

Antonio had tried to placate her when she'd found out, assuring her his was a marriage of convenience, a fortuitous match for the Fabrizios. That *she* was the one he really wanted. In fact, he'd insisted, nothing would change. He would set her up in her own apartment and she would become his mistress.

Chiara had thrown the offer in his face, along with his penthouse key, shocked he would even think she would be interested in that kind of an arrangement. But Antonio, in his supreme arrogance, had been furious with her for walking out on him. Had pursued her relentlessly in the six months since, sending her flowers, jewelry, tickets to the opera, all of which she'd returned with a message to leave her alone, until finally he had.

Her mouth set as she stared out at the darkening night, a bitter anger sweeping through her. She had changed since him. *He* had made her change. She had become tougher, wiser to the world. *She* was not to blame for what had happened, Antonio was. Why should she be so worried about seeing him again?

If this was, as Lazzero had reasoned, a business proposition, why not turn it around to her own advantage? Use the world that had once used her? Surely she could survive a few days in Milan playing Lazzero's love interest if it meant saving her father's bakery? And if she were to run into Antonio at La Coppa Estiva, which was a real possibility, so what? It was crazy to let him have this power over her still.

She fell asleep on the sofa, the TV still on, roused by Kat at 2 a.m., who sent her stumbling to bed. When she woke for her early morning shift at the café, her decision was made.

Di Fiore's was blissfully free of its contingent of fortune hunters when Lazzero met Santo for a beer on Saturday night to talk La Coppa Estiva and their strategy for Gianni Casale.

He'd been pleasantly surprised when Chiara had called him earlier that afternoon to accept his offer. Was curious to find out why she had. Thinking he could nail those details down along with his game plan for Gianni, he'd arranged to meet her here for a drink after his beer with Santo.

Ensconcing themselves at the bar so they could keep an eye on the door, he and Santo fleshed out a multilayered plan of attack, with contingencies for whatever objections the wily Italian might present. Satisfied they had it nailed, Lazzero leaned back in his stool and took a sip of his beer. Eyed his brother's dark suit.

"Work or pleasure tonight?"

"Damion Howard and his agent are dropping by to pick up their tickets for next week. Thought I'd romance them a bit while I'm at it."

"What?" Lazzero derided. "No beautiful blonde lined up for your pleasure?"

"Too busy." Santo sighed. "This event is a monster. I need to keep my eye on the ball."

Lazzero studied the lines of fatigue etching his brother's face. "You should let Dez handle the athletes. It would free up your time."

His brother cocked a brow. "Says the ultimate control freak?"

Lazzero shrugged. He was a self-professed workaholic. Knew the demons that drove him. It was part of the territory when your father self-destructed, leaving his business and your life in pieces. No amount of success would ever convince him it was *enough*.

Santo gave him an idle look. "Did Nico tell you about his conversation with Carolina?"

Lazzero nodded. Carolina Casale, an interior designer by trade, was coordinating the closing night party for La Coppa Estiva, a job perfectly suited to her extensive project management skills. Nico, who'd negotiated a reprieve from the wedding planning to attend the party with a client, had called her to request an additional couple of tickets for some VIPs, only to find himself consoling a weepy Carolina instead, who had spent the whole conversation telling him how unhappy she was. She'd finished by asking how Lazzero was.

His fingers tightened around his glass. *He could not go through another of those scenes.* It was not his fault Carolina had married a man old enough to be her father.

"I'm working on a solution to that," he said grimly. "Tonight, in fact. Speaking of solutions, you aren't giving me too much field time are you? I can feel my knee creaking as we speak."

Santo's mouth twitched. "I'm afraid the answer is yes. We need a solid midfielder. But it's perfect, actually. Gianni plays midfield."

Lazzero was about to amplify his protest when his brother's gaze narrowed on the door. "Now *she* could persuade me to abandon my plans for the evening."

Lazzero turned around. Found himself equally absorbed by the female standing in the doorway. Her slender body encased in a sheer, flowing blouse that ended at midthigh, her dark jeans tucked into knee-high boots, Chiara had left her hair loose tonight, the silky waves falling to just below her shoulder blades in a dark, shiny cloud.

It wasn't the most provocative outfit he'd ever seen, but with Chiara's curves, she looked amazing. The wave of lust that kicked him hard in the chest irritated the hell out of him. She had labeled him a bloody Lothario, for God's sake. Had told him he was exactly the kind of man she'd never get involved with. He'd do well to remember this was a business arrangement they were embarking on together.

Chiara's scan of the room halted when she found him sitting at the bar. Santo's gaze moved from Chiara to him. "*She's* the one you're meeting?"

"My date for Italy," Lazzero confirmed, sliding off the stool.

"Who *is* she?" His brother frowned. "She looks familiar."

"Her name is Chiara. And she's far too nice a girl for you."

"Which means she's *definitely* too nice for you," Santo tossed after his retreating figure.

Lazzero couldn't disagree. Which was why he was going to keep this strictly business. Pulling to a halt in front of her, he bent to press a kiss to both of her cheeks. An intoxicating scent of orange blossom mixed with a musky, sensual undertone assailed his senses. It suited her perfectly.

"I'm sorry I'm late," she murmured, stepping back. "The barista who was supposed to relieve me was sick. I had to wait until the sub came in."

"It's fine. I was having a beer with my brother." Lazzero whisked her past Santo just as his brother's clients walked in. Chiara cocked her head to the side. "You're not going to introduce us?"

"Not now, no."

"Because I'm a barista?" A spark of fire flared in her green eyes.

"Because my brother likes to ask too many questions," he came back evenly. "Not to mention the fact that we don't have our story straight yet."

"Oh." The heat in her eyes dissipated. "That's true."

"Just for the record," he murmured, pressing a palm to the small of her back to guide her through the crowd, "Santo and I started Supersonic from nothing. We *had* nothing. There is no judgment here about what you do."

Her long dark lashes swept down, dusting her cheeks like miniature black fans. "Is it true what Samara Jones said about you and your brother masterminding your business from here?"

His mouth twisted. "It's become a bit of an urban myth, but yes, we brainstormed the idea for Supersonic at a table near the back when we were students at Columbia. We kept the table for posterity's sake when we bought the place a few years later." He arched a brow at her. "Would you like to sit there? It's nothing special," he warned.

"Yes." She surprised him by answering in the affirmative. "I'll need to know these things about you to make this believable."

"Perhaps," he suggested, his palm nearly spanning her delicate spine as he directed her around a group of people, "you'll discover other things that surprise you. Why did you say yes, by the way?"

"Because my father needs the money. I couldn't afford to say no."

Direct. To the point. Just like the woman who felt so soft and feminine beneath his hand, but undoubtedly had a spine of steel. He was certain she was up to the challenge he was about to hand her.

Seating her at the old, scarred table located in a quiet alcove off the main traffic of the bar, he pushed her chair in and sat opposite her. His long legs brushed hers as he arranged them to get comfortable. Chiara shifted away as if burned. He smothered a smile at her prickly demeanor. *That* they would have to solve if they were going to make this believable.

She traced a finger over the deep indentation carved into the thick mahogany wood, a rough impersonation of the Supersonic logo. "Who did this?"

"I did." A wry smile curved his mouth. "I nearly got us kicked out of here for good that night. But we were so high on the idea we had, we didn't care."

She sat back in her chair, a curious look on her face. "How did you make it happen, then, if you started with nothing?"

"Santo and I put ourselves through university on sports scholarships. We knew a lot of people in the industry, knew what athletes wanted in a product. Supersonic became a 'by athletes, for athletes' line." He lifted a shoulder. "A solid business plan brought our godfather on board for an initial investment, some athletes we went to school with made up the rest."

A smile played at her mouth. "And then you parlayed it into one of the world's most successful athletic-wear companies. Impressive."

"With some detours along the way," he amended. "It's a bitterly competitive industry. But we had a vision. It worked."

"Will Santo be in Milan?"

He nodded. "He's the chairman of the event. He'll have his hands full massaging all of our relationships. When he isn't busy doing that with his posse of women," he qualified drily.

"Clearly runs in the family," Chiara murmured.

Lazzero set a considering gaze on her. "I think you would be surprised by the actual number of relationships I engage in versus what the tabloids print. I do need some time to run a Fortune 500 company, after all."

"So actually," Chiara suggested, "you are a choir boy."

A smile tugged at his lips. "I wouldn't go that far."

Chiara expelled a breath as a pretty waitress arrived to take their order. In dark jeans and a navy T-shirt, Lazzero was elementally attractive in a way few men could ever hope to emulate. When he smiled, however, he was devastating. It lit up the rugged, aggressive lines of his face, highlighting his beautiful bone structure and the sensual line of his mouth. Made him beautiful in a jaw-dropping kind of way. And that was before you got to his intense black stare that seemed to dissect you into your various assorted parts.

Which was clearly having its effect on their waitress. Dressed in a gray Di Fiore's T-shirt and tight black pants, she flashed Lazzero a high-wattage smile and babbled out the nightly specials. Without asking Chiara's preference, Lazzero rattled off a request for a bottle of Italian red, spring water and an appetizer for them to share.

She eyed him as the waitress disappeared. "Are you always this...*domineering*?"

"*Sì,*" he murmured, eyes on hers. "Most women like it when I take control. It makes them feel feminine and cared for. They don't have to think—they just sit back and... enjoy."

A wave of heat stained her cheeks, her pulse doing a wicked little jump. "I am not most women. And I *like* to think."

"I'm beginning to get that impression," he said drily. "The 'not like most women' part."

"What happens," she countered provocatively, "when you turn this hopelessly addicted contingent of yours back out into the wild? Isn't that exactly the problem you're facing with Carolina Casale?"

He shrugged. "Carolina knew the rules."

"Which are?"

"It lasts as long as she keeps it interesting."

Her jaw dropped. His arrogance was astounding. Carolina, however, had likely believed she was different—her cardinal mistake. As had been hers.

"She married Gianni on the rebound from you," she guessed.

"Perhaps."

She felt a stab of sympathy for Carolina Casale. She knew how raw those dashed hopes felt. Antonio had married within months of their breakup. Because that was what transactionally motivated men like Antonio and Lazzero did. They used people for their own purposes without thought for the consequences. It didn't matter who got hurt in the process.

The waitress returned and poured their wine. Chiara put the conversation firmly back on a business footing after she'd left. "Shall we talk details, then?"

"Yes." Lazzero sat back in his chair, glass in hand. "La Coppa Estiva is a ten-day-long event. It begins next Wednesday with the opening party, continues with the tournament, then wraps up on the following Saturday with the final game and closing party. We will need to leave New York on Tuesday night to fly overnight to Milan."

Her stomach lurched. She was actually doing this.

"That's fine," she said. "There's a girl at work who's looking for extra shifts. I can trade them off."

"Good." He inclined his head. "Have you ever been to Milan?"

She shook her head. "We have family there, but I've never been."

"The game," he elaborated, "is held at the stadium in San Siro, on the outskirts of the city. We'll be staying at my friend Filippo Giordano's luxury hotel in Milan."

Her stomach curled at the thought of sharing a hotel suite with Lazzero. But of course, they were supposedly together and they would be expected to share a room. Which got her wondering. "How do you expect us to act together? I mean—"

"How do I normally act with my girlfriends?"

"Yes."

He shrugged. "I don't expect you to be all over me. But if there is an appropriate moment where some kind of affection is in order, we go with the flow."

Which could involve a kiss. Her gaze landed on his full, sensual mouth, her stomach doing a funny roll as she imagined what it would be like to kiss him. It would be far from forgettable, she concluded with a shiver. That mouth was simply far too...*erotic.*

Which was exactly how she should *not* be thinking.

"You were right," she admitted, firmly redirecting her thoughts. "I don't have the appropriate clothes for this type of an event. I would make them, but I don't have time."

Lazzero waved a hand at her. "That comes with the deal. We have a stylist we use for our commercial shoots. Micaela's offered to outfit you on Monday."

She stiffened. "I don't need a stylist."

He shrugged. "I can send my PA with you with my credit card. But you would lose the benefit of Micaela's experience with an event like this. Which could be invaluable."

She hated the idea of his PA accompanying her even more than she hated the idea of the stylist. And, she grumpily conceded, a stylist's help would be invaluable given her doubts about her ability to pull this off.

"Fine," she capitulated, "the stylist is fine."

"*Bene.* Which brings us to the public story of *us* we will use."

She eyed him. "What were you thinking?"

"I thought we would go with the truth. That we met at the café."

"And you couldn't resist my espressos, nor me?" she filled in sardonically.

His mouth curved. "Now you're getting into the spirit. Except," he drawled, his ebony gaze resting on hers, "I would have gone with the endlessly beautiful green eyes, the razor-sharp brain and the elusive challenge of finding out who the real Chiara Ferrante is underneath all those layers."

Her heart skipped a beat. "There isn't anything to find out."

"No?" His perusal was the lazy study of a big cat. "I could have sworn there was."

"Then you'd be wrong," she came back evenly. "How long has this supposed relationship of ours been going on, then?"

"Let's say a couple of blissful months. So blissful, in fact, that I just put an engagement ring on your finger."

She gaped at him. "You never said anything about being engaged."

He hiked a broad shoulder. "If I put a ring on your finger, it will be clear to Carolina there is no hope for a reconciliation between us."

"Does she think there is?"

"Her marriage is on the rocks. She's unhappy. Gianni is worried he can't hold her."

"Oh, my God," she breathed. "Why don't you just tell Gianni he has nothing to worry about? That you have a heart of stone."

He reached into his jeans pocket and retrieved a box. Flipping it open, he revealed the ring inside. "I think *this* will be more effective. It looked like you. What do you think?"

Her jaw dropped at the enormous asscher-cut diamond with its halo of pave-set stones embedded into the band. It was the most magnificent thing she'd ever seen.

"Lazzero," she said unsteadily. "I did not sign on for this. This is *insane*."

"Think of it as a prop, that's all." He picked up her left hand and slid the glittering diamond on her index finger. Her heart thudded as she drank in how perfectly it suited her hand. How it fit like a glove. How warm and strong his fingers were wrapped around hers, tattooing her skin with the pulse of attraction that beat between them.

How *crazy* this was.

She tugged her hand free. "You can't possibly expect me to wear this. What if I put it down somewhere? What if I lose it?"

"It's insured. There's no need to worry."

"How much is it worth?"

"A couple million."

She yanked the ring off her hand. "No," she said, setting it on the table in front of him. "Absolutely not. Get something cheaper."

"I am not," he said calmly, "giving you a cheaper engagement ring because you are afraid of losing it. Carolina will be all over it. She will notice."

"And what happens when we call this off?" She searched desperately for objections. "What is Gianni going to think about that?"

"I should have him on board by then. We can let it die a slow death when we get back." He took her hand and slid the ring on again.

"I won't sleep," Chiara murmured, staring at the ring, her heart pounding. Not when she would publicly, if only for a few days, be branded the future Mrs. Lazzero Di Fiore. It *was* crazy. *She* would be crazy to agree to do this.

She should shut it down right now. *Would*, if she were wise. But as she and Lazzero sat working out the remaining details, she couldn't seem to find the words to say no. Because saving her father's business was all that mattered. Pulling him out of this depression that was breaking her heart.

CHAPTER THREE

CHIARA, IN FACT, didn't sleep. She spent Sunday morning bleary-eyed, nursing a huge cup of coffee while she filled out the passport application Lazzero was going to fast-track for her in the morning.

The dazzling diamond on her finger flashed in the morning sunlight—a glittering, unmistakable reminder of what she'd signed on to last night. Her heart lurched in her chest, a combination of caffeine and nerves. Playing Lazzero's girlfriend was one thing. Playing his *fiancée* was another matter entirely. She was quickly developing a massive, severe case of cold feet.

She would be to Italy and back—*unengaged*—in ten days' time, she reassured herself. No need to panic or for anyone to know. Except for her father, given she wouldn't be able to help out at the bakery on the weekends. Nor could she check in on him as she always did every night, a fact that left her with an uneasy feeling in the pit of her stomach.

She chewed on her lip as she eyed her cell phone. Telling her father the truth about the trip was not an option. He would never approve of what she was doing, nor would his pride allow him to take the money. Lazzero, for whom logistics were clearly never a problem, had offered to make an angel donation to her father's business through a community organization Supersonic supported which provided assistance to local businesses.

Which solved the problem of the money. It did not, however, help with the little white lie she was going to have to tell her father about why she was going to Italy. Her father had always preached the value of keeping an impeccable truth with yourself and with others. It will, he always said, save you much heartache in life. But in this case, she concluded, the end justified the means.

She called her father and told him she was going to be vacationing with friends in a house they'd rented in Lake Como, feeling like a massive ball of guilt by the time she'd gotten off the phone. Giving in to her need to ensure he would be okay while she was gone, she called Frankie De-Lucca, an old friend of her father's who lived down the street, and asked him to look in on her father while she was away.

She dragged her feet all the way down to meet Gareth, Lazzero's driver, the next morning for her shopping expedition with Micaela Parker. She was intimidated before she'd even stepped out of the car as it halted in front of the posh Madison Avenue boutique where she was to meet the stylist. Everything in the window screamed *one month's salary*.

Micaela was waiting for her in the luxurious lounge area of the boutique. An elegant blonde, all long, lean legs, she was more interesting looking than beautiful. But she was so perfectly put together in jeans, a silk T-shirt and a blazer, funky jewelry at her wrists and neck, Chiara could only conclude she was in excellent hands. Micaela was, after all, the dresser of a quarter of Manhattan's celebrities.

"Tell me a bit about your personal style," Micaela prompted over coffee.

Chiara showed her a few of her own pieces she'd made on her phone. Micaela gave them a critical appraisal. "I like them," she said finally. "Very Coachella boho. Those soft feminine lines look great on you."

"Within reason." A pang moved through her at the praise. "I have too many curves."

"You have perfect curves. You just need to show them off properly." Micaela handed back her phone. "What other staples do you have in your wardrobe we can work with?"

Not much, it turned out.

"Not a problem," Micaela breezed. "We'll get you everything. Luckily," she teased, "Lazzero's PA gave me carte blanche. He must be seriously smitten with you."

Chiara decided no answer was better than attempting one to that statement. Micaela took the hint and reached for her coffee cup to get started. Her eyes nearly popped out of her head when she saw the giant diamond sparkling on Chiara's hand.

"You and Lazzero are *engaged*?"

"It's brand-new," Chiara murmured, as every assistant in the shop turned to stare. "We haven't made a formal announcement yet."

"You won't have to now," Micaela said drily, inclining her head toward the shop girls. "Half the city will know by noon."

Oh, God. Chiara bit her lip. Why had she agreed to do this again?

Micaela led her into the dressing area and started throwing clothes at her with military-like precision. Telling herself it was the armor she needed to face a world in which she'd been declared not good enough, Chiara tried on everything the stylist presented her with and discovered Micaela had impeccable taste that worked well with her own personal style.

It was when they came to the search for the perfect evening dresses that Micaela got intensely critical. Chiara would be in the limelight on these occasions, photographed by paparazzi from around the world. They needed to be flawless. Irreproachable. Eye-catching, but not ostentatious.

Just the thought of walking down a red carpet made her stomach churn.

By the time they'd chosen purses and jewelry to go with her new wardrobe, she was ready to drop. Looking forward to collapsing at the spa appointment Micaela had booked for her, she protested when the stylist dragged her next door to the lingerie boutique.

"I don't need any of that," she said definitively. "I'm good."

"Are you sure what you have isn't going to leave lines?" Micaela asked.

No dammit, she wasn't. And she wasn't about to end up on a red carpet with them. Marching into the fitting room, she tried on the beautiful lingerie Micaela handed over. Felt her throat grow tighter as she stood in front of the mirror in peach silk, the lace on the delicate bra the lingerie's only nod to fuss.

Antonio had loved to buy her lingerie. Had always said it was because he loved having her all to himself—that he didn't want to share her with anyone else. He'd used that excuse when it came to social engagements too—taking her to low-key restaurants rather than his high-profile events because, she'd assumed, he was deciding whether he should make her a Fabrizio or not, and fool that she'd been, she hadn't wanted to mess it up.

Heat lashed her cheeks. Never again would she give a man that power over her. Never again would she be so deluded about the truth.

Sinking her fingers into the clasp of the delicate bra, she stripped it off. She hadn't quite shed the sting of the memory when Micaela whisked her off to the salon for lunch, hair and treatments.

Dimitri, whom Micaela proclaimed the best hair guy in Manhattan, promptly suggested she cut her hair to shoulder length and add bangs for a more sophisticated look.

A rejection rose in her throat, an automatic response, because her hair had always been her thing. Her kryptonite. Antonio had loved it.

That lifted her chin. She wasn't that Chiara anymore. She wanted all signs of her gone. And if there was a chance she was going to run into Antonio in Milan, she would need *all* her armor in place.

"Cut it off," she said to Dimitri. "And yes to the bangs."

Lazzero was on the phone tying up a loose end before he left for Europe on Tuesday evening when Chiara walked into the tiny lounge at Teterboro Airport. Gareth, who'd dropped her off with Lazzero's afternoon meetings on the other side of town, deposited Chiara's suitcase beside her, gave him a wave and melted back outside. But Lazzero was too busy looking at Chiara to notice.

Dressed in black cigarette pants, another pair of those sexy boots she seemed to favor and a silk shirt that skimmed the curve of her amazing backside, she looked cool and sophisticated. It was her hair that had him aghast. Gone were the thick, silky waves that fell down her back, in their place a blunt bob that just skimmed her shoulders. He couldn't deny the sophisticated style and wispy bangs accentuated her lush features and incredible eyes. It just wasn't *her*.

Wrapping up the call, he strode across the lounge toward her. "What the hell did you do to your hair?"

Her eyes widened, a flash of defiance firing their green depths. "It was time for a change. Dimitri, Micaela's hair guy, thinks it looks sophisticated. Wasn't that what you were going for?"

Yes. *No.* Not if it meant cutting her hair. She had gorgeous hair. *Had* gorgeous hair. He wanted to inform *Dimitri* he was an idiot. Except Chiara looked exactly like the type of woman he'd have on his arm. Micaela had done her job well. *So why the hell was he so angry?* Because he'd liked her better the way she'd been before?

"I'm sorry," he said gruffly. "It's been a long day. You look beautiful. And yes, it's chic...very sophisticated."

Her chin lowered a fraction. "Micaela was amazing. She gave me some excellent advice."

"Good." Catching a signal from a waiting official, he inclined his head. "We're good to go. You ready?"

She nodded and went to pick up her bag. He bent to take it from her, his fingers brushing against hers as he did. She flinched and took a step back. He grimaced and hoisted the bag. He was going to have to deal with that reaction before they landed in Italy or this relationship between them wasn't going to be remotely believable.

He carried it and his own bag onto the tarmac, where the sleek corporate jet was waiting. After a quick check of their passports, they were airborne, winging their way across the Atlantic.

He pulled out his laptop as soon as they'd leveled out. Chiara, an herbal tea in hand, fished out a magazine and started reading.

Together they silently coexisted, seated across from each other in the lounge area. Appreciating the time to catch up and finding it heartily refreshing to be with a woman who didn't want to chatter all the way across the ocean about inane things he wasn't the slightest bit interested in, it wasn't until a couple of hours later that he noticed Chiara wasn't really focusing on anything. Staring out the window in between flipping pages, applying multiple coats of lip balm and fidgeting to the point where he finally sighed and set his laptop aside.

"Okay," he murmured. "What's wrong?"

She dug into her bag, pulled out a newspaper and dropped it on the table in front of him. Too busy to have touched the inch-thick pile of press clippings that had been left on his desk that morning, he picked it up and scanned the tabloid page, finding the story Chiara was referring to near the bottom. It was Samara Jones's weekly column, featuring a shot of Chiara leaving a store, shopping bags in hand.

One Down—One to Go!

Sorry, ladies, but this Di Fiore is now taken. According to my sources, Lazzero Di Fiore's new fiancée was seen shopping in fashion hot spot Zazabara on Monday with celebrity stylist Micaela Parker, a four-carat asscher-cut diamond dazzling on her finger. My source wouldn't name names, but revealed an appearance at La Coppa Estiva was the impetus for the shopping excursion.

Lazzero threw the tabloid down. For once he didn't feel like strangling the woman. It was perfect, actually. Word would get around, Carolina would realize the reality of the situation and his problem would be solved.

The pinched expression on Chiara's face, however, made it clear she didn't feel the same way. "It was the point of this, after all," he reasoned. "Don't sweat it. It will be over in a few days."

She shot him a deadly look. "Don't sweat it? Playing your girlfriend is one thing, Lazzero. Having my face plastered across one of New York's dailies as your fiancée is another matter entirely. What if my father sees it? Not to mention the fact that it's going to be the shortest engagement in history. The press will have a field day with it."

He shrugged. "You knew they were going to photograph you in Milan."

"I was hoping it would get buried on page twenty." Her

mouth pursed. "Honestly, I have no idea how we're going to pull this off."

"We won't," he said meaningfully, "if you flinch every time I touch you."

A rosy pink dusted her cheeks. "I don't do that."

"Yes, you do." *Now*, he decided, was the time to get to the bottom of the enigmatic Chiara Ferrante.

"Have a drink with me before dinner."

She frowned. "I'm sure you have far too much work to do."

"It's an eight-hour flight. There's plenty of time. You just said it yourself," he pointed out. "We need to work on making this relationship believable if we're going to pull this off. Part of that is getting to know each other better."

Summoning the attendant, he requested a predinner drink, stood and held out a hand to her.

Chiara took the hand Lazzero offered and rolled to her feet. She could hardly say no. He would only accuse her of being prickly again. And she thought that maybe he was right, maybe if they got to know each other better she wouldn't feel so apprehensive about what she was walking into. About her ability to carry this charade off.

She curled up beside him on the sofa in the lounge area, shoes off, legs tucked beneath her. Tried to relax as she took a sip of her drink, but it was almost impossible to do so with Lazzero looking so ridiculously attractive in dark pants and a white shirt rolled up at the sleeves, dark stubble shadowing his jaw. It was just as disconcerting as she'd imagined it would be. As if the testosterone level had been dialed up to maximum in the tiny airplane cabin with nowhere to go.

God. She took another sip of her drink. Grasped on to the first subject that came to mind. "What sport did you play in university?"

"Basketball." He sat back against the sofa and crossed one long leg over the other. "It was my obsession."

"Santo too?"

His mouth curved. "Santo is too pretty to rough it up. He'd be running straight to his plastic surgeon if he ever got an elbow to the face. Santo played baseball."

She considered him curiously. "How good *were* you? You must have been talented to put yourself through school on a full scholarship."

He shrugged. "I was good. But an injury in my senior year put me on the sidelines. I didn't have enough time to get back to the level I needed to be before the championships and draft." He pursed his lips. "It wasn't meant to be."

She absorbed his matter-of-fact demeanor. She didn't think it could have been so simple. Giving up her design classes had been like leaving a piece of herself behind when money had been prioritized for the bakery. Lazzero had had his fingers on every little boy's dream of becoming a professional athlete, only to have it slip right through them.

"That must have been difficult," she observed, "to have your dream stolen from you."

A cryptic look moved across his face. "Some dreams are too expensive to keep."

"Supersonic was a dream you and your brothers had," she pointed out.

"Which was built on a solid business case backed up by a gap in the market we identified. Opportunity," he qualified, "makes sense to me. Blind idealism does not."

"Too much ambition can also be destructive," she said. "I see plenty of examples of that in New York."

"In the man who broke your heart?" Lazzero inserted smoothly.

Her pulse skipped a beat. "Who says he exists?"

"I do," he drawled. "Your speech at the café…the fact that you've never given any man who comes in there a fighting chance. You have 'smashed to smithereens' written all over you."

She sank her teeth into her lip, finding that an all-too-accurate description of what Antonio had done to her. "There was someone," she acknowledged quietly, "and yes, he broke my heart. But in hindsight, it was for the best. It made me see his true colors."

"Which were?"

"That he was not to be trusted. That men like him are not to be trusted."

He eyed her. "That is a massive generalization. So he hurt you...so he burned you badly. He is only *one* man, Chiara. What are you going to do? Spend the rest of your life avoiding a certain kind of man because he *might* hurt you?"

Her mouth set at a stubborn angle. "I'm not willing to take the risk."

"Did you love him?"

"I thought I did." She gave him a pointed look. "I could ask you the same thing. Where does *your* fear of commitment come from? Because clearly, you have one."

A lift of his broad shoulder. "I simply don't care to."

"Why not?"

"Because relationships are complicated dramas I have no interest in participating in." He took a sip of his drink. Rested his glass on his lean, corded thigh. "What about family?" he asked, tipping his glass at her. "I know nothing about yours other than the fact that your father, Carlo, runs Ferrante's. What about your mother? Brothers? Sisters?"

A shadow whispered across her heart. "My mother died of breast cancer when I was fifteen. I'm an only child."

His gaze darkened. "I'm sorry. You were close to her?"

"Yes," she said quietly. "She ran the bakery with my father. She was amazing—wonderful, *wise*. A pseudo parent to half the kids in the neighborhood. My father always said most of the clientele came in just to talk to her."

"You miss her," he said.

Heat stung the back of her eyes. "Every day." It was a deep, dark hollow in her soul that would never be filled.

Lazzero curled his fingers around hers. Strong and protective, they imparted a warmth that seemed to radiate right through her. "My father died when I was nineteen," he murmured. "I know how it feels."

Oh. She bit her lip. "How?"

"He was an alcoholic. He drank himself to death."

She absorbed his matter-of-fact countenance. "And your mother? Is she still alive?"

He nodded. "She's remarried and lives in California."

"Do you see her much?"

He shook his head. "She isn't a part of our lives."

"Why not?"

"It isn't relevant to this discussion."

She sat back in the sofa as a distinct chill filled the air. *Not a part of their lives?* What did that mean? From the closed-off look on Lazzero's face, it didn't seem as if she was going to find out.

She slid her hand out of his. Took a sip of her drink. "What other things should I know about you?" she asked, deciding the mood needed lightening. "Recreational pursuits? Likes, dislikes?"

His mouth quirked. "Are you looking for the dating show answer?"

"If you like," she agreed.

He took a sip of his wine. Cradled the glass in his palm. "I train in a gym every morning at six with a fighter from the old neighborhood. That's about the extent of my recreational activities other than the odd pickup basketball game with my brothers. I *appreciate*," he continued, eyes glimmering with humor, "honesty and integrity in a person as well as fine Tuscan wines. I *dislike* Samara Jones."

Her mouth curved as she considered her response.

"You've likely gathered from my speech at the café integrity is a big one for me too," she said, picking up on the theme. "*I*, like you, have little downtime. When I'm not working at the café, I'm helping out at the bakery, which makes my life utterly mundane. Although I do," she admitted with a self-deprecating smile, "have a secret obsession with ballroom dancing reality shows. It's the escapism."

Lazzero arched a brow. "Do you? Dance?"

"No." She made a face. "I'm horrible. It's entirely aspirational. You?"

"My mother was a dancer, so yes. She made us take classes. She thought it was an invaluable social skill."

She found the idea of the three powerful Di Fiore brothers taking dance classes highly entertaining. It occurred to her then that she had no idea what a date with Lazzero would look like. Did he take a woman dancing? Perhaps he whisked them off to Paris for lavish dinner dates? Or were the females in his life simply plus-one accompaniments to his endless social calendar?

Was he romantic or entirely transactional? She sank her teeth into her lip. *That* had nothing to do with a business arrangement, but God, was she curious. If she and Lazzero had ever acted on the attraction between them, how would it have played out?

She decided it was a reasonable question to ask, given their situation. "So what would a typical date night look like for you? So I have some sense of what *we* would look like."

He rubbed a palm over the stubble on his jaw, a contemplative look on his face. "We might," he began thoughtfully, "start off with dinner at my favorite little Italian place in the East Village. Nothing fancy, just great food and a good atmosphere. Things would definitely be getting interesting over dinner because I consider stimulating conversation and excellent food the best primer."

For what? she wondered, her stomach coiling.

"So then," he continued, apparently electing to illuminate her, "if my date decided she'd found it as stimulating as I, we'd likely head back to my place on Fifth. You could assume she'd end up well satisfied...*somewhere* in my penthouse."

Heat flared down low, a wave of color staining her cheeks. She wasn't sure if it was the "somewhere" that got her or the "well satisfied" part.

"I see," she said evenly. "Thank you for that very *visual* impression."

"And you?" he prompted smoothly. "What are your dating preferences? Assuming, of course, they involve the working-class, non-power-hungry variety of man?"

"I'm too busy to date."

He gave her a speculative look. "When *was* the last time you had a date?"

She eyed him. "You don't need to know that. It has nothing to do with our deal."

"You're right," he deadpanned. "I just want to know."

"No," she said firmly. "It's *not relevant* to this discussion."

An amused smile tilted his lips. "You could be out of practice, you realize?"

"Out of practice for what?"

"Kissing," he said huskily, his smoky gaze dropping to her mouth. "Maybe we should try one now and get it out of the way. See if we're any good at it."

Something swooped and then dropped in her stomach. She was seriously afraid she *was* out of practice. *Severely* out of practice. But that didn't mean kissing Lazzero was a good idea. In fact, she was sure it was a very *bad* idea.

"I don't think so," she managed, past a sandpaper dry throat.

"Why not?" His ebony eyes gleamed with challenge. "Or are you afraid of the very *real* attraction between us?"

Her pulse racing a mile a minute at the thought of that sensual, erotic mouth taking hers, she could hardly deny it. She *could*, however, shut it down. *Right now.*

She lifted her chin, eyes on his. "This is a business arrangement between us, Lazzero. When we kiss, it will be toward that purpose and that purpose only. Are we clear on that?"

"Crystal," he murmured. "I like a woman who can keep her eye on the ball."

CHAPTER FOUR

CHIARA'S MIND WAS on anything but business after that heated encounter with Lazzero. By putting the attraction between them squarely out in the open, he had created a sexual awareness of each other she couldn't seem to shake. Which absolutely needed to happen because that attraction had no place in this business arrangement of theirs. Particularly when Lazzero had clearly been toying with her with his own ends in mind—making them *believable* for Gianni Casale.

She retreated to a book after dinner, forcing herself to focus on it rather than her ill-advised chemistry with the man sitting across from her. Night fell like a cloak outside the window. With Lazzero still absorbed in his seemingly endless mountain of work, her eyelids began to drift shut. Giving in to the compulsion, she accepted his invitation to use the luxurious bedroom at the back of the plane and caught a few hours of sleep.

When she woke, a golden, early morning light blanketed the white-capped Italian Alps in a magnificent, otherworldly glow. She freshened up in the bathroom, then joined Lazzero in the main cabin. He'd changed and looked crisp and ready to go in a light blue shirt and jeans, his dark stubble traded for a clean-shaven jaw.

Her heart jumped in her chest at how utterly gorgeous he was. Did the man ever look disheveled?

"We're about to land," he said, looking up from the report he was reading. "Do you want coffee and breakfast before we do?"

She wasn't the slightest bit hungry, still groggy from sleep. But she thought the sustenance might do her good. Accepting the offer, she inhaled a cup of strong, black coffee and nibbled on a croissant. Soon, they were landing in Milan and being whisked from the airport to the luxury hotel Lazzero's Milanese friend, hotel magnate Filippo Giordano, owned near the La Scala opera house.

The Orientale occupied four elegant fifteenth-century buildings that had been transformed from a spectacularly beautiful old convent into a luxurious, urban oasis. Chiara was picking her jaw up off the ground when the hotel manager swooped in to greet them.

"We were fully booked when Filippo made the request," he informed them smoothly. "La Coppa Estiva is always *maniaco*. Luckily, the presidential suite became available. Filippo thought it was perfect, given you are newly engaged."

Chiara's stomach dropped. *This is well and truly on. Oh, my God.*

The stately suite they'd been allocated occupied the entire third floor of the hotel, living up to its presidential suite status with its high ceilings and incredible views of the city, including one from the stepped-down infinity pool on the elegantly landscaped terrace.

Sunlight flooded its expansive interiors as the butler gave them a personal tour. The suite's lush, tasteful color scheme in cream and taupe was complemented by its black oak woodwork, the perfect combination of Milanese style with a touch of the Orient.

Chiara's eyes nearly bugged out of her head when the butler showed them the showpiece of a bathroom, its muted lighting, Brazilian marble floors and stand-alone hot tub occupying a space as large as her entire apartment. But it was the gorgeous, palatial bedroom with its French doors and incredible vistas that made her heart drop into her stomach. *One elegant, king-size, four-poster bed*. How was that going to work?

Lazzero eyed her. "I'd asked for a suite, thinking we'd get one with multiple rooms, but clearly this was all that was available. I'll sleep on the sofa in the bedroom."

"No." She shook her head. "You're far too tall for that. I will."

"I'm not a big sleeper." He shut the argument down with a shake of his head.

They got settled into the suite, Chiara waving off the butler who offered to hang up their things because she preferred to do it herself. After a sumptuous lunch on the terrace, Lazzero went off to work in the office, with a directive she should take a nap before the party because it was going to be a late night.

She didn't have the energy to protest yet another of his arrogant commands. Too weary from only a few hours of sleep, she undressed in the serene, beautiful bedroom and put on jersey sweats before she crawled beneath the soft-as-silk sheets of the four-poster bed. The next thing she knew, it was 6 p.m., the alarm she'd set to ensure she'd have enough time to get ready sounding in her ear.

Padding out to the living room, she discovered Lazzero was outside swimming laps in the infinity pool. Deciding she would enjoy the pool with its jaw-dropping view tomorrow, *minus* what she was sure would be an equally spectacular half-naked Lazzero, she had a late tea, then took a long, hot bath in the sunken tub.

Lazzero came in to shower as she sat applying a light coat of makeup in the dressing room. Keeping her brain firmly focused on the mascara wand in her hand rather than on the naked man in the shower, she stroked it over her lashes, transforming them from their ordinary dark abundance to a silky, lush length that swept her cheeks. A light coat of pink gloss finished the subtle look off.

Makeup and hair complete, she slipped on the silver sequined dress she and Micaela had chosen for the party. Long-sleeved and made of a gauzy, figure-hugging material, it clung to every inch of her body, the sexy open back revealing a triangle of bare, creamy flesh.

She stared dubiously at her reflection in the mirror. It was on trend, perfect for the opening party, but it was shorter than anything she normally wore. Micaela, however, had insisted she had an amazing figure and needed to show it off. She just wasn't sure she needed to show so *much* of it off.

Pushing her doubts aside, she slipped on her gold heels, a favorite purchase from her shopping trip because they were just too gorgeous to fault, and a sparkly pair of big hoop earrings, her one concession to her bohemian style. And declared herself done.

She stepped out onto the terrace to wait for Lazzero. The sun was setting on Milan, the magnificent Duomo di Milano, the stunning cathedral that sat in the heart of the city, bathed in a rosy pink light, its Gothic spires crawling high into the sky. But her mind wasn't on the spectacular scenery, it was on the night ahead.

Her stomach knotted with nerves, her fingers closing tight around the metal railing. This wasn't her world. What if she said or did something that would embarrass Lazzero? What if she stumbled on one of the answers they'd prepared to the inevitable questions about them?

Her mouth firmed. She'd been taking care of herself since she was fifteen. She'd learned how to survive in any situation life had thrown at her in tough, gritty Manhattan which would eat you alive if you let it. Every *day* at the Daily Grind was an exercise in diplomacy and small talk.

Surely she could survive a few hours socializing with the world's elite?

And perhaps, she conceded, butterflies circling her stomach, she was winding herself up for nothing over Antonio. Perhaps he wouldn't even be there tonight. Perhaps he was out of town on business. He ran a portfolio of global investments—he very likely could be.

Better to focus on the things she could control. Another of her father's favorite tenets.

Fifty laps of the infinity pool with its incomparable view of Milan should have rid Lazzero of his excess adrenaline. Or so he thought until he walked out onto the balcony and found Chiara sparkling like the brightest jewel in the night.

Dark hair shining in a silken cap that framed her beautiful face, the silver dress highlighting her hourglass figure, her insanely good legs encased in mile-high stilettos—she made his heart stutter in his chest. And that was before he got to her gorgeous eyes, lagoon-green in the fading light, a beauty mark just above one dark-winged brow lending her a distinctly exotic look.

The tension he read there snapped his brain back into working order. "Nervous?" he asked, moving to her side.

"A bit."

"Don't be," he murmured. "You look breathtakingly beautiful. I'm even forgiving Dimitri for the hair."

She tipped her head back to look up at him, her silky hair sliding against her shoulder. A charge vibrated the air between them, sizzling the blood in his veins. "You don't have to feed me lines," she murmured. "We aren't *on* yet."

His mouth curved at her prickly demeanor. "That wasn't a line. You'll soon know me well enough to know I don't deliver them, Chiara. I'm all for the truth in its soul-baring, hard-to-take true colors. Even when it hurts. So how about we make a deal? Nothing but honesty between us this week? It will make this a hell of a lot easier."

An emotion he couldn't read flickered in her eyes. She crossed her arms over her chest and leaned back against the railing. "Tell me why this deal with Gianni is so important for you, then? Why go to such lengths to secure it?"

He lifted a shoulder. "It's crucial to my company's growth plans."

She frowned. "Why so crucial? Fiammata is a fading brand, Supersonic the rising star."

"Fiammata has a shoe technology we're interested in."

"So you want to license it to use in your own designs?"

His mouth curved. "Sharp brain," he drawled. "It's one of the things I appreciate about you." *Her legs being the other predominant one at the moment.*

She frowned. "What's the holdup, then?"

And wasn't that the multimillion-dollar question? A thorn unearthed itself in his side, burrowing deep. "Fiammata is a family company. Gianni may be having a hard time letting such an important piece of it go."

"As would you," she pointed out, "if it was yours."

"Yes," he agreed, a wry smile twisting his mouth, "I would." He reached across her to point to the Duomo, glittering in the fading light. "There is a myth that Gian Galeazzo Visconti, the aristocrat who ordered the construction of the cathedral, was visited by the devil in his dreams. He ordered Visconti to create a church full of diabolical images or he would steal his soul. Thus the monstrous heads you see on the cathedral's facade."

"Not really much of a choice was it?" Chiara said as she turned her head to look at the magnificent cathedral.

"Not unless you intend to embrace your dark side, no." His gaze slid over the graceful curve of her neck. Noted she'd missed a hook at the back of her dress. *Perhaps more nervous than she admitted.*

He stepped behind her. "You aren't quite done up," he murmured, setting his fingers to the tiny hook. It took a moment to work out the intricate, almost invisible closure, his fingers brushing against the velvet-soft skin that covered her spine.

She went utterly still beneath his hands, the voltage that stretched between them so potent he could almost taste it. Her floral perfume drifting into his nostrils, her soft, sensual body brushing against his, the urge to act on the elemental attraction between them was almost impossible to resist. To set his hands to those delectable hips, to put his mouth to the soft, sensitive skin behind her ear until she melted back into him and offered him her mouth.

But, he admitted, past his accelerating pulse, that would be starting something he couldn't finish because the *only* thing on the agenda tonight was nailing Gianni Casale down, once and for all.

He reluctantly pulled back. Chiara exhaled an audible breath. Turned to look up at him with darkened eyes, her pupils dilated a deep black among a sea of green. "He'll be there tonight? Gianni?" she asked huskily.

"*Sì*. Everyone in Milan will be there." He glanced at his watch. "Speaking of which, we should go or we'll be late."

The sleek Lamborghini Lazzero had borrowed from Filippo made quick work of the drive to the venue. Soon, they were pulling up in front of Il Cattedrale, the historic church where the opening party for La Coppa Estiva was being held.

Turned into a café/nightclub over a decade ago, its stately facade was lit for the festivities, illuminating the cathedral's elegant red brickwork and massive arched front door. Chiara's stomach turned to stone as she took in the scores of paparazzi jostling for position on either side of the stationed-off red carpet, camera flashes snapping like mad as they photographed the arrival of the world's glitterati.

There was the world's most famous Portuguese footballer making his way down the red carpet with his supermodel girlfriend, followed by the eldest princess of a tiny European municipality Chiara recognized from one of the gossip magazines her fellow barista Lucy kept under the counter. The princess's balding, older husband beside her was, Chiara recalled, a huge fan of football.

"Santo will be excited about that," Lazzero murmured as he helped her from the car. "Free publicity right there."

Her damp palm in his, her other clutching the tiny purse that matched her dress, Chiara didn't respond. *What had Micaela said about the etiquette for the red carpet?* Her mind felt as blank as a chalkboard wiped clean.

Lazzero passed the car keys to the valet and bent his head to hers. "Relax," he said softly, his lips brushing her ear. "I will be by your side the entire time."

A current zigzagged through her, one she felt all the way to the pit of her stomach. It didn't get any better as Lazzero straightened and pressed a hand to the small of her back. In a sophisticated black tux that molded his long, muscular frame to perfection, he was undeniably elegant. *Hot.* Utterly in command of his surroundings.

She took a deep breath and nodded. The handler gave them the signal to walk. Lazzero propelled her forward, stopping in front of the logo-emblazoned step-and-repeat banner so the photographers could get a shot of them. The heat from his splayed palm radiated through her bare skin, focusing every available brain cell on those few inches of flesh.

It did the trick in distracting her. Before she could blink, it was over and they were making their way inside the cathedral. Which was *unbelievable.*

Much of the original architecture of the church had been

left intact, stone walls and square pillars made of cream-colored Italian marble rising up to greet the original sweeping balconies of the cathedral. The massive chandelier was incredible, a full story tall, the large canvases on the walls impressive. But the most arresting sight of all had to be the original altar which had been converted into a bar under the dome of the church. Lit tonight in Supersonic red, it was spectacular.

"I've never seen anything like it," Chiara breathed. "It's like we've all come to pray to the gods of entertainment."

Lazzero's mouth twisted. "Exactly what Santo was envisioning. He'll be thrilled."

The crowds were so thick they were difficult to negotiate as they made their way toward the bar, the upbeat music drowned out by the buzz of the hundreds in attendance. Lazzero wrapped a hand around her wrist, guiding her through it as they sought out his brothers who held court at the bar.

Santo, whom she remembered from Di Fiore's, looked supremely sophisticated in a dark suit with a lavender shirt, every bit the blond Adonis the press painted him as. Nico had Lazzero's dark looks, so handsome in a clean-edged, perfect kind of way, he was intimidatingly so.

Both were undeniably charming. "Trust Lazzero to show up with the most beautiful woman in the room when he claims he has been out of circulation," Nico drawled, kissing both of Chiara's cheeks. "Although you picked the wrong brother," Santo interjected, stepping forward and lifting her hand to his mouth. "Why go for the middle brother when you can have the most physically viable of them all? Think of the genetics."

He said it so straight-faced, Chiara burst out laughing. "Yes," she said, "but Lazzero tells me you have a *posse*. I'm afraid that wouldn't do for me."

Santo pouted. "I will give it up when the time comes."

"That will be when you are old and gray." Nico handed her a glass of champagne and Lazzero a tumbler of some dark-colored liquor. Lounging back against the bar, the eldest Di Fiore nodded toward a table beside the dance floor. "Gianni arrived a few minutes ago."

Chiara's gaze moved to Gianni Casale, whose powerful presence stood out amongst the crowd at the table. In his midfifties, he had thick, coarse black hair tinged with gray, expressive dark eyes and a lined face full of character. Impeccably dressed in a charcoal gray suit with a silver-gray tie, he was, she conceded, undeniably handsome still.

Her attention shifted to the woman beside him. She didn't have to wonder if it was Carolina Casale or not because the brunette's eyes were trained on her and the hand Lazzero had rested on her waist. Remarkably beautiful with vivid blue eyes that matched her designer silk dress, dark hair and alabaster skin, the cool elegance she projected was borderline aloof.

She looked, Chiara concluded, as if she'd rather be anywhere than where she was. *Hungry* was the only word she could think of to describe how Carolina looked at Lazzero. She wondered if the other woman had any idea how obvious her feelings were.

Lazzero, on the other hand, looked utterly impassive as he turned around and got the lay of the land from his brothers. When they were suitably caught up, he tightened his fingers at her waist. "We should circulate," he murmured. "You okay with the champagne?"

She pulled in a deep breath. "Yes."

Lazzero spent the next couple of hours attempting to cover off the most important business contacts in the room as he played it cool with Gianni, waiting for the Casales to come to them. He should have been focused solely on business, his game plan with Gianni firmly positioned in his head, but his attention kept straying to the woman at his side.

He was having trouble keeping his eyes off Chiara's legs in that dress, as were half the men in the room. Despite the tension he could sense in her, a tension he couldn't wholly understand given the confidence he was used to from her, she remained poised at his side, charming his business associates with that natural wit and intelligence he had always appreciated about her. It was, he found, a wholly alluring combination.

He was about to acquire another glass of champagne for her from a waiter's tray when Carolina and Gianni approached, Carolina's hand on her husband's arm firmly guiding him toward them.

His ex-lover looked stunning, as beautiful as ever with those icy cool, perfect features, but tonight she left him cold. She had always been too self-contained, too calculating, too bent on getting her own way. Gianni, who'd spent three years putting up with those character flaws, eyed him warily as they approached, his dark eyes betraying none of the undercurrents stretching between them.

"Lazzero." Dropping her hand from her husband's arm, Carolina stood on tiptoe and pressed a kiss to both of Lazzero's cheeks. She lingered a bit too long, and as she did Gianni's eyes flashed with a rare show of emotion.

"Carolina." Lazzero set her firmly away from him so that he could shake Gianni's hand. Releasing it, he drew Chiara forward. "I would like you both to meet my fiancée, Chiara Ferrante."

The color drained from Carolina's face. "I'd heard the gossip," she murmured, her gaze dropping to Chiara's left hand, where the asscher-cut diamond blazed bright. "I thought it must be wrong." She forced a tight smile to her lips as she returned her perusal to Lazzero. "You swore you'd never marry."

"Things change when you meet the right person," Lazzero said blithely.

"Apparently so."

Gianni, ever the gentleman, stepped forward to compensate for his wife's lack of discretion. *"Felicitazoni,"* he said, pressing a kiss to Chiara's cheeks. "Lazzero is a lucky man, clearly."

"Grazie mille," Chiara replied. "It's all very new. We're still…absorbing it."

"When is the big day?" Carolina lifted a brow. "I haven't seen an announcement."

"We're still working that out," said Chiara. "For now, we're just enjoying being engaged."

"I'm sure you are." A wounded look flashed through Carolina's vibrant blue eyes. "You must be very happy."

Lazzero felt a bite of guilt sink into him. He shouldn't have let it go on so long. It was a mistake he would never repeat.

Chiara escaped to the ladies' room after that awkward encounter with the Casales. She felt sorry for Carolina who was so clearly still in love with Lazzero, who hadn't blinked the entire conversation. Because she knew that hurt—that rejection—what it felt like to be discarded for something *better.*

It took her forever to wind her way through the crowd to the powder room. An oasis in the midst of the celebration, it was done in cream and black marble with muted lighting and white lilies covering every available surface. Heading for one of the leather seats in front of the mirror, Chiara ran smack into an older woman on her way out.

An apology rose to her lips. It died in her mouth as she stared at the lined, still handsome face of Esta Fabrizio, Antonio's mother. She froze, unsure of what to do. The older woman swept her gaze over her in a cursory look, not a hint of recognition flaring in her dark eyes. Flashing Chiara an apologetic look, she murmured, *"Scusi,"* then moved around her to the door.

"Is it just you and Maurizio here tonight?" Esta's companion asked.

"Sì," Esta replied. "My son is out of town, so it is us representing the family tonight."

Chiara sank down on the leather seat, relief flooding through her as they left. *Antonio isn't here.* She could put that fear to rest. But quick on its heels came humiliation as she stared at her pale face in the mirror. Esta had looked at her as if she was nothing. But why *would* she remember her?

She'd treated Chiara as if she were a bug to be crushed under her shoe the day she'd shown up unexpectedly at Antonio's penthouse to surprise him for his birthday, only to find Chiara leaving for work. Esta had taken one look at Chiara, absorbed her working-class, Bronx accent and correctly assessed the situation. She'd informed Chiara that Antonio had a fiancée in Milan. That she was simply his American "plaything." The Fabrizio matriarch had added, with a brutal lack of finesse, that a Fabrizio would never marry someone like her. So best if she ended it now.

A bitter taste filled her mouth as she reached for her purse and fumbled inside for her powder and lipstick. Applying a coat of pink gloss and powdering her nose with shaking hands, she willed herself composure. She would *not* let that woman get to her again. The important thing was that Antonio was not here. She could relax.

Now all she had to do was pull herself together.

The party was in full swing when she exited the powder room. The lights had been lowered, the massive chandelier cast a purple hue across the room, the hundreds of smaller disco balls surrounding it glittered like luminescent planets in the sky. High in the ceiling, amidst that stunning celestial display, hung sexily dressed acrobats in beautiful red dresses, hypnotizing to the eye.

Music pulsed through the room, champagne flowed freely as couples packed the dance floor. She headed toward the bar where Lazzero and Santo had ensconced themselves. Almost groaned out loud when Carolina Casale flagged her down, two glasses of champagne in her hand. *That was all she needed right now.*

Carolina handed her a glass of champagne. "I apologize for my behavior earlier. I was caught off guard. I thought I should congratulate you properly. Lazzero and I go a long way back."

"He mentioned." Chiara considered Carolina warily as she took the glass. "*Grazie.* How *do* you know each other?"

"My firm did the interior decorating for Supersonic's offices as well as Lazzero's penthouse when he bought it." A low purr vibrated Carolina's voice. "Lazzero couldn't be bothered with that kind of thing."

Heat seared her skin. She could only imagine how that relationship had started. Carolina walking around Lazzero's penthouse with paint samples in her hand only to find herself in his bed. *Well satisfied*, no doubt.

"How did *you* and Lazzero meet?" Carolina prompted, a speculative glitter in her eyes. "Everyone is very curious about how you did the impossible by catching him."

"We met in a café."

The brunette arched a dark brow. "A café?"

"Where I work." Chiara lifted her chin. "We've known each other for over a year now."

An astonished look crossed the other woman's face. "You're a *waitress*?"

"A barista," Chiara corrected, her encounter with Esta Fabrizio adding a bite to her tone. "Love doesn't discriminate, I guess."

Carolina's face fell at the surgical strike. "Love?" Her

mouth twisted. "I would offer you a piece of advice about Lazzero. He is in *lust* with you, Chiara, not in love with you. He doesn't know *how* to love. So take my advice and make sure that prenup of yours is ironclad."

"Duly noted," Chiara rasped, having had more than enough. "Now, if you'll excuse me, I need to find my *fiancé*."

Santo eyed Chiara as she stood toe-to-toe with Carolina. "Should we intercede?"

"Give it a minute," Lazzero murmured, eyes on the exchange. "Chiara can handle herself."

"That she can." Santo shifted his study back to him. "I remember now where I've seen her before. Chiara. She's the brunette you were chatting up at the *Score* premiere."

"I wasn't chatting her up," Lazzero corrected. "I was saying hello. Her friend won tickets to the launch. I see her every day—it would have been rude not to say hi."

His brother gave him a disbelieving look. "And you're trying to tell me she is all business? That all she does is make your espresso every morning? I don't believe it. Not with that body."

A flash of fire singed his belly. "Watch your words, Santo."

His brother blinked. "You *like* her."

"Of course I like her. I brought her with me."

"No, I mean, you *like* her. You've never once warned me off a woman like that."

"You're overthinking it."

"I think not." Santo gave him a considering look. "She is far from your usual type. I think your taste has improved."

It might have, Lazzero conceded, if Chiara were *his*. Which she was not.

Santo drained his glass as Chiara stalked through the crowd toward them, an infuriated look on her face. "I see a damsel in distress. Off to do my duty. Good luck with *that*."

Santo waltzed off into the crowd. Chiara slid onto the bar stool beside him, her green eyes flashing as she downed a gulp of champagne.

Lazzero eyed her. "What did she say?"

"She is—" Chiara waved a hand at him. "She was *rude*. She told me to make sure my prenup is airtight because it isn't going to last."

"It *isn't* going to last," he said. "This is fake, remember? Why are you so upset?"

She gave him a black look. "She made it clear a barista is *beneath* you."

"That's ridiculous."

"Is it?" Her mouth set in a mutinous line. "Carolina owns her own interior decorating firm. *I* am merely a barista you hired to play your fiancée…someone who couldn't, in a million years, afford to say no to your offer. Someone you would never *consider* marrying." Her eyes darkened. "This is exactly what I was talking about earlier…the games rich people play where people get hurt. Carolina might be a bitch, Lazzero, but she is *wounded*."

A flare of antagonism lanced through him. "I think you have it the wrong way around. I'm doing this so that *no one* gets hurt. If I made a mistake with Carolina, which I might have, it was in letting the relationship drag on for too long. Since I acknowledge I made that mistake, I am rectifying it now by not hurting her further by giving her hope for something that can never be."

She gave him a caustic look. "Exactly what do you think is going to happen if you do commit to a woman? The bogeyman is going to come get you?"

The fuse inside him caught fire. "Speaks the woman who doesn't date?"

"At least I acknowledge my faults."

"I just did," he growled. "And as far as you and Carolina are concerned, you are right, you are *not* in the same class as her. You *outclass* her in every way, Chiara. Carolina is an entitled piece of work who uses everything and everyone in her life to her own advantage. You are hardworking and fiercely independent with an honesty and integrity I admire. So can we please put the subject of your worth to rest?"

Her indignation came to a sliding halt. "So why *did* you date her, then?"

A hint of the devil arrowed through him, fueled by his intense irritation. "She took off her clothes during our consultation appointment at my penthouse. What was I going to do?"

Her eyes widened. "You aren't joking, are you?"

"No."

"I walked right into that one, didn't I?"

"Yes. Now," he murmured, bringing his mouth to her ear, "can we move on? Gianni just sat down at the end of the bar. He's watching us and I'd like to make this somewhat believable."

She blew out a breath. "Yes."

"Bene." He nodded toward her almost empty glass of champagne. "Drink up and let's dance."

She cast a wary eye toward the dance floor, where the couples were moving to the sinuous rhythm of a Latin tune. "Not to this."

"This," he insisted, sliding off the stool and tugging her off hers.

"Lazzero, I don't know how," she protested, setting her glass on the bar and dragging her feet. "It's been years since I took salsa lessons and I was *terrible*. I'm going to look ridiculous out there."

He stopped on the edge of the dance floor and tipped her chin up with his fingers. "All you have to do is let me lead," he said softly. "Give up that formidable control of yours for once, Chiara, because this dance doesn't work without complete and total…submission."

Chiara's heart thumped wildly against her ribs as Lazzero led her onto the dance floor. The feel of his fingers wrapped around her wrist sent a surge of electricity through her, tiny sparks unearthing themselves over every inch of her skin.

This is such a bad, bad idea.

A new song began as they found a free space among the dancers. Sultry and seductive, it brought back memories of the bruised feet and embarrassing silences she'd stumbled through in dance classes. She attempted one last objection as Lazzero pulled her close, clasping one hand around hers, the other resting against her back. "Back on one," he said, cutting off her protest, "forward on five."

She wasn't sure how she was supposed to remember the *first* step with the heat of his tall, muscular body so close to hers, his sexy, spicy aftershave infiltrating her head. But she couldn't just stand there on the dance floor doing nothing with everyone watching, so she took a deep breath and stepped back to mirror Lazzero's basic step.

Her lessons, remarkably, came back immediately, the basic step easy enough to execute. Except she was all out of rhythm and stumbled into him, her cheeks heating.

"Follow my lead," Lazzero growled. "And look at *me*, not at the floor. When I push, you step back, when I pull, you move forward. It's very basic. Follow my signals."

Except that was a dangerous thing to do because his eyes had a sexy, seductive glimmer in them that had nothing to do with a business deal and the champagne had now fully gone to her head, making any attempt at sophisticated steps a concerted effort.

Forcing herself to concentrate, she followed his lead before she fell flat on her face. His grip firm and commanding, he guided her through the steps until she was picking out the basic movement in time to the music.

"Now you've got it," he murmured, as they executed a simple right turn. "See, isn't this fun?"

It was, in fact, with a lead as good as Lazzero. He moved in ways a man shouldn't be able to, his hips fluid and graceful. She started to trust he would place her where she needed to be and gave herself in to the sensual rhythm of the dance. The champagne, fully charging her bloodstream now, had the positive effect of loosening her inhibitions even further as they pulled off some more sophisticated steps and turns.

By the time the song was over, she was having so much fun, she fell laughing into Lazzero's arms on the final turn. Caught up in all that muscle, his powerful body pressed against the length of hers, she swallowed past the racing of her heart as a languorous, slow number began to play. "Maybe we should go get a drink," she suggested, breathlessly. "I am *seriously* thirsty."

"While I have you so soft and compliant and all womanly in my arms?" he mocked lightly, sliding an arm around her waist to pull her closer. "We're actually managing to be convincing at the moment. I'd like to enjoy the novelty before the arrows start flying again."

"I don't do that," she protested.

"Yes, you do." He gave her a considering look. "I think it's a defense mechanism."

"Against what?"

"I'm still trying to figure that out."

She followed him through the slow, lazy steps, excruciatingly aware of the hard press of his powerful thighs against hers, the thump of his heart beneath her hand, *the brush of his mouth against her temple.*

"Lazzero," she breathed.

"The Casales are watching. Relax."

Impossible. Not with the warm touch of those sensual lips on her skin giving her an idea of how they'd feel all over her. The smooth caress of his palm against the small of her back, burning into her bare skin. Definitely not when his mouth traced a path along the length of her jaw.

He was going to kiss her, she registered with a wild jump of her heart. And there was nothing she could do to stop it. Nor could she even pretend she wanted to.

Electric shivers slid up her spine as he tilted her chin up with his thumb, holding her captive to his purposeful ebony gaze. Her breath stopped in her chest as he bent his head and lowered his mouth to hers in a butterfly-light kiss meant to seduce.

This isn't real, she cautioned herself. But it was fruitless, as every nerve ending seemed to catch fire. Lips whispering against hers, his thumb stroking her jaw, he teased and tantalized with so much sensual expertise, she was lost before the battle even began, her lips clinging to his as she tentatively returned the kiss.

Nestling her jaw more securely in his palm, he tugged her up on tiptoe with the hand he held at her waist and took the kiss deeper. Head tilted back, each slide of his mouth over hers sending sparks through her, Chiara forgot everything but what it felt like to be kissed like this. To be *seduced*. As if lightning had struck.

A sound left the back of her throat as her fingers crept around his neck. Clenched tensile, hard muscle. Murmuring his approval, he nudged her mouth apart with the slick glide of his tongue and delved inside with a heated caress that liquefied her insides. Weakened her knees.

She moved closer to him, wanting, *needing* his support. His hand slid to her hip, shifting her closer to all that muscle, until she was molded to every centimeter of him, the languorous drift of his mouth over hers, his deep, drugging kisses, shooting sparks of fire through her.

A low groan tore itself from his throat, the hand he held at her bottom bringing her into direct contact with the shockingly hard ridge of his arousal. She should have been scandalized. Instead, the wave of heat coursing through her crashed deeper, a fission of white-hot sexual awareness arcing through her.

She was so far gone, so lost in him, she almost protested when Lazzero broke the kiss with a nuzzling slowness, his fingers at her waist holding her steady as he dragged his mouth to her ear.

"The song is over," he murmured. "As much as I hate to say it."

The lazy satisfaction in his voice, the beat of a fast new tune, brought the world into focus with shocking swiftness. *What was she doing? Had she lost her mind?* Lazzero had kissed her to prove a point to the Casales. This was just a *game* to him, she simply a pawn he was playing. And she had pretty much thrown herself at him.

Head spinning, heart pounding, she pulled herself out of his arms. "Chiara," he murmured, his eyes on hers, "it was just a kiss."

Just a kiss. It felt as if the earth had moved beneath her feet. Like nothing she'd ever experienced before, not even with Antonio who'd been practiced in the art of seduction. But for Lazzero, it had been *just a kiss*.

Had she learned nothing from her experiences?

She took a step back. Lifted her chin. "*Sì*," she agreed unsteadily, "it was just a kiss. And, now that we've given an award-winning performance, I think I've had enough."

CHAPTER FIVE

JUST A KISS.

Clearly, Lazzero conceded as he drove back to the hotel at the close of the night, that hadn't been the right line to feed Chiara at that particular moment in time. She had given him one of those death glares of hers, stalked off the dance floor and remained distant for the rest of the evening, unless required to turn it on for public consumption.

The chill had continued in the car, with her blowing off his attempts at conversation. But could he blame her, really? A kiss might have been in order, but *that* hadn't been necessary. That had been pure self-gratification on his part.

He should have stopped it before it had gotten hot enough to melt the two of them to the dance floor. Before he'd confirmed what he'd always known about them—that they would be ridiculously, spectacularly hot together. But Chiara's unwarranted, unfair judgments of him had burrowed beneath his skin. And, if he were being honest, so had his need to prove he was not the *last* man on earth she'd ever want, he was *the* one she wanted.

His curiosity about what it would be like to strip away those formidable defenses of hers had been irresistible. To find the passion that lay beneath. And hell, had he found it.

His blood thickened at the memory of her sweet, sensual response. It had knocked him sideways, the feel of those lush, amazing curves beneath his hands as good as he'd imagined they would be. He'd let the kiss get way out of hand, no doubt about it, but he hadn't been the only participant.

Chiara was out of the car and on her way into the lobby as he handed the keys to the Lamborghini to the valet, shocking him with how swiftly she could walk in those insanely high shoes. She had jammed her finger on the call button for the elevator by the time he'd made it into the lobby, her toe tapping impatiently on the marble. It came seconds later and swished them silently up to the third floor.

Kicking off her shoes in the marble foyer of the penthouse, she continued her relentless path through the living room, into the bedroom. He caught up with her before she reached the bathroom door. Curved a hand around her arm. "Chiara," he murmured. "We need to talk."

She swung around, a closed look on her face. "About what? You were right, Lazzero, it was *just a kiss*. And now, if you don't mind, I am going to go to bed. I am exhausted." Her eyes lifted mutinously to his. "*If* I am *off duty*, of course."

Oh, no. Red misted his vision as she pulled out of his grasp and stalked into the bathroom, slamming the door in his face. She wasn't going to go there.

Walk away, he told himself. Shake it off. Deal with this tomorrow when saner heads prevail.

Except nothing about that kiss had been business and they both knew it. It had been a long time coming, *a year* precisely, since he'd walked through the door of the Daily Grind and found Chiara cursing at an espresso machine on a particularly bad day. They *had* something. That was clear. They were consenting adults. What the hell was the problem?

He stalked into the dressing room. Threw his wallet and change on the armoire. The wounded look on Chiara's face in the car filtered through his head. She thought he was playing with her. That this was a *game* to him. Which, admittedly it might have started out as, until he'd gotten as caught up in that kiss as she had been.

Leaving her to stew, he decided as he stripped off his bow tie and cuff links, was not a good idea. Tossing them on the dresser, he rapped on the bedroom door. Walked in. Frowned when he found the room empty, the bed untouched. Then he spotted Chiara on the balcony, her back to him.

Definitely stewing.

He crossed to the French doors. Stopped in his tracks. She was dressed for bed, a factor he hadn't taken into consideration. Which needed to be taken into consideration, because what she was wearing heated his blood.

The simple tank top and shorts were hardly the sexiest nightwear he'd ever seen, covering more of her than most women did on the streets of Manhattan. It was the way the soft jersey material clung to her voluptuous body that made his mouth go dry.

His hands itched to touch, to give in to the craving he'd been fighting all night, but he stayed where he was, framed in the light of the suite.

"It wasn't just a kiss."

His quiet words had Chiara spinning around. An equally spectacular view from the front, he noted, her face bare of makeup, lush mouth pursed in contemplation, her legs a sweep of smooth golden skin that seemed to go on forever.

He set his gaze on hers. "That kiss was spectacular. You and I both know it. I wanted to do it since the first moment I saw you in that dress tonight. Actually," he amended huskily, "since the first day I set eyes on you in the coffee shop. You and I have something, Chiara. It would be ridiculous to deny it."

She swallowed hard, the delicate muscles in her throat

convulsing. A myriad of emotion flickered through her green eyes. "You were toying with me, Lazzero."

He shook his head. "I was satisfying my *curiosity* about the attraction between us. Finding out how it would be. And you were curious too," he added deliberately, eyeing the flare of awareness staining her olive skin. "But you won't admit it, because you're so intent on protecting yourself, on preserving that prickly outer layer of yours, on putting your *labels* on me, you won't admit how you feel."

A fiery light stormed her eyes. "You're damn right I am. I have no interest in becoming your latest conquest, Lazzero. In being bought with a piece of jewelry. In performing ever greater circus tricks to retain your interest, only to be dumped in a cloud of dust when I no longer do. I have *been there* and *done that*."

His jaw dropped. "That's absurd."

"You said it at Di Fiore's. Your relationships only last as long as your interest does." She planted her hands on her hips. "The soul-baring truth and nothing but. Isn't that how you put it?"

He had no response for that, grounded by his own transparency. She tipped her chin up. "Consider my curiosity well and truly satisfied. My *list* ticked off."

His ego took that stunning blow as she turned and stalked inside, effectively ending the conversation. Except which part of it hadn't been true? He was all of that and more.

He followed her inside, stripped off his clothes in the guest bathroom and deposited himself under a chilly shower to cool his body down, still revved up from that almost-sex on the dance floor.

He played by a certain set of rules because that's what he was capable of. He was never going to allow a woman *in*, was never going to commit, because he knew the destructive force a relationship could be. He'd watched his father wind himself in circles over his mother before he'd imploded in spectacular fashion, a roller coaster ride he was never getting on. Ever.

Getting his head tied up in Chiara, no matter how hot he was for her, was insanity with everything riding on this deal with Gianni. He'd best keep that in mind or *he* was going to be the one going down in a cloud of dust.

Pulling on boxer shorts in deference to his company, he braced himself for the far-too-short-looking sofa in the bedroom, the only sleepable surface in the suite other than the extremely comfortable-looking four-poster bed. Which was…*empty*.

What the hell?

He found Chiara curled up on the sofa, a blanket covering her slight form. Her dark hair spread out like silk against the white pillowcase, long, decadent lashes fanned down against her cheeks, she was deep asleep.

Every male instinct growled in irritation. This had clearly been her parting volley. *Clearly*, she didn't know him well enough if she thought he was going to let her sleep there, no matter how amazing that bed looked after the couple of hours of sleep he'd had on the plane.

Moving silently across the room, he slid his arms beneath her, lifted her up and carried her to the bed. Transferring her weight to one arm, he tossed the silk comforter aside and slid her into the bed. She was so deep asleep she didn't blink an eyelash as she shifted onto her stomach and burrowed into the silk sheets. Which gave him a very tantalizing view of her amazing derriere in the feminine shorts.

The reminder of what those curves had felt like beneath his hands, how perfectly she'd fit against him, sizzled the blood in his veins. Revved him up all over again. A low curse leaving his throat, he retreated to the sofa, flicked the blanket aside and settled his hormone-ravaged body onto the ridiculous excuse for a piece of furniture.

His attempts to get comfortable were futile. When he stretched out, his feet hung over the edge, cutting off his circulation. When he attempted to contort himself to fit, his old basketball injury made his knee throb.

The minutes ticked by, his need to sleep growing ever more acute. He had four hours maximum before he had to get up for his practice with a team of world-class athletes who were going to run him into the ground at this rate. He must have been insane to agree to play.

He had shifted positions for what must have been the tenth time when Chiara lifted herself up on her elbow and blinked at him in the darkness. "How did I get into the bed?"

"I carried you there," he said grumpily. "Go back to sleep."

She dropped back to the pillow. A silence followed. Then a drowsy, "Get in the bed, Lazzero. It's as big as Milan. We can share it."

He was off the sofa and in the bed in record time. It *was* the size of Milan and he could restrain himself. Finding a comfortable position on the far side of the bed, he closed his eyes and lost himself to blissful unconsciousness.

Chiara was having the most delicious dream. Plastered against a wall of heat, she was warm and cocooned and thoroughly content after finding the air-conditioning distinctly chilly during the night.

Pressing closer to all that heat, she registered it was hot, hard muscle—hot, hard *male* muscle that was its source. Utterly in tune with the whole picture because she had truly outdone herself with this dream, she pressed even closer.

A big, warm hand slid over the curve of her hip to arrange her more comfortably on top of him. She sighed and went willingly, because he felt deliciously good against her, underneath her, *everywhere*, and it had been so long, so damn long since she'd been touched like this. *Held* like this.

He traced his fingers down her spine, savoring the texture and shape of her. She purred like a cat and arched into him. The sensual slide of his mouth against the delicate skin of her throat stirred her pulse to a drumbeat. Melted her insides. A shiver coursing through her, she turned her head to find the kiss he was offering. *Best dream ever.*

Slow, lazy, decadent, it was perfection. She moved closer still, wanting more. His hand closed possessively over her bottom, a low sound of male pleasure reverberating against her mouth.

Too real.

Oh, my God.

She broke the kiss. Sank her palms into his rock-hard chest, panic arrowing through her as she stared into Lazzero's sleepy, slumberous gaze. Registered the palm he held against her back, the other that cupped her buttock, plastering her against him, exactly as she'd been in her dream.

Except it hadn't been a dream. It had been real. *Good God.*

She pushed frantically against his chest. Scrambled off him. Lazzero eyed her lazily, his ebony eyes blinking awake. "What's the hurry?" he murmured, his husky, sleep-infused voice rumbling down her spine. "That was one hell of a way to wake a man up, *caro.*"

She sat back on her heels. Ran a shaky hand through her hair. "You took advantage of the situation."

"I think you have that the wrong way around," he drawled. "I have been on this side of the bed all night, a fact I made damn sure of. Which means it was *you* who found your way over here." He lifted a brow. "Maybe it was your subconscious talking after that kiss last night?"

Her cheeks fired. "I had no idea *who* I was kissing."

He crossed his arms over his chest and lounged back

against the pillows. "Funny that, because you sighed my name. Twice. I'm fairly sure that's what woke me up."

She searched his face for some sign he was joking. "I did *not*."

His smug expression gave her little hope. She dropped her gaze away from his, utterly disconcerted, but that was an even bigger problem because he was jaw dropping— perfectly hewn, bronzed muscle, marred only by the scar that crisscrossed his knee. Better than she could ever have imagined, his low-slung boxers did little to hide his potent masculinity. Which was more than a little stirred up at the moment. *By her.*

"I am," he murmured, pulling her gaze back up to his, "wide-awake now, on the other hand, if you are looking for my full participation."

Her stomach swooped. Searching desperately for sanity, she shimmied across the massive bed and slid off it. Felt the heat of Lazzero's gaze follow her, burning over the exposed length of her legs. "I need to shower," she announced, heading for the bathroom as fast as her legs would carry her.

"Coward," he tossed after her.

She kept going. He could call her what he liked. If she didn't get her head on her shoulders, figure out how to wrangle her attraction to Lazzero under control, she was going to mess this up, because this was *not* her world and she was hopelessly out of her depth. And since messing this up was not an option, she needed to restore her common sense. *Yesterday.*

Joining the other girlfriends, wives and friends of the players in the VIP seating area at San Siro stadium for the practice proved to offer plenty of opportunity for Chiara to recover her composure. It was packed with women in designer outfits and expensive perfume, sophisticated perfection she couldn't hope to emulate.

Dressed in a pair of white capri jeans and a fuchsia-colored blouse she had knotted at the waist, a cute pair of white sneakers on her feet, she looked the part, but how could she possibly participate in the conversations going on around her? What did she know about Cannes for the film festival or an annual Easter weekend on a Russian oligarch's yacht?

She found herself confined to the outer fringe of the group, the cold shoulder Carolina had given her instigating that phenomenon, no doubt. She wasn't sure why she cared. This wasn't her world, she didn't want it to be her world. But that didn't mean it didn't hurt. That it didn't remind her of the mean girls in school who'd ridiculed her for her hopelessly out-of-date, out-of-fashion clothes.

Putting on the aloof face she'd perfected in school, she positioned herself at the end of the bleacher, pretending not to care. The lovely, bubbly wife of the Western European team captain, Valentino Calabria, sat down beside her, dragging one of the other wives with her as she braved the cold front. "Don't pay any attention to them," Pia Calabria murmured. "It takes years to break into their clique."

Pia kept up a continual stream of conversation as the Americas team took to the field for its practice, for which Chiara was inordinately grateful. It was hard, brutal play as the team geared up for its opening match against Western Europe, sweat and curses flying.

Pia sat back as the play halted for a water break, fanning her face with her purse. "The eye candy," she pronounced with a dramatic sigh, "is simply too much for me to handle today."

"Which you are not supposed to be noticing with Valentino, the *magnifico*, right in front of you," Pia's friend reprimanded drily.

Pia slid her a sideways look. "And you are not doing the same? *Looking* is not a crime."

Chiara's gaze moved to Lazzero. It *was* impossible not to ogle. Intense and compelling in black shorts and a sweaty, bright green Americas T-shirt, he looked amazing.

"Him," Pia agreed, following her gaze to Lazzero, who stood in the middle of the field, wiping the sweat off his forehead with the hem of his T-shirt as he yelled at his teammates to get ready for the kick in. "Exactly. Now, there is a *man*. Those abs… You could bounce a football off of them. And those thighs…" She rolled her eyes heavenward. "*Insano*. No wonder Carolina is going ballistic."

Chiara kept her eyes glued to the field. Thought about that ridiculously amazing kiss she'd shared with Lazzero that morning. It had felt undeniably *right*. As if she and Lazzero had something, exactly as he'd said. She would be lying if she said she wasn't desperately curious to know what it would have been like if she'd let it play out to its seductive conclusion, because she knew it would have been incredible.

You're a senior citizen at twenty-six. Kat's jibe flitted tauntingly through her head. Her life *was* pathetic. She *had* no life. But to take a walk on the wild side with Lazzero, who'd surely annihilate her before it was all over? It seemed patently unwise.

She pushed her attention back to the field, rather than allow it to continue down the ridiculous road it was traveling. Watched as Lazzero's squad executed an impressive series of passes to put the ball in the net.

"Hell." Pia covered her eyes. "They look good. Too good. Valentino is going to be unbearable if they lose."

The practice ended shortly thereafter. Chiara dutifully engaged a cool Carolina in a stilted conversation as she'd promised Lazzero she would so that he could catch up with Gianni before the sponsor lunch. When Carolina blew her off a few minutes later, she found herself at loose ends as Pia drifted off to find her husband.

Giving her father a quick call at the bakery before he began work, she assured herself he was okay, then got up to stretch her legs and go look for Lazzero when some of the Americas team players started to drift back onto the field. Heading toward the tunnel where the players were coming out, she stopped dead in her tracks at the sight of Lazzero and Carolina engaged in conversation in the shadowed passage. Carolina, stunning in a bright yellow dress, was leaning against the wall, Lazzero standing in front of her, his head bent close to hers, his hand on the wall beside her.

Intimate, *familiar*, the conversation looked intense. Sharp claws dragged through her. What were they talking about? Was Carolina trying to convince Lazzero she would leave Gianni for him? She had no doubt the other woman would do so in a flash, more than a bit in love with him still.

The jealousy that rocketed through her was illogical, she knew it. She and Lazzero were putting on a charade. It *wasn't* real. But the visceral emotion sweeping through her was.

She swung away, her insides coiling. Walked into a brick wall. She looked up to find Lucca Sousa, the celebrated Brazilian captain of the Americas' squad steadying her, his hands at her waist. Glancing down the tunnel, Lucca absorbed the scene she'd just witnessed, a frown creasing his brow.

"Nothing to see there," he murmured, pressing a hand to her back and guiding her away from the tunnel. "Ancient history, that is."

It hadn't looked so ancient. It had looked very *present*.

"At loose ends?" Lucca queried, giving the group of football wives a glance.

Chiara shot him a distracted look. "I am not part of their clique."

"Nor do you want to be," he said firmly. "Take it from me. Come—kick a ball around with me before lunch."

He was taking pity on her, she registered, a low burn of humiliation moving through her. Helping her save face. It unearthed a wound she'd buried layers deep, because she knew what it was like to be the side amusement for a man who had more than his fair share of willing participants.

But tall, dark and gorgeous Lucca, as smooth as Lazzero was hard around the edges, refused to take no for an answer. Procuring a ball from the sidelines, he ignored his own personal posse lining up to talk to him and shepherded Chiara onto the field. "Do you play?"

She shook her head. "Only a bit in school."

"That will do." Giving her an instruction to move back a few feet, they dribbled the ball back and forth. A couple of the other players and their wives joined in and they played a minigame at one end of the field, a crowd gathering to watch the good-natured fun. Lucca and she proved decent partners, mainly because he was brilliant and as patient as the end of the day.

Chiara, who hadn't been a bad player in school, still found the precision required to get the ball in the net exceedingly frustrating, particularly after all this time. Lucca stopped the play, moved behind her and guided her through the motion of an accurate, straight kick. It took her a few tries, but finally she seemed to master it.

They played the game to five, Chiara's confidence growing as they went. When their team won the game, she jumped in the air in victory. Lucca trotted over and gave her a big hug, lifting her off her feet. "Don't look now," he murmured, glancing at the sidelines, "but your fiancé is watching and he looks, how do I say it in English...*chateado*. Pissed."

Cheeks flushed, exhilarated from the exercise, she stood on tiptoe and gave him a kiss on the cheek, knowing she was stoking the fire, but unable to help herself. "Thank you. That was so much fun."

"You're good at this," Lucca drawled, his eyes sparkling. "Go get him."

Her stomach turned inside out as she walked off the field toward Lazzero, who was standing on the sidelines, dressed in dark jeans and a shirt, arms crossed over his chest.

"Should we go in to lunch?" she suggested coolly when she reached his side. "It looks like it's ready."

"In a minute." He shoved his hands into his jean pockets, his gaze resting on hers. Combustible. *Distinctly combustible.* "Having fun?" he asked.

"Actually, yes, I was. Lucca is lovely."

"He's the biggest playboy on that side of the Atlantic, Chiara."

"I thought that was you," she returned sweetly.

"He had his hands all over you," he murmured. "We are supposed to be newly engaged—madly in love. You might try giving that impression."

Her chin came up, heat coursing through her. "Maybe *you* shouldn't be canoodling with your ex, then. Everyone saw you, Lazzero. You're lucky Gianni didn't."

He raked a hand through his hair. "Carolina was upset. I was doing damage control."

"So was I. If people were watching Lucca and I, then they weren't watching you. And honestly," she purred, "I don't think there is a woman on the planet who would object to having Lucca Sousa's hands on her, so really, it was no hardship. You can thank me later."

His gaze darkened. "Trying to push my buttons, Chiara?"

She lifted a brow. "Now, why would I do that? This isn't real, after all."

Lazzero attempted to douse his incendiary mood with a cold beer at lunch as he sat through the interminably long, posturing event with all its requisite speeches and small talk. The urge to connect his fist with Lucca Sousa's undeniably handsome jaw was potently appealing. Which was not a rational response, but then again, Chiara seemed to inspire that particular frame of mind in him.

His black mood might also, he conceded, be attributed to Gianni. He'd finally pinned the Italian CEO down before lunch, but their conversation had not been the one he'd been looking for.

He finessed an escape as dessert ran into ever-lasting coffee, promising to meet Chiara at the exit once he'd collected his things. Packing his things up, he ran into Santo on his way out of the locker room.

His brother's eyes gleamed with amusement as he rested a palm against the frame of the door. "Everything under control with your fiery little barista? You look a bit hot under the collar."

"Not now, Santo." Lazzero moved into the hallway for some privacy. "I talked to Gianni."

Santo lifted a brow. "How did it go?"

"Not great," he admitted. "He seems to have some reservations about how the two brands will work together. If our design philosophies will match. But he wasn't saying no. He wants to meet on Tuesday."

"Well that's something." Santo shrugged. "Show him the design ideas we've developed. They're impressive."

Lazzero shook his head. "Those designs are all wrong. I'm not happy with them."

A wary look claimed his brother's face. "This is not the time for your obsessive perfectionism, Laz. The designs are fine. *Use them*. We might not get another crack at him."

"We definitely won't if we use those drawings," Lazzero said flatly. "Gianni will hate them. I *know* him. We need him on board, Santo."

Heat flared in his brother's eyes. "I am clear on that. *I*, however, wasn't the one who decided to go off half-cocked on the annual investor call and tell the world we're going to be the number two sportswear brand when number three was a stretch."

A red haze enveloped his brain. "That damn analyst led me on, Santo. You know she did. She loves to push me."

"And *you* shouldn't have bitten. But that's irrelevant now. *Now* we have to deliver. We go back empty-handed and the financial community will crucify us." His brother fixed his gaze on his. "We both know how fast a rising star can crash, Laz. How it's all about perception. What happens if we start to look as if we've overshot our orbit."

Broken, irreparable dreams and all the inherent destruction that comes with it.

His father had been one of the greatest deal-makers on Wall Street—a risk-taking rainmaker who had made a fortune for his clients. Until he'd taken the biggest risk of all, founded a company of his own on a belief those riches could be his, and lost everything.

He *knew* the dangers in making promises you couldn't keep. In trying to grow a company too far, too fast. Had grown up with its repercussions falling down around him, just as Santo and Nico had. But he also knew his instincts weren't wrong on Volare.

"You need to trust me. We have *always* trusted each other. I can do this, Santo. I can make us number two. You just need to give me the room to maneuver."

His brother studied him for a long moment, his dark gaze conflicted. "I do trust you," he said finally. "That's my problem, Laz. I'm not sure if this obsessive drive of yours is going to make us or break us."

"It's going to make us," Lazzero said. *"Trust me."*

CHAPTER SIX

LAZZERO EMERGED FROM the luxurious office space at the Orientale at close to midnight, having spent the evening consulting with his design team in New York, attempting to come up with some sketches for Gianni that worked. An effort which had not yet yielded fruit, but *had* achieved his dual purpose of staying away from Chiara and his inexplicable inability to control himself when it came to her.

Tracing a silent path through the living room to the bedroom, he found the rumpled bed unoccupied and light pooling into the room from the terrace. Crossing to the French doors, he found Chiara curled up on the sofa, staring out at an unparalleled view of Milan. The moon cast an ethereal glow over the beautiful, aristocratic city, but it was Chiara's face that held his attention—the stark vulnerability written across those lush, expressive features, the quiet stillness about her that said she was in another place entirely.

Dressed in the silky, feminine shorts and tank top she seemed to favor, her hair rumpled from sleep, she looked about eighteen. Except there was nothing youthful about the body underneath that wistful packaging. The fine material of her top hugged every last centimeter of her perfect breasts, her hips a voluptuous, irresistible curve beneath the shorts that left her long, golden legs bare.

His blood turned to fire, his good intentions incinerating on a wave of lust that threatened to annihilate his common sense. *So he had a thing for her. Maybe he had a gigantic thing for her. He could control it.*

Maybe if he kept telling himself that, he'd actually believe it.

She turned to look at him, as if sensing his presence. The emotion he read in her brilliant green eyes rocked him back on his heels. It was impossible to decipher—too mixed and too complex, but he could sense a yearning behind it and it turned a key inside of him. Melted that common sense away into so much dust.

"Did you get your designs figured out?" Her voice was husky from lack of use.

He shook his head. "The team's still working on it." He picked up the hardback book she had sitting beside her, a pencil tucked into the binding, and sat down. "You couldn't sleep?"

"My head was too full."

With what? He looked down at the book he held, a sketchbook of some sort, open to a drawing of a dress. "What's this?"

"Nothing. It's just a hobby. I like to make my own clothes." She reached for the book, but he held on to it and flipped through the sketches.

"These are really good. Do you have formal training?"

"I did a few semesters of a fashion design degree at Parsons."

"Only a few semesters?" He directed an inquisitive gaze at her. "It's one of the best design programs in the country. Why did you stop?"

"We needed to prioritize money for the bakery." She shrugged. "It was a long shot anyway."

"Says who? Parsons clearly thought you had talent."

Her expression took on a closed edge. "The program was insanely competitive—the design career I would have had even more so. It just wasn't realistic."

He snapped the book shut and handed it to her. "The best things in life are the hardest to attain. What was the end goal if you'd continued with your degree? To go work for a designer?"

She shook her head. "I wanted to create my own line of affordable urban fashion."

"A big dream," he conceded. "What was your inspiration for it?"

She drew her knees up to her chest and rested her head against the back of the sofa. "My mother," she said, a wistful look in her eyes. "We didn't have much growing up. The bakery did okay, but there was no room for extras. My father considered fashion a luxury, not a necessity, which meant I wore cheap, department store clothes or my cousin's hand-me-downs. Hard," she acknowledged, "for a teenage girl trying to fit in with the cool crowd.

"Thankfully, my mother was an excellent seamstress. After dinner, when the bakery was closed, she'd brew a pot of tea, we'd spread the patterns out on the floor and make the clothes I wanted." A smile curved her lips. "She was incredible. She could make anything. It was magical to me, the way the pieces came together. There was never any doubt as to what I wanted to be."

"And then she passed away," Lazzero murmured.

"Yes. My father, he was—" she hesitated, searching for the right words "—he was never really the same after my mother's death. He was dark, *lost*. He worshipped the ground she walked on. All he seemed to know how to do was to keep the bakery going—to *provide*. But I wouldn't go out with my friends, because of how dark he would get. I was worried about what he would do—what he *might* do. So, I stayed home and took care of him. Made my own clothes. It became a form of self-expression for me."

His heart contracted, the echoes of an ancient wound pulsing his insides. "He was angry. Not at you—at the disease. For taking your mother from him. For shattering his life."

Her dark lashes fanned her cheeks. "You were like that with your father."

He nodded. The difference was, his father's disease had been preventable. Perhaps even more difficult to accept.

Chiara returned her gaze to the glittering city view. "Designing became my obsession. My way of countering the mean girls at school who made fun of my clothes. My lack of designer labels. Sometimes I would make things from scratch, other times I would buy pieces from the thrift store and alter them—not to follow the trends but to reflect what *I* loved about fashion. Eventually," she allowed, "those girls wanted me to make things for them."

"And did you? After what they'd done?"

She nodded.

"Why?"

"Because anger doesn't solve anything," she said quietly. "Only forgiveness does. Allowing my designs to speak for me."

Lazzero felt something stick in his chest. That struck him as phenomenal—*she* struck him as phenomenal—that she would have that sense of maturity, wisdom, at such a young age.

But hadn't he? It was a trait you developed when you were left to fend for yourself. *Sink or swim. Protect yourself at all costs. Arm yourself against the world.* But unlike Chiara, he had had his brothers. She'd had no one.

For the first time he wondered how, in withdrawing when his mother had left, retreating into that aloof, unknowable version of himself he did so well, what effect that had had on his brothers. What it must have been like for Nico, at fifteen, to leave school, to abandon the dreams he'd had for himself to take care of him and Santo. How selflessly he'd done it. How Chiara had had none of that support and turned out to be as strong as she was.

He picked up her hand and tugged it into his lap. Marveled at how small and delicate it was. At the voltage that came from touching her, the connection between them an invisible, electrical thread that lit up his insides in the most dangerous of ways.

"You need to go back to school," he murmured. "Defeating the mean girls was your mission statement in life, Chiara. Some people search a lifetime for one. You *have* one. If you quit—*they* win."

Her gaze clouded over. "That ship has sailed. My classmates are done and building their careers. I'm too old to start again now."

His mouth twisted. "You're only twenty-six. You have plenty of time."

"Speaks the man who put Supersonic on the Nasdaq by the time he was twenty-five."

He shook his head. "You can't compare yourself to others. Santo and I had Martino, our godfather, to back us. To *guide* us. And Nico, who is every bit as brilliant."

She slanted him a curious look. "Was Martino family? What was the relationship between him and your father?"

He shook his head. "Martino and my father were on Wall Street together. Two of the biggest names in their day. Intense competitors and the best of friends."

"Was that where your father's alcoholism began? I've heard stories about the pressure…the crazy lifestyle."

"It started there," he acknowledged. "My father was levelheaded. Smart. Just like Martino. They both swore they'd get out once they'd made their money. Martino, true to his word, did. He founded Evolution with his wife, Juliette, and the rest is history. My father, however, got sucked into the lifestyle. The *temptations* of it.

"My mother," he continued, "didn't make it easier for

him by taking full advantage of that lifestyle and spending his money as if it were water. When Martino finally convinced my father to leave, he was intent on proving he could do it bigger and better than Martino. He bet the bank and his entire life savings on a technology start-up he and a client founded that never made it off the ground."

"And lost everything." Chiara's eyes glittered as they rested on his.

"Yes."

"Did Martino try and help your father? To pull him out of it?"

His mouth flattened. "He tried everything." *Just as they had.* Pouring bottles down the sink. Hiding them. Destroying them. Nico walking their father to AA every night before he'd gone to evening classes. None of it had worked.

Chiara watched him with those expressive eyes. "When did Martino take you under his wing?"

"After my father's funeral. My father was too humiliated to have anything to do with Martino when he was alive. Martino had conquered where he had failed. He refused all help from him. They had," he conceded, staring up at the scattering of stars that dotted the midnight sky, "a complex relationship as you can imagine."

Chiara didn't reply. He looked over at her, found her lost in thought. "What?"

She shrugged a slim shoulder. "I just— I wonder—" She sighed. "Sometimes I wonder if that's why my father withdrew after my mother died. Because I reminded him too much of her. We were mirror images, she and I."

"No." He squashed that imagining dead with a squeeze of his fingers around hers. "You can't take that on. People who are mired in grief get caught up in their own pain. It's as if they're in so deep, they can't dig their way out. They try," he acknowledged, "but it's as if they've made it to the other side, they're clawing their way to the surface, but they can't make it those last few feet to get out."

Her eyes grew dark. "Your father couldn't climb out?"

He nodded. And for the first time in his life, he realized how angry he was. How furious he was that his father who had always been superhuman in his eyes, his *hero*, hadn't had the strength to kick a disease that had destroyed his childhood. How angry he was that, in his supreme selfishness, his father had put his grief above *them*. At those who had created such a culture of reckless greed, his father had been unable to resist, tempted by sirens he didn't have the strength or desire to fight.

"You can't blame yourself," he told her. "This is about your father's inability to put you first, which he *should* have done."

"He did in a financial sense," Chiara pointed out.

"But you needed the emotional support, as well. That's just as important to a fifteen-year-old. And that, he didn't give you."

She sank her teeth into her lip. "Maybe I didn't give him what he needed, either. He was so lost. I didn't know what to do. I keep thinking maybe if I'd gotten him some help, if I'd done *something*, he wouldn't be the way he is. As if he's half-alive. As if he'd rather not be."

Her eyes glittered with tears, unmistakable diamond-edged drops that tugged hard at his insides. The defiant tilt of her chin annihilated his willpower completely. "Chiara," he murmured, pulling her into his arms, his chin coming down on top of her head, her petite body curved against his, "this is not on you. It's about him. You can't find his happiness for him. He has to find it himself."

"And what if he doesn't?"

"Then you were there for him. That's all you can do."

He thought she might pull out of his arms then, a palpable tension in her slight frame. Which would have been the smart move given the chemistry that pulsed between them. Instead, heaving a sigh, she curled closer. Her jasmine-scented hair soft as silk against his skin, the silent, dark night wrapping itself around them, it was a fit so perfect, his brain struggled to articulate it. For once in his life, he didn't even try.

His mouth whispered against the delicate curve of her jaw in an attempt to comfort. The rasp of his stubble against her satiny skin raked a shiver through her. Through *him*.

She went perfectly still. As if she'd forgotten how to move, how to breathe. His palm anchored against her back, her softness pressed against his hardness, his brain slid back to that lazy, sexy kiss this morning. The leisurely, undoubtedly mind-blowing conclusion he would have taken it to if it had been his call.

His blood thickened in his veins, his self-imposed celibacy over the past few months slamming into him hard. His fingers on her jaw, he turned her face to his. Her dark lashes glistening with unshed tears, her lush mouth bare of color, the flare of sensual awareness that darkened her beautiful green eyes was unmistakable. The kind that invited a man to jump in and drown himself in it.

Vulnerable. Too vulnerable.

"Lazzero," she murmured.

This isn't happening.

He lifted her up and carried her inside. In one deft move, he sank his fingers beneath the silky hair at her nape and whisked his arm from beneath her thighs until she slid down his body to her feet, the rasp of her ripe curves against his sensitized flesh almost sending him up into flames.

He doused the vicious heat with a bucketful of cold determination. Because this, *this* could not happen right now. His brain was far too full and she was too damn fragile.

He reached up to tuck a rumpled tendril of her hair behind her ear. "It's late," he rasped. "Go to sleep."

Turning on his heel, he headed for the study and a response from his New York team before he changed his mind and gave in to temptation.

He had a problem. A big one. Now he had to figure out what to do with it.

Chiara woke late, her body still adjusting to the time difference, her mind attempting to wrap itself around the intimate, late-night encounter she'd had with Lazzero the night before. She eyed the unruffled side of the bed opposite her, indicating Lazzero had not joined her. Which actually wasn't the worst thing that could have happened given how he'd walked away last night, shutting things down between them.

Her stomach knotted into a tight, hard ball. She kicked off the silk comforter in deference to the already formidable heat and stared moodily out at another vivid blue, cloudless perfect day through floor-to-ceiling windows bare of the blinds she'd forgotten to close. She might be able to excuse herself for her slip last night because she'd been so vulnerable in the moment, but she couldn't escape the emotional connection she and Lazzero had shared. How *amazing* he'd been.

She buried her teeth in her lip. She had poured her heart and soul out to him last night. Her hopes, her dreams. Instead of brushing them aside as her father had done, pointing to her mother who'd barely been eking out an income as a seamstress before she'd met him, or Antonio, who had advised her she'd be lost in a sea of competition, Lazzero had validated her aspirations.

Defeating the mean girls is your mission statement in life. If you quit—they win.

She'd never thought about it like that. Except now that she had, she couldn't stop. Which was unrealistic, she told herself as a distant, long-ago buried dream clawed itself back to life inside of her. Even with the bakery on a solid financial footing, the rent was astronomical. She'd still need to help her father out on the weekends because he couldn't afford the staff. Which would make studying and working impossible.

She buried the thought and the little twinge her heart gave along with it. It was easy to think fanciful thoughts in Lazzero's world, because he made everything *seem* possible. Everything *was* possible for him. But she was not him and this was not her world.

She conceded, however, that she had misjudged him that day in the café. Had tarred him with the same brush as Antonio, which had been a mistake. Antonio had been born with a silver spoon in his mouth, recklessly wielding his power and privilege, whereas Lazzero had made himself into one of the most powerful men in the world *despite* the significant traumas he'd suffered early on in life. He was a survivor. Just like her.

It made him, she acknowledged with dismay, even more attractive. It also explained so much about who he was, *why* he was the way he was, that insane drive of his. Because he would never be his father. Never see his world shattered beneath his feet again. It also, she surmised, explained why Lazzero was a part of the community angel organization in New York—it was his way of helping when he had been unable to help his father. Another piece of the man she was just beginning to understand.

Then there was last night. He could have used their intense sexual chemistry to persuade her into bed—but he had not. He had walked away instead. Exactly the opposite of what Antonio had done when he had seduced her with his champagne and promises.

Promises Lazzero would never give because he was clear about what he offered a woman. About what he had to give. Which would likely, she concluded, heat blanketing her insides, be the most incredible experience of her life if she allowed it to happen. Which would be *insane*.

She needed coffee. Desperately. She slipped on shorts and a T-shirt and ventured out to the kitchen to procure it. *All* problems could be solved with a good cup of java.

Making an espresso with the machine in the spotless, stainless steel masterpiece of a kitchen, she leaned against the counter and inhaled the dark Italian brew. She had nearly regained her equilibrium when Lazzero came storming into the kitchen dressed in jeans and a T-shirt, a dark cloud on his face. Sliding to an abrupt halt, he scorched his gaze over her fitted T-shirt and bare legs. Back up again.

"Make me one of those, will you?"

Heat snagged her insides. "You might try," she suggested with a lift of her chin, "'please make me one of your amazing espressos, Chiara. I am highly in need.'"

"Yes," he muttered, waving a hand at her. "All of that."

She turned and emptied the tamper into the garbage, relieved to escape all of that mouthwateringly disheveled masculinity. Took her time with the ritualistic packing of the grinds, because she had no idea where she and Lazzero stood after last night. How to navigate this, because it felt as if something fundamental had changed between them. Or maybe it was just *her* that felt that way?

Having artfully packed the tamper with the requisite perfect, round puck, she set the coffee to brew, turned around and leaned a hip against the counter. "You've been up all night?"

Lazzero raked a hand through his rumpled hair. "The designs are not what they need to be."

"When is your meeting with Gianni?"

"Tuesday."

She took a sip of her coffee. Considered his combustible demeanor from over the rim of her cup. "I have a thought."

He gave her a distracted look. "About what?"

Definitely past the moment, he was. "Volare," she elaborated. "I was looking at the Fiammata shoes when I was window-shopping yesterday. The way they are marketed. They're selling a dream with Volare, not a shoe. A *lifestyle*. The ability to fly no matter who you are. Your designs," she said, picking up one of the sheaf of drawings he'd left on the counter, "need to reflect that. They need to be aspirational."

He eyed her contemplatively. "You may have a point there. The designs are *functional*. That's what I don't like about them. Fiammata's approach is very European. Quality of life seems to predominate here. Which, in today's market," he allowed, "might appeal to the American consumer." He slanted her a speculative look. "What would you do with them?"

Chiara found her sketchpad in the bedroom and brought it back to the kitchen. Setting it on the island, she began sketching out a running shoe that was more aspirational than the one Lazzero's designers had done. Something she could see herself wearing.

"Something like this," she said, when she was finished. "Smoother lines. As if the shoe allows you to soar no matter who you are or what you do."

Lazzero rubbed a palm over the thick stubble on his jaw. "I like it, but I think we can go even further with it if that's the direction we were to take. Can you give it the sense that it has wings? My scientists can make sure the aerodynamics work. It's the impression that counts."

She altered the image so it looked even sleeker, with an emphasis on the power of the front of the shoe. Made the back end less clunky. "Like this?"

Lazzero studied it. "Now it's too aspirational. Too ethereal. It needs to be *real* at the same time it's inspirational."

She eyed him. "Are you always this perfectionistic?"

"Sì," he drawled, his gaze glimmering as it rested on

her. "With everything I do. It can be a good quality, I promise you."

Heat pooled beneath her skin, his well-satisfied comment slicing through her head. She wished he'd never said it because she couldn't get it out of her head.

She bent her head and fixed the drawing. Back and forth they went, building off each other's ideas, Lazzero relentlessly pushing her to do better, pulling things out of her she hadn't even known she had. Finally, they finished. She massaged her cramping hand as he examined the drawing from every angle. If he didn't like this version, she decided, he could do it himself.

"I love it," he said slowly, looking up at her. "You're insanely good, Chiara."

A glow warmed her insides. "It's rough."

"It's fantastic." He waved the drawing at her. "Do you mind if I get my New York team to play with the idea? See what they come up with?"

She shook her head. "Go ahead."

He prowled toward her. Dipped his head and grazed her cheek with his lips, the friction of his thick stubble against her skin, the intoxicating whiff of his expensive scent, unearthing a delicious firework of sensation in her. "Thank you."

She sank back against the counter, watching as he strode toward the living room.

"Oh, and, Chiara?"

Her pulse jumped in her throat as he turned around. "Mmm?"

A wicked smile curved his lips. "You make a mean espresso."

CHAPTER SEVEN

"Santo cielo."

Pia shaded her eyes from the bright sunlight slanting through the roof of San Siro stadium as the referee added two minutes to the Americas versus Western Europe game, the teams locked two-two in the tense, bitter rivalry being played in front of eighty thousand screaming fans. "I can't bear to watch," her Italian friend groaned. "Valentino is going to be *impossibile* if this ends in a tie."

Chiara, thankful for the one and only ally she had, kept her thoughts to herself. She knew how important this game was to Lazzero. Had witnessed how dedicated he was to the REACH charity he supported in Harlem that kept kids off the street and on the court, the cause he was playing for this week. More layers to the man she had so inaccurately assessed at the beginning of all of this.

Who, along with his penchant to care deeply for the things that mattered to him, had a seemingly inexhaustible appetite for social connection if it contributed to the bottom line. The foreign correspondents' dinner on Saturday, cocktails at the British embassy on Sunday, a dinner meeting with the largest clothing retailer in the world last night at a posh Italian restaurant where they'd consumed wine expensive enough to eat up her entire monthly budget.

Plenty of opportunity for Lazzero to put his hands on her in those supposedly solicitous touches that sent far too much electricity through her body and plenty of opportunity for her to like it far more than she should.

She sank her teeth into her lip as Lazzero took the ball on the sidelines. It had been all business all the time. Which was exactly as it should have been. What she'd signed up for. What she'd *asked* for. Why then, did she feel so barefoot? Because the way she felt when she was with Lazzero made her feel alive in a way she hadn't for a very, very long time? Because feeling *something* felt good?

Her palms damp, her heart pounding, she watched as Lazzero yelled instructions to his teammates, then threw the ball in. Off the Americas team went, roaring down the field. Three neat passes, the final one from Lazzero to Lucca, and the ball was in the net.

The crowd surged to its feet with a mighty roar, Chiara along with it. One last fruitless drive by the Western Europe team and the clock ran out, signaling victory for the Americas. Lazzero, looking utterly nonplussed by his assist in the winning goal, turned and trotted off the field where he and Lucca were enveloped in a melee of congratulations.

Pia groaned. "There goes my chance for romance tonight. You, on the other hand," she said, tugging on Chiara's arm, "must go down to the field. It's La Coppa Estiva tradition to give the winning players a kiss. The television cameras love it."

Oh, no. Chiara dug her heels in. She was *not* doing that. But as the other wives and girlfriends filed onto the field, she realized she had no choice. Getting reluctantly to her feet, she left her purse with Pia and made her way down the stairs.

Lazzero eyed her as she approached, an amused light dancing in his dark eyes. *Thump* went her heart as she took him in. Sweat darkening his T-shirt, his hair slicked back from his brow, his game face still on, he was spectacular.

She pulled to a halt in front of him. Balanced her hands

on his waist as she stood on tiptoe to brush a kiss against his cheek. "Congratulations," she murmured. "You played a fantastic game."

He caught her jaw in his fingers, the wicked glint in his eyes sending a skitter of foreboding through her. "I think," he drawled, "they're going to expect a bit more than that."

Spreading his big palm against her back, he bowed her in a delicate arch, caged her against the unyielding steel frame of his powerful body. Her breath caught in her throat as he bent his head and took her mouth in a pure, unadulterated seduction that weakened her knees.

Her arms wound around his neck out of the pure need to keep herself upright. But then, her fingers got all tangled up in his gorgeous thick hair, *she* got all tangled up in the dark, delicious taste of him and the way he incinerated her insides, and the *plink, plink* of the camera flashes faded to a distant distraction.

Dazed, disoriented, she rocked back on her heels when he ended it, the hand he had wrapped around her hip holding her steady. Light blinding her eyes, a chorus of wolf whistles and applause raining down around them, she struggled to find her equilibrium.

Lazzero swept his sexy, devastating mouth across her cheek to her ear. "It almost felt as if you meant that, *angelo mio*."

She was afraid she might have.

"Finally got your priorities straight." Lucca issued the jab as he waltzed past, his posse trailing behind him. "You look amazing, *querida*. As always."

Lazzero's face darkened. "I can still put my fist through your face, Sousa."

Lucca only looked amused as he headed to a television interview with Brazilian TV. Chiara looked up at Lazzero, her heartbeat slowing to a more normal rhythm. "How did your meeting with Gianni go?"

His combustible expression turned satisfied. "He loved the sketches. Due in large part, to you. He's invited us to a dinner party on Friday night to discuss the partnership further."

She smiled. "That's amazing. Congratulations."

He retrieved the towel he had slung over his shoulder and wiped the sweat from his brow. "I thought I'd take you out to say thank you. Celebrate."

"With the team, you mean?"

"No," he said casually, slinging the towel over his shoulder. "Just us. I figured you'd had enough socializing. And, I have a surprise for you."

A *surprise*? A break from the relentless socializing? She was most definitely on board.

A slither of excitement skittered up her spine. "What should I wear?"

He shrugged. "Something nice. Wear one of your own dresses if you like. We can just be ourselves tonight."

It was a directive Lazzero might have reconsidered as he and Chiara stood on the tarmac at Milano Linate Airport in the late afternoon sunshine, her light pink dress fluttering in the wind. Empire-waisted and fitted with flowing long sleeves that somehow still left her shoulders bare, it was designed with multiple layers of some gauzy type of silk that looked as if she was wearing a flimsy scarf instead of a dress.

Which only came to midthigh, mind you, exposing a sweep of bare leg that held him transfixed. He was having dreams about those legs and what they would feel like wrapped around him, and that dress wasn't helping. The image of what he would like to do with her wasn't fit for public consumption.

Chiara gave him a sideways look as she proceeded

him up the steps into the jet. "You told me to wear what I wanted."

"I did and you look great." He kept his description to the bare minimum. "The dress is fantastic."

Her mouth curved into a smile that would have lit a small metropolis. "I'm glad you think so. It's one of mine."

The impact of that smile hit him square in the chest. *He was screwed*, he conceded. So royally screwed. But then again, he'd known that the moment she'd told him her story. When she'd quietly revealed her plan to defeat the mean girls of the world. It explained everything about the sharp, spiky skin that encased her. The fierce need for independence. The brave face she put on for the world, because he'd been exactly the same.

The difference between him and Chiara was that he had taught himself not to care. Made himself impervious to the world, and she had not. Which *should* label her as off-limits to him. Instead, he had the reckless desire to peel back more of those layers. To find the Chiara that lay beneath.

They flew down to the boot of Italy to Puglia, known for its sun, sea and amazing views. Sitting in the heel of the boot, it was tranquil and unspoiled, largely untouched by the masses of tourists who flocked to the country.

"It's stunning," Chiara breathed as they landed in Salento, nestled in the clear waters of the Adriatic, its tall cliffs sculpted by the sea.

"A friend of mine has a place here." Lazzero helped her down the steps of the jet, afraid she would topple over in those high heels of hers, which also weren't helping his internal temperature gauge. "It's unbelievably beautiful."

Her dress whipped up in the wind as they walked across the tarmac. He slapped a hand against her thigh as a ground worker stopped to stare. "Can you please *control* this dress?"

Hot color singed her cheeks. "It's the wind. Had I known

we were *flying* to dinner, I would have chosen something else."

And that would have been so, so sad. He ruthlessly pulled his hormones under control as he guided her to the waiting car, allowing her to slide in first, then walked around the car to climb in the other side. The town of Polignano a Mare, perched atop a twenty-meter-high limestone cliff that looked out over the crystal-clear waters of the Adriatic, was only a short drive away.

Known for its cliff diving, jaw-dropping caves carved out of the limestone rock that rose from the sea, as well as its excellent food, it held a wealth of charm as the sunset bathed it in a fiery glow. Suggesting they leave the car behind and walk the rest of the way to their destination to enjoy the view, Lazzero caught Chiara's hand in his.

Her gaze dropped to where their fingers were interlaced. "We're not in public," she murmured. "You don't have to do that."

"Sheer force of habit," he countered blithely. "Don't be so prickly, Chiara. We're holding hands, not necking in the street."

Which brought with it a whole other series of images that involved him backing her into one of the quaint, cobblestoned side streets and taking exactly what he'd wanted from the very beginning. Not helpful when added to *the dress*.

She left her hand in his. Was silent as they walked through the whitewashed streets toward the sea, the lanes bursting with splashes of fluorescent color from the vibrant window boxes full of brightly hued blooms. Then it was him wondering about his presence of mind, because the whole thing felt right in a way he couldn't articulate. Had never experienced before.

The Grotta Nascondiglio Hotel, carved out of the magnificent limestone rocks, rose in front of them as they neared the seafront. Chiara gasped and pointed at something to their right. "Are *those* the cliff divers? Good heavens, look where they're diving from."

They were high—twenty meters above the ground, diving from one of the cliffs that flanked the harbor below. But Lazzero shrugged a shoulder as they moved closer to watch. "It's perfectly safe. The water is more than deep enough."

"I don't care how deep it is," Chiara breathed. "That's *crazy*. I would never do it. Would you?"

"I promised my friend who lives here I would do it next year with him."

Her eyes went wide. "No way."

A smile pulled at his lips. "Sometimes you just have to take the leap. Trust that wherever it takes you, you will come out the other side, better, *stronger* than you were before. Life is about the living, Chiara. Trusting your gut."

Chiara's brain was buzzing as Lazzero escorted her inside the gorgeous Grotta Nascondiglio Hotel. It might have been the challenge he had just laid down in front of her. Or it could simply have been how outrageously attractive he looked in sand-colored trousers and a white shirt that stretched across his muscular torso, emphasizing every rippling muscle to devastating effect.

He didn't need anything else to assert his dominance over the world, she concluded, knees a bit unsteady. Not even the glittering, understated Rolex that contrasted with his deeply tanned skin as he pressed a hand to her back and guided her inside the restaurant. The aura of power, *solidity*, about him was unmistakable, his core strength formed in a life that had been trial by fire.

The warm pressure of his palm against her back as they walked inside the massive, natural cave unearthed an excitement all of its own. It was sensory overload as she looked around her at the warmly lit room that opened onto a spectacular view of the Adriatic.

"Tell me we have a table overlooking the water," she said, "and I will die and go to heaven."

Lazzero's ebony eyes danced with humor. "We have a table overlooking the water. In fact, I think it's that one right there."

She followed his nod toward a candlelit table for two that sat at the mouth of the cave, the only one left unoccupied. The only thing separating it from a sheer, butterfly-inducing drop to the sea was the cast-iron fence that ran along the perimeter of the restaurant. Chiara's stomach tipped over with excitement. It was utterly heart-stopping.

The maître d' appeared and led them toward their table. She slipped into the seat Lazzero held out for her and accepted the menu the host handed her. Pushing her chair in, Lazzero took the seat opposite her.

"Not exactly a little hole in the wall in the East Village," she murmured, in an attempt to distract herself from the thumping of her heart.

A speculative glimmer lit his dark eyes. "Are you calling this a *date*, Chiara Ferrante?"

Her stomach missed its landing and crashed into her heart. "It was a joke."

His sensual mouth curved. "You can't even say it, can you? Are you going to run for the hills now that we've gotten that out of the way?"

"Are you?" she asked pointedly.

"No." He sat back in his chair, the wine list in hand. "I'm going to choose us a wine."

He did not ask her preference because, of course, that wasn't how a date with Lazzero went. His women felt feminine and cared for. And she found herself feeling exactly that as he took control and smoothly ordered a bottle of Barolo.

It was, she discovered, a heady feeling given she'd been the one doing the taking care of for as long as she could remember.

"So," Lazzero said, sitting back in his chair when their glasses were full. "Tell me about this urban line of yours. What kind of a vision do you have for it?"

She snagged her lip between her teeth. "You really want to know?"

"Yes. I do."

She told him about the portfolio of designs she'd been working on ever since she was a teenager. How her vision had been to design a line for both teenagers and young women starting out in the work force, neither of whom had much disposable income.

"Most women in New York can't afford designer fashion. Most are like me—they want to be able to express their individuality without blowing their grocery budget on a handbag."

Lazzero made a face. "I've never understood the whole handbag thing." He pointed his glass at her. "How would you market it, then?"

"Online. My own website, which would include a blog to drive traffic to the retail store. The boutique online fashion retailers… Keep it small and targeted."

"Smart," he agreed. "The trends are definitely headed that way. Very little overhead and no in-store marketing costs."

He swirled the rich red wine in his glass. Set his gaze on hers. "I was speaking with Bianca, my head designer, this morning when I signed off on the sketches. She mentioned to me how talented she thought you were."

Her insides warmed. "That's very nice of her to say."

"She's tough. It's no faint praise. Bianca," he elaborated, "heads up an incubator program in Manhattan, the

MFDA—Manhattan Fashion Designer Association. You've heard of it?"

She nodded. "Of course. They nurture new talent from the community—offer bursaries for school and co-op positions in the industry. It's an amazing mentoring program."

"I told Bianca your story. She wants to meet you." Lazzero's casually delivered statement popped her eyes wide-open. "If you are interested, of course. It would just be for a coffee. To see if you'd be a good fit for the group. There are no guarantees they'd take you on, but Bianca holds a great deal of sway."

Her stomach swooped and then dropped. "It's impossible to crack, Lazzero. Some of the most talented kids at school never made it in."

"They're looking for people with vision. You have one." He shook his head. "You don't second-guess an opportunity like this. You embrace it. See where it goes. It may go somewhere. It may go nowhere. But at least you tried."

She bit the inside of her mouth. She had only been dabbling at the drawing the past few years. What if she'd lost her technique? What if she didn't have *it* anymore? And then there was the part where she'd never get another chance like this.

"It's just a coffee," Lazzero said quietly. "Think about it."

She nodded. Sat back in her chair, her head spinning, and took a sip of her wine. The fact that he believed in her enough to do that for her ignited a glow inside of her. But it wasn't just that. He had invited her opinion about the sketches, had valued her input. He valued her for *who* she was. When was the last time someone had done that?

He might be every bit as much of a playboy as Antonio was, but that, she realized, was where the similarities between the two men began and ended. Lazzero was fascinating and complex, the depth to him undeniably compelling.

He was brutally honest about who he was and what he had to offer a woman, which Antonio had never been.

What he'd said that first night about her had been right. She *was* afraid to get hurt again. Was afraid to admit how she felt about him. But denying this connection between them wasn't getting her anywhere.

A flock of butterflies swooped through her stomach. What if she were to walk into this thing with Lazzero with her eyes wide-open? No wild, dreamy expectations like she'd had with Antonio. Just the cold hard reality that when she and Lazzero went back to New York, it would be over?

It was a heady thought that gained momentum as the conversation drifted from politics to the entertaining stories Lazzero had to tell about the mega-million-dollar athletes he worked with. As she sipped the delicious, full-bodied wine. Absorbed the heart-stoppingly romantic atmosphere as the waves crashed against the cliff below.

And then there was the way Lazzero kept holding her hand as if it was the most natural thing in the world. The brush of his long, muscular legs against the bare skin of her thighs that sent shivers of excitement through her. The way his gaze rested on her mouth with increasing frequency as the night wore on.

She didn't want to feel dead inside anymore. She wanted to walk into the fire with Lazzero. To know every thrilling moment of it. To not look back and wonder *what if.* Because she *wasn't* the same girl she'd once been. She was tougher. Wiser. And she knew what she wanted.

Somewhere along the way, between a discussion of the current state of the EU and the choice of decadent dessert, she lost the plot completely.

Lazzero's gaze darkened. "I have a question," he asked huskily, eyes on hers. "When are we getting to the necking part of the evening?"

Her insides fell apart on a low heated pull. "Lazzero—"

He lifted his hand. Signaled their waiter. Five minutes later, he had the bill paid and something else the waiter had placed in his hand. Extending a purposeful hand to her, he navigated the sea of tables to the exit with an impatience that had her heart slamming into her breastbone. But he didn't lead her toward the entrance, he directed her toward the elevators instead.

"Aren't we getting the car?" she breathed.

"No." Jamming his thumb on the call button Lazzero summoned the elevator. *A key*, she identified past her pounding heart. He had a key in his hand.

She could have cried out with frustration when the elevator doors opened to reveal two couples inside. She smiled politely at them, her knees shaking. Lazzero, noticing her less-than-steady stature, slid an arm around her waist and pulled her back against his hard, solid frame. Which was like touching dry timber to a match. By the time they stopped at their floor, she was trembling so much, she could hardly breathe.

Open slid the elevator doors. Out she and Lazzero stepped. Down the hall he strode, her hand in his. There didn't seem to be any other rooms on this floor, just the one door Lazzero stopped in front of at the end. Expecting him to use the key, she gasped as he backed her up against the wall instead, his mouth dipping to take hers in a hot, hard kiss, one that promised a wildness that echoed the shaking in her knees.

His hand wound around a thick chunk of her hair, he angled her head until he had her exactly where he wanted her, then plunged deeper, until they were consuming each other with a ferocity that was terrifying in its intensity.

When they finally came up for air, they were both breathing hard. Lazzero dragged his mouth up to her ear. "You are so beautiful," he murmured. "Tell me you want this, Chiara."

A moment of complete and utter panic consumed her. She drew back, a handful of his shirt in her fingers. Took a deep breath and grounded herself in his dark, hot gaze. In the man, she was learning, she could trust without reservation. Reaching up, she traced the hard, sensual line of his mouth with her fingers and nodded.

His eyes turned to flame. His brief fumble with the key before he got it into the lock wiped away the last of her reservations. Door unlocked, he picked her up, wrapped her legs around him and walked through the door, kicking it shut.

Wild for her in a way he had never experienced before, Lazzero backed Chiara up against the wall and picked the kiss up where he had left off. Trailing openmouthed caresses down the elegant line of her neck, he sank his teeth into the vein that throbbed for him. Her gasp rang out, hot, needy.

Tempted beyond bearing, he slid his hands beneath the gauzy silk of her dress and cupped her bottom. *Silk.* She was wearing silk panties beneath the dress—light, sheer wisps of nothing. Sliding his hands over her bottom, wanting, *needing* to feel her against him, he lifted her, altered the angle between them so that he was cradled in the heat between her thighs. She gasped as the still-covered length of his erection parted her softness through the silk of her panties.

"God, Lazzero. That feels—"

He smoothed a thumb over the juncture of her thigh and abdomen. She arched against him, his hot, hard length rubbing against her center.

"How?" he whispered, his voice rough. "How does it make you feel?"

"So good," she whimpered. "It feels so good. So *hot.*"

He uttered a string of curses. *Slow it down*, his brain warned. Slow it down or he'd be buried in her in about five seconds flat and that was not how this was going to go. Not when the thought of having her was blowing a hole in his brain.

His heart threatening to batter its way through his chest, he sucked in a breath. Unwrapped her legs from around his waist and eased her down his body until her feet touched the floor, the slide of her curves against him hardening him to painful steel. Confused, Chiara stared up at him, her green eyes dazed with desire.

"We need to slow it down," he said huskily, snaring her hand and leading her into the suite, "or this is going to be over way too fast."

The suite, he discovered, was like something straight out of a fantasy. Carved out of the same limestone rock as the rest of the hotel, the circular room was finished with exposed brick and a mosaic-tiled floor illuminated by the soft glow of the lamp that had been left on for them.

Not to be outdone by the view from the restaurant, a luxurious sitting area offered a spectacular view of the sea through the open French doors and the terrace beyond. It was, however, the massive bed dominating the space that held his attention.

He sat down on it. Drew Chiara between his parted legs. His blood fizzled in his veins as he scoured her from head to toe.

"I don't know what to touch first," he admitted huskily. "You are so stunning you make my head want to explode."

Her eyes darkened to twin pools of forest green. She apparently knew exactly what *she* wanted to touch. Hands trembling, she moved her fingers to the buttons of his shirt. Worked her way down the row until she'd reached the last, buried beneath his belt. Dragging his shirt from his pants, she undid it, spread her palms flat against his abs and traced her fingers over each indentation and rise of muscle.

"You are insane," she murmured.

His stomach contracted, a rush of heat flooding through him. Not as insane as he was going to be if he didn't touch her soon. Shrugging off the shirt, he threw it to the floor. Hands at her waist, he turned her around and lowered the zip on her dress, exposing inches of creamy, olive skin as he sent the dress fluttering to the floor in a cloud of dusky-pink silk.

"Step out of it," he instructed, heart jamming in his chest.

She kicked the dress aside and turned around. Absorbed the heat of his gaze as it singed every inch of her skin. The soft, full, oh-so-kissable mouth that had driven him wild from the beginning. The delicate pink bra and panty set she wore that did little to hide the lush femininity beneath.

He sank his hands into her waist and lifted her to straddle him, her knees coming down on either side of his. Cupping her head with the palm of his hand, he brought her mouth down to his. Devoured her until she was soft and malleable beneath his hands and as into this as he was.

Needing to touch, to discover, he dropped his hands to her closure of her bra. Undid it and stripped it off, dropping it to the floor. Her curves, heavy and rose-tipped, filled his hands. Drunk on her, unable to get enough, he traced circles around her flesh with his thumbs, moving ever closer to the swollen tips with every sweep of his fingers, but never where she wanted it, until she groaned and pushed herself into his hands.

"Like this?" he asked softly, rubbing his thumbs over the distended peaks, enflamed by her response. She gasped and muttered her assent. He rolled the hard nubs between his fingers until she was twisting against him, restless and needy.

"You want more?" he murmured. "Show me where."

A wave of color stained her cheeks. "Lazzero—" she whispered.

"Show me."

She sank her teeth into her lip. Spread a palm against her abdomen, low, where those tiny pink panties barely covered her femininity. His blood surged in his veins. Tempted beyond bearing, he covered her palm with his, his eyes on hers. "You want me to touch you?"

Her cheeks turned a deeper, fiery red. Then came a tiny nod. He almost lost it right there, but somehow, he held it together. Easing his fingers beneath the waistband of her panties, he cupped her in his palm. Waited while she got used to his intimate possession, her beautiful green eyes dilating with heat. Then, sliding a finger along her slick cleft, he caressed her with a lazy stroke. Felt his heart slam in his chest at how wet, how aroused she was.

"You feel like honey," he murmured, taking her mouth in a lazy kiss at the same time as he rotated his thumb against her sweet, throbbing center. "Like hot, slick honey."

She moaned into his mouth. He kept teasing her until she was even hotter, slicker, aroused to a fever pitch. Then he slid a finger inside of her—slowly, gently, watching the pleasure flicker across her face as he claimed her with an intimate caress.

"You like that?"

"More," she whispered, arching her back.

Her uninhibited, innocent responses affected him like nothing he could remember, the blood raging in his head now. He slid deeper, each gentle push of his finger taking him further inside her silky body. The feel of her velvet flesh clenching around him was indescribable. She was tight and so damn hot. *Heaven.*

"That's it," he encouraged thickly as she moved into his touch, inviting it now. "Ride me, baby. Take your pleasure."

She closed her eyes. He tangled his tongue with hers, absorbed every broken sound until her harsh pants became desperate. "Lazzero—" she breathed.

He slid two fingers inside of her. Pumped them deep. Once, twice, three times, and she came apart in his arms.

Chiara wasn't sure how long it took her to surface, her bones melted into nothing as his strong arms held her upright. When she finally returned to consciousness, she found herself drowning in the dark glitter of satisfaction in his black gaze.

He had given her extreme pleasure, but had taken none for himself. The tense set of his big body beneath her hands was testament to the control he had exerted over himself. But now it was stretched to the limit.

Emboldened by what they'd just shared, wanting to give him the same pleasure he'd just given her, she dropped her hand to the hard ridge that strained his trousers. Reveled in the harsh intake of air he sucked in. "I think we should abstain from that right now," he murmured, clamping his hand over hers.

"I want to touch you," she said softly, her eyes on his. "Let me."

He considered her for a moment, and then his hands fell away. She curled her fingers around the button of his pants. Released it from its closure. Her fingers moving to his zipper, she lowered it, working it carefully past his straining erection.

The air was so hot and heavy between them as she reached inside his briefs and closed her fingers around him, it was hard to breathe. He was insanely masculine—like smooth, hard steel. Moving her hands over him, she stroked him, petted him, her body going slick all over again at the thought of having him. *Taking* him.

With a low groan, Lazzero rolled off the bed and divested himself of the rest of his clothes. The sound of a foil wrapper sounded inordinately loud in the whisper-quiet room. Prowling back to the bed, he kissed her again, eased her back into the soft sheets with the weight of his body and stripped the panties from her.

An ache building inside of her in a deeper, headier place, she cupped the back of his head and brought his mouth down to hers.

Luxurious, intimate, the meeting of their mouths went on forever. Sliding his hand around the back of her knee, Lazzero curved her leg around his waist. Settled himself into the cradle of her thighs until his heat was positioned against her slick, wet flesh. Her stomach dissolved into dust. He was big. *So big*.

"We go slow," he murmured, reading her expression. "Tell me how it feels, *caro*. What you like."

She arched her hips, desperate for him. He slid a palm beneath her bottom, raised her up and slipped the velvet head of him just inside her, his big body shuddering. "So tight," he said raggedly, "so good. How does that feel?"

"Amazing." She barely got the word out past the pounding of her heart. "More."

He sank inside of her a little bit more. Retreated, then pushed deeper, each stroke giving her time to adjust to the size and girth of him. Gentle, so patient, he tried *her* patience.

She closed her hands around his rock-hard glutes and pulled him deeper. A muttered curse leaving his mouth, he grasped her hips and claimed her with a single, powerful thrust that filled every part of her. Tore the breath from her lungs.

Never had she felt so possessed, so full of *everything*. Mouth glued to his, her air his air, they set a frantic rhythm together until they melted into one. Until she felt herself tighten around him, the pleasure threatening to shatter her all over again.

"That's it." Thick, hoarse, the guttural edge to Lazzero's voice at her ear spurred her on. "Let go."

His big body flexed above her, his muscles bunching as he shifted his position to deepen his thrusts. The connection they shared as his dark gaze burned into hers was so electric, so all-encompassing, it froze her in place. So much more than just the physical, it was the most intimate, soul-baring experience of her life.

Slowly, deliberately, he ground against her where she needed him the most. The delicious friction of his body against hers sent her over the edge with a sharp cry. An animal-like groan leaving his throat, Lazzero unleashed himself and took his pleasure, claiming her so deeply all she saw was white-hot stars as they shattered into one.

CHAPTER EIGHT

CHIARA EMERGED FROM a sex-induced haze to find herself plastered across Lazzero's muscular chest, her legs tangled with his, his heart pounding beneath her ear in almost as wild a rhythm as hers. She had the feeling he was as thrown off balance by what they'd just shared as she was, but he didn't say anything, just stroked a lazy path down her spine with his palm.

Her stomach dipped, settling somewhere around the rocky shore below. She'd just had wild, ridiculously hot sex with Lazzero, the depth of the connection they'd shared frightening in its intensity. She had not only walked *into* the fire, she'd drowned herself in it. She didn't feel dead anymore, she felt unnervingly, terrifyingly alive, like someone had mainlined adrenaline through her veins. As if she'd denied herself this depth of feeling, of *connection*, for so long, it was complete and utter sensory overload.

But there was also fear. Fear she'd spent a lifetime avoiding these feelings. That the one time she'd slipped and allowed herself to be this vulnerable, she'd been destroyed. Fear that it was Lazzero that was making it so scary. Because he was an insane lover. Because she had liked him for a long time and refused to admit it.

Because of how he made her *feel*.

She buried her teeth in her lip. Forced herself to stay in the moment. To absorb it, rather than run from it, because she'd been doing that for far too long and she'd promised herself *this* was not going to be about that. This was about finding a piece of herself again that she'd lost.

"What?" Lazzero's hand stilled on her spine, as if he could read the shift in her emotion.

She buried her teeth deeper into her lip. "Nothing."

He rolled her onto her back and sank his fingers into her hair so that she was forced to look at him. "You are far too easy to read. You have smoke coming out of your ears. Regrets already?"

"No. It was perfect. I—" She shook her head. "Making myself vulnerable isn't the easiest thing for me. You were right about that. It's easier to hide behind my layers—to not engage, rather than let myself feel."

His midnight gaze warmed. "You were engaged just now. You made me a little insane for you, Chiara. Or did you miss the part where we almost didn't make it to the bed?"

A flush crept up her body and warmed her cheeks. She had *not* missed that part. She had been there for every mind-blowing second of it. She'd *liked* that he'd almost lost control. That she could do that to him. That he had been just as crazy for her as she had been for him. It made her feel less self-conscious about the way she felt.

Lazzero ran a finger across the heated surface of her cheek. "Give me five minutes," he murmured, "and I will refresh your memory."

Her gaze slipped away from his, unable to handle the intensity of the moment. Moved over the magnificent length of his muscled body, bathed in the glow of the lamplight. It warmed another part of her entirely, every inch of the honed, sinewy muscle on display, the scar that crisscrossed his knee his only imperfection.

She traced her fingers over the raised ridge of the scar. "What's this?"

"An old basketball injury."

"The one that ended your career?"

"Yes."

When no further information was forthcoming, she sank back on her elbow to look at him. "I sat beside your old basketball coach at lunch yesterday—Hank Peterson. He was wonderful. Full of such great stories. He told me you come to talk to his kids at the REACH program."

A ghost of a smile touched his mouth. "Hank is a legend. I met him when we moved to Greenwich Village. He used to coach a league at The Cage, one of the most famous streetball courts in New York that was right around the corner from our house. It was mythical, where *dreams* are made—where some of the greats were born. I used to ditch my homework and play all night. Until they turned the lights off and Hank sent me home."

Her mouth curved. "I used to do the same thing with my sketching. I was supposed to be doing my homework while my parents finished work at the bakery. Instead, my mother would come home to a whole lot of drawings in the back of my notebook and very little else. It used to drive her crazy."

"At least she cared," he murmured. "That's a good thing."

She frowned. "Yours didn't?"

"There was no one home *to* care. My father was drinking by then and my mother had left. Nico," he allowed, "used to lecture me to study. He was all about school and learning. But I was hopelessly obsessed."

Her eyes widened. *His mother had left?* "I thought she remarried when your father died."

Lazzero shook his head. "She walked out on us when I was fourteen."

Chiara was shocked into silence. *What mother would leave her children like that? When everything was falling*

apart around them? When her children were at their most
vulnerable and needed her most of all?

"Was your father's alcoholism an instigator in her leaving?" she asked, trying to understand.

"My mother was a sycophant," he said flatly. "She fell
in love with my father's money and she fell out of love with
him when he lost it."

She bit the inside of her mouth. "I'm sure it wasn't quite
that simple."

"It was just that simple." He tucked his hands behind his
head, an expressionless look on his face. "My mother was
a dancer trying to make it on Broadway when she and my
father met. She wanted a career, the glitz, the glamour. She
didn't want a family. When she got pregnant with Nico, my
father thought he could change her mind. But he never did.
He spent their entire marriage trying to keep her happy,
which in the end failed miserably when he imploded and
she walked out on him."

She absorbed his harshly issued words. "That's only one
side of the story," she said huskily. "I'm sure it couldn't
have been easy on your mother to give up her career. Her
dream. And your father," she pointed out, "sounds as if he
was extremely driven. As if he had his own internal demons to battle. Which couldn't have been easy to live with."

"No," Lazzero agreed evenly, "it wasn't. But he was
a man. He was focused on providing. He was hurt when
he couldn't make her happy. His pride was damaged. He
spent more and more time at work, because he didn't want
to be at home, which eventually devolved into the affairs
he had to compensate. Which were not in any way excus-
able," he qualified, "but perhaps understandable, given she
drove him to it."

That struck a raw note given what Antonio had done to
her. "Nobody drives anyone to do anything," she refuted.

"Relationships are complicated things, Lazzero. You make a choice to love someone. To see it through."

His eyes glittered. "Exactly why I choose not to do it. Because any way you look at it, someone always messes it up."

She absorbed his intense cynicism. "So basketball," she murmured, seeking to dispel some of the tension in the air, "became your outlet. Like sketching was for me?"

He nodded, sifting his fingers through her hair and watching it in the play of the light. "If I was on the court, I wasn't dealing with the mess my life was. With the shadow of a man my father had become. But I also," he conceded, his gaze darkening, "fell in love. There's a magic about the game when you play it on the streets of New York—an unspoken devotion to the game we all shared. By the time I'd won my first tournament for Hank, I knew I wanted to play basketball for a living."

Her mouth curved. "Hank said you were always the first and last on the court."

"Because I wasn't as physically gifted as some of the other players," he acknowledged. "I didn't have the size some of them did, nor the jumping ability. I had to work harder, *want it more* than all the rest. But I was smart. I could read the court and I built my career around that. I won a division championship for Hank in my junior year at Columbia."

A college career which, according to Hank, had been limitless in its possibilities. Until he'd injured himself.

She curled her fingers around his knee. "Tell me about it? What happened."

He lifted a shoulder. "There isn't much to tell. I was chasing a player down on a breakaway in a key divisional play-off game. I jumped to block the shot, felt something pop in my knee. Shatter. When I tried to stand up, I couldn't. I'd torn the two main ligaments that hold your knee together. It was almost impossible for the surgeons to put it back together."

Her throat felt like gravel. "That must have been devastating."

"It was what it was."

His standard line. But she knew now it hadn't been so simple. "Hank said you were an exceptional player, Lazzero. That you'd been scouted by three professional teams. It had to have hurt to have that taken from you."

A shadow whispered over the clarity of his gaze. "What do you want me to say, Chiara? That I was shattered inside? That watching every dream I'd had since I was eight go up in a puff of smoke tore me apart?"

She flinched at the harsh edge to his voice. Pushed a hand into the mattress to sit up and stare out at the sea, a dark, silent mass beyond the French doors. Maybe she'd been looking for the truth, given she'd poured her heart and soul out to him on the terrace that night. But that was not what this was, she reminded herself, and she'd be a fool to forget it.

Lazzero exhaled an audible breath. Snared an arm around her waist and pulled her back against him, tucking her against his chest.

"I was in denial," he said quietly. "I refused to believe it would end my career. I went for a second opinion and when that doctor told me I would never play at that level again, I set out to prove him wrong. It took me almost a year and hundreds of hours of physio to accept the fact that I was never coming back. That it was *over.*"

A hand fisted her chest. "You didn't give up," she said, absorbing the hard beat of his heart beneath her ear. "Not like I did."

"Giving up wasn't an option. It was everything to me."
Sometimes dreams are too expensive to keep.
Her blood ran jagged in her veins. Suddenly, he made so

much sense to her. Lazzero's world had dissolved beneath his feet, not once, when his father had imploded and his mother had walked out, but twice, when his basketball career had disintegrated beneath his feet on a painful stroke of fate. But instead of allowing himself to become bitter and disillusioned, he'd created Supersonic. Built a company around the sport he loved.

"Hank says you are a great mentor to the kids," she said huskily.

A lift of his shoulder beneath her. "It gives them something to shoot for if a pro basketball career doesn't work out for them. Unfortunately, the statistics are stacked against it."

Her heart did a funny twist. She hadn't needed another reason to like him this much. Because falling for Lazzero wasn't on the agenda in this walk on the wild side of hers. And maybe he decided that too, because before she could take another breath, he had rolled her onto her back, speared a hand into her hair, and there was no escaping the sparks that sizzled and popped between them.

"I think that's enough talking," he murmured, lowering his mouth to hers. "Now that I've gotten you where I want you, I intend to take full advantage of it."

She sucked in a breath, only to lose it as he covered her mouth with his, his kiss dragging her back into the inferno with relentless precision. A gasp left her throat as he slid his tongue inside her mouth, mating with her own in a fiery dance that signaled his carnal ambitions.

It was pure, dominant male at its most blatant and she loved it. Her hands found the thick muscle of his back and shoulders as she surrendered to the hunger that consumed them both.

Her last coherent thought was that it had been worth every second. Exactly as she'd known it would be. And maybe she was in way, way over her head.

* * *

An opera at the stunning Teatro alla Scala in Milan was hardly the thing to put a girl firmly back on her feet after she'd just embarked on a wild, passionate affair with a man who was most definitely out of her league. Chiara, however, attempted to do exactly that the following evening as she and Lazzero attended a private performance of Verdi's *La Traviata* at the beautiful, iconic theater.

An opportunity for the sponsors of La Coppa Estiva to entertain their international guests in a glamorous, glitzy affair that had been enjoyed by the Milanese upper crust since the eighteenth century, she and Lazzero were to host a German retail scion and his wife in their private box.

She thought Micaela had gotten her outfit just right, the ankle-length sleek scarlet dress with its asymmetric cut at the shoulder glamorous, yet understated, a red lip and sparkly heels her only accessories. It was Lazzero in a perfectly tailored black suit, his ebony hair worn fashionably spiky tonight, a five o'clock shadow darkening his jaw, that was making her pulse race.

His touch lingered just a little bit longer than before, the possessive glimmer in his eyes as they worked the crowd doing something funny to her insides. *As if they were lovers.* Which, in fact, they were, a mind-boggling detail she was just beginning to wrap her head around.

Then it was the spectacular theater that was stealing her attention. Six rows of gold stuccoed boxes sat stacked on top of each other in the oval theater, soaring high above the packed crowd below. The massive, Bohemian crystal chandelier was incredible, as was the sumptuous elegance of their box with its red velvet, silk and gilded stucco interior. Since she knew nothing about opera, having never attended one in her life, Chiara nestled her viewing glasses in her lap and scoured the program so she would know the story, but soon the lights were dimming and the curtain came up and she lost herself to the performance instead.

She was hooked from the very first second. Transfixed by the elaborate sets, the hauntingly beautiful music and the poignant story of Violetta Valéry, the heroine of Verdi's opera.

Violetta, a courtesan, knows she will die soon, exhausted by her restless life. Alfredo Germont, played by a handsome, world-famous tenor who strutted across the stage in the opening act, has been fascinated by Violetta for a very long time. When he is introduced to her at a party, he proposes a toast to true love. Enchanted by his candid and forthright manner, Violetta responds with a toast in praise of *free* love.

Enamoured though she may be, Violetta decides there is no room for such emotion in her life and walks away from Alfredo. But she can't quite seem to put him out of her head and eventually, the two embark on a passionate love affair.

Tears filled Chiara's eyes as she watched Alfredo awaken Violetta's desire to be truly loved. They slipped silently down her cheeks amidst the beautiful music. She brushed them from her cheeks, afraid to watch, because she knew what was to come. As in all of the great, tragic love stories it seemed, disaster was about to befall the two lovers.

Alfredo's father, a wealthy aristocrat, pays a visit to Violetta to convince her there can be no future for her and his son. That she is destroying Alfredo's future by encouraging his love, and that of his sister, as well, to marry into the upper echelons of society.

Heartbroken, Chiara watched as Violetta left Alfredo to return to her old life, telling him she didn't love him to set him free. Alfredo, grief stricken and racked with jealousy and hurt at Violetta's supposed betrayal, stalked across the stage as the music reached its crescendo and proposed a duel with her paramour to end the second act.

"Ooh," said the German CEO's wife as the lights came up for the intermission. "It's so good, isn't it?"

Chiara nodded, frantically rifling through her purse for a tissue. Lazzero offered her the handkerchief from his front pocket, a cynical look on his face. She ignored him as they made their way out into the elegant foyer with its fluted columns and crystal chandeliers, her head still caught up in the story. Absorbing its nuances.

Violetta's story had struck so many chords in her, she wasn't sure which one to consider first. How much the character reminded her of herself with her determination to escape her emotions. How she hadn't been good enough for Antonio. How swept up she was becoming in Lazzero. What would happen in the end, because Violetta had to die, didn't she? Would her and Alfredo's love be forever thwarted?

When her opera companion excused herself to the ladies' room, Chiara slipped out onto one of the Juliette balconies to regain her equilibrium while Lazzero introduced the German CEO around. The tiny balcony, set apart from the larger one that was buzzing with activity, boasted a lovely view of the lit Piazza della Scala.

She leaned back against the stone facade of the building and inhaled a deep breath of the sultry, summer night air. It was as far removed from her life as she could possible imagine. And yet, there was something so real about the moment. So revelatory.

She had not been living for far too long, that she knew. But was it worth the consequences that Violetta had feared to fully embrace this new world of emotion? To reap the greatest rewards that life had to offer? She hadn't quite determined the answer to that question when Lazzero stepped out onto the balcony, two glasses of Prosecco in his hands.

She lifted a brow. "You're not networking until you drop?"

"Hans saw someone he knew." He handed her a glass of Prosecco. "I thought you might need this. You looked a little emotionally devastated in there."

A wry smile pulled at her mouth. "It's a beautiful story. I got a little swept up in the emotion. Although you," she conceded, "did not seem quite so captivated. Which part of your jaded view of love did Verdi offend?"

"Not all of it," he drawled, leaning a hip against the wall. "I thought Violetta was spot-on. I'm all for the concept of *free love*. Everybody walks into it with realistic expectations. Nobody gets hurt. Her critical mistake was in buying into Alfredo's vision—into a fantasy that doesn't really exist."

"Who says?" she countered lightly. "My parents had it. They were madly in love with each other."

"So much so that your father is in the dark place that he is?" Lazzero tipped his head to the side. "Some would call that an unhealthy kind of love. A *devastating* kind of love."

She couldn't necessarily disagree with the observation, because loving that deeply had consequences. She had lived with them since she was fifteen. She knew what it was like to be loved and what it felt like to have that love taken away. Had convinced herself she was better off without it after Antonio. But she also believed her parents had shared something special and somewhere, deep down, if she were to be completely honest, she knew she wanted it too.

She met Lazzero's cynical gaze. "You're talking about your parents. That *messy*, kind of love you are so intent on avoiding?"

"They were a disaster from start to finish," he said flatly. "My father fell in love with an illusion rather than the reality of what he got. This," he said, waving a hand toward the doors, "could be their story tonight. And you see how well it turned out for Violetta and Alfredo."

She shook her head. "Violetta *loved* Alfredo. What they had was real. It was his father that messed it up."

"And look how easily she was swayed. One might say she was simply looking for a way out. That she never truly committed."

"She was being selfless. She wanted to set him free. You make a choice to love someone, Lazzero. You *choose* to commit."

"Or you choose to marry for the wrong reasons." He tipped his glass at her. "My mother married my father for the money. Carolina married Gianni on the rebound. Violetta needed to be rescued. Does anyone ever marry for the *right* reason? Because they want to spend their lives together?"

"Violetta's case was different," she disagreed. "For her to set Alfredo free was, in my opinion, the ultimate act of love on her part."

"And what happens when she is gone?" Lazzero lifted a dark brow. "Do you think Alfredo is going to applaud himself for the decision he made when his heart has been smashed to smithereens?"

Exactly as his father's had been? Her insides curled at the parallels. "Maybe," she offered huskily, "he will feel lucky to have experienced that kind of love *once* in his life and he will have that to hang on to when she's gone. Maybe, as much pain as my father is in, he wouldn't trade what he and my mother had for the world."

Lazzero rested an inscrutable gaze on her.

"What?"

"You," he murmured. "I never would have guessed you are a closet romantic with that prickly exterior of yours."

She shrugged. "I'm merely trying to make a point. *You* are the one who said to me that tarring all men of a certain bank balance with the same brush is a mistake. Maybe," she suggested, "lumping all relationships into the same category is an equal error in judgment."

He pushed away from the wall and caged her in with a palm beside her head all in one lazy movement. "So," he drawled, his eyes on hers, "is that what is on offer to Mr. Right? Chiara Ferrante's heart if a man is willing to go *all in*?"

Her breath stalled in her chest. He was so gorgeous, so dark and brooding up close, it was impossible to think. "Stop playing with me," she murmured. "You are inherently skilled in the art of deflection, Lazzero."

"Who says I'm playing? Maybe I'm accepting your challenge. Maybe I just want to know the answer."

"Maybe," she breathed. Because she wasn't sure if she was ready to open herself up again to the full gamut of that emotion she so feared. To the possibility she might be rejected again—that she wouldn't be *good enough*. But maybe that was the risk you had to take. To know, that if you jumped, you were strong enough to handle whatever came on the other side.

"What I *think*," Lazzero murmured, his dark gaze glittering as it rested on hers, "is that you and I have a good thing, Chiara. Honest, up-front, with all of our cards on the table. And *that* is why it works."

Right, she told herself. That was exactly what this was. And she could handle it. Absolutely she could.

"Although," he said softly, lowering his head to hers so their breaths melded in a warm, seductive caress, "I didn't come out here to debate Verdi with you."

Every kiss, every caress, every heart-stopping moment of pleasure from the night before swept through her in a heady rush. "Oh," she breathed, her heart thumping in her chest. "Why did you?"

"Because I wanted to do *this*." He closed his mouth over hers in a lazy, persuasive possession that stormed her senses. She let her eyes flutter shut. Stopped thinking entirely as her fingers curled around the lapel of his jacket, a gasp of warm air leaving her lips as her mouth parted beneath his sensual assault.

The sound of the intermission bell ended the seductive spiral. "We should go back in," Lazzero murmured, nuzzling her mouth.

"Yes," she agreed unsteadily, taking a step back. "Although I'm not so sure I want to see Violetta shatter Alfredo's heart."

CHAPTER NINE

THE THOUGHT OF a dinner party at Villa Alighieri, Gianni Casale's stunning estate in Lake Como, was a much less intimidating prospect for Chiara than many of the events she and Lazzero had attended thus far. She had created the sketches for Volare the Italian CEO had fallen in love with, she had accepted Bianca's offer for coffee which could take her life in a whole new direction and she was knee-deep in a spectacular affair with Lazzero that showed no signs of cooling.

If she was being unwise, foolhardy, in thinking she could handle all of this, telling herself she wasn't in as deep as she was, she brushed those thoughts aside, because being with Lazzero was the most breathtakingly exciting experience of her life, she felt ridiculously alive and it was the headiest of drugs.

Striving for an elegance and composure to match the evening, she chose a midlength, black wrap dress. Simple in design, it was the gorgeous material that made the dress, the light jersey clinging to her body in all the right places, the deeply cut V that revealed the barest hint of the swell of her breasts its only overtly sexy note.

Chiara had loved it because of the huge, red hibiscus that fanned out from her waist, transforming the dress from ordinary to extraordinary. A splash of vibrant color on a perfectly cut canvas.

Adding a dark cherry gloss to her lips and delicate high heels that matched the exotic bloom, she left the golden tan she'd acquired to do the rest of the work, her final touch a series of layered silver bracelets.

Lazzero spent the entire drive up to Lake Como on a conference call, in full mogul mode. It wasn't until they'd parked at the marina and taken possession of the boat that would transport them to Villa Alighieri, that she claimed his attention, his gaze roving over her in a starkly appreciative appraisal that brought a flush to her cheeks.

"You look like an exotic flower come to life," he murmured, brushing a kiss against her cheek. She took in his tapered, light gray pants and lavender shirt as he stepped back. They did everything for his dark good looks and little for her pounding heart that felt as if it might push right through her chest.

On any other man, the pastel color might have come off as less than masculine. On Lazzero, it was a look that would send most women slithering to the ground.

"You don't look so bad yourself," she said breezily, the understatement of the year. But clearly, she needed to do something to diminish the way his eyes on her made her feel. As if this was more than a charade. As if she wanted to fling caution to the wind. Which was so *not* what she should be doing.

His dark gaze trailed lazily over her face. Read the emotions coursing through her as he always seemed to do. "I am," he drawled, "worried about the hair, however."

She produced a scarf from her evening bag. "I was warned." Draping it around her head, she secured the ends beneath her chin in Jackie O fashion before Lazzero handed her into the boat and brought the powerful speedboat rumbling to life. Soon, they were off, headed toward Villa Alighieri, which was perched at the end of a wooded promontory on the far end of the lake, accessible only by boat because the privacy-conscious Gianni liked it that way.

The sun threw up slender fingers of fire into a spectacular vermillion sky, the air was crisp and cool on her skin, the spray of the seawater as they sped across the lake salty, invigorating, life affirming in a way she couldn't describe. Or maybe, she thought, butterflies swooping through her stomach, that was just the way Lazzero made her feel—as if she'd woken up from a life of not really living.

When a particularly strong gust of wind caught her off guard, she swayed in her high heels. Lazzero caught her wrist in his fingers, tugged her to him and tucked her in front of him at the steering wheel. His mouth at her ear, he pointed out the sights, the husky edge to his voice raking across her nerve receptors, backed up by the hard press of his amazing thighs against hers. By the time he cut the throttle and they pulled up to the wide set of stone steps that led up to Villa Alighieri, Chiara was so caught up in him she couldn't see straight.

Lazzero threw the rope to one of the valets who stood waiting, then lifted her out of the boat and onto the steps, his hands remaining on her waist to steady her as her legs adjusted to solid ground. Drawn by the smoky heat in his eyes, she stared up at him, the muscles in her throat convulsing.

"Dammit, Chiara." He raked a gaze over her face. "You pick a hell of a time to go there, you know that?"

You don't pick *these things*, she thought unsteadily, sliding her hand into his as he led her up the path toward the cream stuccoed villa, which rose up out of the spectacular, terraced gardens.

"This is unbelievable," she murmured. *"Heaven."*

"Gianni named it after his favorite poet—Dante Alighieri—who wrote *The Divine Comedy.*"

Her lips curved. "My father loves *The Divine Comedy.*"

He'd been trying to get her to read it for forever. She thought it appealed to the philosopher in him.

He was quiet as they took the winding path through the gardens up to the loggia. But she knew how critical tonight was for him. Read it in the tense set of his face. Which meant she needed to be focused on the task at hand.

"Who's going to be here tonight?"

He threw her an absentminded look. "A few of the Italian players and their wives. A fairly intimate group from what I could gather."

Which it turned out to be. Mingling under the elegant loggia which offered a breathtaking view of the lake and the islands beyond from its perch on the highest point of the promontory, were perhaps a dozen guests.

Carolina and Gianni materialized to greet them. Lazzero slid a proprietary hand around her waist, but Carolina, it seemed, had elected to sheath her claws tonight. Which made it easier for Chiara to let down her guard as she met the Italian players and their wives and girlfriends, as well as Gianni's daughter from his first marriage, Amalia, a beautiful, sophisticated blonde.

The friendly rivalry between Lazzero and the Italian players inspired good-natured jokes and predictions about who would win the tournament, headed for an Americas, Western Europe collision in the final the following day. By the time they'd finished the cocktails, Chiara was relaxed and enjoying herself, finding Amalia, in particular, excellent company.

It was as they were about to sit down to dinner at the elegantly set table for twelve that Amalia's beautiful face lit up. *"Eccoti!"* she exclaimed, walking toward the house. *There you are.* "I thought maybe you were grounded by the bad weather."

Amalia's husband, Chiara assumed, who'd been in London on a business trip. She turned to greet him, a smile on her face. Felt her heart stop in her chest at the sight of the tall, dark-haired male brushing a kiss against Amalia's cheek, the jacket of his sand-colored suit tossed across his shoulder.

It could *not* be. *Not here. Not tonight.*

Amalia came back, her husband's hand caught in hers. "Antonio," she said happily, "please to meet you Lazzero Di Fiore, a member of the Americas team and a business associate of my father's, and his fiancée, Chiara Ferrante."

"Please *meet.*" Antonio corrected her English, but his eyes never left Chiara. "*Mi dispiace.* I'm sorry I'm late. We were grounded for an hour."

"You're not late," Amalia said, wilting slightly at the correction. "We were just about to sit down to dinner."

"*Bene.*" Antonio held out a hand to Lazzero. "A pleasure," he drawled in perfectly accented English. "Congratulations on your engagement."

Chiara swayed on her feet. Lazzero tightened his arm around her waist, glancing down at her, but her eyes were glued to the man in front of her. His raven-dark hair, the lantern jaw she'd once loved, the piercing blue eyes that exuded an unmistakable power, an authority that was echoed in every line of his perfectly pressed, handcrafted suit. But it was his eyes that claimed her attention. They were the coldest she'd ever encountered.

How, she wondered, *had she never noticed that?*

Lazzero extended his hand to Antonio. Greeted the man who had once been her lover. Who had smashed her heart into so many pieces she'd wondered if she would ever be able to put herself back together again.

Panic pushed a hundred different flight routes through her head. What was she supposed to do? Admit she knew him? Deny it completely? The latter seemed preferable with his wife standing at his side. Antonio, however, didn't miss a beat. Focusing that cold, blue gaze on her, he bent to press a kiss to both of her cheeks. "Lazzero is clearly a lucky man," he murmured. "When is the big day?"

It was as if he'd asked her the exact date and time a meteor was going to hit the earth and blow them all to smithereens. Lazzero gave her a quizzical look. She swallowed hard and gathered her wits. "Next summer," she murmured. "So many people rush their engagements. We wanted to enjoy it."

"Indeed," agreed Antonio smoothly. "Marriage is a lifelong commitment. A serious endeavor. Amalia and I did the same."

Oh, my God. A flare of fury lanced through her. He had not just said that. *A lifelong commitment. A serious endeavor. He* had been willing to break those vows before he'd even embarked on his marriage. He had *planned* on taking a mistress, without deigning to fill her in on the plan. And why? Amalia was beautiful, charming, funny, *with* the impeccable breeding Antonio required.

Gianni joined them, giving Antonio's arm a congenial squeeze. "A good introduction for you," he said to Lazzero. "The Fabrizio family is the largest stakeholder in Fiammata outside of the family. That's how Antonio and Amalia met. You should pick his brain over dinner. He can give you some excellent perspective on the company."

Lazzero nodded and said he would do exactly that. Chiara attempted to absorb the panic seeping through her like smoke infiltrating a burning building. Of course it made complete sense that Antonio owned a stake in Fiammata, she acknowledged numbly. He ran one of Europe's largest investment houses, with a slew of marquee clients across the globe.

Lazzero bent his head to hers as they waited to be seated at the elegant table under the loggia, his lips brushing her cheek in a featherlight caress. "What's wrong?"

"Nothing." She forced a smile past her pounding heart. "I think that cocktail might have gone to my head."

"You should watch the wine, then. It was a hot day."

She absorbed the concern in his ebony gaze. The *warmth*. It was like looking into a mirror of the man. She always knew exactly where she stood with Lazzero—good or bad—just as he'd promised from the beginning.

She did not turn down the excellent Pinot Grigio that was served with the appetizer, desperately needing the steadying edge it gave her nerves. Seated between Amalia and Lazzero, with Antonio directly opposite her and Gianni beside him, she attempted to regain her composure as the men talked business and Amalia chattered on. But it was almost impossible to concentrate.

Antonio kept staring at her, making only a cursory attempt at conversation. Which made her agitated and furious all at the same time. She took a deep sip of her wine. Steeled herself as she pulled her gaze away from his. She was going to do exactly what she'd told herself she would do in this situation. She was going to move past it like the piece of history it was. She was not going to let Antonio get to her and she was not going to let her disarray affect this evening for Lazzero.

Somehow, she made it through the leisurely seven-course meal that seemed to stretch for an eternity on a hot, sultry night in the Lakes, the wine flowing as freely as the delicious food, which Chiara could only manage a few bites of. By the time the *dolce* was served, and Gianni claimed Lazzero for a private conversation over a *digestivo* of grappa, she was ready to crawl out of her skin.

She chatted fashion with Amalia, who was quite the fashionista with the budget she had at her disposal. When Carolina claimed Amalia to speak with someone else, Chiara secured directions to the powder room at the bottom of the loggia stairs and retreated to repair her powder and gloss. A tension headache pounding like the stamp of a sewing machine in her head, she took her time, aware Gianni and Lazzero might be a while and unable to face the thought of yet more social chitchat.

When she could delay no longer, she headed back upstairs. Almost jumped out of her skin when Antonio cut her off at the bottom of the stairs.

"We need to talk," he said grimly.

A thread of unease tightened around her chest, then unraveled so fast her heart began to whirl. "No we don't. We were done the day I walked out of your penthouse. There's nothing to talk about."

He set his piercing blue gaze on her. "I disagree. We can either talk about it here or up there," he said, nodding toward the loggia and the sound of laughter and conversation.

She stared at him, sure he was bluffing. But just unsure enough she couldn't risk it. Nodding her head, she followed him to a viewing spot near the water that sat under the shade of an enormous plane tree, cut in the shape of a chandelier.

He leaned back against the tree. "You look different. You've cut your hair."

Chiara tipped her chin up. "It was time for a change."

He eyed her, as if assessing the temperature in the air. "You don't love him, Chiara. You don't go from being madly in love with me to madly in love with another man in the space of a few months."

"It's been six months," she said quietly. "And I was never in love with you, Antonio." She knew that now when she compared her feelings for him to the ones she had for Lazzero. "I was *infatuated* with you. Bowled over by your good looks and charm. By the attention and care you lavished on me. I thought I meant something to you. When in reality, I never did."

He rubbed a hand over his jaw. Shook his head. "I *was*

in love with you, Chiara. I told you my marriage to Amalia was a political one. Why can't you get that through your head? Why do you keep pushing me away when we could have something?"

She shook her head, everything crystal clear now. "She is beautiful. Lovely, charming, funny. How can she not be enough for you?"

"Because she isn't you." He fixed his gaze on hers. "You are *alive*. You are fire and passion in bed. You do it for me like no other woman ever has, Chiara."

The blood drained from her face at the blunt confirmation of everything she'd known, but hadn't wanted to believe. "So I was good enough to warm your bed, but I wasn't good enough to stand at your side?"

"It wouldn't have worked," he said quietly. "You know that. I needed the match with Amalia. It works. But I hadn't given up on you. I thought you'd be over it by now. I was going to come see you next month in New York when I'm there."

"Save yourself the trouble." Her chin lifted as she slammed the door shut on that piece of her life with devastating finality. "I am in love with Lazzero, Antonio. I am marrying him. We are *over*."

"You don't mean that," he countered, his dark gaze flashing. "You're hurt. A ring on your finger isn't going to increase your value, Chiara. Not to a man like Di Fiore. You'll still be a possession to him. What's the difference if you're his or mine?"

It stung, as if he'd taken a hand to her face. "He is ten times the man you are," she said flatly, refusing to show him how much it hurt. "You can't even make the comparison. And you're wrong, I do care about him."

Which was scarily, undeniably true.

Frustration etched a stormy path across Antonio's handsome face. "What do you want me to do, Chiara? Walk away from Amalia? You know I can't do that."

Her heart tipped over and tumbled to her stomach. He actually *believed* she still wanted him after everything he'd done?

"I want you to leave me alone," she said harshly. "I want you to forget we ever existed."

"Chiara—"

She turned on her heel and walked away.

Lazzero emerged from his after-dinner chat with Gianni infuriated by the Italian's perpetual game of hard to get. Now that he and the Fiammata CEO were aligned when it came to the design sensibility of a potential Supersonic Volare line, Gianni had turned his focus to price and how much he expected to be compensated for Volare. Which was astronomical—far more than Lazzero had offered—and also utterly ridiculous for a single piece of intellectual property.

Firmly immersed in the black mood that had overtaken him, he sought out Chiara. When she wasn't in the group enjoying after-dinner drinks, he looked for her downstairs, concerned she wasn't well. He was about to give up, thinking they'd missed one another, when he found her in one of the viewing areas that overlooked the lake. With Antonio Fabrizio, who hadn't taken his eyes off her all dinner, a liberty he had been content to allow because Chiara was beautiful and he couldn't fault Fabrizio for thinking so.

Tempering his rather insanely possessive streak when it came to Chiara, he started toward the two of them, only to have Chiara turn on her heel and walk toward him, her face set in a look of determination.

"Whoa." He settled his hands on her waist as she nearly walked through him. She blinked and looked up. "Sorry," she muttered, an emotion he couldn't read flaring in her green eyes. "I didn't see you there."

He tipped her chin up with his fingers. "You okay? You look pale."

She nodded. Waved a hand toward Fabrizio, who was making his way up the stairs. "Antonio was just showing me his boat. The *Amalia*. It's quite something."

He studied the play of emotion in her eyes. "You sure?"

"Yes. I am tired though. Do you think we can leave soon?"

Her request mirrored his own desire to end the evening before he self-combusted. Setting a hand to her back, he guided her upstairs where they made a round of goodbyes and said thank you to the Casales.

It was dark on the boat trip back across the lake. This time, he spent the journey focusing on getting them safely back to shore rather than putting his hands on Chiara, doing the same on the stretch of highway back to Milan. She was quiet the whole way, perhaps suffering from the headache Amalia had given her aspirin for. Which worked for him, because he needed to get his antagonism with Gianni out of his system.

Curving a hand around her bare thigh, he focused on the road. Thought about how easy the silences were between them. How easy it was to be with *her*.

She was smart as he'd known, talented as he'd come to find out and compelling in a way he couldn't describe— the most fascinating mix of innocence, toughness and a fierce strength he loved. With more secrets hidden beneath those protective layers, he suspected, glancing over at her shadowed face in the dim light of the car. He shouldn't want to uncover them as much as he did, but the desire was undeniable.

When they arrived back to the Orientale forty-five minutes later, he threw his jacket over a chair and followed Chiara into the dressing room where she stood removing her jewelry. Their sexy moment on the boat infiltrating his head, he came to a halt behind her. Set his hands to her voluptuous hips, his mouth to her throat. "Head better?"

She nodded. Tipped her head back to give him better access, an instinctive response he liked. He pressed a kiss to the sensitive spot between her neck and shoulder. Registered the delicate shiver that went through her.

He should really go work. Crunch some numbers to try and make Gianni's preposterous demands make sense, but he'd been so hot for her from the moment they'd stepped off that boat tonight, he needed to have her. And maybe once he had, he could pry what was wrong out of her in bed. *Fix it.*

He pulled her back against him so she could feel his arousal pressed against her. Her heady gasp made him smile. With a sigh, she melted back into him, the bond between them undeniable. *Incomparable.*

He scraped his teeth across the pulse pounding at the base of her throat. Slid a hand inside the wrap front of her dress and curved it possessively around her breast. Her little moans as he stroked the silky button to an erect peak had him hard as titanium. Setting his hands on her thighs, he slid them up underneath the sleek material of her dress until he found the soft skin of her upper thighs.

"God," he murmured, his mouth against her throat. "You make me so hot for you, Chiara. Like no other woman has… I can't think when I'm around you."

She went stiff as a board. "What did you just say?"

He paused. Racked his brain, numbed with lust. "I said you make me hot for you. Like no other woman does. It's true. You do."

She pulled out of his arms and swung to face him so fast it made his head spin. Set a smoldering green gaze on his. "I am more than just an *object*, Lazzero."

He eyed her warrior pose, arms crossed over her chest, cheeks flushed with arousal. "Of course you are. You know I appreciate everything about you."

Her mouth set in an uncertain line. He swore and shoved his hands in his pockets which only increased his agony. His mother had perfected the hot and cold routine. He'd watched his father spin like a hamster on a wheel trying to keep up. He was *not* doing this tonight. No matter how much he wanted her.

He dug his fingers into the knot of his tie, stripped it off and tossed it on the armoire. "I need to work," he bit out. "Get some sleep. We can talk in the morning."

He saw the hurt flash through those beautiful eyes. Steeled himself against it as he turned on his heel and left. Which was the sane thing to do, because lust was one thing. Getting emotionally involved with her another thing entirely. Particularly when he had already gone way too far down that path.

Chiara paced the terrace, her thoughts funneling through her head fast and hard, like a tornado on rapid approach. Lazzero had requested honesty at the start of all of this. She should tell him. *But why?* her brain countered. Antonio wasn't anyone's business but her own. She'd made it clear it was over a long time ago. It was Antonio's problem if he couldn't accept it. It *was* history. What use would it be to dredge it up?

She kept pacing under the luminous hanging hook of a moon, a tight knot forming in her chest. She and Lazzero *had* something—a fledgling bond they were building she was afraid to break. She'd felt it on that boat tonight. She was falling for him and she thought he might feel something for her too. Unless she was reading him all wrong, she conceded, which she could be because she'd done it before.

Would he understand if she told him the truth about Antonio? Or would he judge her for being as naive as she'd undoubtedly been when it came to him?

There didn't seem to be a right answer. Lost in a circular

storm of confusion, she finally went inside, removed her makeup and stood under a long, hot shower in the steam room, hoping it would ease the tension in her body and provide clarity to the questions racing through her head. But she only felt worse as she dried herself off and put on her pajamas.

She had completely overreacted to what Lazzero had said. Had allowed her history with Antonio to rule her when Lazzero had proven every which way but Sunday how highly he thought of her. And here she was, ruining it all.

She curled up in the big, king-size bed in the shadow of the beautiful silver moon. But her heart hurt too much to sleep.

Lazzero went over his financials in the study. But no matter which way he spun the numbers, they simply didn't make sense. Which left him in an impossible position. Pay more for Volare than it was worth and put Supersonic's growth in jeopardy, or walk away from the deal and admit to the analysts who ruled his future he had been too hasty in his predictions for that rapid growth he'd promised, an admission—as Santo had stated so bluntly—they would crucify him for.

Neither of which he considered options. Which left his only choice to call Gianni's bluff and force him to make a deal. Which wasn't at all a sure bet given the competitors the Italian CEO had hinted he had waiting in the wings—a British sportswear giant the one that worried him the most.

Painted into a corner of his own making, he pushed to his feet, poured himself a glass of whiskey and carried it to the floor-to-ceiling windows that overlooked the city. Gianni he would solve. He was banking on the fact that there wasn't a company in America right now hotter than Supersonic. That the Fiammata CEO was so enamored of his dominant US market share, his offer would outshine the others.

Chiara, on the other hand, was a puzzle he couldn't seem to decipher. The scene they'd just acted out was a perfect demonstration of everything he'd spent his life avoiding. Exactly what happened when you got invested in someone. It got messy. *Complicated.*

Except, he conceded, taking a sip of the whiskey, Chiara was different. She wasn't a practiced manipulator like his mother had been, nor was she a drama queen like Carolina. She was honest and transparent—real in a way he'd never encountered. And something was wrong.

Sure, he might have needed to blow off some steam tonight, but she had never been an object to him. *Ever.* And she knew it. She had been just as into him on that boat tonight as he had been to her, her reaction to him in the dressing room way off.

He polished off the Scotch, battling his inner instincts as he did so. He should stay away. He knew it. But his inability to remain detached from Chiara was a habit he couldn't seem to break.

The bedroom was plunged into darkness when he walked in, the glow of the moon its only light, spilling through the windows and splashing onto the silk-covered bed. Chiara was curled up in it on her side of the mattress, but he could tell she wasn't sleeping from the rhythm of her breathing. Shucking all of his clothes except his boxers, he slid into bed.

Silence.

Sighing at the tension that stretched between them, he reached for her, curving an arm around her waist and pulling her into his warmth. *"Mi dispiace,"* he murmured, pressing a kiss against her shoulder. "I am in a filthy mood because of Gianni. He has me running in circles."

Chiara twisted in his arms to face him. Propped herself

up on her elbow. "No—" she said on a halting note, "—it was me. I let my baggage get the better of me. I'm sorry. It wasn't fair to you."

Dark hair angled across her face, skin bare of makeup, eyes glittering like twin emerald pools, she was impossible to resist. He ran a finger down her flushed cheek. "How about you tell me what happened earlier? Because I don't think that was about *us* and what we have here."

An emotion he couldn't read flickered through those beautiful eyes before she dropped back onto the pillow and fixed her gaze on the ceiling. "It's hard to explain."

"Try," he invited.

She waved a hand at him. "It's always been about the way I look. Ever since high school. While the girls were making fun of my clothes, the boys wanted me for what was underneath them, which only made the girls more vicious to me. I didn't know how to handle it, so I retreated. Which was fine, because mostly, I was at home with my father. But also because I didn't trust. I didn't believe anyone would want me for who I was, so it was easier that way.

"Then," she said, twisting a lock of her hair around her finger, "I finally met someone that I thought did. I opened myself up to him. Trusted him. Only to realize he had no intentions of letting me share his life. He only wanted me in his bed." She pursed her lips. "What you said tonight reminded me of him. Of something he said."

His heart turned over. He'd known that son of a bitch had done a number on her. He'd like to find him and take him apart piece by piece. But hadn't he objectified her too with his offer to come to Italy? With his suggestion he *gloss her up*? To make her fit into his world? Except he'd always seen more in Chiara than just her undeniably beautiful packaging. Had always known there *was* more to her if he could just manage to peel back those layers of hers. And he'd been right.

He caught her hand in his. Uncurled her tight fingers to lace them through his own. "You know I care about you," he said gruffly. Because he did and he wanted her to know that.

She nodded. Eyed him silently.

"What?"

"Gianni," she murmured. "You're letting him make you crazy, Lazzero. Why not develop the technology yourself if he's going to be like this?"

The far too perceptive question stirred the frustration lurking just beneath the surface. "Because I don't have the time," he said evenly, tempering his volatile edge. "Acquiring Volare means we can put the shoe into production immediately. Meet our steep growth trajectory."

"And if Gianni won't sell it to you? What do you do then?"

A muscle jumped in his jaw. "I'll cross that bridge when and if we come to it."

"Maybe," she suggested quietly, "if Gianni *doesn't* work out, it's time to get back to your roots. To make it about the passion again."

He arched a brow. "Who says the passion's missing?"

"I do." She shook her head. "I saw your face at Di Fiore's that night, Lazzero, when you talked about starting Supersonic. How you came alive when we were doing those sketches… You say you don't dream anymore, but you and Santo *had* a dream to make the best products out there for athletes. Because you *are* athletes. Because it's in your blood. *That* is what you should be doing. Not running circles around Gianni Casale."

"It's not that simple," he said curtly. "Dreams grow up. I run a multibillion-dollar business, Chiara. I've made promises to my shareholders I need to keep. This isn't about sitting down in the lab with my engineers playing house. It's about making my numbers."

Her chin lifted. "I'm not talking about playing house. I'm talking about following your passion, just as you've been pushing me to do." She waved a hand at him. "I've been thinking a lot about what you said this week. About what I want out of life. Sometimes dreams *are* too expensive to keep. And sometimes they're all you have."

And now she was threatening to blow up his brain. "I don't need a lecture right now," he said softly, past the shimmering red in his head. "I need some sleep. Tomorrow's a big day."

"Fine." She lay there staring at the ceiling.

He let out a pained sound. "What?"

"I just think if you dish it out, you should be able to take it."

His blood sizzled in his veins. "Oh, I can take it," he purred, eyes on her pajamas, which tonight, had big red kisses plastered across them. "But I'm trying to keep my hands off you at the moment. At *your* request."

Her white incisors bit into her lip, her eyes big as they rested on his. "I thought you wouldn't be in the mood now."

The vulnerable, hesitant look on her face hit him square in the solar plexus. "Baby," he murmured, "if there's a planet in this solar system where I wouldn't want you in that outfit, you're going to have to find it for me."

A river of color spread across her face, a smoky heat darkening her gaze. "Lazzero—" she breathed, her eyes on his.

He pushed a hand into the bed and brought himself down over her. Bracing himself on his palms and knees, he lowered his mouth to her ear. "Say it," he murmured, "and I will."

And so she did, whispering her request for him to make love to her in a husky voice that unearthed a whole new set of foreign emotions inside of him. Ones he had no idea how to verbalize. And then, because actions had always spoken louder than words and he wanted to show her what she did to him, *on every level*, he deified her instead.

Caging her sexy, amazing body with his, he moved his mouth over every centimeter of her satiny skin until her pajamas impeded his progress and he stripped those off too. Exploring every dip and curve, he trailed his mouth over the taut, trembling skin of her abdomen, found the delectable crease between hip and thigh.

Chiara sucked in a breath, fisted her hands in the bedspread. He could tell she loved it when he did this to her. It made her wild for him. But she was also at her most vulnerable—stripped open and exposed to him. And that was exactly the way he wanted her right now. He wanted to obliterate the distance she'd put between them earlier and put them back exactly where they belonged.

He spread her thighs with firm hands. Slid a palm beneath her bottom and lifted her up to him. Her delicate, musky scent made his head spin. He blew a heated breath over her most intimate flesh. Felt her thighs quiver. Heard the rush of air that left her lips. It set his blood on fire.

He explored her first with his mouth and then with his fingers, caressing every pleasure point with a reverent touch. Her tiny whimpers of pleasure, the clutch of her fingers in his hair, threatened to incinerate him.

"Look at me." His throaty voice dragged her out of the vortex, her eyes stormy and hazy as they focused on his. "When you are like this, stripped bare, Chiara, when you allow yourself to be *vulnerable*, you are insanely beautiful."

Her eyes darkened. Drifted shut. He spread her wider with his hands. Feasted on her, devoured her until she was shaking beneath him. He had meant to dismantle her. Instead he dismantled himself as he mercilessly ended it with the hard pull of his mouth on the most sensitive part of her. It tore a cry from her throat, her broken release reverberating through him.

His skin on fire, his heart pounding in his chest, he crawled up her sated, limp body, clasped her arms above her head and, his hands locked with hers, took her in a slow, sweet possession that lasted forever.

Something locked into place as he watched her shatter alongside him. A piece of him he'd never accessed before. A piece of himself he hadn't known existed. He thought it might be the point of no return.

She fell asleep in his arms, her dark lashes fanning her cheeks. He held her, his breath ruffling the silky hair that slid across her cheek. But sleep eluded him, what she'd said about Gianni turning through his head. Maybe because he thought there might be a grain of truth in what she'd said. That he *had* lost his passion somewhere along the way and it had become all about the business. That all he *knew* was how to keep on pushing, because what would he find if he stopped?

CHAPTER TEN

WITH A HEART-STOPPING Americas team win—the first ever for the squad—in the history books at La Coppa Estiva that afternoon, Chiara dressed for the closing party amidst a buoyant air of celebration. To be held at one of the swishest hotels in the city, it was pegged to be the bash of the year.

Smoothing her palms over her hips, she surveyed her appearance in the black oak mirror in the dressing room at the Orientale. She'd spent far too long choosing her dress, vacillating between the two choices Micaela had given her until she'd finally settled on a round-necked, sleeveless cream sheath that showed off the olive tone of her skin and made the most of her figure.

She thought Lazzero would appreciate the sexy slit that came to midthigh. Which was going to be the *last* time she allowed herself to think like that, because tomorrow it was back to reality. Back to their respective lives. And maybe, if everything worked out with Bianca, exciting new possibilities for her. Hoping for more with Lazzero, when she knew his capabilities, would be a fool's errand. Asking for a broken heart.

Except, she conceded, her heart sinking, it might already be too late. That somewhere along the way, the charade had faded and reality had ensued and this relationship had morphed into something exciting and real and she *didn't* want it to end.

If her head told her it was impossible to fall in love with someone so quickly, her heart told her otherwise.

As if she'd summoned him with her thoughts, Lazzero blew into the dressing area, a towel wrapped around his hips, a frown marring his brow. Clearly used to maximizing every minute of the day, he went straight for the wardrobe.

Her eyes moved over his shoulders and biceps bulging with thick muscle, down over abs that looked as if they'd been carved out of rock, to the mouthwatering, V-shaped indentation that disappeared beneath the towel. He was the hottest man she'd ever encountered. Being with him had been the most breathtakingly exciting experience of her life. But he was so much more than that, the glimpses he'd given her into the man that he was making her want *more* of him, not less.

He shot her a distracted glance. "Do you have any idea where Edmondo put the shirt to my tux?"

"In the far closet," she said huskily. "Closest to the door."

He stalked over to the closet. Snared the shirt off the hanger. "*Perfetto.* Now if I can just find my bow tie, we're in business."

She pointed to a drawer. He bent and rustled through it, straightening with the black tie in his hand, a victorious look on his face. "Amazing. How did I ever do this without you?"

She couldn't actually answer that because he'd been serious all day. Too serious, avoiding any kind of personal interaction after that amazing night they'd shared. Except when she'd literally forced him onto the bed to ice his knee after he'd limped away from today's brutally physical match. His eyes had turned to flame then, a suggestion she could ease his pain in another way entirely rolling off his tongue. To which she'd replied they had no time.

And now he was back to serious. As if maybe he'd rethought everything, decided she'd been exactly the kind of high-maintenance female he avoided like the plague last night and it was best to dump her before they got back to New York.

She couldn't read him *at all*. It was making her a little crazy.

Lazzero shifted his distracted survey to her. "You okay?"

She nodded.

"Bene." A smile creased his cheeks. "You look incredible. I'll be ready in five."

The crowds were thick outside the Bvlgari Hotel, located in a renovated, eighteenth-century Milanese palazzo just around the corner from the Orientale. There was that same intimidating red carpet to walk, that same unnerving need to be *on*, but tonight Chiara was too distracted to pay it much heed, relying on the hand Lazzero had resting on the curve of her back to guide her through the throngs of guests and hangers-on.

The party was in full swing in the meticulously landscaped gardens where trees and hedges created a series of open-air rooms. Lit in La Coppa Estiva blue, the buoyant crowd was buzzing under the influence of one of Italy's most famous DJs, a celebratory atmosphere in the air. Soon, she and Lazzero were caught up in it, acquiring glasses of the champagne that was flowing like water while they made the rounds.

The only minor ripple in the celebration was the appearance of Antonio as he worked the party with his international contacts, minus Amalia who had come down with a cold. Chiara blew off his attempt to talk to her when Lazzero was waylaid by Carolina and one of the other organizers, and determinedly ignored him from that point on.

Pia, accompanied by a surly Valentino, who'd been a part of the losing team, soon came up to whisk her off to the dance floor.

"I need you," Pia said. "He's making me crazy."

Chiara smiled. Looked up at Lazzero. "Okay?"

"Yes," he drawled, subjecting her to one of those looks that could strip the paint from a car. "But don't go far. I need to be able to look at you in that dress."

A flush stained her skin as he bent to brush a kiss against her cheek. *"Go."*

She frowned as he straightened, visibly favoring his left leg. "You should stay off that knee."

"And how," he murmured, dropping his mouth to her ear, "will I get you to play nursemaid if I do?"

"You don't need a nursemaid," she said saucily. "You need to be able to walk tomorrow."

Lazzero watched as Chiara turned on her heel and followed Pia into the crowd. He couldn't take his eyes off her in that dress. The sleek design molded her fabulous figure like a glove and the slit that left an expanse of silky skin bare every time she moved was an invitation to sin.

His head fully immersed in the woman who had just walked away from him, it took him a moment to realize Santo had materialized at his side, sharp in black Armani.

"Sorry?" he said on a distracted note. "What did you say?"

"I said, 'Well if it isn't the man of the hour…'" Santo clapped him on the back. "That was a genius of a final play, *fratello*. Aren't you glad you played?"

Lazzero muttered something in the affirmative. Santo eyed him, a glitter in his eyes. *"Dannazione."*

"What?"

"The dark knight has fallen."

"What the hell are you talking about?"

"Her." Santo nodded at Chiara's retreating figure. "Your barista. You are ten feet under. *Fully brewed.* In case you hadn't noticed."

He had. He just had no idea what the hell to do about it. He'd been thinking about it all night. He should let Chiara walk away. Call it a scorching-hot affair done right. Nobody gets hurt. Everybody wins. *His specialty.* Because Chiara didn't play by the same rules as him. And maybe that was the real reason he'd stayed away from her as long as he had.

And then he'd invited her to come to Italy with him. Had kissed her, made love to her and crossed every line in the book. Which left him exactly where?

"I need a drink," he said flatly.

"A celebratory drink," Santo agreed.

Ensconcing themselves at the bar, they exchanged their fruity glasses of champagne for an excellent measure of off-list smoky bourbon as they recapped the game in glorified detail.

It hit him like a knife edge how much he'd missed the adrenaline that had once been his lifeblood. The *buzz* that came from being on the firing line in a pivotal match.

Competition was in his blood—it was what he thrived on. The *purpose* that had once fueled his days, because if he'd been on the court nothing else had mattered.

Building Supersonic had fulfilled that competitive edge. The need to *conquer.* But somewhere along the way the rush had faded. Carrying the weight of a team, of a school, on his back might rival the necessity to keep ten thousand people in a job, but his soul wasn't in it the way it had once been. Chiara had been right about that.

He watched her on the dance floor with Pia. Wondered what it was about her he couldn't resist. She was beautiful, yes. But he'd dated scores of beautiful women. Chiara was *real* in a way he'd never encountered before. She challenged him, made him think. He was *better* when he was with her. Happy even, a descriptor he would never have used with himself.

If the truth be known, he went into that damn café every

morning because he wanted to see her. Because he didn't feel half-alive when he was around her. And the thought of them going back to the status quo with Chiara serving him an espresso in the morning with one of those cool, controlled expressions on her face made him a little nuts. But what, exactly, did he have to offer her?

She deserved someone who would be there for her. An *Alfredo*. Someone who would offer her that true love she was looking for. Someone who would be that solid force she needed to shine. Who would prove to her she would always be *enough*.

Which was not him. He had never been *that guy*. So why the hell did he want to be so badly?

When he couldn't help himself any longer, he left his brother to the devices of a beautiful redhead and sought Chiara out on the dance floor.

Chiara tipped her head back to look up at Lazzero as they danced, her pulse racing at the banked heat in his gaze. He'd been staring at her the whole time she'd been on the dance floor with Pia, his desire for her undeniable. But maybe, she acknowledged, a hand fisting her chest, that was all it was.

He slid a hand to her hip in a possessive hold. Tugged her closer. "Do you know what I was thinking the opening night when I was holding you like this?"

"What?"

"That I wanted to ditch the party and have you until the sun came up." His gaze darkened. "I am crazy about you, Chiara. You know that I am."

Her heart missed a beat. She'd been so scared she'd been imagining it. Building it up in her head like she'd done before. Getting it all wrong. "You don't want to end this when we get back to New York?"

He shook his head. "I think we should see each other

back in New York. See where this goes. If," he qualified quietly, "you want that too."

She sank her teeth into her lip. "What do you mean, 'see where this goes'?"

"I mean exactly that. We explore what we have. See where it takes us." He shook his head. "I'm not good at this, Chiara. I could mess it up. But I don't want to lose you. *That*, I know."

Her knees went weak. He wasn't making any promises. She could end up with her heart broken all over again. Was likely setting herself up for it. But everything she'd learned about Lazzero made her think he was worth it. That if she was patient, she might be able to breach those tightly held defenses of his. That maybe she could be *the one*.

A whisper of fear fluttered through her belly at the thought of making herself that vulnerable again. Because Lazzero, she knew, could annihilate her far worse than Antonio had ever done. But the chance to have him, to *be* with him, to hold on to that solid force he'd become for her, was far too tempting to resist.

She stood on tiptoe and kissed him by way of response. A long, slow shimmer of a connection, it was perfection. But soon it grew hungrier, *needier*, the flames between them igniting.

Lazzero enclosed the nape of her neck with his hand and took the kiss deeper, delving into her mouth in a hot, languid joining that stole her breath. She settled her palms on his chest. Grabbed a handful of his shirt. Every hot breath, every stroke, every lick, sensual, earthy, built the flames higher.

Tracing a path across her jaw and down to the hollow of her throat, Lazzero pressed an openmouthed kiss to her pulse. It was racing like a jackhammer. He flicked his tongue across the frantic beat, shifted his hands lower to shape her against his hard male contours. A gasp slipped from her lips.

He pulled back. Surveyed her kiss-swollen mouth. "I think this time we *are* leaving," he murmured. "The song's over, *caro*. Go get your things."

Lazzero propped himself up against the bar while Chiara collected her wrap, a supreme feeling of satisfaction settling over him. He was strategizing on all the different ways he would take her apart until she begged for him, when Antonio Fabrizio slid into place beside him at the bar and ordered a Scotch. Turning to face the Italian, he reluctantly switched back into networking mode.

"Enjoying yourself?" he murmured lazily.

"Sì." Fabrizio reclined his lanky frame against the bar, his gaze on Chiara's retreating figure. "Beautiful, isn't she? The most beautiful woman in the room, no doubt."

Lazzero stood up straighter. "I think so," he agreed evenly. "But then again, she's my fiancée, so I would."

"Still," the Italian drawled, "a man would be hard-pressed to resist."

And now he'd had it. Lazzero's blood sizzled, the amount of bourbon warming his blood doing little to leash his temper. He'd been okay with the man admiring Chiara last night, but really, enough was enough. Given, however, Gianni had let it slip that the Fabrizio investment house was one of Fiammata's largest stakeholders, he needed to keep it civil.

"Luckily," he said icily, "I don't have to." He waved a hand at the other man. "I have a suggestion, Fabrizio. You have a beautiful wife. Perhaps you should go home and lavish some attention on her."

The Italian lifted a shoulder. "Amalia is a political match. Unexciting in bed. Chiara, on the other hand, is not."

Lazzero froze. *"Scusi?"*

Fabrizio set a cold, blue gaze on him. "You didn't know? She was mine before she was yours, Di Fiore. Or didn't she tell you that?"

He was lying, was his first thought. But he had no reason to lie. Which meant he was the one in the dark here.

"When?" he grated.

Fabrizio shrugged. "It ended before Christmas. I was engaged to Amalia. Chiara didn't like playing, what do you Americans call it…*second fiddle* to my fiancée, so she broke it off. Gave me an ultimatum—it was Amalia or her." The Italian tipped his glass at Lazzero. "As far as her being in love with you? Highly unlikely given she made a habit of telling me she was in love with me every morning before I left for work."

Lazzero's head snapped back. Fabrizio was telling him he'd had an affair with Chiara months ago? A man she'd calmly pretended she'd never met last night when they'd been introduced. An *engaged man*.

Except she hadn't been calm, he recalled. She'd been off from the moment Antonio Fabrizio had shown up at that party. Had blown off his concern for her as a case of fatigue. His brain putting two and two together, he rocked back on his heels. Fabrizio was the man who'd broken her heart?

A dangerous red settled over his vision. He had just poured out his feelings to her. Had just told her he was crazy about her. And she had lied to his face. Did he even *know* her?

"I get it," Fabrizio murmured. "She's *insano* in bed. Almost worth putting a four-carat ring on her finger."

It was the "almost worth it" that did it. Lazzero had Fabrizio by the collar of his bespoke suit before he knew what he was doing. Blind fury driving him, he balled his hand into a fist and sent it flying toward the Italian's face. Anticipating the supreme satisfaction of watching it connect with that arrogant, square jaw, he found his hand manacled just short of its destination.

"What the hell are you doing?" Santo said, wrapping an arm around him and hauling him backward. "Have you lost your mind?"

Fabrizio straightened the lapel of his suit as a shocked crowd looked on. Picked up his Scotch and shifted away from the bar, his eyes on Lazzero. "By the way," he drawled. "I nudged Gianni in the direction of the British deal. It has a more global scope."

His parting volley hanging in the air, the Italian sauntered off into the crowd. Enraged, Lazzero pulled at Santo's grip to follow him, but his brother held him back. Directed a furious look at Lazzero. "What the hell is wrong with you? He's a key stakeholder in Fiammata, for God's sake."

Lazzero shrugged him off. Raked a hand through his hair. "He's an arrogant bastard."

"So you decided to *hit* him?"

A frisson of fury lanced through him. "No," he bit out. "That was for something else."

"Well, whatever it is, you need to get it together. Everything hinges on this deal, Laz. Or have you forgotten?"

Lazzero's mouth thinned. "He baited me."

"Which appears to be your Achilles' heel," his brother observed. "Perhaps food for thought as you do some damage control here."

Chiara claimed her wrap, practically floating on air. A sharp bite of anticipation nipped at her skin as she made her way back through the crowd to where Lazzero was waiting for her at the bar.

Her progress painfully slow, she looked up to catch his eye. Noted he was deep in conversation. The tall, dark male he was talking to shifted to pick up his drink. *Antonio*, she registered. Which would have been fine. A social chat perhaps. *Business*. Except for the expression on Lazzero's face.

Oh, my God.

Heart pounding, she quickened her pace, desperate to intervene. But the crowd was too tightly packed, her high heels allowing her to move only so fast. By the time she made it to the bar, Santo was hauling Lazzero away from Antonio after some type of an altercation. Antonio, who looked utterly unruffled, straightened his suit, said something to Lazzero, then melted off into the crowd.

She came to a sliding halt in front of the two brothers. Santo said something to Lazzero, a heated look on his face, then stalked off. He looked just as furious as his brother. *Or maybe not.* Lazzero looked *livid.*

"What happened?" she breathed.

Lazzero's face was a wall of concrete. "We are not talking about it here."

She didn't argue because the rage coming off him in waves was making her knees weak. Clutching her purse to her side, she practically ran to keep up with his long strides as they found Carolina and the other organizers of the party, thanked them, then walked the couple of blocks back to their hotel.

When they entered their suite, Lazzero peeled off his jacket and threw it on a chair. Whipping off his bow tie, he tossed it on top of his jacket and walked to the bar to pour himself a drink. Carrying the glass to the windows, he stood looking out at a shimmering view of a night-lit Milan.

Chiara kicked off her heels and threw her wrap on a chair. Her throat too tight to get words past it, her brain rifled through the possible scenarios of what had just happened. Which were too varied and scary to consider, so she stood, arms hugged around herself, and waited for Lazzero to speak. Which he finally did.

"Why didn't you tell me about Fabrizio?"

She blanched. Felt the world fall away from beneath her feet. "I didn't think it was anyone's business but my own," she said, managing to find her voice as he turned to face her. "Antonio and I were over months ago. It was history to me. I didn't see the point in bringing it up."

"You didn't see the point?" His voice was so quiet, so cold, it sent a chill through her. "Because you had an affair with a man who *belonged to someone else*?"

The blood drained from her face. "I didn't have an affair with him. I didn't know he was engaged, Lazzero. He lied to me. I told you what happened last night."

"You didn't tell me it was *Antonio Fabrizio*!" He yelled the words at her with such force she took a stumbling step backward. "Fabrizio is one of Fiammata's largest stakeholders, Chiara. There are three, equally strong deals on the table for Volare. That son of a bitch told Gianni to take the British offer over ours."

Oh, good God, no. The blood froze in her veins. She had known Antonio was angry. That he wasn't one to concede defeat. But she'd been so sure the fact that she was engaged to Lazzero would have driven the point home that she was unavailable. Which, she admitted numbly, had been a gross miscalculation on her part.

"I'm so sorry," she said dazedly, sinking down on the arm of the sofa. "I can't believe he did this."

His gaze glittered like hard, polished ebony. "What were you two talking about by the lake, then? If it's *over*?"

She sank her teeth into her lip. "It's complicated."

"Enlighten me," he growled.

She pressed her palms to her cheeks. Dropped her hands to her sides. "I met Antonio at a party last summer in Chelsea. It was a sophisticated crowd—I was completely out of my league. Worried about my father. You know what it's been like. Antonio—he pursued me relentlessly. He wouldn't give up. He swept me off my feet, made all sorts of promises and within weeks we were living together.

"I thought we had something. That he loved me. Until one morning when I was leaving the penthouse for work, I bumped into his mother. She'd come to surprise Antonio for his birthday—to do some Christmas shopping. She told me Antonio had a fiancée in Milan. That I was just his American plaything."

Her stomach curled at the memory. "I was crushed. *Devastated*. I gave Antonio his key back that night and told him I never wanted to see him again. He was furious. Refused to take no for an answer. He kept sending me flowers, theater tickets, jewelry. Kept calling me. I sent it all back, told him I wanted nothing to do with him. Finally, a couple of months ago, he stopped calling."

Lazzero watched her with a hooded gaze. "And last night?"

"Antonio followed me when I went to the washroom. He said he hadn't given up on me. That he thought I'd be over Amalia by now and he was going to come and see me in New York the next time he was in town."

"Because he wants you back."

A statement, not a question. One she couldn't refute, even with the recrimination written across Lazzero's face. "Yes," she admitted. "He wants me to be his mistress. He asked me what I wanted—if I wanted him to leave Amalia, because he couldn't. I told him I was engaged to you. That I loved you. That I wanted him to forget we ever existed, because I want nothing to do with him."

"He *said* you disliked playing second fiddle to Amalia. That you, in effect, had given him an ultimatum—it was her or you."

Her breath left her in a rush. "That's a lie," she rasped. "He is on a seek and destroy mission. If he can't have me, no one will."

"Why bother?" Lazzero murmured. "I get that all men love you, Chiara, but Fabrizio is a powerful man. He could have any woman he wants."

Her stomach curled at the insinuation she wasn't worth pursuing. That she had somehow *invited* Antonio's attention last night. That she was in some way responsible for what had happened.

"Antonio is entitled," she said quietly, fingers clenching at her sides. "He *does* think he can have anything he wants. I think you forget you're the one who walked into the café and threw that insane amount of money at me to come with you, Lazzero. You're the one who wouldn't take no for an answer. *I* never wanted to be any part of this world."

"Because he is here."

"Yes," she snapped back at the look of condemnation in his eyes, "because he is here. I put him out of my life, Lazzero. I had no idea he was married to Amalia. I was in complete shock last night at the dinner party. But never once did I give him any encouragement that there might still be something between us. You know how I feel about you."

"I don't *know* anything," he lanced back. "I have no idea what the hell to believe, because you lied to my face, Chiara." He pointed the Scotch at her. "I gave you every opportunity to tell me what was wrong last night. Every opportunity you needed. And you told me you were tired. That *nothing* was wrong."

Her stomach dropped, like a book toppling off a high shelf. She should have told him. She had known he had trust issues. Had known he'd let down his walls for her. Had known she'd been playing with fire by not telling him. And still, she had done it.

"I was afraid to lose you," she admitted softly. "Afraid you wouldn't understand."

A choked-off sound of disbelief ripped itself from his throat. "So you did the one thing guaranteed to make that happen? *Maledizione*, Chiara. You know my history on this. I thought we *had* something here. I thought we were building something together. I thought we were different."

"We are," she blurted out, her heart in her mouth. "I'm falling for you, Lazzero. You know that."

"How would you even know *who* you're in love with?" He waved a hand at her. "A few months ago it was him. Now it's me. Do you just turn it on and off at will? Like a tap?"

Her stomach contracted at the low blow. At the closed-off look on his face, getting colder by the minute. "I was never in love with him," she said evenly, her chin lifting. "I *thought* I was. How I feel for you is completely different."

He shrugged that off. "Trust was the one thing that was nonnegotiable in this. You knew that."

"Lazzero," she said huskily, "it was an error in judgment. *One* mistake."

"Which could bury me." He raked a hand through his hair. Eyed her. "Is there anything else I should know? Any other powerful men you have slept with who can annihilate my future?"

Her breath caught in her throat. "You did *not* just say that."

He pushed away from the bar and headed for the study. "I need to go research the competition. See if I can salvage this."

The finality of it, the judgment written across his face said it all. Whatever she said, it wasn't going to be enough.

"Why did you try and hit him?" She tossed the question after him because she had to know.

He turned around, mouth twisting. "He suggested you were *almost* worth a four-carat ring. I was defending your honor, fool that I am."

CHAPTER ELEVEN

CHIARA DIDN'T SLEEP. She lay awake all night in the gorgeous four-poster bed, numb, *frozen*, as she waited for Lazzero to join her. But he never did, pulling one of his all-nighters in an attempt to salvage the deal. And what, she conceded miserably, staring up at the beautiful crystal chandelier, would she have even said to him if he had?

She *should* have told him about Antonio. She could never have predicted what Antonio had done—was still in utter shock that he'd done it. But she had known about Lazzero's trust issues. And instead of believing in what they had, in what they were building together, she'd reverted back to her old ways. Had allowed her insecurities to rule. And in doing so, she'd destroyed everything.

Sleepless and bleary-eyed, she boarded the jet for their flight home to New York the following afternoon. Lazzero devoted the entire journey to his effort to discredit his British competition, which left such a sick feeling in her stomach, she hadn't slept there, either.

If she hadn't known it was over the night before, she knew it was when Lazzero bid her a curt farewell on the tarmac, he and Santo en route to a sports fund-raiser, not one speck of that warmth he usually reserved for her in his gorgeous, dark eyes. She gave him back the ring, unable to bear wearing it a moment longer, only to have Lazzero wave his hand at her and tell her to keep it. *He couldn't take it back and she needed the money.*

It had been all she could do not to throw it at him. She told him instead that she couldn't be bought, that she'd never been for sale and shoved the ring in his hand. Then she'd allowed Gareth, whom Lazzero had handed her off to, to shepherd her into the Bentley for the drive home.

Her carpe diem moment seemed foolish as the car slid smoothly off into the night. She had told herself it was a mistake to accept Lazzero's offer. To allow herself to fall for him. Then she'd gone ahead and done it anyway and fool that she'd been, she'd started to buy into the fairy tale. Of what she and Lazzero could be.

Her chest throbbed in a tight, hot ache as the headlights from the other cars slid across her face. She'd opened herself up exactly as Lazzero had challenged her to—had shown him who she truly was—had taken that leap—only to have him walk away as if what they'd shared had meant nothing. As if *she* wasn't worth the effort. Which might hurt the most of all.

The sun was sinking in a giant, red-orange ball when she arrived at her apartment in Spanish Harlem, bidding the city a sultry, crimson adieu. Gareth, a gentleman to the end, helped her up the three sets of stairs to her door and made sure she was safely inside before he melted back into the sunset like the former special agent he likely was.

The apartment was hot and stuffy, empty with Kat working the closing shift. She dumped her suitcase in the living room, too exhausted to even think about unpacking, because then she would have to look at all those beautiful clothes and the memories that came with them. About the man who'd just walked away from her without a backward glance.

She called her father instead as she made a cup of herbal tea, anxious to talk to him after a week of trading messages. Only to find him bubbling over with the news of a visit by the Five Boroughs Angel Foundation the previous afternoon, in which Ferrante's had been the recipient of an angel investment that would cover the bakery's rent for the remainder of the year.

He'd been so happy and relieved, he'd gone over to Frankie DeLucca's to celebrate. It was almost enough to peel away a layer of her misery as she signed off and promised to see her father the following evening.

She carried the tea into the living room, intent on numbing her brain with one of her dancing shows. But the stiflingly hot room felt like a shoebox after the palatial suite at the Orientale, the sound from her downstairs neighbor's TV was its usual intolerably loud level and the window box air conditioner refused to work.

As if nothing has changed. Except everything had. And maybe that's why her chest felt so tight. Because she'd gone to Italy as one person and come back another. Because of Lazzero.

The tears came then, like hot, silent bandits slipping down her cheeks. And once they started, they wouldn't seem to stop. Which was ridiculous, really, because, in the end, what had Lazzero been offering her? The same no-strings-attached arrangement as Antonio had? A few more weeks of being starry-eyed while she fell harder for a man who had a questionable ability to commit?

She staggered to bed, flattened by jetlag. Rose the next morning with a renewed sense of determination. She was tougher than this. She wasn't going to let Lazzero Di Fiore crush her. She was going to go to this coffee with Bianca and *crush it*. Because if there was one thing Lazzero had taught her, it was that she couldn't depend on anyone else to make her dream happen. That had to come from her.

She met Bianca at the Daily Grind before her shift began. A tall, Katharine Hepburn–like bombshell, Bianca was as tough as Lazzero had described, but also inspiring, brilliant and full of amazing ideas as they looked through her portfolio. When Bianca glanced at her bare left hand for what seemed like the fiftieth time, Chiara waved it in the air. "We broke up," she said shortly. "It was all my fault."

It was the same line she used with the girls at the café when Bianca disappeared out the door with a promise to get back to her with the committee's decision. When a week passed with no sign of Lazzero and his habitual order of a double espresso, her heart jumping every time the bell on the door rang, because maybe he would change his mind. Maybe he would apologize. But it never happened.

Eyes trained on his computer screen, Lazzero pulled the coffee that his PA, Enid, had just delivered within striking distance while he scanned the contents of the email he'd just gotten from Gianni. Only to discover the wily Italian had changed the rules of the game. *Again.*

His mind working a mile a minute at the implications of what the Fiammata CEO was proposing, he lifted the espresso to his lips and took a sip. Almost spit it out.

It was the final straw.

"Enid!" he bellowed, pushing to his feet and heading out to Reception, cup in hand. "What the hell is this?" He arched a brow at her. "Do we not have an espresso machine and do you not know how to use it?"

His exceedingly young, ultraefficient PA, who couldn't be more than twenty-five, gave him a wary look as if considering which angle with which to avoid this new threat. "We do," she agreed evenly, "and I do."

"Then maybe you can try again," he suggested, dumping the cup on her desk. "Because this is filth. *F.I.L.T.H.*"

Enid calmly got to her feet, scooped up the cup and headed toward the kitchen. Santo strolled out of his office, a football palmed between his hands. "Jet lag getting to you?" he asked pointedly.

"Gianni," Lazzero muttered. "He just got back to me."

Santo followed him into his office. "What did he say?"

"'After much consideration,' he's decided to split the global rights for Volare. Supersonic is to receive the North American license, Gladiator, the rest-of-world global rights. Provided we are agreeable with the price tag he has attached to the offer."

"Which is?"

Lazzero named the figure.

Santo blinked. "For the North American rights? That would stretch us."

More than stretch them. It would eliminate other growth opportunities he wanted to pursue. *Close doors.* On a bet that Volare would move heaven and earth for them.

He walked to the window. Looked out at a glittering Manhattan, the sun gilding the skyscrapers the palest shade of gold. If America was the land of opportunity, New York was the epitome of the American Dream. He'd seen it from both sides now—knew what it was like to live one step away from the street with a paralyzing fear as your guiding force and what it was like to have it all. How easily it could flip—in the blink of an eye—with one wrong move.

With one mistake.

He locked his jaw, ignoring the pain riding beneath his chest, because *they* were over and he was better off this way. But that didn't mean she hadn't made him think.

"We're not doing it." He turned around and leaned against the sill, his eyes on Santo. "We take the reputational hit. We tell the analysts it's going to take us a bit longer than we anticipated to make it to number two, and we do it ourselves. The way we do it best."

A wealth of emotion flickered through Santo's dark eyes. "There will be a storm. You know that."

He nodded. The investment community *would* crucify them for missing their targets for the first time in the company's history. There would be that analysis their star had risen too far, too fast. But he hadn't created this company to have it ruled by a bunch of number crunchers in their high-priced offices.

He lifted a shoulder. "We ride it out. We were bound to hit one someday."

Santo palmed the football in his hands. "Okay," he said finally, a rueful smile tilting his lips. "We do it ourselves. We go back to our roots. Tell Gianni to go to hell."

His blood buzzed in his veins. It felt *right* for the first time in forever.

Enid came in with the new espresso. Set it on Lazzero's desk and beat a hasty retreat. Santo eyed the coffee. "You going to do something about that?"

"About what?"

"Your barista."

Lazzero scowled. "What makes you think I need to?"

"Because I've never seen two people try *not* to look at each other as hard as you two did on the plane. Because she lights you up in a way I've never seen before. Because you haven't shaved in a week, you look terrible and you're hurting and you won't admit it." Santo crossed his arms over his chest and cocked a brow. "Have I covered it all?"

Quite possibly. Which didn't mean he wasn't still furious with her.

"You're crazy about her," his brother said quietly. "What's the problem?"

What wasn't? That she had violated the one code of honor he lived his life by, the trust he'd needed to convince himself they could be different. That he'd been *all in for her*, confessed his innermost thoughts and feelings to her when she hadn't shown him the same respect? Because it had felt like the most real thing he'd ever had, when in reality it had been as fake as every other relationship he'd known.

He pushed away from the sill and headed toward his desk. "It was never going to work. She was a temporary thing."

"Good to know," Santo said lazily. "Because I think she's amazing and if you don't go after her, I will." His brother gave a laconic shrug. "I'll give her some time to get over your jaded, broken heart, of course, but then I will."

Lazzero had to smother the urge to go for his brother's throat. He knew he was baiting him and still, the soft taunt twisted a knot in his gut.

He missed her. In the morning giving him sass from the espresso machine...when he walked into the penthouse at night, filling his empty spaces...and definitely, plastered across his bed sketching in those sexy pajamas of hers. But trust and transparency were essential to him.

Santo sauntered out of his office wearing a satisfied look, having stirred him up exactly as he'd known he would. He attempted to anesthetize himself with yet more work alongside the weak, tepid garbage Enid had produced yet again, but he couldn't seem to do it.

The first Monday after the Labor Day weekend was always madness at the Daily Grind. The students were back, relentless in their search of a caffeine injection as they juggled an unfamiliar, highly resented wake-up call, while the flashy-suited urban set struggled to get back to reality after a weekend spent in the Hamptons. And then, there was Sivi, currently having a meltdown over her broken romance with a Wall Street banker who'd ended things over the weekend. Chiara had fixed half a dozen of her messed-up orders already, which wasn't helping her ability to cope with the massive lineup spilling out the door.

"You know what I think?" Sivi announced, handing her

three cups marked with orders of questionable reliability. "*I* think Ted has been reading Samara Jones. I think he decided to dump me because the Athertons' pool party was on the weekend. I was just a *summer shag.* I looked good in a *bathing suit.*"

Kat snorted as she made change for a customer. "Men have been systematically dumping women in Manhattan for little to no reason since the beginning of time. The whole concept of a summer shag is ridiculous."

"Oh, it's a real thing," interjected a twentysomething-blonde regular in the lineup. "The event I held last week? Seventy-five percent of the men came with a plus one. My Fall Extravaganza in a couple of weeks? *Fifty percent.*"

"It's an epidemic," said her friend, a perky, blue-eyed brunette. "My roommate found her kiss-off gift in his underwear drawer over the weekend. She's trying to decide whether to stick around or not."

"At least she got a kiss-off gift," grumbled Sivi. "I loved him, I mean, I really *loved him*, you guys. The BlackBerry in bed? No problem. Football all Sunday? I did my nails. And the snoring? It was like the 6-train coming through the walls. But I excused it all for him because he was *just that good in bed.*"

Oh, my God. Chiara wanted to put her head in her hands, but she had two espressos and an Americano to make, and now a frowning customer was shoving her drink back across the counter. "This is *not* what I ordered. I ordered a *triple venti, half-sweet, nonfat caramel macchiato.*"

Chiara counted to five. Sivi waved a cup in the air. "Are there *any* men left in Manhattan who have serious intentions when it comes to a woman?"

"I do," intoned a husky, lightly accented voice. "Although I might have gone about it the wrong way."

Chiara's heart lurched. She looked up to find the owner of that sexy, familiar voice standing in the lineup, all eyes on him as he answered Sivi's question. Which might also have something to do with the way Lazzero looked. Dressed in a severely cut pinstripe suit, a snowy-white shirt and a dark tie, he was so sinfully good-looking, she could only clutch the cup in her hand and stare, her brain cells fried with the pleasure and pain of seeing him again.

She'd missed him. God, she'd missed him.

Memories of their last meeting bled through. She pulled in air through a chest so tight it hurt to breathe. Lowered her gaze and started remaking the macchiato with hands that shook, because he was not doing this. He was damn well not doing this right here and right now.

But, oh, yes, he was. "I am guilty," Lazzero said evenly, "of being *that guy*. Of callously discarding a woman without a second thought. Of believing a piece of jewelry could buy a weekend in the Hamptons. Of thinking my money could acquire anything I wanted."

The perky brunette drank him in from the tip of his sleek, dark head to his custom-made Italian shoes. "I can't say I would have said no."

"Until," Lazzero continued, his eyes on Chiara, "I met the one woman who was immune to it. Who convinced me that I was *wrong*. That I wanted more. And then I was scrambling," he admitted. "I tried every which way but Sunday to show her how different the man was beneath the suit. And then, when I finally did, I screwed it up."

Chiara's stomach swooped, skimming the shiny surface of the bronze, tiled floor. She set the cup down before she dumped espresso all over herself. Took in Lazzero, intensely private Lazzero, who was loath to talk about his feelings, talking to her as if there was no one else in the room. Except the entire front half of the lineup was watching them now and the café had gone strangely silent.

"We are over," she said quietly. "You made that very clear, Lazzero."

"It was a mistake." A stubborn strength underlaid his tone. "You need to give me another chance."

Like he had her? She dumped the misguided macchiato in the sink, her heart shattering all over again at how completely he'd taken her apart. "I don't *need* to do anything. I no longer make coffee on command for you, Lazzero. I no longer serve as your decorative piece on the side and I definitely don't have to forgive you so that I can once again become as expendable as one of your high-priced suits."

"I'm not interested in having you on a temporary basis," Lazzero said huskily, stepping over to the counter. "I'm interested in having you forever. I walked away from the deal, Chiara. Nothing is right without you."

She stared at him, stunned. *He'd walked away from the deal? Why would he do that?* She noted the dark shadows in his eyes then, the white lines bracketing his mouth, the dark stubble on his jaw. Not cool, collected Lazzero. Another version entirely.

"I'm in love with you, Chiara." He trained his gaze on hers. "Give me another chance."

"I don't know about you," said the brunette, "but he had me at the pinstriped suit."

"Yes, but it was necessary to make him grovel," said the blonde. "Not that we know what he did."

Chiara's heart was too busy melting into the floor at the naked emotion blazing in Lazzero's eyes to pay them much heed.

"And now that we have that decided," said a disgruntled-looking construction worker at the front of the line, "could we please have some coffee here? Some of us have to work for a living."

Chiara stared blankly at the drink orders in front of her. Kat waved a hand at her. "*Go.* You are clearly now useless, as well. Sivi—you're on the bar with Tara. And for heaven sakes, try and get it right."

Chiara had to run to keep up with Lazzero when he took her hand and dragged her out of the café and into the bright morning sunshine. Breathless, she leaned against the brick wall of the coffee shop and stared dazedly up at him. "Did you mean that? That you love me?"

"Yes," he said, setting a palm against the wall beside her. "Although the speech was not intentional. You have a way of provoking a completely irrational response in me."

Happiness bloomed inside of her, a dangerous, insidious warmth that threatened to envelop her completely. She bit her lip, held it in check. "What do you mean you walked away from the deal? Why would you do that?"

"Because you were right. Because somewhere along the way, I *had* lost my passion and I needed to get it back. It's what gets me out of bed in the morning. Or *in it* at night," he murmured, his eyes on her mouth. "Which has also been extremely empty. Too empty because I'd let the best thing that's ever happened to me walk out of my life."

The blaze of warmth in his eyes threatened to throw her completely off balance. She spread her palms against the warm brick wall and steeled herself against the desire to throw herself in his arms. "You hurt me with those things you said, Lazzero. Badly."

"I know." He traced the back of his knuckles across her cheek. "And, I'm sorry. If I had been in my right mind, I would have seen the truth. That Antonio had made a wrong decision in letting you go and was doing everything he could to get you back. Instead, I let him push all my buttons. I was blind with jealousy. I thought you might still love him, because he is clearly still in love with you. And I was angry," he allowed, "because I thought what we had was real."

"It *was* real. I should have trusted you, but you needed to trust me too, Lazzero. It goes both ways."

"Yes," he agreed, "but in the moment, that breach of

trust confirmed everything I thought I knew about relation-ships—that they are messy, complicated things better off avoided. Proved us as false as every other relationship in my life had been. That I was the fool, because there I was, letting a woman play with my head, exactly as my father had done time and time again."

Her stomach curled. "I wish I could take it all back," she whispered. "I hate that I let my insecurities get to me like that."

He shook his head. "I should have realized why you'd done what you'd done. I *did* after I cooled off. No man had ever proven to you he was deserving of your trust. *I* was still hedging my bets by offering you a no-strings-attached relationship when I knew how I felt about you."

"About that," she said, her heart swelling as she lifted her fingertips to trace the hard line of his jaw because she couldn't resist the need to touch him any longer, "how can you be in love with me when you called it a fantasy that doesn't really exist that night at the opera?"

"Because you challenge every belief I've ever had about myself and what I'm capable of," he said huskily. "I've been walking around half-alive for a long time, Chiara. Think-ing I was happy—telling myself I didn't need anyone. Until you walked into my life and showed me what I was miss-ing. In *every* aspect."

She melted into him then, unable to help herself, her fingers tangling in his hair to bring his head down to hers. "I love you," she murmured against his mouth.

Passionate, perfect, the kiss was so all consuming nei-ther of them noticed Claudio ambling past them into the café, a newspaper tucked under his arm. "Took you two long enough," he muttered. "I really don't get modern court-ship at all."

EPILOGUE

Nico Di Fiore married Chloe Russo in a simple, elegant ceremony at the majestic, storied St. Patrick's Cathedral on Christmas Eve in Manhattan. Dubbed one of the must-attend society events of the season, the nuptials drew guests from around the globe, including many of the famous personalities who represented the face of the Evolution brand.

Chloe, who had chosen the date because Christmas Eve had been her father's favorite night of the year, walked down the aisle in a showstopping, tulip-shaped, ivory Amsale gown which left an inspired Chiara dying for a sketchpad and pencil, dress designs dancing in her head.

The five hundred guests in attendance remarked on Chloe's serene, Grace Kelly–like beauty and timeless elegance. *A dark-haired version*, they qualified. Mireille, who preceded Chloe down the aisle in a bronze gown that matched the glittering metallic theme of the wedding, was her blonde equivalent.

Nico looked devastating in black Armani, as did his two groomsmen, Lazzero and Santo, whom Samara Jones cheekily underscored from her position in the gallery, had been on her summer must-have list. Humor, however, gave way to high emotion when Chloe began to cry the moment she reached Nico's side, overcome by the significance of the evening. Nico held her until she stopped, which hadn't left a dry eye in the house.

Then it was off to the magnificent Great Hall of the Metropolitan Museum of Art in Central Park for the lavish dinner reception and dance. With its immense domes, dramatic arches and marbled mosaic floor, it was suitably glamorous for the sophisticated crowd in attendance.

Chloe had wanted it to be a party, for the guests to dance the night away and celebrate. Which it surely was. As soon as dinner was over, the lights were dimmed to a sparkling gold, and the festivities began with the bride and groom's first dance to Etta James's "At Last," sung by LaShaunta, the famous pop star who fronted Chloe's wildly popular perfume Be.

Chiara found herself caught up in the romantic perfection of it all. With Lazzero consumed by his best man duties, she danced with partner after partner as the live band played. But all night long, she felt his gaze on her in the shimmering, sequined, off-the-shoulder dress she'd chosen especially for him, its glittering latte color somehow apropos.

Mireille, Chloe's sophisticated, irreverent sister she was growing to love, gave Chiara an amused glance after one such scorching look as they stood on the side of the dance floor, recovering with a glass of vintage champagne. "He's so crazy about you, he doesn't know which way is north and which way is south."

Chiara's heartbeat accelerated under the heat of that look. She knew the feeling. And it wasn't getting any more manageable, it was only getting worse, because Lazzero had been there for her every step of the way as she'd taken on the coveted incubator position with Bianca and worked to prove herself amidst so much amazing talent. Through her decision to go back to school. He'd come to mean so much to her, she couldn't actually articulate it in words.

"I never thought I'd see it," Mireille mused. "The Di Fiore brothers fall. Nico, I get. He was always the nurturer and he was always in love with Chloe. But Lazzero? I thought he was *untakeable*. Until I saw him with you."

So had she. Her gaze drifted to Santo, entertaining a bevvy of beauties on the far side of the dance floor. "What about Santo? Do you think he'll ever commit?"

A funny look crossed Mireille's face. "I don't know. There was a girl…a long time ago. Santo was madly in love with her. I think she broke his heart."

Chiara rested her champagne glass against her chin, intrigued. "Is there any chance they'll get back together?"

"I would say that's highly unlikely."

She was about to ask why when Mireille, clearly deciding she'd revealed too much, changed the subject. "Your dress is amazing. Is it one of yours?"

Chiara nodded.

"I need one for Evolution's Valentine's event." Mireille tipped her glass at her. "Would you make me something similar?"

"Of course." Chiara was beyond flattered. Mireille was a PR maven, one of the highest-profile socialite personalities in New York. *Everyone* noticed what she was wearing.

She was still bubbling over at the idea when Lazzero came to claim his dance, his official duties over for the evening. The champagne popped and sparkled in her veins as she tipped her head back to look up at him. "Mireille loves my dress. She asked me to make her one for Evolution's Valentine's event. Can you believe it?"

"Yes." He brushed his lips against her temple in a fleeting caress. "The dress is amazing, as are you. Speaking of which," he prompted, "when are you finishing up work at the bakery?"

"Next week. My aunt Gloria called me today to tell me she's retiring. She's going to take on my shifts at the bakery to give herself something to do, which is so perfect," she bubbled, "because my father adores her. It'll be so good for him. Oh," she added, "and the *jaw-dropping* news? My father is playing *briscola* at Frankie DeLucca's house on Friday nights. Can you believe it?"

Lazzero smiled. "Maybe you going to Italy was exactly what he needed."

"Yes," she agreed contemplatively, "I think it was."

She chattered on until it became clear Lazzero wasn't really listening to her, that absentminded look he'd been wearing all night painted across his face.

"Have you heard a word I've said?" she chastised.

"Yes." He shook his head at her reproving look. "No," he admitted. "I need some air," he said abruptly. "Do you need some air?"

She looked at him as if he was mad. It was December and her flimsy dress was not made for this weather. But she knew Lazzero well enough now to know that when he needed to talk, she needed to listen.

They collected their coats and walked hand in hand out into a winter wonderland, Central Park covered in a dusting of snow that made it look as if it had been dipped in icing sugar. It was magical, as if they had the park all to themselves. She was thinking it had been the *perfect* idea, when Lazzero tugged her to a halt in a pretty clearing flanked by snow-covered trees.

She tilted her head back to look up at him. But now he was holding both her hands in his, and she thought she could detect a slight tremor in them, and her heart started to hammer in her chest. "Lazzero," she breathed, closing her fingers tight around his. "What are you doing?"

He rested his forehead against hers for a moment, took a deep breath, then sank down to one knee. Her legs went so weak at the sight of him there, she thought she might join him.

He delved into the inside pocket of his dark suit. Pulled out his fist. Uncurled his fingers. Her breath caught in her chest as the moonlight revealed the magnificent asscher-cut diamond in his palm.

Her ring. The ring she'd dreamed about. The ring she wanted back. Desperately.

Her eyes brimmed with tears that spilled over and ran down her cheeks. A frown of uncertainty crossed Lazzero's face. "You like the ring, don't you? I've been going back and forth all week on it. I thought maybe I should buy you another, but I bought this one for you. Because it reminded me of you. Full of life, vibrant, *impossibly strong.*"

She stifled a sob. *He* made her feel strong. Impenetrable. Bulletproof. As if she could take on the world.

"I love the ring," she managed to choke as she shoved her hand at him. He slid the ring on, the heavy weight of it sliding a piece of her heart back into place.

His face smoothed out. "I'm no Alfredo," he said huskily. "But I want to have that once-in-a-lifetime love with you, Chiara. I want to be the guy who's always there for you. The one who never lets you down. *If* you will do me the honor of becoming my wife."

Her fingers tugged at the lapels of his coat. Rising to his feet, he collected her against him and kissed her until she was breathless. And then buttons on coats were a problem in their haste to get closer to each other. When that proved too frustrating an exercise, Lazzero swung her up into his arms and carried her out of the park.

"You're giving up your job at the café tomorrow," he commanded, lifting his hand to flag a taxi on Fifth Avenue.

"You just want me to make you coffee every morning," she accused, a massive smile on her face.

"Yes," he agreed, his face an arrogant canvas of satisfaction, "I do. But only if it comes with you."

* * * * *

LET'S TALK
Romance

For exclusive extracts, competitions and special offers, find us online:

- **f** MillsandBoon
- 🐦 @MillsandBoon
- 📷 @MillsandBoonUK
- ♪ @MillsandBoonUK

Get in touch on 01413 063 232

JOIN US ON SOCIAL MEDIA!

Stay up to date with our latest releases, author news
and gossip, special offers and discounts, and all the
behind-the-scenes action from Mills & Boon...

 @millsandboon

 @millsandboonuk

 facebook.com/millsandboon

 @millsandboonuk

It might just be true love...

GET YOUR ROMANCE FIX!

Get the latest romance news, exclusive author interviews, story extracts and much more!